MY FAVORITE VIEW

BOOK TWO IN THE MINT CREEK RANCH SERIES

HILARY DARTT

ALSO BY HILARY DARTT

The Mint Creek Ranch Series

My Favorite Story

My Favorite Place

The Seedling Homestead Series

A Summer of Wonder

A Dream of Home

A Promise of Forever

The Intervention Series

The Dating Intervention

The Marriage Intervention

The Motherhood Intervention

The Garden Club Series

Jasmine's Pact

Studying Sequoia

Just Holly

MY FAVORITE VIEW

BOOK TWO IN THE MINT CREEK RANCH SERIES

HILARY DARTT

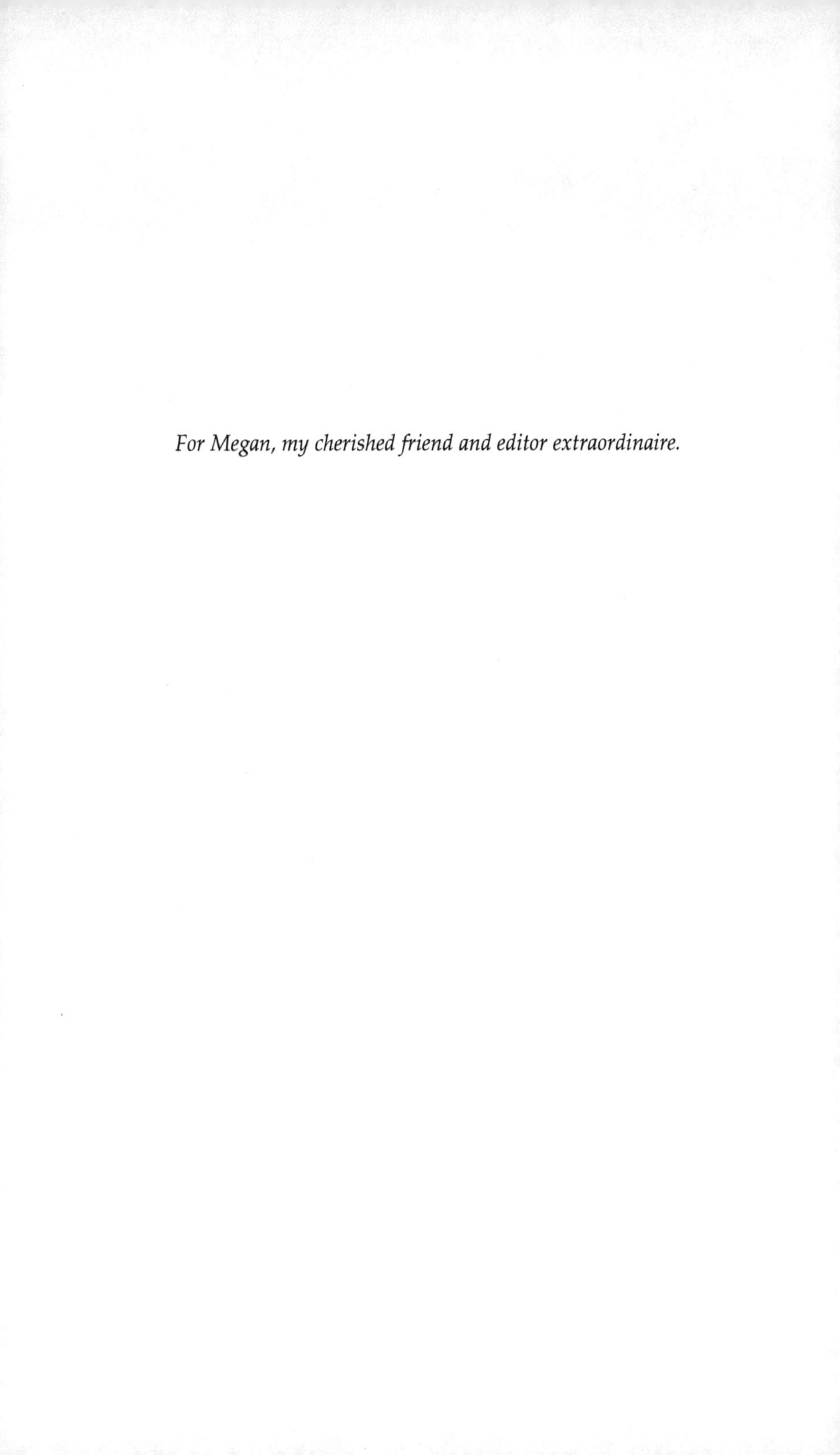

For Megan, my cherished friend and editor extraordinaire.

CHAPTER ONE

MONTANA

MONTANA HART HAD WOKEN up next to Sawyer Nelson countless times.

This time was different. She always opened her eyes first, and lay there watching him sleep, memorizing and re-memorizing his features.

His long, thick eyelashes. The strong line of his jaw. His smooth chest, his chiseled abs, his — that was always where she stopped. Because every time, her watching him woke him up and brought him to attention. And then she would notice it, and he would see her notice it. And then they would make love. And then they would swear they would never make love again.

But it never took.

One late-summer Saturday morning, when the sun didn't slant through the windows until just before six, Montana woke up next to Sawyer, and she kept her eyes closed.

That's how she knew it would be the last time they spent the night together. For real.

She didn't want to look at him … to see the mistake she made, yet again, after promising herself she wouldn't. How was she ever supposed to quit Sawyer Nelson if she couldn't bring herself to quit him? There was so much between them. History. Love. Heartbreak.

At one point, Montana thought she couldn't live without him. But he didn't feel the same way.

She thought back to the night before, to the hours and moments that led up to them returning together to Sawyer's place after a long … *hiatus* is what he would call it (with a drawl). Something of a "break."

They were celebrating. Cody Davis, who was like a brother to both of them, proposed to Tessa Kincaid, the reporter who'd moved to town three months before.

The group of them — Cody and Tessa, Montana and Sawyer, and their friend Trace Walker — went out for drinks. The mood was festive. Lots of laughter, the clinking of glasses and beer bottles as they made one toast after another — first, to a long, happy life together for the newly engaged couple, then to many fun adventures, and eventually to what someone called a "whole passel of little children."

Montana was happy for Cody and Tessa. She and Cody grew up together on the Mint Creek Ranch, thick as thieves. And since Tessa joined the *Daily Dispatch* three months before and worked in tandem with Montana covering Cody's bull-riding championship tour, they'd become close friends.

But for every toast, Montana felt a twinge of … *wistfulness* was probably the best word to describe it. Every time Cody and Tessa looked at each other, Montana could practically *feel* the connection. Their gazes met and their eyes lit up. They looked so happy. Content. In love. And all night long, Montana remembered how badly she wanted that with Sawyer.

She couldn't tell whether Sawyer felt the same way she did, or if he was relieved she hadn't lassoed him in. He avoided eye contact with her for most of the night. A couple times, when she caught him looking at her, he looked away, his eyes coming to rest on anything else: his beer bottle, the bartender, Cody and Tessa slow dancing in the middle of the dance floor.

The two lovebirds were the first to leave. Trace stuck around for a little while to lament the loss of Cody from the world of singledom, but then he left, too, and it was just Montana and Sawyer. They sat at the bar, neither of them speaking over the loud country-rock music, an empty stool between them. And in what she thought was a poetic moment, Montana imagined their history occupying that stool: sitting between them, keeping them from being together.

"What are you doing after this?" Sawyer asked her after a while.

It always went like that. Montana never said what she *should* say: "Going home and straight to bed." Instead she answered like she did that night: "Nothing. What about you?"

And then, just like always, Sawyer smiled at her. His eyes crinkled at the corners, and his lips curved upward. Like always, Montana knew that her "nothing" would turn into her going home with Sawyer.

With them came the truth: even though she acted like she didn't have anything better to do, going home with Sawyer was the only thing Montana wanted to do.

At Sawyer's house, in his arms, was the only place she wanted to be. At least, until the next morning.

There they were, the morning after Cody and Tessa's engagement, and for the first time ever, Montana didn't want to have lazy morning sex. She did want to run home to steep in her own regret. She finally opened her eyes, and allowed herself one lingering look at this man — her first love, her first everything — then she slipped out from between the sheets and into the kitchen, where she scribbled a note. Then, she went right through the front door. Boots and jeans in hand, she slid into the safety of her car.

Traveling away from Sawyer's, she thought about the vow she'd made the night before. Seeing Cody and Tessa so happy at the prospect of spending the rest of their lives together, Montana pledged to end things with Sawyer — for good this time. She deserved the same happiness Tessa and Cody had. And, so did Sawyer. But they couldn't have it together. Once, years ago, he made it clear that he didn't want that with Montana. It was time to let him go. It was the best thing for both of them.

Montana pulled into the tiny parking spot beneath her tiny apartment. She trudged upstairs, still barefoot. Once inside, she put on the teakettle. Then she went into her bedroom to take off Sawyer's t-shirt. She folded it and put it at the very back of her closet.

She could still taste Sawyer's lips on hers, smell his skin. She could feel his unshaven cheek against hers, his hands on her breasts, him inside of her as their bodies rocked together. The lovemaking was always different, yet so familiar. The touches, the sensations. Each time, it felt exciting and wonderful and exactly like home. Which was why saying goodbye felt nearly impossible.

Montana felt the first tear slip down her cheek. Then the next. She brushed them away and took a sip of her tea. It was lukewarm. She wondered how long she'd been sitting there. Her phone rang and her body protested when she got up to retrieve it from the kitchen. She was sore and bone-tired. Montana felt a quick flash of disappointment when she saw Tessa's name on her screen, and not Sawyer's. But then relief took over.

"What are you doing?" Tessa wanted to know.

Montana burst into tears. "Just throwing myself a little pity party."

"What happened? If Sawyer —"

"No, no. It was mutual. It's just that after seeing you and Cody together last night, I got to thinking. I wanted that — what you guys have — for as long as I can remember. With Sawyer. But it's clear the two of us can never have it. So, I think it's time to end things between us. For good this time."

"Oh, Montana."

———

SAWYER

SAWYER ALWAYS SLEPT like the dead when Montana was beside him. Her absence that morning woke him from a sound sleep, and he found that her side of the bed was already cold. He wondered how she managed to sneak out, and how long ago she left.

The night before felt different. As he remembered it — the way his body fit with Montana's, the way she clung to him, like she needed him — he felt himself standing at attention.

For about half a minute, he wondered why she hadn't woken him up like she often did, so they could make love again in the morning. But then his rational side chimed in and reminded him of the expression he'd seen on her face when they were all together at the Watering Hole.

Sawyer knew Montana better than anyone ... maybe even better than he knew himself. Even though she was genuinely happy for Tessa and Cody, she was heartbroken. Because — they both knew this — she'd spent most of her life wanting wedded bliss with Sawyer. But then he'd gone and acted like the biggest damn fool and made the biggest mistake of his life. He didn't want to think about that night, years ago, just before she left for college.

That's why she clung to him last night. She was remembering that, too. She would probably never forgive him, and besides, she deserved better.

And that's why, when she took off earlier that morning, she was undoubtedly thinking, *I'm gonna quit Sawyer Nelson. For good this time.*

He could hear it, in her cute cowgirl twang (he didn't know where she'd picked it up; she'd lived in Prescott, Arizona, her whole life). She *always* said she was going to quit him. But she never did.

The smell of coffee drifted into the bedroom. That was his cue: time to get up. He, Trace, and Cody were supposed to ride fence that day, and they planned to start at daybreak. He dragged himself out of bed and pulled up the comforter. His mom would never approve of such a halfhearted job of making the bed, but he didn't care. At that moment, he wanted coffee. And morning sex. Since he was getting only one of those, he made a beeline for the kitchen.

An envelope sat on the counter, and he could see Montana's loopy handwriting on the back of it. She'd probably grabbed a piece of junk mail off the stack. He smiled, and was still smiling when he read her words: *That was the last time.*

She'd left notes before, but never like that. Sawyer swore as he tore the envelope in half without even checking its contents. He dropped the halves in the trash, filled his mug, then carried his coffee back to the bedroom and found some clothes to put on. He noticed Montana hadn't left the shirt she'd worn to bed. Under normal circumstances, that would make him happy. But these weren't normal circumstances. She had left this morning without so much as a goodbye, which, really, was more of a goodbye than any words she could say.

Sawyer drove his truck over to the Mint Creek Ranch's main barn. He loved the ranch. It held so many childhood memories. But he hadn't *earned* it; he'd inherited his portion from his parents. He wanted something of his own, and when he had that, he would put a barn right next to his main house. That way, he could keep his horse there and ride out from home. He'd rather be horseback than in a fancy truck any day, he thought as he pulled up.

Trace was already there, saddling up his horse, Heidi.

"You're looking rested this morning. I take it you and Montana didn't go home together?"

Even though Sawyer's heart cracked just the tiniest bit as he thought again of how Montana had left that morning, he gave Trace his best cocky smile. "Oh, I went home with her. And *then* I got a really good night's sleep."

He would never admit to Trace that he just slept better when Montana was there, no matter how many times they had sex.

"You're a glutton for punishment, man."

"Hey," Sawyer said, anything but eager to repeat this conversation, again, especially because it hit close to home. "When's the last time *you* went home with anyone?"

Trace checked the fit of his horse's saddle and then swung himself into it. "That's none of your business."

He rode right out of the barn. Chuckling, Sawyer shook his head and went to work on his own horse, Whistler.

"I'll tell you what, boy. I think Montana really means it this time."

The horse nickered and Sawyer thought he might feel some sympathy. Then Sawyer decided he was being overly sentimental. He finished saddling up and rode out to the breezeway to join Trace, who had switched to business mode.

His gaze narrowed, and running along the fence line, he said, "So I guess we're starting in the northwest corner. Then going east, then south."

"When do you suppose Cody will join us? Or *do* you suppose he'll join us?"

Trace smiled. "Maybe not. He and Tessa were probably up all night. You know what they say about the Mint Creek Ranch boys."

"I haven't heard anyone say much of anything about *you* lately," Sawyer said.

"I'm just building the mystery, my man. What's with you today, man? You've got some mean in you."

"Nothing, man."

Trace raised an eyebrow at Sawyer. "Okay."

"Shut up."

"What? All I said was 'okay.'"

"Yeah. I know what you meant."

Even astride his horse, Trace had a way of putting his hands on his hips that emanated exasperation.

"Fine," Sawyer said. Whistler shook his head and snorted and Sawyer said, "Montana left me a note this morning. Said last night was the last time we're going home together."

Another raised eyebrow from Trace (and maybe a silent "I-told-you-so"). "Think it's for real this time?"

Sawyer nodded. "I think it is."

The sound of an engine cut through the buzz of the cicadas.

"Speak of the devil," Trace said as Cody's truck pulled in.

Within a few minutes, the three of them were headed for the north-west corner of Mint Creek Ranch, their horses at a full gallop. Cody's dad, Tom, would follow them in his all-terrain vehicle in just a few minutes with the equipment to make any necessary repairs.

The ride would take about fifteen minutes. The big spread, and the way his body fell into a natural rhythm to match the horse's strides, meant Sawyer could think. Even though two hundred acres gave everyone plenty of space, and Sawyer had never felt crowded before, home seemed claustrophobic lately. Sawyer urged Whistler to run faster, and he wondered if he was trying to outrun that feeling.

Even as a little kid, he had a need for speed. He could remember all the parents teasing him about it (while his mother prayed out loud that he wouldn't get himself killed). He'd never been afraid to gallop, to all-out canter on his horses.

Whistler was his first independent purchase, unrelated to the Mint Creek Ranch. He did his research, found a ranch in Montana that boasted long lines of fast, strong, smart ranching horses. He paid top dollar. And it was worth it. Whistler could outrun just about any of the other horses on the ranch and outmaneuver any cow. He was so easily trainable and over the past couple of years he and Sawyer had begun to move as one. Sometimes it felt like they could read each other's minds.

That's why they'd done so well on the rodeo circuit.

For the past year or so, Sawyer had been thinking maybe Whistler's success was an indicator from some higher power that he could do things on his own. Yes, he'd always been part of this insepa-rable trio — the three guys, plus Cody's sister Annie — and he wouldn't trade that for anything. But sometimes, especially when he was agonizing over the mistakes he'd made, he thought he maybe needed to completely revamp his life. Have something all his own.

If he couldn't have Montana, maybe he could find happiness some other way.

By that time, Sawyer and Whistler had reached the starting point for the day's fence riding. Thinking time was over. He dismounted as fast as he could and leaned against the fence so it would look like he'd been waiting a long time when Cody and Trace got there. It was an old joke, something they'd done since they were kids and raced every-where. When they were really little, they raced on foot. Then ponies, and eventually, real horses. Whoever got there first would always fling himself on the ground and act like he'd been waiting for ages.

Sawyer started it. They used to read some version of the tortoise and the hare, where every time the tortoise encountered the hare, the hare was relaxing after a quick jaunt ahead. Now, it was tradition.

After a couple of minutes, Cody and Trace brought up their horses.

"Got a bee in your saddle?" Cody asked. "You took off like your pants are on fire."

"He says Montana's quitting him," Trace said to Cody.

"Yeah?" Cody said. "He always says that."

Yeah, Sawyer thought. *But this time, I think it's for real.*

MONTANA

THE FIRST TIME Montana and Sawyer got married, they were six years old and in first grade. One of the girls in Montana's class made her a veil and two rings out of construction paper. It was a spring day, the kind of morning where you could just feel the warmth of the sun cutting through the cool air. Montana and Sawyer stood facing each other, a gentle breeze pulling her veil off her shoulders. The veil- and ring-maker acted as officiant.

"Do you, Montana Hart, take Sawyer Nelson to be your husband forever and ever, as long as you both shall live?"

Montana remembered looking into Sawyer's twinkling brown eyes and thinking she wanted nothing more than to be his wife forever and ever. "I sure do."

"And do you, Montana Hart, promise to hug Sawyer Nelson every morning, and kiss him goodnight every night, forever and ever, as long as you both shall live?"

Montana thought there was nothing she would want to do more. Ever. Not even eat ten ice cream cones a day. "I sure do."

Sawyer's smile got just a little bit bigger.

"And do you, Sawyer Nelson, promise to hug and kiss Montana every single day until you both are old and gray?"

Sawyer looked at the little girl, surprised. Maybe he'd never thought of Montana as an old-and-gray lady before. But then he seemed to accept the idea because he shrugged and nodded. "I guess I do."

"And do you promise to love her forever and ever, as long as you both shall live?"

Sawyer looked back at Montana, and Montana's heart soared inside her chest.

"I sure do."

The teacher on recess duty blew her whistle. And they didn't even get to kiss. But later that night, during chore time on the ranch, Sawyer made it official. Montana was in the barn milking one of the cows. Sawyer came up to her, carrying one of the milking stools. He set it down next to hers, and while she milked, he said, "I never got to kiss the bride. Do you reckon I could do it now?"

Montana stopped milking and closed her eyes. She figured Sawyer was leaning toward her and she waited, lips puckered. Then, quite without warning, his stool tipped over and he fell straight forward, tipping over her pail of milk.

They didn't share their first kiss until a few years later, but Montana didn't consider it a *real* kiss: Sawyer drummed up the courage to do it only because Trace and Cody dared him to.

After school one day, they all climbed on the bus. Instead of cramming three boys to a seat like they usually did — leaving Montana to her own spacious spot — Sawyer rushed to sit with her, and Cody and Trace got into the seat behind them.

Montana heard some giggling, and while she wasn't sure what to make of it, she did wonder what they were up to. The boys were always playing some prank or another. It had long since stopped bothering her. A few times, one of them kicked the back of the seat. Montana ignored that. Finally, just before they got to their stop, she found out what all the noise was about. Sawyer said her name, and when she turned to look at him, he leaned in and gave her a quick peck on the mouth.

Later, he admitted it had been a dare, and Montana came to suspect that Trace and Cody wanted to kiss girls, too, but didn't have anyone willing.

They shared a couple more kisses while they were still in elementary school.

But Montana remembered, with the kind of clarity that pulled at her heartstrings, their first *real* kiss—the first time a kiss actually made her think about what came next, the first kiss that sent a fluttery feeling through her torso and right down between her legs.

They were fifteen, sophomores in high school. Freshman year had put a bit of a strain on their relationship, with him asking Suzette O'Hannon to the spring dance. But sophomore year was a new year.

It was homecoming, and a crazy set of circumstances had opened the door for Sawyer to play quarterback on the varsity team that night. As was his competitive nature, he played like a varsity player. A real expert. Every pass he threw made it into a receiver's waiting grasp and he earned hundreds of yards and a handful of touchdowns for the team. Montana still got chills thinking about it. The game was spectacular.

Afterward, Montana was standing with a group of their mutual friends, waiting outside the gym for the homecoming dance to begin. The football team came up from the field and Montana's eyes automatically sought Sawyer, like they always did. There he was, grinning so broadly Montana couldn't help but grin, too. And sure enough, his eyes met hers within a fraction of a second. It was always that way.

They had spoken over the past couple months — their paths were always crossing since they were both residents of the Mint Creek Ranch — but they hadn't been alone together, or even hung out as a couple, in forever. Maybe even a year. So Montana was completely caught off guard when Sawyer broke from the pack and walked right up to her, his newly broad shoulders squared. He held his helmet in his left hand, and he wrapped his right hand around the back of her neck and kissed her. That moment was everything. Fireworks. Goosebumps. The freshest lemonade on the hottest day. And, it was sex. Montana could taste it. Unable to resist, she kissed him right back.

Someone on the football team whistled, and someone else hollered, "Get a room, Nelson!"

Sawyer ended the kiss and when Montana opened her eyes, she could practically see the flames in his. He gave her another smile, cocky mixed with something dangerous, and then he jogged off to join his teammates.

It wasn't long after that that Montana and Sawyer made love for the first time.

While fall at Mint Creek Ranch always bustled, and there were chores to be done to ready the place for winter, Montana took a weekend job at the pumpkin festival at a nearby farm. She let kids into the corn maze and helped them find their way out. She ran the pony rides and weighed pumpkins. She sold cotton candy and helped sticky-fingered little ones into the hayride.

She loved it, and she couldn't think of any other way she'd rather earn money. She came home from every shift downright weary. One night, she made her way back to Mint Creek Ranch and decided to spend a few minutes relaxing. She climbed up the ladder inside the barn and let herself down into the loft.

It was a cozy spot. All the Mint Creek Ranch kids used it not only as a fort, but also as a place for some alone time. When she dropped down onto the floor, she noticed someone sitting at the other end, feet dangling over the edge. She squealed and jumped, surprised to find someone else appear at that hour. Sawyer was laughing when he turned and looked at her. "Gave you a real good scare, didn't I?"

"You scared me half to death! My heart is fairly beating out of my chest!"

Sawyer chuckled and as graceful as a tiger, he got to his feet and came toward her.

———

ONCE MONTANA FELL in love with Sawyer — none of that baby stuff from first grade, but real, grown-up love in third grade — she knew she would marry him one day, for real. So throughout their childhood and teenage years, through all the ups and downs, she didn't worry herself. Some days, she hated him for putting a frog in her lunchbox or sneaking under the bleachers with Mindy Larrabee or taking Suzette O'Hannon to that spring dance freshman year. But even then, she loved him. Every time she thought about her future, Sawyer was in it. He was the man across from her at her wedding altar, the one with whom she chose paint colors and cabinets and light fixtures and kitchen countertops. He was the father of her children, and boy, would they be the cutest around.

For her, it was just a matter of time until they got married. For him, though, maybe it wasn't a certain thing.

CHAPTER TWO

IF GROWN-UP Montana felt certain of one thing, it was that she wanted to create a life of her own, separate from Sawyer.

But.

She didn't really know how to begin, mentally. So, one morning, she took herself to the library to peruse the self-help section. Rows upon rows of books in every color lined the shelves. *Healing from Trauma, Ending Codependency, Starting Over.* Montana huffed out a sigh. How would she know whether any of them were worthwhile? She drummed her fingertips on her thighs. Then, she pulled out a book at random. She liked the color of the cover — a mint green. Like mint chip ice cream. The title, *Get Over Yourself,* felt a bit abrasive. If she were going on a journey, she wanted a warm and fuzzy tour guide. She didn't even open the book before placing it back on the shelf. The one next to it caught her eye. *On Your Own.*

"Hmm," Montana said. "Sounds apropos." She pulled it out and opened it. She liked what she saw in the table of contents: *Why this book? What do you want? How will you get what you want?*

Feeling a little braver, Montana closed the book and held it against her body while she looked for a couple more. After a few minutes, she had settled on two: *Finding You* and *Your Most Important Relationship.*

It didn't escape Montana that those titles could also belong on the covers of romance novels. She checked out, and as she went back to her car, she thought about what she'd seen as she flipped through the books.

One common theme: cooking for yourself. Although she often opted to cook rather than eating out, she never really took the time to make elaborate meals if she were the only one eating. It was always something like grilled fish with steamed vegetables or some kind of greens bowl.

Sure, when Sawyer was there, she would go all out.

But she deserved a great meal, too, didn't she? Something luxurious and aromatic and deeply satisfying. Something that took a long time to make. If she expressed her love for Sawyer through cooking, then why wouldn't she do the same for herself? She set her books on her passenger seat.

Feeling emboldened, she said to herself, "Next stop: grocery store."

While driving, she let herself get lost in thinking about what she could make.

"Spaghetti," she said, hearing the reverence in her voice. Spaghetti would be perfect. It was comfort food. She could make it as simple or complicated as she wanted to. And she wanted to make it complicated: load it up with vegetables and seasonings and spicy meat. She could buy a fresh-baked loaf of French bread and a bottle of wine. Good wine. Expensive wine (okay, so a twenty-dollar bottle probably didn't qualify as "expensive" for most people. But it was four times what she'd spend on a typical day).

She ran through the list of what she'd buy: pasta, bell peppers, a head of garlic (which she would roast in the oven! Her mouth watered), a yellow onion. Zucchini? Spicy Italian sausage, of course.

She couldn't think of the last time she had homemade spaghetti. She parked, then took her notebook out of her purse and wrote down her list before getting out of the car.

At the entrance of the grocery store, she saw a couple of kids sitting on the ground, a cardboard box between them. Being a photojournalist required a significant amount of curiosity. She couldn't help herself — she took a few steps closer and peered into the box. Involuntarily, she let out an, "Aww."

Half a dozen wiggling, fuzzy puppies squirmed around in the bottom of the box.

"Want to hold one?" The little girl looked up at Montana with a twinkle in her eye. She probably knew she'd found a softy.

"I don't think I can pass that up." A second later, the little girl was pressing a fat, soft puppy with fur the color of chocolate into her hands. Montana cradled it against her chest and it licked her chin. Charmed, she said, "How old are these guys?"

The little boy, who Montana assumed was the girl's brother, said, "They're seven weeks old, ma'am. Our mama said if we don't find them a home, she's going to take them to the Humane Society. It's our fault Magpie — that's their mama — got out of the yard and ran the neighborhood."

"Aw, our mama did not say that! He's just saying that so you'll feel bad and take one. Our mama said if we don't find them a home our daddy's gonna divorce all three of us."

"Which," the brother said, "is not true. He wouldn't really divorce us. But he would be very, very unhappy."

"And then our mama would be very, very unhappy," the sister said, her tone so perfectly matching her brother's that Montana had to laugh, which encouraged the puppy to lick her chin again and paw at her chest.

If there was anything that signified an independent life, it was getting a pet of her own, Montana thought. What would Sawyer think of that? A girl who had her own dog didn't need anything from a guy like Sawyer. But was getting a dog just to spite your boyfriend — scratch that; *ex*-boyfriend — really the best reason to adopt a pet? Even Montana had to admit it wasn't. But was that the only reason she wanted a puppy?

No, Montana had always wanted a dog. When she was a kid, the Mint Creek Ranch always had dogs. But they were ranch dogs. Friendly, but busy working most of the time. At the end of each day, they ate dinner at the barn and flopped down on their mats. She could never have her own because her mom was deadly allergic. Suddenly, that childlike desire welled up in Montana's chest. She *wanted* this puppy.

"You know what? I'll take him. Can you guys hang onto him for a few minutes? I've got to buy my dinner. And, I guess, some puppy food."

The kids looked at each other and grinned. They both seemed to be thinking they'd nailed her as a sucker. And she was perfectly okay with that.

"Does he have a name yet?" she asked them.

"We call him The Rock," the boy said. "You know, like the wrestler who's an actor now. He's a real tough guy."

"But you don't have to keep the name," the sister rushed to say. "He's your dog now. You can name him whatever you want."

He's your dog now. Montana tucked him under her right arm and scratched behind his ear with her left hand. He licked her face again and she giggled. She set him back in the box.

"Okay. Keep an eye on him for me? I'll be right back."

List in hand, she made her way through the store as quickly as she could. Then she ran over to the pet supplies aisle. She chose the same brand of food they always had at the ranch. She added a leash and collar and a few toys to her cart. The grocery store didn't have any dog beds on hand, so she'd have to go to the pet store within a day or two. She made her way to the cash register. When she got back outside, relief overwhelmed her. She hadn't even realized she was worried about her dog. But there he was, being thrust at her in the hands of the little girl.

"Here you go, ma'am. He's all yours." Montana took him. She pushed her cart with one hand and held the puppy in the other, fending off tears of happiness all the way to her car. When she finally got her groceries in the trunk and settled into the driver seat with The Rock on her lap, she burst into a full-on cry. Maybe it was silly, but she felt like she'd taken a major step toward creating her new life.

SAWYER

IT WAS time to commit to the bachelor life. A real split from Montana meant Sawyer was going to have to fend for himself. The first step was to stock his pantry. He usually went day by day, hoping somehow, he and Montana would cross paths and end up eating dinner together. But, that wouldn't be happening much from now on.

So he made his way to the grocery store, a heavy feeling in his stomach, like he'd swallowed about a hundred fishing sinkers. Sawyer had never been much for cooking. He could *do* it; his mom had insisted all the boys learn how to cook, so they wouldn't grow up to be "worthless husbands" (her words, which made his dad laugh, since he didn't do much more than heat up canned soup). But he didn't enjoy it like some people did.

Cody always said there was something satisfying about throwing a steak and some potatoes on the grill. And Trace imagined himself as some gourmet cook, coming up with complicated sauces and 100-ingredient rubs for meat he smoked. But Sawyer preferred not to spend more than five minutes cooking a meal.

He was so lost in thought that he didn't even realize he'd parked right next to Montana's car until he was out of his seat and around the bed of his truck. When he saw her shabby little hatchback, he stopped in his tracks. He was about to turn around and move his car, but he forced himself to keep walking. This was a small town. He was going to run into her and he might as well get used to it. He spotted a few books on her passenger seat. And, because he'd be curious about books on anyone's seat — absolutely not because he wanted to know exactly what *she* was reading — he took a closer look. He didn't know what to make of the titles. He could see only the spines of the two books on the bottom, but the top book, *Your Most Important Relationship*, had a tagline about how developing your relationship with yourself would lead to a happier, fuller life.

Part of Sawyer, the part that still ached at her desire to stay away from him, wanted to sneer. But another part of him, the part that still loved her and wanted to be part of her happy, full life, felt a spasm of panic. She *was* serious. She was really going to create a life without him.

Although he'd just reminded himself that he was going to see her around town, he told himself then that didn't mean he couldn't try to avoid her. He walked across the parking lot to the entrance farthest from their cars. Then, he made a beeline for the canned food section, knowing she almost never ate canned foods. He rushed through adding soups and pastas and chili to his cart. Then, head down, he strode as quickly as he could over to the freezer section (which Montana also avoided). He tossed in a bunch of frozen dinners. The cashier at checkout raised an eyebrow at him and didn't even try to start a conversation.

That's right, he thought. *I'm a loser. A lifetime bachelor.*

He checked his watch. He'd been in the store for ten minutes, which meant Montana was probably done and gone. It was likely safe to use the entrance closer to his car. And her car. He hoped with all his might that her car was gone.

When he walked out the door, he nearly tripped over a couple of kids who were sitting on the ground with a cardboard box between them. The little boy was struggling with the box. At least, that's what Sawyer thought until he saw that the kid was trying to push a rowdy puppy back in.

"Need a hand?" The boy put a hand over the puppy's entire head and shoved it down with a little more force.

"No thanks, mister. This one just wants to escape."

"And I told him," said the little girl, all big-sister bossiness, "if that puppy runs into the parking lot, she's going to get squished. Like a bug."

Sawyer knelt down to see the puppy in question.

Montana

AS SOON AS Montana got home, she realized she hadn't put much forethought into the logistics of having a puppy at home (and maybe she should have). She had dinner to cook and wasn't sure what to do with the dog. She couldn't leave the little guy roaming all over the house. Carrying him tucked under her right arm, she dug through the coat closet and found a cardboard box she'd saved, just because it was a really good box.

"I knew this would come in handy," she said, remembering the way Sawyer had raised a skeptical eyebrow at her when she'd flattened it for storage.

"Perfect." She reassembled it and set it next to the kitchen door, put a folded towel on the bottom, and set the dog on the towel.

Next, she put on some music. Jazz seemed just right for the occasion. Sophisticated. Fitting for a mature, independent woman. The expensive wine smelled heavenly. She reread the label, which promised notes of oak and cherry. After pouring a glass, she let it sit while she filled a pot with water.

On the first sip, her knees went weak with pleasure.

"Who needs a man when you have expensive wine, huh, boy?" she said to the dog, who wagged his tail and scratched at the side of the box.

A girl could really get used to this, Montana thought. The sound of the knife chopping vegetables on the wooden cutting board, the smell of the oil heating in the saucepan, the sizzle of the meat.

"Garlic," she said. That, too, smelled heavenly. Startled to find her wine glass empty already, she refilled it. The puppy was still in his box, curled up into a tiny little ball in the corner. A swell of love overcame Montana and she felt the sting of tears. That was *her* puppy. Her baby. People weren't really supposed to feed dogs spaghetti, but she thought about sharing a plate with her new baby.

While the sauce simmered and the pasta boiled, Montana lit some candles on her small dining table. It wasn't for romance, but for ambience. This was how women of luxury lived. Why shouldn't she enjoy delicious candlelit dinner on her own?

A while later, she dished up her food, careful to indulge every one of her senses as she did. The fresh-baked French bread felt soft against her fingertips and she could smell the yeast when she cut into it. She let the steam from the pasta brush over her face, and she savored the creamy taste of butter when she licked it off her fingertips. The music flowed through her body. Once everything was on the table, including her bottle of wine, Montana went to sit down. Then she had a thought, and went to get the puppy. She put his box on the chair next to hers. Even though he still slept soundly, she felt like she had company. It was perfect.

———

Sawyer

THERE WAS something innately depressing about heating up a can of ravioli or a tray of frozen steak, Sawyer decided as he headed for home. Fortunately, before he made it there, his phone rang.

"Want to come over for dinner?" Cody said without preamble. "I'm throwing a few steaks on the grill."

Sawyer smiled. The invitation was probably Tessa's doing. She felt so bad for both Sawyer and Montana that she kept insisting Cody invite them over for dinner. Separately, on alternating days.

"Actually, I just picked up some dinner at the store."

"You cooking?"

Sawyer had to laugh at the doubt in Cody's voice. "Just some soup or something."

"Spent some time in the canned goods aisle, did you?"

Sawyer couldn't get away with anything. "The freezer aisle, too. If you must know."

"Well, I've saved you from the misery. Go put your Single Man dinners, or whatever they're called, in the freezer and come over. Tessa insists."

Once he got home, Sawyer realized his mistake in accepting Cody's invitation. What was he going to do with this puppy ... not just during dinner, but all day, every day? Maybe getting a dog was a mistake. He supposed he could bring it to work like the ranch hands always did. He could teach it to ride his horse, he thought, his amusement growing. It was a great idea. He looked over at the little fur ball, sitting on the passenger seat.

"Riding shotgun already. You're my co-pilot."

He could've sworn the dog smiled at him. If Montana were there, she would say it was some kind of energy. A cosmic smile. She loved that stuff. But he needed to stop thinking about what she'd say or think ... she wasn't there, he reminded himself. They were going their separate ways, for good this time.

At home, he stacked his meals in the freezer and left the cans on the kitchen counter. He grabbed a beer cooler and put in a few beers, then a bottle of wine for Tessa.

When he got to Cody's house, he didn't even bother knocking. He never had. But as he stepped across the threshold, beer cooler in one hand, the puppy in the other, he thought maybe he should start.

Cody was no longer a bachelor, living alone. What if he and Tessa were — well, it could be any number of things. Luckily, at that moment, they were in the kitchen, Tessa on a barstool at the counter and Cody standing across from her, rubbing seasoning into three juicy steaks.

"Party's here," Sawyer said.

Cody flashed him a grin, then froze. "What's that you've got there?"

"Beer. Oh, and wine."

"No, in the other arm."

"Oh, this?" Sawyer lifted the pup so Cody could see her. "New sidekick. Doesn't have a name yet, though."

Tessa was already pulling the dog from the crook of Sawyer's arm, kissing her on the head.

"What a cutie," she said. "Where'd you get her?"

"Grocery store." He offered her the lopsided smile he knew melted all the ladies' hearts, and she smiled back.

"What in the world do you plan to do with her all day while you're working?" Tessa wanted to know.

Sawyer shrugged. "She'll just tag along. Anyway, Cody, those steaks look so fresh they're practically still bleeding."

"Damn straight. Just got them today from the llama farm."

Tessa looked at Cody, her eyes wide with alarm. Cody laughed.

"Just kidding. I got them from Bright Star."

Tessa swatted Cody on the shoulder.

"These things are just about ready to go," Cody said. "Want to come out on the deck with me?"

Sawyer winked at Tessa. "I was thinking about staying in here and using my dog to charm your fiancée. Maybe even steal her. But I guess I can go out on the deck with you. Let me grab a beer."

"While you two do that, I'll whip up my super-secret dessert special," Tessa said.

"Watch out, Cody. She starts baking, and I'll really want to steal her."

A cutting board balanced on one hand, Cody came around the end of the counter and gave Tessa a long, deep kiss that had even Sawyer blushing.

"No danger of that," Cody told Sawyer, winking.

Although Tessa rolled her eyes, her smile showed her happiness. She scratched the puppy's head one last time and handed her back to Sawyer. He set her on the floor, and she trotted along after the men, tripping over her too-large paws every few steps.

Just like that, Sawyer Nelson was in love.

CHAPTER THREE

"YOU NEED A NAME," Montana said to her puppy the morning after bringing him home. They'd suffered through several restless hours the night before, until Montana finally gave in and brought the dog into her bed.

She couldn't believe how well she'd slept with the warm little body snuggled up to her shoulder (between potty trips to the deck). They'd just been outside, and they were lying in bed again, the puppy grasping the edge of the sheet between his sharp teeth, pulling on it with all the force his tiny body could muster.

"Monster," Montana said. "That's a good name for you." The puppy barked, then, and Montana laughed. "Big voice for such a tiny guy."

Suddenly, she wondered what size this baby would be as an adult dog. "I should have thought to ask those kids how big your parents are."

Unfazed, the puppy continued pulling on the sheet, growling with an unexpected ferocity. "You singing?" Montana asked, stroking the puppy behind the ears. She held up a finger. "I've got it. Cash. You know, like the singer. Johnny. Your voice sounds just like his."

Cash released the sheet and cocked his head to one side, as if he were listening.

"Yes. It suits you perfectly. Cash it is."

Now that Cash had calmed down, Montana took a few minutes to really look at him. Fur the color of chocolate and eyes of amber, he was just about the cutest thing she'd ever seen. Although his paws were so massive, he may end up rivaling the ponies she'd ridden as a kid … and so far, he ate like a small horse, too.

She moaned. "Why couldn't I have run into a couple of kids giving away toy poodles or something?"

Her apartment was suitable for now, but this dog was going to outgrow it any day. Even then, he started to whine, and she assumed he was hungry. He followed her into the kitchen, and she coaxed him into a sitting position while she poured his food.

"Maybe you'll just stop growing in a month or two," she said to Cash as he gobbled up the kibble. He paused his eating to look at her and wagged his tail before resuming. She rubbed his back and went to get dressed for work.

"I'm so glad I'm going to take pictures of dogs instead of going to the City Council meeting," she told Cash. "What can I wear that won't be ruined if a dog slobbers on it?" she said to herself as she slid shirts, dresses, and skirts along the rod in her closet.

She found City Council meetings boring (they were pretty much the least photogenic of all her assignments). She was a little bummed to miss this one, though. Her friend, Abby Flores, owned a construction company. Although she'd already built several commercial projects in town, she had a new one in mind: a housing development on the property adjacent to the Mint Creek Ranch. During that day's meeting, she'd present her vision to the City Council members, who would later vote on whether she could build the subdivision on the parcel.

Montana remembered the day Abby had run up to her in the grocery store, eyes bright and cheeks rosy with excitement.

"You won't believe this!"

At the time, they didn't know each other very well, and Montana thought it was a little strange that Abby would approach her like that. But they'd shared a good rapport as Montana photographed Abby's construction projects, and Montana was instantly intrigued by the sense of being let in on a secret.

"I won't believe what?"

Abby gripped Montana's arm. "I bought it! I put in an offer, and they accepted it! We're going to be neighbors!"

"Neighbors? You bought a house, here? I thought you wanted to stay in Utah."

On an exhale, Abby said, "I do. Short-term. But this? This is long-term. I have a vision, Montana! And I'm going to make it happen. Oh my gosh, this is so unlike me. I bought a piece of property, and I have no idea if I can make it work!"

Naturally, Montana had insisted then and there that they go for a celebratory drink and a more detailed explanation. Over champagne and then wine, Abby revealed that she'd always wanted to build a rural housing development, and that she'd been absolutely unable to pass up the Williamson Valley property when she laid eyes, and feet, on it.

Yes, she'd have to jump through lots of hoops and navigate tons of red tape, but finding and buying the property was the first step.

Cash came tumbling into the closet then, interrupting Montana's memory of that day and bringing her back to the present moment, in which she was tired of wearing summer work clothes and couldn't decide on an outfit appropriate for dog slobber and the blistering end-of-summer heat.

Abby's proposal for rezoning her land would be a tough sell: most of the ranchers in Williamson Valley (the home of Mint Creek Ranch) were against any kind of development in the area. Trace was one of them. He'd seen the rezoning presentation on the meeting agenda and was all fired up about it. Montana knew Trace had no idea who was making the presentation, but him finding out was going to be interesting.

Abby had kept a low profile as she worked on the commercial projects.

"I like my work to speak for itself," she told Montana the first time Montana went out to a job site to take photos for the paper. "I'd rather you didn't get me in any of the pictures."

And Montana could respect that.

So, even though Trace was aware of the commercial projects Abby had completed over the past few months, he probably had no idea who Abby was. He was in for a rude awakening at the meeting, Montana thought. As much as she loved Trace, he could be a bit old-fashioned. He *hated* the idea of Abby's development (even though he didn't yet know it was *her* development), and had spent the past several days complaining to Sawyer and Cody about it.

But because Montana hated conflict, she couldn't bring herself to tell either Trace or Abby that a rivalry was likely ... besides, she certainly didn't want to be caught in the middle.

She returned her focus to her outfit. While going through her skirts for what felt like the millionth time, a piece of clothing dropped to the floor. When she picked it up, she recognized it right away: it was the skirt Sawyer bought for her at a rodeo in Albuquerque a few years back. He wasn't always the most romantic or sentimental, so when he returned from Albuquerque and presented her with a cute little gift bag, she was touched. And when she saw that he had picked out a skirt for her, she was thrilled. It was long and soft and contained just about every color from the rainbow. Some of the sections had little glass beads on them and others had mirrored sequins.

She held the skirt up to her face and inhaled, trying to remember when she'd worn it last. Feeling sentimental, she slipped out of her sweatpants and into the skirt, adding a thin t-shirt and a pair of sandals, and hoping she wouldn't cross paths with Sawyer that day.

Montana carried Cash to the bathroom and couldn't resist scratching his neck one more time. He licked her fingers, and his tail thumped against the floor before she closed the door.

Those sentimental feelings still running strong, Montana decided to stop for a coffee at Brew. And, for the first time since Abby moved to Prescott, Montana saw her by chance, leaning against the back of her truck in the parking lot. Montana parked next to the truck.

"Good morning," she said as she got out of her car.

"I hope it is," Abby said.

Montana shut her car door. "Is the brilliant and fantastic Abby Flores nervous? That's not like you."

"I am. And I know, it's not."

"But you've already got the property. What are you nervous about?"

Abby sighed. "I don't know. I mean, you know as well as I do that not everyone loves the idea of any new development out in Williamson Valley. I want official approval, right? But more than that, I want real, genuine approval. It's that age-old desire, right? I want people to like the projects. To like *me*."

Immediately, Montana thought of Trace. And then she thought she might throw up. Trace would never like Abby. She cleared her throat. "I get that. Just give them time. Once they get to know you and see what you have in mind, they'll like you."

"I hope you're right."

Side by side, the two of them walked into the coffee shop. Abby stared up at the menu, looking dazed. Montana squeezed her arm, and she shook her head and offered a weak smile.

Montana winked at her. "Let me get your coffee for you. Relax. You'll be fine. Just remember to smile."

Montana wished she could go with Abby to the meeting, but the humane society hadn't been able to move her appointment. She left her friend with one final hug, and said, "I'll call you after. You'll be great."

———

THE HUMANE SOCIETY shoot took just as long as a City Council meeting would have, but provided exponentially more entertainment. Montana went back to the *Daily Dispatch* newsroom to process her photos.

"Hey, did you make it to that City Council meeting, by chance?" Stanley Stephenson, editor in chief, approached her desk.

She shook her head and turned her monitor so he could see what she was working on. "Puppy pictures."

"Ah, that's right," he said. "Well, I hear the meeting was a doozy. Your buddy Trace got all worked up."

Montana felt sick again. "Figures."

"It's going to run as a Page One story, so I was hoping you could get some shots of Abby Flores."

Montana nodded. "Sure."

"All right. Thanks. I've got a lunch, so I'll see you later."

After choosing a few of the best dog photos, Montana uploaded them to the server. Then, because curiosity pulled at her, she pulled up the replay of the City Council meeting.

As she watched on her computer screen, people filed in and sat down. Montana recognized most of them. Prescott was a small town. There was Mama Martin, owner of the llama farm, and old Farmer Hernandez.

The mayor, who ran the meetings, tapped his gavel on the table in front of him. "It's nine a.m. Let's get started."

After all the typical welcome and business items, it was Abby's turn to speak. Her hands clasped together at her waist were the only giveaway that she was nervous. She handed a flash drive to the City's technology person and within a few seconds, her slideshow was projected onto a screen at one side of the room. Abby went and stood next to the screen. Someone dimmed the lights. The audience hushed.

Montana held her breath.

Abby took a deep breath and began speaking. "I'm here today to begin the process of rezoning the property at Williamson Valley and Saddle Horn Roads. I'd like to divide the property into twenty parcels, each one five acres. I believe these larger parcels will allow us to maintain the character and integrity of the area. I'd like to share with you my proposed plans, and the finalized designs for the different models."

No one spoke, so Abby went on. "First slide, please."

An image appeared on the projector screen: a drawing of the rolling hills so familiar to Montana, dotted with houses. "As you can see, the way I've situated the houses will allow for maximum space and privacy, and it shouldn't impact the neighbors or the flow of traffic, because I've put in new roads here and here."

Still, no one spoke.

"Okay," Abby said. "I'll show you the models now, so you can get a feel for how the development will really look. Next slide, please."

Montana inhaled, held her breath.

"This is the forest cottage model," Abby said. "It's the smallest of the four models, with options for two or three bedrooms."

It was adorable, Montana thought. Perfect. Exactly what a person would see in the forest. In a fairytale. Montana was in love. It was so charming, with its peaked roof and little square windows in front. The rendering showed little flower boxes underneath the windows, stuffed with bright blooms. Montana used her imagination to fill in all the other details: the welcome mat, some colorful Adirondack chairs, her car in the garage. And her dog! Little Cash, all grown up, running around the front yard.

Abby went on to describe the other three models. Some of the Williamson Valley property owners, including Trace, got up to speak. Montana got the vague impression they didn't want the Council to approve the rezoning. But she had stopped listening. All she could think about was the cottage. *Her* cottage. She already had a new dog. It only made sense that she would get a new place. By the end of the meeting, she had made a very important decision. She was going to buy a house. Not just any house. One of Abby's.

———

THE CITY COUNCIL meeting was over and Montana's computer screen was blank. She clicked out of the Internet browser and closed her eyes. Her vision was there, plain as day. Although her fingers itched to pick up the phone and call Abby immediately, she knew it wouldn't hurt to sleep on her big decision.

Home ownership was on her mind immediately when she woke up, though, so she called Abby and scheduled a photo shoot, out at the property that would be the Sunset Valley subdivision. In a rush to see the space in person, she got there before Abby did.

"Thank you so much for doing this," she said when Abby got out of her truck. "You're making my life so much easier. To tell you the truth, I hate photographing City Council meetings. I'd much rather meet someone out here where at least there's scenery."

Abby turned in a full circle. "Yes, there's definitely scenery, isn't there?"

Montana rested the camera on her hip. "So what brings you to Williamson Valley property ownership?"

The question sounded awkward to her own ears, but Abby didn't seen to notice.

"Oh, I'm sure you've heard that it's, you know, just a burning desire to completely ruin the atmosphere Williamson Valley. Sorry. It's just that this is pretty much my dream project. This is my dream property. I'd like to live here, myself. The last thing I want to do is ruin it."

Montana took a deep breath and squeezed Abby's arm. "Don't let Trace get to you. He's averse to change. It's not you."

"I take it you're a Prescott native, too? That's how you know Mr. Walker?"

Mr. Walker. Montana laughed. "Yes, I'm a native. And I've never called Trace 'Mr. Walker' a day in my life. We literally grew up together, running every inch of the Mint Creek Ranch as kids. Along with Cody Davis and Sawyer Nelson. Trace is like a brother to me. I love the heck out of him, but I also know he can be a little … or a *lot* hardheaded."

A series of emotions ran over Abby's face and Montana felt like she'd said the wrong thing; she'd implied she would be on Trace's side. She rushed to say, "Oh, my gosh. I can read every thought you're thinking right now. Don't worry. I'm nothing like Trace. Okay, maybe we have a few things in common. But let's just say I'm a little more open-minded than he is. I watched the online replay of your presentation at the meeting, and I can see the potential in what you're envisioning for your development. And, goodness knows, I could use another girlfriend. Seems like I'm always surrounded by men. Trace will come around."

At that last part, Abby made a face, and Montana laughed. "I know. Maybe he won't. But even if he doesn't, you and I can still be friends, right?"

Finally, Abby smiled. "In that case, I'd love to show you my sketches. This is totally preliminary, since the City Council hasn't even approved the rezoning yet. But it'll give you an idea of what I'm thinking."

Back at her truck, Abby pulled the printed versions of the drawings out of the cab and spread them on the tailgate. Montana stood next to her, her excitement growing. Obviously, Abby had put a lot of thought into designing the subdivision.

"Oh, I see," Montana said. "You've got the houses situated here for maximum privacy, right? The little hills will be between the houses, so neighbors won't be able to see into each others' windows. And this bank of windows is south-facing, right?"

Once they'd looked at the last page, Montana beamed at Abby. "This is going to be amazing. I just know it's going to happen."

Abby beamed back. "Thank you. You don't know how much that means to me."

"You know what?" Montana said. "This lighting is really nice. Why don't I get a couple pictures of you right here, with the property in the background? Maybe a few beside the truck, with the drawings, and a few without the truck?"

With natural beauty and confidence, Abby was an easy subject. After about ten minutes, Montana said, "I think I've got what I need, here. Thanks again for meeting up. I'm sure you have a lot going on."

"No more than you do, I'm sure. Actually, it's good you got me out of the house. I've been obsessing over these drawings, and I need to stop by a couple of job sites this afternoon."

"I just want to say, you did great this morning," Montana said.

"Really?" Abby said. "I was so nervous! And then, when all those people spoke at the end … I don't know. Do you think I did okay?"

"I do," Montana said, smiling. "In fact, you did so well, I want to take you out to lunch."

"Is this actually a pity invite?"

Montana laughed. "Absolutely not. It's actually more of a proposal."

Interest sparked in Abby's eyes. "I'm in. Where do you want to go?"

"How about the Burger Shack?"

"Sure," Abby said. "I'm famished. I could use a nice juicy burger right now."

"And a beer," they said in unison.

A few minutes later, they'd settled into a red-and-white-striped booth at the Burger Shack and ordered a couple of beers. They made small talk while they waited for their drinks and food.

As soon as the server returned, the women clinked their bottles together and Abby said, "Okay. Dish."

For a few seconds, Montana debated waiting until their server delivered their food. *She* was the nervous one this time.

What if Abby didn't think it would work? Montana was going to need her buy-in. She decided she might as well just launch in, while her emotions were still high after imagining living in that adorable cottage.

"Well?" Abby asked. "I can sure see your wheels turning. What are you thinking?"

Montana took another deep breath. "I want to buy one of your houses."

It was a big declaration. Abby knew Montana lived in an apartment the size of a postage stamp. She probably assumed Montana couldn't afford to buy a place, much less one of the homes in a brand-new development in the most expensive area of Prescott. Plus, Abby could undoubtedly tell, from the way Trace glared at her through the entire City Council meeting, that he hated the idea of her development. And Montana had grown up with Trace, on the very land he thought he was defending.

Montana held her breath. If she was surprised, Abby didn't show it. She tilted her head. "I mean, I love my own designs, but that's just ego. Are you serious?"

"Serious as a heart attack."

Speaking of heart attacks, Montana felt like she was about to have one. Her heart was about to beat right out of her chest.

"Well."

"I'm not sure what that means."

"First and foremost, I'm flattered. To have someone with your sense of taste wanting to buy one of my houses? That's really amazing."

"But."

Abby shrugged. "But, you *are* part of the Mint Creek Ranch crew. You're practically a sister to Trace, who, as we saw today, is completely against me putting in this development."

"I didn't hear a word of what he said."

"You didn't?"

"I was gone, off in lala land, imagining buying one of your houses."

"Wow," Abby said.

"You don't know how much it would mean to me to buy a cottage," Montana said, reaching across the table to take hold of Abby's hands. "Yes. I am a Mint Creek Ranch girl. But anyone with half a brain can see that what you're doing is going to be amazing."

Abby raised an eyebrow, and Montana said, "I mean, Trace has half a brain, but only just. And, apparently, not where you're concerned."

"Oh, I can't tell you how good it feels to hear you say that," Abby said. "Even though I believe, from the bottom of my heart, that this development is going to be amazing, and an asset, and make Mint Creek Ranch and all of Williamson Valley even more special, Trace had me questioning my sanity. I thought maybe I was wrong. I thought maybe it would feel too crowded, that the development would be an eyesore in Williamson Valley."

"Are you kidding me?" Montana said. "I mean, I love Trace. And he has a good head on his shoulders. But he's wrong! I can't believe you let what he was saying get to you."

"I've always considered myself a pretty confident person," Abby said. "But for some reason, Trace gets under my skin."

An imaginary lightbulb illuminated over Montana's head. Each of them, apparently, got under the other's skin ... what could it mean? But no. It was impossible. Montana tapped her fingers on the tabletop. Abby looked down at the motion. Montana stopped and took another drink. This was not the right time to bring up that possibility. She needed to stay on track. But she *did* make a mental note to come back to it.

"Anyway. Back to the matter at hand," Montana said. "I'm not your regular buyer."

Abby waited, patient. Montana took another quick sip of her beer. "I have quite a bit saved up. But maybe not enough for a real down payment. And I'm not sure if I can get a traditional loan. I know this is going to be a really big ask. But I was wondering if we might be able to make some kind of deal. Like, where I buy directly from you, with special terms."

On the drive over here, Montana had worked this all out, scribbling notes on a piece of paper at red lights. She pulled that piece of paper out of her purse, unfolded it, and smoothed it before turning it around so Abby could read it.

"Fact is, I don't know how much one of your houses even costs. I mean, I get that there's a base value and certain things are considered add-ons. But I was thinking maybe I could make a down payment with everything I've got saved up. And then, I could take photos for your marketing. I could run any sort of marketing campaigns. That was my second major in college, you know? I don't know how much that would be worth to you, but I know how much I typically charge. I figured you would want to do some marketing, and I don't know if you've hired anyone yet. But I know this town. I know its people. And I know I could bring in some buyers. I grew up here. I grew up in Williamson Valley, right next door to your development. I know everything that makes it wonderful. I —"

"Montana. Montana, wait." Abby's eyes bored holes into Montana's. "Yes. The answer is yes. I will do whatever it takes to help you get into one of my houses."

Yes? "Yes?" Montana's heart was beating so hard, she could hear the sound of it in her ears.

"Yes!"

She jumped out of the booth and slid in next to Abby, giving her a squeeze around the shoulders. "That's it? You don't want to work out all the details? Like, how I'll pay you, how I'll run your marketing, how many buyers I'll bring in?"

Abby waved a hand, dismissing Montana's concern. "I'm not worried about it. I know where you live."

Montana tightened her hug. "Thank you! Thank you so much. Thank you to infinity. You have no idea how much this means to me."

"Well, you're giving me a pretty good idea."

The server was back with their food. "Are we celebrating? Should I bring dessert?"

Montana felt tears threatening to spill over her lower lids. She dashed them away with her fingertips. After the server left, she returned to her side of the booth.

"Actually, marketing is something I've been thinking a lot about," Abby said. "I have no idea what to do when it comes to that. I mean, I have my phone, but I don't have a nice camera like yours. And I did think about asking you to take some pictures for me, but I didn't want to impose. I know you already work full-time. I didn't know if you would want a whole separate job."

"Are you kidding me? There's nothing I want more. And," Montana said. "As you can see, *I'm* not afraid of imposing."

She took a big bite of her burger. She'd never tasted anything so wonderful. Abby looked about as delirious as Montana felt.

Abby smiled and picked up her own burger. "I'm glad. As much as it means to you to live in one of the cottages, it means a lot to me, too. I mean it."

"Good. I'm going to need a big yard for my new puppy. I've got to think about fencing for him."

"Wait. Your new puppy?"

Montana filled Abby in on Cash, and how she'd realized he was going to quickly outgrow the apartment.

"Perfect, then! This is divine timing."

For a few minutes, they ate in silence.

A house. She was going to own a house! She, Montana Hart, was going to be a homeowner. With a dog and a yard, and even a garden. And without a man. Perfect.

"So," Abby said. "Have you been thinking about my marketing?"

Montana was ready for this. She *had* been thinking about Abby's marketing. She nodded, swallowing her food. "I have. I think the first thing you need to do is create some social media accounts. And get some great photos we can use. We can repurpose things. But we're going to need a lot of photos and a lot of copy … you know, the words."

Abby nodded. "I know what copy is."

"Also, I think we need to come up with a theme for your campaign. Like, the main message."

Abby nodded. "Okay. We might be getting a little ahead of ourselves. We still need rezoning approval. But I'll start brainstorming. You know, I'm so glad you brought up this idea. I'm so used to doing everything on my own. It's the one thing I love and hate about myself. It's so hard for me to rely on people. To admit that I need help. So thank you."

Montana could relate. The youngest of all the Mint Creek Ranch kids, she had always been on a mission to prove that she could do everything the bigger kids could do.

"Well, I guess we're in this together, now."

Abby squealed, surprising Montana. They both laughed.

Montana checked her watch. "I'd better go. I've got to get your amazing photos uploaded so we can print them in tomorrow's paper."

Abby groaned. "Do you have to? I'm afraid I'm going to get hate mail from Trace."

"Just tell him to shove off. That's my first marketing tip for you."

"You're hired."

———

THE MOMENT MONTANA got into her car to leave the Burger Shack, she squealed.

Abby had invited her to meet up after work later to drive out to the property. Montana was going to choose the lot she wanted. Her own lot!

She could hear Sawyer's reasonable voice in her mind: "Calm down, Montana. Even if she's marked out the lots, the City Council hasn't approved rezoning. Don't count your chickens."

"Chickens, schmickens," she said into the empty space of her car.

She was giddy, drunk on excitement, on possibility. Drunk on independence. She turned up the music and belted out the lyrics to one of her favorite country songs. Before she knew it, she was dancing, drumming her thumbs on the steering wheel, her head swinging. As she came into downtown, she stopped at a red light around the corner from the *Daily Dispatch* office. Turning up the music even louder, she continued to sing and dance. She heard a honk, then. The friendly double-tap broke through her joy-induced haze. She looked over to see who was honking.

"Of course."

It was Trace. Who, aside from being like a brother to Montana, considered Abby his mortal enemy. Well, Montana thought, since she was going to be in cahoots with Abby, he'd probably consider himself Montana's mortal enemy as well. But at the moment, she didn't care. She wouldn't let Trace rob her of her joy.

She swallowed, hoping to quell the rise of panic in her torso.

Then she gave him a friendly wave, just a wiggle of the fingers, and went right on with her singing and dancing. She glanced over one more time and saw him shaking his head, smiling.

"Go ahead and laugh, Trace!" she hollered, even though he couldn't hear her.

The light turned green. She accelerated through the intersection and thought, *Go ahead and laugh. But I am starting my new life and nothing can stop me.*

CHAPTER FOUR

SAWYER COULD REMEMBER the exact moment he knew Montana was the only woman he would ever love. They were seventeen. It was the last day of school before winter break their junior year. As soon as that final bell rang, Sawyer, Cody, Trace, and Montana piled into Cody's old truck. It was so warm for December that Sawyer and Montana decided to ride in the bed, leaning against the cab, legs stretched out in front of them. Sawyer could feel the heat from the metal through his jeans. His body touched Montana's from shoulder to ankle. The sun's rays, unusually strong that day, cast shadows of Montana's lashes onto her cheeks.

She laced her fingers through his, just like she did whenever they were together. Sawyer looked down at their joined hands and noticed, not for the first time, how perfectly they fit.

Hers were petite, and her fingernails were these perfect little squares. When she painted them, they looked like Chiclets. His hands were the opposite. In fact, Cody and Trace often made fun of his "block hands." At the moment, they looked like part of something magical. Even as that floated through his mind, Sawyer laughed at his own sentimentality. That was a goofy thing to think about — holding hands being magical. But then he looked over at Montana, and she was looking at him, smiling. Like she was thinking the exact same thing he was.

"What are you thinking about?" he asked her.

"Just that I'm hoping you'll meet me in the loft later."

Okay, so she wasn't thinking about their magical hand-holding. But she was thinking about having sex with him, and wasn't that magical, too?

Because it was Friday and the day before winter break, all the families gathered together at Cody's parents' house for a big feast. Even as a kid, Sawyer knew those nights were special. Not everyone got to grow up in a loud, happy, loving extended family like he did.

Sawyer and Montana sat side by side at the big dining room table. Even while the room buzzed with the sounds of talk and laughter and silverware clinking on plates, Sawyer couldn't focus on anything other than Montana. She was telling him about an art project she was working on — a sculpture she wanted to enter into a statewide competition. He kept thinking about her hands, smoothing the clay, shaping it. Then he pictured his own hands, smoothing over her skin, and he could hardly eat because he was so anxious to get to the loft. It felt like forever before dinner was over.

As usual, the kids rushed through cleanup. Sawyer most of all, but no one noticed how anxious he was to get out of the house. Looking back, Sawyer couldn't remember exactly what he said to Trace and Cody and Cody's sister, Annie — probably something about making themselves scarce — but, like good friends, they disappeared.

To avoid tipping off the parents, Sawyer left a few minutes before Montana. In the hay loft, he spread a few blankets on the floor and lit a couple of the lanterns they kept in the barn. The sun had set by that time, and the barn was already a little chilly. He added a blanket to the stack and rubbed his hands together for warmth.

"A fireplace up here would be real nice, right about now," he said into the silence, and he was surprised that he could see his breath in front of his face. An image materialized: he and Montana making love in front of a fire. The more he thought about it, the harder his erection became. By the time she climbed the ladder, it was excruciating.

"Waiting for me?" she asked.

In answer, he pulled down his pants and stepped out of them to walk toward her.

Montana gasped and covered her mouth with one hand. Her eyes twinkled, though, and he knew she was amused and aroused: behind the twinkling, there was a smoldering.

They didn't speak after that. Her boots came off first. Next, she took off her layers, peeling the sweater away from her body, and then the shirt. When she unhooked her bra, revealing her sweet, firm breasts, he groaned. She slid her skirt over her hips and let it pool on the floor at her feet, and then did the same with her underwear.

Sawyer stood there in a trance. Still smiling, she moved toward him and grabbed the bottom edge of his t-shirt. Her fingertips on his bare hips sent a shiver over his skin. Then, the two of them were laying on the blankets, facing each other. Her fingertips trailed up the side of his body and back down. Although his lower half begged to plunge into her — how warm and glorious that would feel — he didn't. He took his time, exploring every soft curve, every smooth line. He used his hands and his mouth on all her delicious parts and when she groaned, finally, begging without words, he brought his face to hers and kissed her. They both had their eyes open, and in that moment, he entered her. She cried out, and he felt her body pulsing around him in release.

His own release came almost instantaneously, and after he finished shuddering, his face buried in her hair, he chuckled. "Wow. I guess I'm pretty good, aren't I?"

She stroked the back of his neck, giving a little laugh of her own.

"Well, I guess you are." He moved off of her and pulled her close, so they were spooning. And that was the moment. Montana was it for him.

They both fell asleep within a few minutes.

Sawyer slept so soundly, and when he woke in the morning, he knew it had snowed. The air had that special quality: heavy, perfect silence. And it was *cold*. So cold the tips of his ears were practically numb.

Ever since he was a little kid, Sawyer loved to look at the snow. Even as a teenager, he couldn't resist slipping out of the makeshift bed in the hay loft to look through a knothole. And boy, had it snowed. More than he had ever seen at once. Three feet, maybe even four. He debated for a couple of seconds. Should he wake Montana so she could see it, or let her sleep?

A shout outside, followed by a *thunk* somewhere very close to his eyeball — a snowball hitting the side of the barn — made the decision for him. *Thunk.*

Just as he looked at Montana, she stretched, and the blanket fell away from her bare arms and upper back. Sawyer started to go hard right away, seeing her skin like that. But another snowball hit the side of the barn.

Montana pulled the blanket back up under her chin and said, "Go on. They're not gonna stop until you go out there and have it out with them. I'll be waiting when you get back."

Shivering now — the air in the loft was frigid, and he could see his breath — Sawyer pulled on his clothes, including the heavy jacket he'd worn the night before. He climbed down the ladder and poked his head through the open door. Cody and Trace, engaged in their own snowball fight, didn't see him. He ducked down and started packing snowballs. Working quickly, he set them in a pile, hoping to have a nice arsenal built up before Trace and Cody noticed he was out of the barn. He remembered there were gloves in the barn only after he made a couple of dozen snowballs and his fingers were numb. When he returned, hands gloved and tingling as they warmed up, he gave a loud whistle. Trace and Cody froze. Then they sprang back to life, running through the snow, lifting their legs high to get through the drifts. Their progress was slow, which gave Sawyer time to throw his snowballs at them, rapid fire. He let out a long, loud war cry as he did, and the two of them yelled, laughing, holding their arms up in front of their faces as he pelted them. Within a couple of minutes, he was out of ammunition. Cody and Trace charged, then, picking up giant piles of snow and throwing them at him as they got close enough.

The snow was soft, and it sparkled in the post-storm sunshine. For the next half hour, the three of them fought, throwing clumps of snow, packing hard snowballs, hiding behind whatever they could — the tractors, the old farm trucks, and sections of fence. Then they decided to build a snow fort, and they made giant blocks of ice using a horse trough as a mold. Before long, they had a curved wall about six feet wide and six feet tall. Although the sun shone, the air was still so cold, they figured the fort would keep for the rest of the day. They also figured they were famished.

Cody and Trace trudged off to their houses to change clothes and rustle up breakfast and Sawyer went back into the barn and climbed the ladder to the loft. The sight of Montana lying there took his breath away. He took off his own wet clothes and slid between the blankets behind her, feeling so much tenderness for her. He just wanted to hold her.

Then she shrieked and scooted away from him.

"Sawyer Levi Nelson! You are freezing cold! Get your own blanket. This instant!"

Sawyer chuckled and did as he was told. He tucked Montana's blanket behind her body and then slid back into position behind her.

"That's better," she said. "I suppose those other two hoodlums went to get some breakfast?"

Sawyer nuzzled Montana's neck, inhaling the sweet scent of her shampoo. "Sure did."

"Well, I reckon we'd better do the same."

Sawyer could think of something he'd rather do. But his skin was still cold. And he knew she wouldn't let him touch her until he warmed up. So, he contented himself with nibbling on her ear and running his hand over her butt through the blankets. He was hungry. And, he could lay there forever with her. And *that* was the moment: Montana Hart was the only woman for him. Forever. But instead of saying so out loud, he said, "I'm famished."

———

YEARS LATER, Sawyer still thought about Montana every morning when he woke up on the Mint Creek Ranch. Each and every square inch of the property held a memory of her. Her scent clung to the furniture. The image of her body lingered, a ghost on his couch, in his bed, in his shower, walking across the deck.

One Sunday morning, his dog — still nameless — woke him up with a few ferocious barks.

"Okay, okay," he said, rubbing the sleep from his eyes as he rolled to a sitting position. After pulling on his sweatpants, he set her on the floor. She followed him, doing her best to get a grip on the leg of his pants.

"You've got a voice on you, that's for sure," Sawyer said, heading straight for the back door. He'd learned quickly that taking even a couple of minutes to start the coffee was a mistake.

As he opened the back door, the dog howled.

"Dolly," he said. "That's it. That's your name."

She looked up at him, and he could swear she was smiling again. She trotted outside.

In the backyard, as always, he looked to Montana's favorite chair.

Years before, when she first decided to leave for college, it was like she'd taken the axe they used for splitting logs and cleaved his heart right in half. And not just his heart, but his entire being. After a time, her physical absence was a relief. But within a few weeks, he started noticing that even though she wasn't around, working the ranch with them, he felt her everywhere. He couldn't escape it.

Then she graduated, got her fancy degree, and came back. Sure, she had her own place off the ranch, and she had her job at the *Daily Dispatch*. But she was around again. And she was his, at least some of the time.

Until she wasn't. She was quitting him.

Suddenly, Sawyer realized Dolly (yes! The name fit perfectly) was sitting at his feet, looking up at him. He bent to scratch her behind the ears, and kept thinking about Montana as they walked back into the house.

Since the other morning, when that thing, whatever it was, had shifted between them, and he knew he'd never hold Montana in his arms again, he felt like he had to get off the ranch. The only way to get over her was to get off this property. He had to stop living with his memories.

So, he decided, he would start looking for a new place. The idea at once thrilled and terrified him. He set the coffee to brew, played a long game of tug-of-war with Dolly, and settled on the couch with his tablet and a mug.

He told himself that searching for properties for sale was just for kicks. He told himself he was just looking, daydreaming. And, as he looked at pictures and prices and maps, he told himself he just might have a panic attack.

Mint Creek Ranch was the only home he'd ever known. Moving away would be like — well, it would be like leaving a nest where he'd been warm and protected his whole life. But he was no baby bird, and anyway, he was just looking. Browsing. Kind of like window shopping. Dolly, in her bed on the floor next to the couch, made a few pitiful barking noises. She was still asleep, and clearly dreaming. He wondered what puppies dreamed about. And then he wondered what

Montana would think of his puppy. Then he kicked himself for thinking about Montana and what she would think of his puppy. It didn't matter. She would love the puppy. She probably wouldn't even make it sleep on the floor. She'd probably let it right up on the couch with her.

"Focus, Sawyer," he said.

There were lots of properties for sale, according to the Internet. Some of them were pretty nice, too. He didn't want a place in town, even though he'd always liked the look of the old, cozy houses. It would feel too claustrophobic. He needed a place where he could breathe. Someplace like Mint Creek Ranch, but that wasn't infused with his memories of Montana. He narrowed his search, entering the ZIP Code that encompassed Williamson Valley, the home of Mint Creek Ranch. If he could at least be neighbors with Cody and Trace, he thought he could survive moving away.

There were a couple of properties he recognized, one of them a gorgeous ranch property he'd driven by a million times. It had everything: a great well, windmills and solar panels, and irrigation. But it was too far out. It would take him thirty minutes just to get to the grocery store. Absently, he continued to scroll and click, scroll and click.

Then he saw it: a listing for a custom-built home, in the unit right next to Mint Creek Ranch. He wasn't sure exactly where the property was, and the listing didn't give a specific address. It did contain renderings of several different models. Each one of them was striking in its own way. There was a little cottage, and a huge château. There were a couple of in-between models, too. Sawyer felt his excitement growing.

Every property in the area was a few hundred acres, which meant that while he'd have his own space, he'd still be within riding distance of his first home. There was a number to contact the seller. Sawyer picked up his phone, then set it down. He'd wait until the next day — nobody worked Sundays in Prescott. It wasn't like a big city where the commerce ran twenty-four seven, which was part of what he loved about it. He pulled up the image of the cottage again and sent it to the printer. A few minutes later, he hung it on his fridge with a magnet he'd gotten from his favorite saloon.

Not because he would forget to call about it, but because the prospect of having his own place, where he could make brand-new memories and have a completely fresh start, was something he wanted to think about every time he walked into the kitchen.

———

THE NEXT MORNING, Sawyer pulled up at the Mint Creek Ranch arena just before eight. He was set to practice team roping with Trace after morning chores, but he was more excited about the prospect of buying a new place than he was about team roping. Still, he had to focus. The Turquoise Circuit had just ended and they didn't have any competitions for a while, but they'd learned from experience that a pair of team ropers could get too much rest. So they made a point of practicing at least twice a week.

When he got out of his truck, he saw that Cody and Trace were already there, horses saddled.

"Am I late?" Sawyer asked as he walked up.

"No," Cody said, and Trace added, "We're just early. Neither of us could sleep last night. We both decided to drag ourselves out of bed before sunrise."

"Better than tossing and turning all morning," Cody said.

"You guys should've called me," Sawyer said.

But he didn't mean it. He'd enjoyed his morning, his daydreaming, his time with his dog. At that thought, he froze. His dog. He'd left the poor girl in the car. There was no way to play it off like he'd meant to do it, so instead, he made a point of being silly, doing an exaggerated pivot turn and heading back to the truck. When he opened the driver's door, his fat little puppy waddled over, her tail wagging a million miles an hour. He lifted her to his chest, and she went to work licking the underside of his chin. He laughed and spluttered and gently pushed Dolly's face away from his.

"That's the great thing about dogs," Cody said. "You can forget them in your car and they still love you. Unconditional love is a real thing with them, unlike with the ladies. Right, Sawyer?"

Sawyer used his free hand to give Cody the middle finger as he walked to the barn to introduce Dolly to Whistler.

He lifted Dolly up to Whistler's eye level, and the horse snorted. He turned his head, his left eye focusing in on this new, furry creature. Dolly seemed completely nonplussed. Relaxed and pliable, she lounged in Sawyer's hands like she'd seen many horses in her short life.

"Whistler, Dolly. Dolly, Whistler. The two of you are going to have to get acquainted. No spooking each other, you hear?"

The horse's massive nose moved closer to the puppy, and just when it got close enough, she licked it. Whistler huffed again, and Dolly wiggled.

A few minutes later, Sawyer had Whistler saddled, and he held Dolly under one arm as he swung into the seat. He settled her on the saddle in front of him, then immediately wondered how long the setup would last. He had no idea how big Dolly would get.

"At some point, you're going to have to run beside us, girl," he said.

When he rode out to the arena, the guys laughed at him, which was pretty much par for the course. The three of them laughed at each other whatever chance they got. A few hours later, after weekend chores, it was time for practice.

"Well, what are we doing today, ladies?" Sawyer asked.

"I thought we could just do a couple of drills," Trace said.

"Why don't you let me hold your dog while I time you?" Cody said. "Apparently, I'm going to have to get used to holding babies. Tessa wants a whole bunch of them."

Again, laughter ensued, this time at Cody's expense.

"You sucker!" Trace said. "First you propose. And now you're getting wrangled into having a whole bunch of kids!"

Cody just smiled, and Sawyer felt a surge of jealousy. He loved Cody, and he was so happy Cody was happy — his best friend was on top of the world. He had just won the bull riding championships and proposed to the woman of his dreams, and he was getting ready to start a new life with her. But Sawyer recognized the pang in his chest. He wanted that too.

He handed the puppy over and Cody held her in his arms. The puppy took to licking Cody's chin.

Cody guided his horse to the edge of the arena while Trace and Sawyer went into the pasture to round up some steers. The two of them had always been such a great team. Clockwork, a well-oiled machine, all of that. They didn't even need to speak — Trace went right, Sawyer went left, and they shaved off a few head of cattle and herded them back to the arena. Cody had the chute open and within a matter of seconds, the cattle were in a smaller pen, with one in the chute.

Steer after steer, Sawyer and Trace practiced. They ran the routine again and again. All of it felt so familiar: the sound of the chute opening, the beating of the cattle's hooves on the arena floor. The smells of the horses sweating and the saddle leather. Trace's commands to his horse. Their movements were smooth and their times were great. Steer up, steer down. Up, down. Up, down.

So why did Sawyer suddenly feel like he wasn't at home here? It was strange. After about forty-five minutes, Trace, Sawyer, and their horses were sweating.

"Ready for a break?" Cody asked.

"If by a 'break,' you mean a beer, I'm ready." Sawyer said.

"Is it even noon yet?" Trace wanted to know.

"Close enough," Sawyer said, and nodding, Cody said, "I happen to have some beers right here."

Cody dismounted, the puppy still tucked safely under his arm, and walked over to a cooler at the edge of the arena, from which he pulled out two cans.

"Hey, you're pretty good at holding a baby and getting beers," Sawyer said.

Cody just rolled his eyes and tossed one to each Trace and Sawyer before grabbing another for himself.

"This is about the most refreshing beer I've had in a long time," Sawyer said.

"It is," Trace said. "But don't enjoy it too much. I think our friend Cody here might be trying to butter us up for something."

Cody, obviously buying time, set Dolly on the ground. All three men watched her waddle around, sniffing every square inch of the arena floor.

"You might be right."

"Oh," Trace said, and Sawyer said, "Bottoms up. I hope you brought a whole six pack."

The two of them gulped down their beers, and Cody chuckled. He retrieved another can for each of them. As they opened them, he said, "Well, you two probably are smart enough that you already know this. But apparently, a proposal means a wedding. Tessa and I are planning one."

"I think I'm gonna be sick," Trace said, and when Cody shot him a dark look, he said, quickly, "Just kidding, man." He punched Cody on the shoulder. "That's exciting. I suppose the beers are bribery. You're going to want our help."

Cody nodded. "That's right. More than anything, I need your moral support. I mean, I couldn't be happier to be marrying Tessa. It's just — a wedding, all that attention, all the planning, all the decisions about minutiae, like what color tablecloths ..."

His voice trailed off.

Sawyer knew what was going on. Cody was nervous. Not about the wedding itself, but about the inevitable media attention in would draw.

Too much media attention had been a problem for Cody about a year ago. An over-ambitious reporter had unknowingly revealed the location of Cody's sister, Annie, who had returned to Prescott to hide from her abusive ex-boyfriend. The reporter had done a cute little write-up of how Cody and Annie spent a night out on the town, getting out Cody's pre-competition jitters. The jerk ex-boyfriend saw the newspaper article and traveled to Prescott to hurt Annie.

The timing was disastrous: it was right before the final night of Cody's bull-riding championships.

Cody, so shaken by what the media attention had almost done to his sister, refused to participate. He had a real shot at the buckle, but he fled to San Diego and hid out at the beach until the championships were over. He spent the next nine months hiding from the spotlight.

But then he decided to take another run at the tour. Naturally, the editor of the local newspaper, the *Daily Dispatch*, wanted to cover his experience. Cody was a hometown star, Prescott's sweetheart. Cody agreed — as long as he vetted the reporter who would be covering him. The human resources team at the newspaper's parent company searched high and low for someone who fit Cody's strict criteria. Tessa was the clear choice. She was only missing two of the most important criteria — a few decades of age, and a penis — but she was also the only one naïve enough to accept the job, which came with a travel bonus, per diem, and room and board, but without any details about why it was so cushy.

Before meeting as reporter and subject, Tessa and Cody met as two single people at the annual rodeo dance. Minimal introductions and maximum chemistry combined for a surprise the next day, when Cody realized Tessa was the reporter who would be spending the next three months with him. He thought she was totally hot — and he almost had her fired. But, good sense prevailed. They fell in love, and the rest was history.

"I get it, man," Sawyer said. "I would be nervous, too. But I'm sure Tessa understands, and she's willing to keep it low-key?"

Cody sighed. "Yes. Absolutely. In fact, she's agreed to have it here, at the ranch."

Sawyer and Trace nodded. "So, you need our help getting everything set up," Trace said.

"Yes," Cody said. "But that's not the part I'm worried about. That's not the reason for the beers."

Uh oh. Sawyer was getting a bad feeling about this.

"The thing is, we're putting together a little team. The Kincaid-Davis Wedding Planning Team."

As Cody's eyes darted back and forth between Sawyer's and Trace's, Sawyer felt his heart pounding. He knew what was about to happen. He was like a man with his head in one of those executioner's blocks. The saw blade was being lowered. And he had to stand there and take it like a man.

"See, Tessa has a vision. And she's asked Abby to design the setting."

Next to him, Trace spluttered, spitting out his beer. Sawyer felt a rush of relief. Thank goodness. It was Abby who was going to help with the wedding, not —

"And Montana will be helping with the decorations."

"Welp," Trace said. "Sounds like you've got it covered. You don't need us."

Good recovery, Sawyer thought. He pounded Trace on the back.

Cody chugged the rest of his first beer, crushed the can, tossed it into the cooler, and grabbed his second beer. He chugged that, too, and said, "You guys are the muscle. It's your job to make Tessa's vision — with Abby's plans and Montana's design — come to life."

There was no way Sawyer could say "no." Cody was like a brother to him. Which meant he was going to be spending the next several weeks — or months — working side by side with Montana. The woman he hated to love.

CHAPTER FIVE

MONTANA THOUGHT she was excited before. But that feeling paled in comparison with what she experienced when Abby drove her onto the land that would soon be her own property. She could hardly breathe.

As if Abby could sense that, she put a hand on Montana's arm and said, "Breathe."

Cash, seated on Montana's lap, licked Abby's arm.

Montana laughed and did as she was told, taking a long inhale and letting the breath out slowly. "It's just —"

"Breathtaking, right?"

Montana nodded. Abby stopped the truck, and the three of them got out. Montana set down the puppy and took a moment to absorb it all. From where she stood, she was surrounded by the lush green fields of Williamson Valley. To the west, Granite Mountain rose, spiny against the sunset. A few leafy trees, still full, shimmered in the evening sunlight. Far off, Montana heard a cow lowing. Cash's ears perked up at that, and he gave a low growl and little bark before pouncing through the grass again.

While it all felt similar to her experience growing up on Mint Creek Ranch — peaceful, serene, picturesque, like waking up in a calendar scene every day — Montana thought owning a piece of property would give her a whole new feeling. She would wake up on a piece of land that *belonged* to her. Nothing and no one had ever truly, truly belonged to her. She thought Sawyer had, but she was wrong. He belonged to Mint Creek Ranch. But she didn't. She closed her eyes and imagined her little cottage in front of her.

"Oh Abby, I can't thank you enough. How can I ever repay you?"

Cash, an obvious empath, picked up on Montana's joy. He romped back over to her and licked her toes.

Just as Montana opened her eyes, Abby came toward her, arms out for a hug.

"No need. I can see it on your face. Just knowing that you're going to love this place as much as I do means the world to me. And now that you're seeing it like I have, I hope you can trust that I have the best of intentions. I'm not looking to develop this place, to make a bunch of cookie-cutter houses, run down the water table, any of those things. I just want people to be able to enjoy it as much as I do."

Abby stepped back and gestured for Montana to get back in the truck.

"Come on, I want to show you your choices. You're the first buyer, so you get first dibs."

Riding around with the windows down and breeze blowing back her hair, Montana had never felt so happy. She loved everything about the view: the tiny horses that dotted the neighboring fields, the silver ribbon of a creek that wound its way across the valley, and the smell of grass and hay as the wind rushed over her.

As they drove along, Abby pointed out the different plots, which were marked at the corners with stakes.

"I think all the lots are great. But some of them are, you know, prime real estate. This one here, it's at a lower point. Which, you might think means it doesn't have the views. But look how green this grass is growing through here. If you wanted a garden, this would be a great place for it."

Did Montana want a garden? Absolutely. Hadn't she always loved flowers? She didn't have to be practical and grow vegetables, if she didn't want to. But *flowers*. Wouldn't that be something?

"I would love to have a garden," she said, and then she laughed because she sounded so enthusiastic.

"And this one here is a bit higher in elevation. It does have a killer view, right?" Abby stopped the vehicle and pointed to the west, where the setting sun shot bright rays into the sky against a vivid sunset. It was spectacular.

"It does have the view."

Abby nodded, all business. "Look at the ground. Just the slightest elevation change and the earth is more arid here. I'm not sure things would grow as well. I mean, you could grow stuff, but it would require a little more work."

Montana nodded. As a homeowner, she was going to have to think about these things.

Abby moved on, driving to the next lot. "This one is kind of tucked back up against a hill. I like that it affords a little more privacy. If you built back into these little swells, no one could see in through your windows."

"Wow," Montana said. "I've got a lot to consider." She felt a momentary flicker of overwhelm. Each of the considerations Abby mentioned seemed important. But which was the *most* important? Which should take top priority?

She was about to ask when Abby stopped again. "This is the next lot."

And right then, in that very moment, Montana knew. It was her lot. Her new home. It had the little hills and the rich, dark green valley. And, if she could build the house just so, she would still be able to see Granite Mountain.

"Stop," she said as a whole new feeling of exhilaration swelled up inside her body. She couldn't contain it. She jumped out of the vehicle, set Cash down, and started running. She felt her shoes come off her feet, and she kept running anyway, her puppy frolicking along beside her. The grass was so soft and the sun was so warm, even as low as it was. Montana ran and ran and ran. She was laughing, throwing her head back from time to time with the joy of it all. When she finally tired herself out, she flung her body down on the soft earth and rolled around. Cash took that as an invitation and covered her face in puppy kisses. Laughing, Montana ran her palms over the grass, let the spikes go between her fingers. Then she jumped up and ran back to where Abby was waiting, a bemused expression on her face.

"You sure this is it?" she said. "Because I really can't tell if you like it."

Montana laughed with glee, again. She threw her arms out and spun around. "I'm sure. I'm positive. This is it. All the other lots were beautiful, but this one — it just speaks to me."

"I should say so," Abby said. "I have something for you."

"For me?" What could Abby possibly have for her? *She* should have something for *Abby*. From the back of the truck, Abby pulled out her backpack. She unzipped it and brought out a flag about the size of a piece of printer paper and attached to a little silver stake. Abby handed it to Montana. She pulled a Sharpie out of the front pocket of her overalls. "Here. Write your name on the flag. Then you get to stake your claim."

"Stake my claim? Like, I get to stick this flag in the ground and claim it?"

Abby smiled. "Exactly."

Montana smoothed the flag over her thigh, uncapped the Sharpie, and wrote, *Montana and Cash*. She put the lid back on the pen and handed it to Abby. When she went to hand her the flag, Abby put up her hand. "Nope. You get to do it. Go stake your claim, my friend."

"Come with me. We'll do it together."

Montana grabbed Abby's hand, and with Cash trotting ahead of them, they walked over to the place where Montana had flung herself on the ground just a minute before.

"Right here?"

"Right here."

"Well, get to it."

Grinning from ear to ear, Montana lifted her hand high, the stake firmly in her grip. "I hereby declare this my land. My home. And Cash's."

She plunged the stake into the ground and felt tears in her eyes as she watched her flag blow gently in the breeze.

"Well, I guess that's it," she said to Abby.

Abby wrapped an arm around Montana's shoulders. "That's it. We'd better go. It's almost dark."

Reluctant to leave, Montana gathered her puppy and climbed into the truck. As they drove away, Montana looked over her shoulder until her new property was out of sight.

"Just remember," Abby said when she'd finally turned around, "nothing's official until we get through the red tape."

"I know," Montana said, vowing not to let herself feel deflated. "I know."

———

MONTANA

MONTANA'S A NEW BEST FRIEND, Tessa Kincaid, was about to have her dream wedding. Not *Tessa's* dream wedding — Montana's.

She was happy for Tessa, she thought as she turned into the Mint Creek Ranch, heading to Cody's parents' house for a planning meeting with Tessa, Abby, and Cody's sister, Annie. But she was also heartbroken for herself.

How many times had Montana planned a Mint Creek Ranch wedding? At least a hundred. In every plan, she and Sawyer got married on the property where they grew up, together (except for the one plan where they eloped to a tropical island). She always knew she wanted to get married in this place that held so much meaning for her.

And finally, a wedding was happening there. But it wasn't hers.

Part of her felt like maybe it was time to let her dream go. After all, she and Sawyer weren't ever going to say, "I do," were they? Another part of her, though, still thought about how she would do things, the choices she would make. As she drove, she envisioned the dance floor under the big cottonwood trees. Fairy lights in the branches. Those high-top tables around the edges, glasses of champagne on every one.

Sighing as she let that vision go, she parked and looked down at everything she had to carry in, shoved onto the passenger side floorboard. There was the grocery bag with the wine and cheese. And her binder-style wedding planning notebook. And the puppy, who sat on the seat, wagging his tail at her.

"I have to admit, Cash," she said, "I dramatically underestimated the amount of work it took to raise up a puppy." He barked at her in response, and she said, "You're just about the sweetest thing. Look at you, talking back to me. You're so smart, you know that?"

And she wasn't like the parent of a human child, stretching the truth to make him feel good about himself. She meant it. He was almost potty-trained. He looked up when she said his name and he came whenever she called him. But it wasn't all sunshine and rainbows. If she left him alone, even for a moment, he got into mischief. He was fast, too. Once she got distracted editing some photos for an assignment. She forgot to pay attention to what he was doing, and when she remembered and realized he had been quiet for a while, she found him just outside the bathroom door, shredding a roll of toilet paper. Another time, she forgot to put him in his crate when she went to take a shower. When she emerged, he had chewed a hole in one of her favorite wool socks. He gave her a look so adorable that it was impossible to be mad at him. Exasperated, yes. But mad? No.

At the moment, because he hadn't quite mastered the art of walking on a leash, it would be easier to just carry him in. She hadn't told Tessa about her new furry family member just yet, and she was a little bit afraid of Tessa's reaction. In Montana's situation, adopting a puppy might seem irresponsible. After all, she lived in a tiny apartment. And she worked full-time. Who was she to think she could raise a puppy? In fact, Montana had considered leaving him at home, so she could avoid the uncomfortable situation. But she didn't want to feel rushed during what should be a fun event.

The evening was about Tessa. So, here she was, with too much to carry and a wiggly puppy to boot. Maybe if she took him in first. Then she could have Tessa watch him while she made a second trip.

"Yes. That's what I'll do, you little monster. That way you can't tear up the passenger seat while I'm inside."

She lifted Cash out of the seat and held him against her chest as she got out of the car. He took this as an invitation to lick her face like crazy. He was still at it when they got to the front door, and she was giggling so hard she couldn't even compose herself to knock. The door swung open. Tessa was already smiling, and when she saw the puppy, she said, "Dolly?"

Montana was confused by her friend's reaction. Why would Tessa think she knew Cash's name? And where did "Dolly" come from? Tessa looked as confused as Montana felt.

"Good guess, but this is Cash," Montana said. "Isn't he cute?"

"Cash? Oh. He looks exactly like — maybe I shouldn't say. It's just that —"

"He looks like what?" Montana wanted to know.

Tessa bit her lip. She seemed nervous. Finally, she explained, the words tumbling out in a rush: "It's just that Sawyer just got a puppy. Dolly. She looks just like yours. I mean, now that I know it's two different puppies, I can see the differences. Dolly is a little darker in the chest. And Cash has bigger paws." Now, her eyes, round with shock, met Montana's. Sure enough, she said, "This dog is going to be huge, you know that?"

Montana didn't know quite how to feel, other than somewhat deflated. For all her nervousness, she'd wanted Tessa to be charmed by her puppy. But it seemed as though Sawyer had stolen her thunder. Tessa had probably been charmed by Dolly.

And, what?! *Sawyer* had a puppy?! *She* was getting a puppy, in part so she could separate herself from Sawyer. So what in the world was *he* doing getting a puppy?

"Here," she said. She handed Cash to Tessa, who finally acted as charmed as Montana had imagined she would.

"Would you mind holding him for a minute? I've got to get a bunch of stuff out of the car. I don't have enough hands."

Tessa's voice switched to baby-talk mode. "Of *course* I don't mind! Of *course* I would love nothing more in the *world* than to hold this tiny furball! Boy, you are just about the cutest thing I've ever seen. You look exactly like your sister."

Grinding her molars together, Montana turned on her heel and headed back to the car. She gathered everything she needed and by the time she returned to the kitchen, Tessa had set Cash down and given him a bowl of water. Abby was there, too, looking so sexy in her construction boots and white tank top, it was unfair. The woman didn't even have to try.

"I'm so glad you brought Cash," Abby said.

"Wait!" Tessa said. "Abby knew about Cash and I didn't? How did you get to find out?"

Montana and Abby looked at each other. Montana started to panic. She wasn't planning to tell anyone about her plans to build a house until it was actually a reality. But then Abby, smooth as butter, said, "We ran into each other downtown one day when she was walking him."

That did the trick.

"Oh, okay. I guess you're off the hook, then. I'm just so glad I got to meet him. I can't believe you didn't tell me the instant you got him. I *am* his aunt, after all."

"Oh, my gosh, I would have, but he's nonstop. I didn't realize how much work he'd be," Montana said. "I can't leave him alone! And between eating and going to the bathroom and chewing up toilet paper, I'm running around like a chicken with its head cut off!"

Tessa laughed and bent to pet Cash. "I guess I'll have to forgive your mama, right?"

There, Montana thought. Everything was right with the world. Tessa was excited about her puppy and claiming him as her nephew. Abby was keeping her secret. And, Sawyer had a puppy, as well. Well, that wasn't quite right. But there was nothing she could do about it now. It was time to focus on Tessa and her upcoming wedding.

Annie came in the door then, a whirlwind of long blond hair, spicy perfume, laughter, and hugs.

"Now that we're all here," Tessa said, "I think a toast is in order."

A flurry of activity ensued as Abby opened a bottle of wine while Tessa took down wine glasses.

Annie was the first to speak once everyone held a glass: "I can't tell you how many times I hoped my brother wouldn't marry a particular girl," she said. "But when I first met Tessa, it was love at first — well, that's a lie. We met on strange terms. When I first got to know Tessa, it was evident that she loves Cody. And when I saw them together, it was obvious that he loves her. They're perfect for each other. I couldn't ask for a more wonderful sister-in-law. And I couldn't be happier to help plan this beautiful wedding. Cheers to Cody and Tessa!"

"Cheers!" they all said.

"Let's eat," Tessa said. "I'm *starving*."

Montana wondered, with another pang of envy, if Tessa was pregnant. Then she dismissed the thought. A girl could be hungry without being pregnant.

"I'll be honest with you guys," Tessa said as they began filling plates with cheese, crackers, grapes, and deli meats.

Montana froze. Was she going to announce she was pregnant?

Tessa went on, "All I care about is marrying Cody. I mean, I want the wedding to be fun, but no pressure. The flowers, the decorations, the favors, the food … those are all just icing on the cake. The ceremony is what matters."

Montana felt giddy with relief.

"I mean, I do care about the songs. Cody and I will pick those out together. What I'm trying to say is, please don't feel any pressure as a member of the Kincaid-Davis Wedding Planning Team. I just want this to be *fun*. The whole point of asking for your help is so we could spend time together. Abby, I hope you'll design a cute little gazebo, because I want the pictures to look nice. And, Montana, I would love your advice on which flowers you think we should use to decorate it. Because you have such a good eye for that stuff. And Annie, you're so good with fashion. You're the go-to expert for the color coordination. And I want the people we do invite to think everything looks nice. But all that being said, I just want this to be fun. That's it!"

They raised their glasses, clinked them together again, and sipped.

"So when is the big day, anyway?" Abby asked.

For the first time, Tessa looked apprehensive. She took one of the fancy green olives off the tray on the counter and popped it into her mouth. "Two months from today." The kitchen went still. Montana gulped.

"Is it for a —" Abby paused. Then, she gulped, and went for it: "Is this a shotgun wedding? Are you knocked up?"

Tessa burst out laughing. "Oh my gosh, I can totally see why it might look that way. But no! Absolutely not. We've been very careful. I didn't even realize I was ready for a husband. And I'm definitely not ready for a baby."

A fresh wave of relief washed over Montana. If Tessa *were* pregnant, Montana would be happy for her. But, she thought as her heart rate slowed back to normal, she would also be jealous. For years, she'd thought of nothing other than starting a family with Sawyer. And if Tessa walked right in and made a baby with Cody after knowing him for only a fraction of the time Montana knew Sawyer, Montana's heart would break. Just a little. Okay, maybe more than just a little.

Abby and Annie were laughing, too. Montana forced something like a laugh, but it fell flat to her own ears.

"Speaking of big news," Abby said.

Montana shot her a warning look. Abby just winked in response. "Wait. I think this is going to require another toast."

Montana's hands were shaking as she picked up the wine bottle and topped off all the glasses. The women turned to Abby.

"I have my first buyer," she said. Annie gasped.

Tessa gave a long whistle, then shouted, "Congratulations!"

Afraid that if she spoke, she'd let something slip, Montana raised her glass.

CHAPTER SIX

SAWYER

IN THE PROCESS of building up a decent daydream for himself, one weekend, Sawyer decided to take a drive. Not a meandering, aimless drive. But a drive to the 5D Ranch in Utah. The trek would take about eight hours, so he set out just after lunch on Friday. He didn't tell anyone. He just packed his truck, turned off his phone, and skipped town. If Cody and Trace knew where he was going, they'd want to know every last detail. Not only that, they'd want to come with him.

But this was something he had to do on his own.

The sun was directly overhead as he drove out of town, following a hunch. One year during the local rodeo, Sawyer, just eight at the time, noticed that all the really mean bulls shared the same brand: the Lazy R.

"They come from a long line of mean cattle," his dad said when he mentioned the observation. "They've got mean in their blood. You ever get a chance to ride a Lazy R bull, you take it, son."

Over the course of the next couple of years, two or three other brands showed up in the mix, their bulls giving cowboys the rides of their lives.

"Those ranchers are smart," Sawyer's dad said. "They paid the Lazy R to have their bulls breed with their cows. Now you see how it works — the Double K bulls are fast *and* mean. Like twisters. And the Yellow Star bulls are smart as whips."

"And mean?" Sawyer said.

"And mean," his dad confirmed. Elbows on the arena fence, he looked down at Sawyer and winked. "You're getting the hang of this, son." He tapped his temple. "You've got real smarts, you know that?"

Sawyer basked in the rare compliment. His dad was loving, but not affectionate. He had high expectations, and certainly didn't "cry all over the place" when Sawyer met them.

After that conversation, Sawyer paid even more attention. He followed the lines of the cattle at different ranches, paid attention to how their offspring turned out. Sometimes he'd think he'd like to see the offspring of a cow from one ranch and a bull from another, and sure enough, he'd find out the ranchers wanted to see it, too.

The more he pictured having his own place with property, the more he thought he could be a rancher. He could breed championship bulls. It could be more than a hobby. It could be his livelihood.

He couldn't compete forever, he thought as he drove north, leaving houses behind him and making his way through fields dotted with low junipers. He loved the rodeo, but he was getting old as far as competing went. He could practically hear his joints creaking when he got out of bed every morning. He still had a few good years in him, but what then?

"Well, Mr. Nelson," he said to himself, "you start your own cattle company."

He liked the sound of that. The shrubs and tall grasses of the high desert gave way to the grassy fields of southern Utah. Sawyer looked in his rearview mirror. He couldn't even see Prescott anymore. A slight pang of panic hit.

No, he would never leave Prescott, but he *was* ready for something of his own. He wondered what Cody and Trace would say. They think he was crazy, probably. But what did they know?

Well, they must know something. Cody was about to get married, and he seemed about the happiest Sawyer had ever seen him. And Trace always seemed perfectly content with the way things were. He had happiness figured out and didn't want to change a thing.

Still, Sawyer thought as the sun sank lower in the sky, he wasn't ready to tell his friends just yet. He was still in dreaming mode, and he didn't want them bringing in any logic. That would come later.

For the time being, Sawyer would just dream his little dream and enjoy it.

Finally, at exactly eight p.m., he pulled into the motel where he'd made a reservation. It was nothing fancy, just a long, low brick building. A couple of other cars sat in the parking lot, but the place definitely wasn't packed. *Good.* He would have a quiet night, get some rest, and feel refreshed for his meeting first thing in the morning. Crickets chirped and the stars sparkled bright in the dark sky.

In the lobby, a tired looking young woman stood behind the desk. After she got his name and took his ID and credit card, he asked her, "Know of any place I can get a good breakfast around here?"

She didn't even look up when she responded. Which was good. He wasn't as famous as Cody, but almost, simply by association, and he didn't want word getting out that he was visiting other ranches.

"There's Mabel's, across the street. They have a good short stack. And then there's the Country Kitchen, just down the road."

Sawyer thanked her, took the room keys she set on the counter, and headed for his room. It was at the back of the building, which meant he wouldn't hear the traffic going by, and it contained just the basics: a bed, a nightstand, and a bathroom. Sawyer smiled with satisfaction. Perfect. He didn't need anything fancy. Just a place to put his head on a pillow and get a good night's sleep.

First, though, he needed a few minutes to decompress. He took off his boots and sat down on the bed with his back against the headboard. He crossed his legs and turned on the TV. But after flipping through a couple of channels, he couldn't get into anything. He had the urge to call Montana, which was out of the question. And because he wasn't ready to tell Trace and Cody what he was up to, he couldn't call them, either.

He didn't even bother turning his phone on. For the first time, building his dream alone felt … lonely.

———

MABEL DID HAVE a good short stack, especially when it was a side dish to complement a giant four-egg meat lover's omelette. If Sawyer's loneliness had dampened his spirits a little the night before, the good, hearty breakfast with strong, hot coffee lifted them.

Diego, the first of the five Ds who made up the 5D Ranch, agreed to meet Sawyer at eight-thirty in the ranch's main building. When Sawyer walked through the door five minutes early, Diego was waiting for him. A broad, stocky man about twice his own age with a dark mustache and twinkling eyes, he held out his hand as soon as Sawyer walked in.

"Welcome, Mr. Nelson. I have to tell you, I'm surprised to have one of the Mint Creek Ranch boys asking for a meeting. And you were a little cryptic on the phone, no?"

Sawyer decided then and there that he liked Diego. He always admired a man who was so straightforward.

"I wasn't trying to be cryptic, but I can see why you thought so. To tell you the truth, I'm not even sure what I'm after. But I do know that I've been watching your bulls for years. I've always admired your cattle, and the choices you make with breeding. You've got fine stock, here."

Diego beamed. "Always start with flattery, that's my motto. I like you already."

He chuckled, and Sawyer couldn't help but laugh right along with him. "Thank you for the compliments. We work hard to ensure a good bloodline, and I think you've bought a few of our bulls, haven't you?"

"We have," Sawyer said. "Storm Chaser, Curly, and, what was it? Diego Junior?" Again, Diego erupted into laughter. "Yes, yes. Diego Junior. I'm sure that was it. What can I do for you, my friend?"

"Like I said, I didn't mean to be cryptic. And what I'm about to tell you is ... well, not exactly top-secret. But it's something I haven't shared with anyone else."

Diego's expression took on interest. He mimed zipping his lips shut and locking them. "You have my word. I won't discuss our meeting with anyone."

Sawyer nodded. "Thank you. I'm thinking about — wow, it feels strange to say it out loud. I'm thinking about getting my own place. Maybe even starting my own cattle company. You're the first person I thought of. Like I said, I like the way you do things. I was wondering if I might be able to spend a little time here, learn from the best. And I wanted to talk with you about what kind of deal you could give me on a few head of cattle. Obviously, I'll need to start small. I don't have a ton of cash to invest in a whole herd or anything just yet. But I want to start with the best."

While he was talking, Diego gestured for him to follow. He led the way out of the office. "Yes," he said when Sawyer finished. "Absolutely. Start with the best, especially if you're going to start small. And I do believe you're in the right place for that. I'm positive we can work something out. Come on, let me show you around."

A Ranger was parked out front, and the men climbed in. As Diego drove them around the property, Sawyer found himself even more impressed than he had been before. First off, the place was huge. And it was well-kept. The fields were lush and green. The barns and buildings looked freshly painted. Although he knew for a fact that the 5D Ranch was home to thousands and thousands of cattle, they didn't look crowded at all. The cows grazed peacefully, as if they lived in some sort of paradise. While Sawyer took in the scene, Diego shared his story.

"You may or may not know that I'm a fifth-generation cattle rancher. My great, great grandfather bought this particular property one hundred years ago. Actually, the current property is about half the size of the original ranch. But, as you know, things change."

Diego looked at Sawyer and winked. Sawyer nodded. Things did change. And, although it seemed like people often talked about change as a negative, Sawyer thought it could be a good thing. Not change for the sake of change. But change for the sake of growth. If — no, *when* — he started his own venture, he would grow.

Back when he was a teenager, and he thought growth was as simple as moving away from your family and starting your own life, he used to imagine starting a ranch with Montana. She was such a mother hen on the Mint Creek Ranch, always tending to the baby cows even though all the adults told her they didn't need tending to. Cows were great mothers that didn't need human interference. But Montana couldn't help herself. Every time a calf was born, she was there. Even if it meant staying up all night. Every time a calf stood on its shaky legs for the first time, Montana cried. It was pretty damn cute. Sawyer wondered what Montana would think of him starting his own line of cattle. Then, he wondered why he couldn't stop wondering what she'd think.

"Here we are," Diego said, parking the Ranger next to a barn (if Sawyer was counting right, this was the fifth barn he'd seen). "This is the nursery. It's nothing like the high-tech nurseries in today's hospitals."

It was set apart from the other structures on the property, nestled back in the foothills behind the ranch. From outside, he guessed there were maybe ten stalls on either side of the walkway. When Diego slid open the giant door at one end, Sawyer noticed how smoothly it rolled on his rails — more proof that this property was well taken care of. The 5D Ranch was definitely something to aspire to. Inside, the barn was quiet. Sawyer could hear the usual animal sounds: the shuffling of feet, breathing, lapping of water.

They walked down the aisle, and Sawyer noticed the cows at the other end of the barn were heavily pregnant. He whistled.

"I know," Diego said. "Glad that's not me. We're expecting a handful of babies any day now. It was a cold winter, eh?"

Sawyer wondered how the ranch staff would manage all the births. He figured they had least one veterinarian on call. He had so many questions, and he wanted to ask them all. He knew the value of a good mentor, and Diego obviously knew what he was doing. But, he didn't want to impose on him, or take advantage of the rancher's kindness.

At the other end of the barn, mother cows were bedded up with their babies. If Montana were there, she would be saying, "Awww," every time they passed a stall. For his part, Sawyer thought they were cute enough. But guys didn't usually say that sort of thing to each other. He settled for, "Those are some good-looking calves. Strong."

Diego grunted. "Out of the ten you see here, only about half will be good for breeding. Maybe less."

Sawyer didn't have to ask what Diego did with the other five. They would wind up on people's dinner tables. Looking into the eyes of these newborn cows, framed by their long lashes, Sawyer thought of Montana yet again. She's gone through a whole period, maybe two or three years, when she didn't eat beef, because she'd fallen in love with a calf that didn't quite make the cut.

Sawyer stopped short when he saw the calf in the last stall before they reached the end of the barn. It leaned against his mother and looked right at him. It had fawn-colored fur, like coffee with a little too much milk in it. It wasn't as skinny as some of the other calves he'd seen. But neither the fur nor the calf's sturdiness were what drew Sawyer's attention. No, it was the eyes. The way this newborn crea-ture looked right at Sawyer. He had an almost knowing expression. Wise. Sawyer blinked. The calf blinked back. Sawyer laughed. Diego slapped him on the shoulder. "I think that guy's trying to tell you something."

"It seemed that way, didn't it?"

Diego leaned forward, elbows on the top edge of the stall door. He made a clicking sound with his mouth and both the cow and the calf walked over to him.

He scratched the cow behind the ears. "You have a beautiful son there, Daffodil."

The cow leaned into Diego's scratching.

"She's pretty tame, isn't she?" Sawyer said.

Diego glanced at him. "She is. I've had her for years. Just about as sweet as they come. She's probably got one more pregnancy in her. She's given us several great breeders."

Sawyer crept closer, kneeling down so he was on level with the calf. He was surprised it didn't back away. But it didn't come any closer, either. It just stared him right in the eye again, without blinking.

"Would you look at that. I don't know if I've ever seen that before," Diego said. "That's a real kick in the pants."

Sawyer straightened up and the two of them made their way out of the barn and back to the Ranger. As they drove back toward the office, Diego said, "Well, I think you've seen the lay of the land. All the high points anyway. There are tons of acres of pasture. And if we drove out there, you'd see all the cattle grazing. But that's about it."

As they drove once again, Sawyer said, "This place looks practically brand new."

"Takes a whole team to keep it looking like this. We rotate through the projects, season by season. So everything gets refreshed and repaired at least once a year. Fencing, the barn, irrigation, all the fields."

While Sawyer admired the operation, he was sure he didn't want something quite so big.

"Would you like to stay for dinner?"

Sawyer checked his watch. "Dinnertime already?"

"Well, not quite. But we do eat early around here. I would say it's cocktail hour. Care for a drink?"

"Don't mind if I do."

Inside the ranch house Diego shared with his wife, Sara, the two men had a long conversation over the best bourbon Sawyer had ever tasted. They talked about cattle, roping, and bull riding, and even Cody and Tessa's upcoming wedding.

"I never thought I'd see a Mint Creek Ranch boy settle down," Diego said.

It stung a little. Even a year ago, Sawyer would have been proud, having considered that a compliment. But at the moment, wasn't he considering settling down in his own way?

"Well, it happens to the best of us."

Diego's eyes twinkled with mischief when he said, "Come to think of it, I never thought *I'd* settle down, either. If you'd told my eighteen-year-old self that I would end up running the 5D Ranch, I would've laughed you right out of town. I was going to move to the big city, become an executive, and run a business. I mean, one where they wear suits and ties. But things change, don't they, Sawyer?"

With that, Sawyer felt like Diego really saw him. It was as if the older man knew exactly what Sawyer was going through, what he would go through. He felt like they'd come to an understanding.

He nodded. "Yes, Diego. They sure do."

———

SPENDING a full day at the 5D Ranch gave Sawyer the clarity he needed.

He wanted it.

He didn't want exactly what Diego had. But he wanted his own ranch. And he wanted it to be on the property he found on the Internet. Although he'd told himself he would spend the eight-hour drive home from Utah the next day thinking about his decision, he'd made up his mind while he sipped bourbon with Diego.

Because they did eat dinner early, Sawyer was back to his motel room by seven that evening. And although he didn't normally go to sleep that early, he found he was exhausted, and he fell into bed and slept hard.

The next morning, he woke before the sun came up. The restaurants weren't yet open, so he snagged a coffee and a breakfast burrito from the gas station and hit the road. An hour passed before he saw the golden edge of the sun peeking over the horizon. He felt so sure, more certain than he had felt of anything in a long time.

His ranch needed a name — a brand. Something he felt proud to say out loud. Something that conveyed quality. He'd have to think on that.

About halfway home, he stopped to fill up the truck's gas tank and grab lunch. Before he got on the road again, he took out his tablet and pulled up the listing for the empty lot. He knew he was unlikely to get an answer since it was Sunday, but he dialed the number anyway, while he sat in the gas station parking lot, a soggy sandwich in one hand.

Sure enough, the phone rang, but no one answered. An automated recording told him whoever owned the phone was unavailable, and he hung up without leaving a message. He'd call first thing in the morning.

The sun was higher in the sky. He wondered what the guys were up to. Sunday morning … they were probably enjoying a giant breakfast. It was a Mint Creek Ranch tradition.

Building his own ranch meant Sawyer could make his own traditions. Was it possible for him to stick with the old ones, too? What would everyone say if he moved out and then showed up on a Sunday morning for breakfast? Years ago, Sawyer's need to be part of something safe and secure — the Mint Creek Ranch — had caused him to lose what was potentially the most important relationship in his life.

Although he wanted his own cattle ranch, he hoped that finally leaving the fold wouldn't cause him to lose any other relationships. Cody and Trace had been a source of stability pretty much forever. And, Sawyer knew, they would continue to be. Not only had they made a "blood brothers" vow when they were nine, promising they'd be friends forever, but also, they *had* been friends forever. Their lives intertwined. It was as if none of them could exist without the others. So, Sawyer told himself, even if Cody and Trace didn't understand at first, they would come around.

———

BECAUSE HE'D BEEN UP SO EARLY, Sawyer hit the sack early Sunday night and woke even earlier on Monday. It felt like forever before the numbers on his phone screen read eight a.m.

As soon as he saw the double zeroes, he dialed the number on the listing for his new ranch property. This time, someone did pick up, and he felt a jolt of shock run through his entire body when he realized who it was. He would recognize her voice anywhere.

"Abby Flores," he said.

"Yep, that's me."

Sawyer cleared his throat. *Abby Flores?*

How in the world had he not realized the property he fell in love with belonged to Abby Flores? The woman was Trace's archrival. Sawyer certainly couldn't buy a piece of property from her. He glanced at the printout from the listing, which he'd propped on his nightstand.

Or could he?

Actually, if he did buy a piece of property from her, he would be as close to Mint Creek Ranch as he could be. Separate, but close.

"Hello?"

Sawyer swallowed. He cleared his throat again, and made a huge effort to sound professional. "Oh, hello. Sorry. Technical difficulties."

"That's okay. How can I help you?"

Sawyer's armpits tingled. He was nervous. Not only because of what he was about to do, but also because of who he was about to do it with. If Trace found out — Sawyer swallowed. If Trace found out, Sawyer would wind up with a bloodied nose and a black eye and who knows how many broken bones. Trace had a mean right hook. And as far as he was concerned, Abby Flores was some kind of demon. Sawyer took a deep breath. Surely, the two of them would come to terms? From what any of them could tell, Abby planned to build that development whether Trace liked it or not.

"Hello?"

"Right. This is David Davidson with Davidson holdings." It was all Sawyer could do to stop himself from laughing a giddy, anxiety-fueled laugh. "My client was interested in a piece of property you're selling. I believe it is parcel number seven in unit twenty-one?"

"Oh, wonderful. That parcel is still available. Would your client like to come out and take a look at it in person?"

Sawyer didn't need to. He knew exactly where it was. He had seen the pictures. He had ridden through it a million times. The lot was perfect.

"He's an out-of-town buyer," Sawyer said. "He may send out an agent. I was just inquiring as to whether the parcel is still available. Let me check with him, and if he wants to send someone out, I'll get back with you. In the meantime, how do I hold this parcel? Are you taking deposits?"

Sawyer thought he heard a choking noise. But when Abby spoke again, her voice sounded strong and sure. "Yes. I'm taking deposits. You can mail a cashier's check."

She gave him a P.O. box and an amount. Hand shaking, he wrote down the details. If he didn't know Abby, he might think this sounded like a scam. She had the machine in motion, but it sounded like she wasn't expecting buyers so early on.

Even if his friends ended up ditching him over this — which Trace very well might — he could befriend Abby Flores. If he remembered correctly, she'd told Montana that she planned to live in her new development. So they would be neighbors. Maybe they could trade a cup of sugar for a couple of eggs.

After they hung up, Sawyer jumped off the couch and pumped his fist. Dolly, who was gnawing on a bone in the middle of the living room, stopped to look at him, head cocked.

Sawyer ran over and gave her a good belly rub. "Good news, girl! We're getting our own place. But first, we've got to go to the bank."

A few minutes later, Sawyer and Dolly stood in front of the bank's locked doors, disappointment hanging over Sawyer's head like a dark cloud.

"Actually," he said to the dog, "this is a good thing. I would have marched right in there and gotten a cashier's check with my name on it."

For an instant, he thought of mailing her a stack of cash, but he decided against that almost immediately. Instead, he thought, he'd get a money order from the grocery store and put a fake signature on it.

No one would be the wiser. Abbie could still cash it at her bank.

An hour later, Sawyer was dropping the envelope, money order inside, into the mailbox in downtown Prescott. He couldn't wait. This was the most exciting thing he'd ever done; the first step in creating his dream life.

CHAPTER SEVEN

AS SMALL AS PRESCOTT WAS, Montana knew it was only a matter of time before she and Cash ran into Sawyer and his puppy. It took just more than a week.

Monday at lunch, although Montana wanted nothing more than to snuggle into bed and take a nap (she had worked late and then had early shooting assignments for the _Daily Dispatch_), she opted to be a responsible puppy parent. She ran home, collected Cash, and took him for his daily walk around the Courthouse Plaza.

She'd taken to eating while they walked, which meant her meals were limited to things she could eat with one hand, like a wrap or a burrito. Bleary-eyed, she strolled around the Plaza, Cash trotting along beside her. These days, one of his ears stood up while the other folded over, and he moved with his chin slightly lifted, which gave him a jaunty look. Every time Montana saw his ears, her heart melted, no matter how bleary-eyed she felt. So there she was, heart melting, eyes on her dog's ears, mouth full of food, when Cash suddenly stopped and dropped into what Montana recently learned was a "play bow": front end down, front legs outstretched, butt in the air, tail wagging. His whole body wagged. He stood up, and then bowed again.

Montana looked down the sidewalk to see what the pup was so excited about, and sure enough, there were Sawyer and his puppy, who, as Tessa said, looked very much like Cash. She was adorable. No matter how Montana felt about Sawyer (and to be fair, her feelings about Sawyer were completely jumbled up, contradictory, and complicated), she couldn't help but fall in love with Cash's sister instantly.

"Well, hello there," she said.

Even as she knelt down to pet her puppy's sister, Sawyer was responding. "Well, hello."

He quickly seemed to realize she hadn't been greeting him.

"This is Dolly," he said. "I take it that's Cash?"

Montana used the dogs, who were now growling and pouncing and jumping around, as an excuse not to look up at Sawyer. "Yep."

"Tessa's right," he said. "They look a lot alike."

As much as she didn't want to talk to Sawyer face-to-face or eye-to-eye, the puppies were too rambunctious for Montana to remain kneeling. So, she stood up and put her hands on her hips. Since she was holding one end of Cash's leash, his movements jerked her around while she stood there. Finally, she made eye contact. And, exactly as she was dreading, she was hit with a longing so strong, she almost flung herself at him. It was like being punched right in the stomach.

"Well, hello to you, too," he said.

She smiled. "Hello."

Would this feeling ever go away? Not just the feeling itself — desperation to belong to him again — but also the intensity of that feeling?

Would she ever stop wondering if things would have turned out differently if she had acted differently? If she hadn't proposed all those years ago? If she hadn't tried to force him away from Mint Creek Ranch before he was ready? The answer was probably no. Montana took a step back.

"Lunch break," she said. She hooked a thumb over her shoulder toward the *Daily Dispatch* office.

"Errands."

They stood there, looking at each other. Before, they might have walked over to get a lemonade together. Before, she could've left her puppy with him. But this wasn't before.

"I'd better get going." Montana turned around.

Cash was too wrapped up in play to follow her, and she tugged on his leash. He didn't budge. She called his name, but he continued growling at Dolly. Going for efficiency, she bent down and picked him up. And as they walked away, he struggled to get out of her arms, back to his sister.

"I know, buddy. Me too."

———

SAWYER

SAWYER'S SECRET was bubbling up inside of him. He wanted nothing more than to share it with someone. And when he saw Montana on the Courthouse Plaza, he almost told her everything. How he wasn't ready to leave Mint Creek Ranch ten years ago, but he was ready now. How he was so sorry about the way things turned out. How he missed her. How, even while he was planning his new, independent life, she kept slipping into his vision.

Every time he thought about how the house would be laid out, or where he would put the little garden with the chicken coop, he imagined her there, sipping her tea on the couch, tending to the plants, collecting the eggs. And after finding out she had adopted Dolly's brother, the puppies entered his daydreams, too.

Before today, he'd pushed those visions aside. He told himself, countless times, that they'd never materialize.

But that was before he saw her reaction to him. Yes, she'd said she was quitting him, but he could tell from the moment she set eyes on him that day that she was still in love with him.

In that instant, he saw her anew in those visions. Naked in his bed. Kissing him good morning.

Then, she shuttered her eyes and hid the emotion. Even if she wanted something with him, she'd never let herself have it again.

They walked away from each other, heading in opposite directions. He guessed she was going to drop off her dog at her apartment, and he was taking his back over to the Mint Creek Ranch to work with Trace and Cody. As they headed back to his truck, Dolly kept stopping and looking back. It broke Sawyer's heart.

That afternoon, he, Trace, and Cody planned to measure out the wedding space at the Davises' house so they knew exactly where to put the altar, the chairs, the tables, and the dance floor. Then, after the measuring, they'd tackle some old-fashioned chores: mucking stalls, repairing gates in the barn, and cleaning water troughs.

Dolly was still too small to jump into the truck on her own, so he lifted her in. She curled up on the passenger seat, and as he drove, Sawyer reminisced.

As teenagers, they'd hated those chores. They thought that because their families owned the Mint Creek Ranch, they were above that kind of thing. But as an adult, Sawyer saw the simple beauty in it, especially after visiting the 5D Ranch. The simplest of chores played a major role in the entire property running smoothly.

Nothing at Mint Creek Ranch was to the same scale as the 5D, but it was kept up just as well, thanks in large part to the values the boys' parents had instilled in them. Trace and Sawyer's parents had long since sold their shares of the ranch back to the Davises and moved away. Sawyer's mom wanted to live on a river, and Trace's dad wanted to retire to Florida.

Sawyer looked forward to seeing all of them at Cody and Tessa's wedding. He wasn't looking forward to facing his mom after she realized he and Montana called it quits for good. She'd always loved Montana, and even though she didn't want her son getting married at eighteen, Sawyer knew she'd consider Montana the one who got away.

She'd said as much when they broke up after that proposal: "I'm not saying the two of you should get married now. You're not even adults yet, for goodness' sake. But if you can't see that the two of you are made for each other, you're a damn fool."

Sawyer parked at the main house, climbed out of his truck, and lifted Dolly down. Together, they walked around to the side of the house where Cody was standing, under the old cottonwood tree where the tire swing hung.

"So this is the place, huh?"

"This is the place. At first, I was thinking of putting the gazebo right under the tree. But now I'm thinking it might be nice to put it over to the side. And then we can get some pictures under the tree."

Sawyer held up both hands, as if he were framing in the scene. "Yes, I think this would make a nice photo. You look very svelte."

"Shut up, man. You know how the ladies like pictures."

"Well, I do know that."

Suddenly, Sawyer was thrown back in time. He and Montana were sixteen and she had just saved up enough to buy her own fancy camera: a high-tech thirty-five millimeter with interchangeable lenses. It was so futuristic at the time that none of the local stores carried it, so the two of them headed down to Phoenix on a camera-buying expedition. They stopped at the gas station for sodas and snacks, then drove down the mountain. It was before the days of GPS or mapping apps, so they used a real paper roadmap to navigate to the camera store downtown. As the storekeeper showed Montana how to use the camera, Sawyer watched her, noticing how absorbed she was in the whole process, and worrying for a moment that she might fall more in love with the camera and taking pictures than she was with him.

But then she put his mind at ease: every time the storekeeper showed her a different feature, she looked up at Sawyer and grinned at him as if to say, "Isn't this the greatest?"

Before he knew it, Sawyer felt just as excited as he thought Montana did. After the storekeeper rang her up and she handed over all that hard-earned cash, she practically danced out of the store.

They drove through a burger place to grab dinner and then headed back up the mountain. It was summer, so the sun was just beginning its descent when they got back home. Just as he'd expected, Montana insisted on taking some pictures. She zipped around the property, from one place to another — the pasture, the barn, the hayfield, the hay barn, the creek — snapping her way through roll after roll of film.

Sawyer followed her, pointing out angles, asking questions about the f-stop and the aperture. They chatted, mostly about photography. And then, she turned the camera on him. And the way she studied him so carefully before taking each picture, he felt like the luckiest guy alive. Here she was, this beautiful, artistic, confident girl, discovering her passion and involving him in it.

Any twinges of jealousy he had in the camera shop dissolved. After she forced him to model for her for about a half-hour, he eased the camera from her hands and put her in the spotlight. It was the hour of golden light. The sun cast a warm glow on everything. It shone on the side of Montana's face, illuminating the ends of her eyelashes and long hair. Sawyer looked through the viewfinder and was captured by her beauty. And even while he took those pictures —

in which she was fully clothed — he imagined taking naked pictures of her. But then they would have to get them developed and someone else would see them.

Still, just thinking about what she would look like, the sun sweeping across the skin on her chest, her breasts, her shoulders, he felt himself growing hard. And once he finished the roll of film, he put the lens cover on the camera and tucked it in its bag. He led her up the ladder to the hay barn attic and they made love. Sweet but urgent. Tender but hungry. Passionate and —

Suddenly, Cody interrupted his thoughts. "Geez, man. Where'd you go?"

All at once, Sawyer's jeans felt too tight. Oh, to be a teenager again.

"Sorry, man. Just a little trip down Memory Lane. To answer your question, yes, I think you should leave some space between the tree and the gazebo. It's a great place for pictures."

Fortunately, Trace walked up just then, saving Sawyer from having to explain what, exactly, that trip down Memory Lane included.

Trace, the organized one, brought a clipboard, and the three of them measured and drew diagrams and measured some more and drew more diagrams. By the time they were done, they had a good sense of where everything would be.

And, Sawyer had a pretty good sense that he was going to need some kind of release. He thanked the heavens they had planned on doing manual labor.

———

MONTANA

"WHAT ARE YOU DOING?"

Montana jumped. She hadn't even realized Stanley Stephenson — her boss and a friend of the Mint Creek Ranch boys — had come into the *Daily Dispatch* newsroom. He stood behind her, looking over her shoulder at her computer monitor … and her decidedly non-work-related activity: creating social media posts for Abby's new subdivision. *Her* new home.

She wasn't worried about getting in trouble, despite the fact that she was on the clock.

No, she was worried about Stanley's nosy nature. It had carried him up the ranks from his position as an editorial assistant at an even smaller daily paper to that as a hard-nosed journalist and then to his current role as editor-in-chief. It also gave him the superpower to uncover her secret. Especially because she'd practically revealed it right there in the office.

Stupid, she thought. *Stupid, stupid, stupid.*

Her first impulse was to click out of the graphic design program she was using, but then she quickly decided that would be too obvious.

"Just some design work," she said finally, after listening to an imaginary clock tick-tocking in her mind. She rushed to add, "Sorry. I know I shouldn't be working on it here, but I just had an idea, you know? And I felt like I needed to implement it before the inspiration left me. I think it's done, now, though."

She saved her work and closed the program. And, as she expected, she didn't fool Stanley.

Moving with a lithe grace that made her jealous, Stanley grabbed the back of an office chair from a nearby desk and twirled it into place across from her.

He sat, crossed his legs, put an elbow on his knee, and rested his chin in one hand. His eyes bored into hers. "Tell me what you're really doing."

She sighed. "I'm really doing graphic design."

He inhaled, ready to interrupt, and she held up a hand. "I am doing graphic design for Abby's new subdivision."

At that, his eyes widened. "Does Trace know?"

"No."

"And that's not all, is it? I can see it on your face. I can read you like a book, Montana Hart."

Caught. Montana knew she could trust Stanley. They'd worked together on many news-related projects where secret-keeping was the name of the game.

"You're right. That's not all," she said. "But you can't tell *anyone* what I'm about to say."

He crossed his heart with one manicured pointer finger.

She gulped and took the plunge. "As a matter of fact, I am buying one of her houses."

Saying it like that, out loud, caused a massive wave of emotion to swell up in Montana's torso.

If it were possible, Stanley's eyes went even rounder. Before he could answer, her phone rang. She saw Abby's name and snatched it off the top of her desk — but Stanley saw it, too. They'd been friends forever, so she wasn't surprised when he didn't excuse himself.

"Hey, Abby."

"I just had the best idea!" Abby said.

Sitting up straighter, Montana felt her eyes flick over to rest on Stanley's face. Maybe she should step into the stairwell to have this conversation. Or, maybe not. Keeping this secret from Sawyer, Trace, and Cody was going to be hard enough. Plus, she'd probably have to make phone calls about it from the newsroom every so often, and she couldn't be running off to the stairwell every time.

"What is it?"

"As soon as I have five buyers," Abby said, "I'm going to start a club. I'll come up with a catchy name for it. But I'm going to invite all the original buyers to be on a sort of committee, to help decide on the direction of the rest of the development."

"That *is* a great idea. And I'd be honored to be on it. But I don't really know if I belong, since, you know, I'm not technically a real buyer."

"Oh, you absolutely are a real buyer," Abby said. "You're the first person to come to me and say that you really wanted to live in my development. So, you're also a founding member of the heretofore unnamed owners' committee."

"I love it. So who else is on it? Anyone I know?"

"I haven't met any of them in person," Abby said, "but so far, no names I recognize. Which doesn't mean much, since you've been in town way longer than I have. Anyway, I'll send you a list. I'm out on the property now, so don't hold your breath. It'll be tomorrow before I can get it to you."

"Sounds great. As you know, I'm *really* looking forward to this. Not just the committee, but having my own place. With Cash."

"I'm looking forward to it as well," Abby said.

They said "goodbye," and even before she set her phone down on her desk, words were tumbling out of Stanley's mouth.

"I take it that was Abby Flores?" He plowed on. "Wow, am I in on a *big* secret."

Montana looked up at Stanley. Impeccable as always, he wore corduroy pants, a blue plaid button-up shirt, and a dark-red vest with a matching bow tie. He was one of only a few openly gay men in Prescott, and everyone loved him.

"The biggest. But I trust you."

Stanley raised his eyebrows. "Sure that's safe? You know I love a big scoop."

She shrugged and turned back to her computer. "Yes, it seems that I am."

Stanley laughed, loud and boisterous. On the way back to his office, he said, "I'll just never get enough of you, Montana. You can trust me. Lips are sealed. And dare I say congratulations?"

She didn't answer. But a couple of hours later, Stanley left the office with a quick "BRB," and returned with a miniature bottle of champagne and a box of cookies from the Cupcake House. He held them out, an offering. "Congratulations. I'm beyond proud of you."

Overcome by emotion, Montana stood up and threw her arms around Stanley. "Thank you," she said. "Thank you so much. It feels so good to share this news. I haven't told anyone else. I know they're going to be mad, at least at first. I'm procrastinating. But I'm so excited. This is a really big step for me."

"It *is* a really big step for you, and I know the crew will understand. No matter what, you're going to need space for that monster of a dog."

"It's nice to see your practical side."

Stanley winked. "As you know, I have a good balance of the practical and the impractical."

"Well, I guess that's true."

Stanley kissed her on the cheek. "Your secret is safe with me."

Montana trusted Stanley, but she knew she couldn't keep the secret from her other friends for much longer. At the very least, she was going to have to tell Tessa. And when she did, Tessa would have to tell Cody. And, things being as they were, Cody would feel like he had to tell Trace and Sawyer. Montana just had to make sure she was ready for that. She didn't know why she was so worried about them thinking she was being foolish or making a huge mistake.

Or, maybe she did know why. Maybe it was because when, all those years ago, she wanted to marry Sawyer, he told her she was being foolish.

"We can't just go and get married, right now, at eighteen. We don't have anything in place for a life together. It would just be foolish."

She'd heard those words over and over in her mind throughout the past ten years. And every time, they made her question whether she was truly capable of creating her own life.

CHAPTER EIGHT

Montana

THE FOLLOWING Saturday morning Montana woke under a heavy blanket of dread. It was the first official Kincaid-Davis Wedding Planning Team workday. Normally, Montana lived for this type of thing. She loved manual labor, the physical demands of swinging a hammer, lifting, carrying, building. She always had. While some of her friends in junior high got squeamish if they slept over and had to help muck the horse stalls, Montana always liked breaking a sweat.

It wasn't the work she dreaded; it was the team, she thought as she tried to muster up the energy to get out of bed. She would be fine if it were an all-girls workday. But it was a whole team day. With only two months to plan the wedding, they needed all hands on deck. She would likely be working side by side with Sawyer for several hours. When they were teenagers, that was fun. They used to have some of their best conversations as they chopped wood or brought loads of hay to the barn. But they weren't teenagers anymore. Montana couldn't decide if it was worse that they wouldn't be alone. If they were, at least she could give him the silent treatment in private. But as it was, she was going to have to be civil to him.

"All right, Hart, you've spent enough time wallowing," she said, her voice echoing against the walls in her empty bedroom. "Time to rise and shine."

As soon as she threw aside the covers and stood up, Cash whimpered from his crate. She let him out and gave him a little scratch behind the ears.

"You want to come with me to the workday?" The puppy wagged his tail and followed her as she walked to the back door to let him out. Sometimes (often), she wished he would answer.

Montana hadn't planned to shower. But, she thought as she filled Cash's bowl with puppy food, since she'd woken up thinking about Sawyer, she figured she'd better. If she was going to work with him all day, she might as well make him miss her. So what if she used a little extra of the shampoo she knew he liked? She'd remind him what he was missing out on.

She made sure to be punctual, and pulled into the Davises' circular driveway at the same time as Abby. Montana hurried to park and grab her puppy so they could walk in together.

"Good morning," Abby said as she walked up. "And good morning to *you*." Her voice rose a couple of octaves as she greeted Cash, who licked her face.

"I guess I don't have to ask you if you're ready for a morning of manual labor," Montana said. "You're used to this stuff."

"What you should ask me is whether I'm ready to spend the morning with Trace Walker."

Montana arched an eyebrow at Abby. "And are you?"

"Nope. Not even a little. I just wish he didn't hate me so much."

Oh, I don't think he hates you, Montana thought. But she kept her mouth shut. She didn't need to interfere where Trace and Abby were concerned.

"I have just the solution," Montana said. "How about you hang out with Sawyer and I'll hang out with Trace?"

"I like the way you think," Abby said.

They reached the main house and walked around to the back, where Tessa and Cody were waiting, seated on a bench. Each of them held a coffee cup. Montana felt yet another pang — not jealousy so much as wistfulness. What she wouldn't give to sit with the love of her life on a bench, matching mugs in hand.

"Gold stars for the two of you," Tessa said, standing to hug them. "You're the first to show up on team workday."

Abby smiled. "I don't think I've ever gotten a gold star before. I feel honored."

"Well don't get used to it."

Trace appeared, and Montana kicked herself for not hearing him come up behind them. Although she'd missed his entrance, she didn't miss the way his eyes met Abby's, smoldering, for an instant, before he blinked away the attraction.

"Trace Walker!" Montana said. "You stop acting like a big jerk right this instant."

"Well, good day to you, too, Montana. I see the claws are out this morning."

Montana decided ignoring him was the best course of action. She turned to face Tessa and Cody.

"I'm going in to get some coffee," Trace muttered. The kitchen's screen door slammed behind him.

"I don't know what's gotten into him," Cody said in a stage whisper.

Montana inclined her head toward Abby. Cody winked at her. Ah, so he saw the same thing Montana did. She smiled. It could be fun to watch this unfold. If Trace could ever stop being a jerk.

"Well," Trace drawled as he returned, a cup of steaming coffee in hand. "I guess we're just waiting on Sawyer now."

Where was Sawyer, anyway? Not that it was any of Montana's business. But usually, he ran right on time. All the Mint Creek Ranch kids did. Their parents instilled the value of timeliness from the moment they could walk. The only reason he'd be late was because —

"Morning, everybody."

The sound of Sawyer's voice did something to Montana's body. Always had. It was like a balm, soothing her anxiety and nerves. Even while her body practically melted at the sound of his voice, anger overtook her mind. How could he be late on a day like today?

As if he were trying to ruffle her feathers, he drawled, "Long night," while looking right at her. Indignation blew up inside her body.

She couldn't help herself. *Long night?* She felt her lip curl into what was surely an ugly sneer. "Pretty irresponsible, considering you are part of this team."

While everyone else's mouths hung open, Sawyer had the perfect comeback. "If you must know, Montana, my sweet, darling puppy kept me up all night. I think she ate something out in the yard. And boy, was she paying for it. I called the vet's after-hours number, and they told me to feed her some rice and plain chicken. I think I finally got her feeling better. But let's just say I've been knee-deep in shit all night long."

Well. That put Montana in her place. She felt ashamed for assuming he'd been with a woman. And, judging by the look on his face, he knew it — and he liked that she'd been jealous. Her face burned hot.

"Oh. Sorry."

With that, Cody and Tessa stood up.

"Right," Cody said. "We're all here now. Should we get started?"

Still fuming, Montana resolved to keep her mouth shut for the rest of the day.

———

SAWYER

IT WAS CHILDISH, but Sawyer felt a considerable thrill that Montana not only assumed he spent the night with another woman, but also (and more importantly) that she was upset by it.

He couldn't quite put his finger on the reason he enjoyed it. Things were over between them. For good. But still. Could a guy derive a little satisfaction from the fact that his ex was jealous? Sure he could. She was so damn cute, her face flaming with embarrassment and anger.

"First order of business," Cody said, rubbing his hands together. "We've got to clear this area."

He gestured to the space west of the giant cottonwood tree behind his parents' house. Trace whistled.

"I know," Cody said, surveying the space, which the Davsises had used as an unofficial storage area over the years. Stacks of wooden pallets, unused flower pots, rolls and sections of fencing, old shipping crates, and empty barrels told countless stories about the Mint Creek Ranch's history. And they all had to be moved.

Sawyer remembered playing hide-and-seek there when they were kids. A place with this many nooks and crannies made for an awesome playground.

"You're thinking hide-and-seek, right?" Trace asked.

"Yep," Sawyer said. "I'm also thinking, judging by Cody's expression, that he thinks we've got a long day ahead."

"Well, that's true," Cody said.

Sawyer whooped. "Let's get at it, ladies and gentlemen. Let's get this done before the sun goes down!"

At that moment, Cody's mom, Elaine, came out of the kitchen and held the door for Cody's dad, Tom, who carried out a giant cooler and set it on the table.

"Elaine said we had to provide sustenance. So here you go. Sodas all around." He cupped a hand around one side of his mouth and said in a stage whisper, "And I might've thrown in a couple beers."

Elaine swatted him on the arm. "That'll slow 'em down, Tommy!"

Tom winked at Cody. Sawyer knew Elaine didn't really mind the beers. She was thrilled about the wedding. Not only because she was marrying off her son, either.

As Tom walked back into the house, he confirmed it, grumbling, "Aw, you know you're just happy there's finally an excuse to get this junk moved. Beers or not."

The truth was, Sawyer thought, it really was the best place on the ranch for a wedding. Just beyond the area they were clearing today, Mint Creek ran through the property. In the afternoon, the sun would shine so nicely through the leaves on the trees.

In pairs, the Kincaid-Davis Wedding Planning Team got to work. They lifted trash items onto a big trailer, which Tom would haul away the following week. They stacked fence panels in the bed of Cody's truck and drove them in loads to the barn, where they'd serve as the walls of a new corral. They shoveled gravel to flatten out the ground. Meanwhile, the two puppies loped and leaped and wrestled and tore around the property like they owned the place, a big ball of fur and energy and too-large paws.

Sawyer quickly noticed that every time he went to pick something up, Abby was there. And, everywhere Trace went, Montana seemed to follow.

He knew without a doubt that Montana and Abby had planned this. Montana had most definitely wanted to avoid spending time with him. And, because of the way Trace acted around Abby, she probably wanted to avoid him, too.

Well, Sawyer thought, as he and Abby lifted a stack of wood pallets to carry to the trash trailer, it worked out just fine for him.

Even though he shouldn't, he found himself watching Montana from afar. Mid-morning when she took off the flannel she wore over her tank top, he just about groaned out loud. The neckline dipped just low enough that he could see the rise of her breasts. And all he could think about was holding those breasts in his hands while she rode him, arching above him.

"Are you okay?" Abby asked.

At the other end of the stack of pallets, she looked at him with a mixture of concern and amusement.

"Yeah," Sawyer managed. "Just got a cramp, that's all."

He could tell she didn't buy it. She raised an eyebrow at him.

"Need to take a break?"

Sawyer shook his head, and they kept walking toward the trailer. Just when they got there, Elaine stopped them before they could load the first stack. "Why don't you guys set those pallets over there? I was thinking maybe we could have a little bonfire tonight. I thought maybe we could make s'mores. Like we did when you were kids."

Sawyer's mouth watered. He smiled at Abby as they moved over to one side to set down the pallets.

Sawyer didn't care what Trace thought about Abby Flores. She was a damn hard worker, and tough, too. She could lift nearly as much as Sawyer could. Even when they took a heavy load, she didn't complain or ask for a break. She just soldiered on. She wasn't hard to look at, either, with her doe-like eyelashes and wide smile. Sawyer could see why she got under Trace's skin. As they walked together back to the junk pile, Abby said, "I've never had s'mores before. Are they any good?"

Sawyer stopped walking. "What? You've never had s'mores?"

Abby shook her head, shrugged. "Nope. My family, we didn't grow up doing any of that kind of stuff. It's not like I was deprived or anything. We just never had s'mores."

"Well, I guess we'll have to rectify that," Sawyer said.

They grabbed another stack of pallets and as they walked it over to where they set the first stack, Sawyer watched Montana out of the corner of his eye. One of the things he loved most about her was that she looked like the most delicate girl he'd ever seen. Yet she was tough as nails. Maybe not as strong as Abby, but just as capable. Even as she and Trace worked together to shovel a pile of gravel into an oversized wheelbarrow, Sawyer admired the way the muscles in her arms and back rippled. He licked his lips. The next second, he tripped over a rock and almost went down. It was all he could do to keep himself from falling, and taking Abby with him.

"I know you think you're over her. Moving on. All of that," Abby said with a knowing smile. "But any fool can see you're not."

Sawyer wasn't sure how to respond. So he didn't. He didn't even know what to think about what Abby said. Was he over Montana? Even if he wasn't, was that so unreasonable? How long did it take to erase a lifetime's worth of being completely head over heels for someone? More importantly, did he even want to erase that? Maybe he *wasn't* over Montana. And maybe he didn't want to be.

When every time you looked at a woman, you wanted to hear her laugh, take her in your arms, protect her, and make love to her, was that really something to throw away?

Sawyer didn't think so. But he doubted he'd ever be able to convince Montana otherwise.

———

Montana

JUST AS SHE'D promised she would, Elaine expressed her gratitude to the Kincaid-Davis Wedding Planning Team for the clearing of the junk pile.

First, she fed the whole crew dinner. She pulled out a frozen lasagna and had it ready just before the sun went down. Then, while everyone washed dishes, she made a giant pot of hot chocolate.

As she passed out the steaming mugs, she said, "I added just enough peppermint Schnapps to relax your tired muscles!"

Finally, she said to Tom, "Now, light those ugly pallets on fire and burn them to the ground."

Within fifteen minutes, the fire roared, casting a circle of warmth and light big enough that all the members of the Kincaid-Davis Wedding Planning Team fit inside it, laughing and talking, recounting stories from the day.

At one point, Montana noticed she had unconsciously moved

closer to Sawyer. Or had he moved closer to her? Not that it mattered. They were now almost touching.

Her body was aware of the fact before her mind even registered it. She could feel him there. Between them, an energy existed, whether she liked it or not.

As Tessa once told her, Montana and Sawyer were like magnets. Half the time, they were drawn to each other, and the other half they repelled one another. Tonight, the energy drew them together. She shivered.

"Cold?"

His voice, close to her ear, was husky, and she didn't know if it was because he was aroused, like she was, or if it was because he was tired after a long night with his dog. Both puppies, exhausted after a day of romping around together, lay at their feet, snoozing.

"No," Montana said. "Just got a shiver."

A dozen years ago, Sawyer would have wrapped his arms around her. In fact, he would have done the same a dozen *weeks* ago. And Montana couldn't explain to herself why she ached so badly for him to do so at that moment.

Before she realized it, her shoulder was touching his upper arm. She didn't bother moving away. Even if the two of them weren't going to be close friends anymore, their bodies would always remember each other, wouldn't they? She took another sip of her hot chocolate, letting the liquid warm her from the inside out.

"It's going to be a great wedding," Sawyer said. "I'm so happy for Cody and Tessa."

"Me too," Montana said, her throat tightening.

If you're so happy, she asked herself, *then why do you feel like you want to cry?*

CHAPTER NINE

Montana

MONDAY MORNING, the first email in Montana's inbox was from Abby, with the subject line: *Sunset Valley First Owners Club.*

Montana, still in bed, gasped and tapped to open the message, which read:

Hello Montana,

Welcome to the Sunset Valley First Owners Club.

Congratulations!

As one of the first property owners in the development, you have the opportunity to help define its direction. I believe that while we all have a similar vision of what we want the development to be, it is from our varied perspectives, experiences, and ideas that our new community will truly flourish.

Attached you will find a list, including contact information, of the members of this very exclusive club. I would like to have our first meeting two weeks from today at 4 p.m. Consider it a Happy Hour. I will provide drinks and refreshments. There will be no formal agenda; it is simply a chance for us to get to know one another.

Please reply to this email and let me know if you will be able to attend. I sincerely hope to see you there.

In gratitude,

Abby Flores

With every word she read, Montana's excitement grew. Her heart fluttered against her ribcage and she placed a hand on her chest to slow it down.

"I'm going to be a property owner," she whispered. And not only that, she was going to have the chance to help make the development amazing.

She couldn't wait. It seemed that Cash couldn't, either. He stood in his crate, his whip of a tail hitting the bars repeatedly as his whole body wagged.

Montana got out of bed and released Cash, who stopped between every couple of huge bounds to wag at her until they reached the front door and she clipped on his leash. They walked down the stairs and out to their usual morning potty spot.

While Cash did his thing, Montana opened the email attachment — the list of the first five buyers.

There was Abby, whose name was first on the list, followed by Montana's. The third name, José Suarez, was unfamiliar to Montana. She recognized the fourth: Jacob Austin. This wasn't a surprise. Jacob always liked to be on the forefront of the newest things in town. Back when they built the first penthouse apartments in downtown Prescott, he snatched one up as soon as they became available. Now, maybe he was looking to settle down. Enjoy the country life.

The fifth name on the list was a corporation rather than an individual: the Leaning S Ranch. *The Leaning S Ranch?* Montana's mouth went dry. Her vision went blurry. She swore her heart stopped beating.

"The Leaning S Ranch?" Cash stopped digging at the root of the little cherry tree and looked up at her, head cocked. The Leaning S Ranch didn't exist. Not in real life — yet. That ranch existed only in one place: Sawyer Nelson's imagination. Unless Montana didn't know Sawyer as well as she thought she did, he was the fifth buyer in the development.

Cash barked, and Montana realized she'd completely frozen. She dropped her hand, which she had put over her mouth at some point, then forced herself to take a deep breath, and then another.

Why didn't Abby tell her?

Why didn't *Sawyer* tell her?

How did she not know what was happening?

And — she could hear suspenseful music in her mind: *dun dun*

DUN — what was she going to do? She couldn't possibly live just acres away from Sawyer for the rest of her life! That's why she'd moved away from Mint Creek Ranch in the first place.

Shock and surprise exited stage left, and indignation entered.

This — buying one of Abby's properties — was *her* idea! It was supposed to be completely separate from Sawyer!

With a shaking hand, Montana picked up her phone. She almost couldn't dial. Abby picked up right away, and Montana could hear the excitement in her voice when she said, "Did you get it? Did you get my email?"

Montana's excitement from just moments before was gone. In its place: anger. "I got it."

"What's wrong?"

"Abby. Why didn't you tell me?"

"Tell you what? I told you about the club."

That's when it struck Montana. Abby had no idea who owned the Leaning S Ranch. And Sawyer? He probably wanted to keep it that way. That's why he used the ranch name instead of his own.

A fresh wave of thoughts occurred to Montana then. Why on God's green earth would Sawyer purchase property from Abby? Sawyer's best friend, Trace, would be livid if he knew. What was Sawyer thinking?

"Abby. Do you know who owns the Leaning S Ranch?"

Silence.

"No," Abby said slowly. "I've never heard the guy's name. He paid his deposit with a money order. I've never seen him in person. He sounds nice on the phone, though."

"He sounds nice," Montana said, trying to keep her voice even. "But does he sound familiar?"

Again, silence.

"I mean, no?" Abby said, finally.

"The Leaning S Ranch doesn't exist. Not yet, anyway. But I know who owns it."

The realization must have dawned on Abby, then, because she spoke the next word as Montana said it: "Sawyer."

"Montana. I didn't know. I swear."

Montana forced herself to take another breath. A deep one. "I believe you. I don't think he wanted you to know it was him. And I can only imagine the reaction he's having right now, seeing my name on the list, too."

Suddenly, the hilarity of the situation hit Montana. She started laughing.

"Montana?"

"This," she gasped between fits of laughter, "is the definition of irony. I don't even know what to say. I'll call you later."

As soon as she hung up, her phone rang. She cursed herself for not removing Sawyer's profile picture from his contact information in her phone. Because there she was, looking down at his smiling face. His eyes, as green as the grass in her favorite meadow, sparkled back at her.

She might as well get the conversation over with. Besides, she had a lot of questions.

SAWYER

WHEN MONTANA ANSWERED THE PHONE, Sawyer could hear laughter in her voice. He couldn't imagine what was so funny. As surly and irritable as he was feeling at the moment, he spat, "What's so funny?"

"How did you know I was laughing?"

"Woman. I know you practically as well as I know myself. Now tell me what's so damn funny."

He should have known his attitude would make her want to toy with him. She always loved to, as she put it, "get his goat."

"You wouldn't believe the email that just showed up in my inbox."

So, she knew. Leave it to Montana to think of this as some sort of cosmic joke. That was the problem. She believed the universe was always conspiring. She didn't believe in mistakes. But it seemed like he'd made one. This was supposed to be *his* pursuit. A Montana-free pursuit.

"Glad you think it's so funny."

He heard her sigh and instantly knew her feelings on the topic were much more complicated. In fact, she sounded downright weary when she responded.

"It's just — how do I put this into words?"

Sawyer loved and hated the familiarity with which she spoke. It drove him crazy how they could go from being best friends one instant to virtual strangers the next. At the moment her tone conveyed the kind of honesty and compassion that meant they were best friends.

"For a while now," she said, "I've been thinking I wanted to get a real house. I didn't know exactly what that would look like. But … "

Her voice kind of trailed off, and he knew she was deciding which words to use. What to tell him and what to keep to herself.

"Suffice it to say, I wanted a fresh start. Something all my own. It started with the puppy. Then, one morning, I was covering the City Council meeting where Abby was making a presentation. And she put on a slideshow. I can't describe how I felt when I saw the cottage. It was just —"

"Like home." He finished her sentence.

There was a pause, and he knew she was nodding. "Yes. Exactly."

That's how I've always felt about you, Montana, he wanted to say. But he didn't. He wanted to tell her how he had the same sense when he saw the lot for sale on the Internet. It wasn't a home with Montana, but it was the next best thing.

"Trace —" Montana began, and Sawyer said, "Doesn't know."

"I think he might kill me. Might kill both of us," Montana said, that edge of humor creeping back into her voice. "But I really think Abby has a good concept going. And I think once Trace sees it in person, he'll feel a lot better about it. But, in this instance, I just had to think of myself. I've been … floundering. Feeling lost. Until this."

Sawyer ran a hand through his hair.

"You're right. Trace is going to kill us."

"The Leaning S ranch, huh?" she said.

Again, he heard compassion in her voice. She knew. She understood that for Sawyer, this was the beginning of fulfilling a lifelong dream. She would never judge him for setting out on his own. "Yeah. Finally."

"Well, you're not going very far from home, are you?"

He chuckled. "No. To tell you the truth, I felt like I needed a fresh start, too. Something of my own. I've been just browsing the real estate listings online. You know, for fun. And then I saw this. The view, right? And I had that same feeling. So I called. I didn't know it was Abby's property, and I didn't realize quite how close it was to home. I got an automated voicemail and left a message. Between the moment I saw the listing and Abby's return phone call, I fell in love with the place. I printed up a picture and put it on my fridge. Trace and Cody haven't even seen it. You won't tell them, will you?"

"I won't tell them if you won't. I'm not quite ready to tell them yet, either."

Neither of them spoke for a minute. Sawyer could hear Montana breathing, and the sound and rhythm set off a memory of lying next to her in bed, watching her breathe.

"Well," they both said.

Montana spoke next. "I guess I'd better go. I'm a very busy member of the Sunset Valley First Owners Club. As you know, my days are very full."

Again with the humor. When he first picked up the phone to dial Montana, Sawyer felt angry, agitated. Now, he felt at peace with his decision. Why didn't things always work this way between them?

"Montana?"

"Yeah?"

"I'm happy for you."

"I'm happy for you, too, Sawyer. I really am."

They disconnected, and, not for the first time, Sawyer wished they were going through this process together. In a way, they were now. But they were doing it in parallel, rather than in tandem. And even though he was thrilled about his future, he also felt just the tiniest bit sad.

MONTANA

LATER THAT DAY, Abby texted Montana and invited her to lunch. As soon as they sat down, Abby said, "So, you acted like I was doing you a big favor by giving you a deal on your new house, right?"

Montana nodded. "Absolutely. You are."

Abby drummed her fingertips on the table. "Well, I have a favor to ask you."

"Anything," Montana said.

Abby's eyes narrowed. "Anything?"

Again, Montana nodded. "Anything."

"Are you free this Friday night?"

"Honey, these days, I'm free every Friday night."

"That's good," Abby said. "Because I need you to join me on a double date. A double-blind date."

A date? Montana hadn't been on a date in as long as she could remember. Maybe there were a couple in college, after she and Sawyer went their separate ways. But none of them were standouts.

This had the potential to be fun. Grinning, Montana shrugged. "Okay."

"Okay?" Abby still looked doubtful.

"Yeah. Why not? I'm doing new things in all these other areas of my life. A puppy, a new house, the Sunset Valley First Owners Club. Why not go on one date with a new guy?"

"I like your attitude," Abby said. "Thank you so much. One of the guys on my crew, Dylan, he's been trying to set me up with his friend for a year. He says we'd be perfect together. I've been telling him no all this time, but now I've run out of excuses, and I feel like I should just get it over with. It's not that I don't want to date anyone. But dating is just so —"

"Awkward?" Montana said.

Abby nodded. "It is. And with Sawyer up in your space for the next few months, with the wedding planning and the home owner-ship, I figured you could use a good distraction. Last time Dylan asked me, I said I didn't really feel safe going on a date with someone I didn't know at all. Now he's suggested a double date, so I can bring a friend. I agreed, praying you would, too."

The more Montana thought about it, the better the idea seemed. Wasn't this serendipity? What if this guy turned out to be incredible?

"Do you know anything about these guys?" she asked Abby.

"I just know they work in I.T."

Montana had never dated anyone who worked in I.T. She preferred her men rugged. But, maybe it was time for a change.

MONTANA WAS SO busy with work that week, Friday evening was there in what felt like no time. Abby made all the arrangements. They were going to Tito's, a restaurant with a live band and a dance floor.

Feeling a little nervous — nervous-excited, maybe? — she headed home from work to change and get ready.

She stood in her closet, feeling at a loss. It had been so long since she dressed to impress anyone other than Sawyer.

She thought back to the night a few months ago, when she took Tessa to the rodeo dance, and Tessa met Cody. One night. One night was all it took to change the trajectory of Tessa's life.

Could this be that night for Montana? Some random, double-blind date? At her feet, Cash picked up a ballet flat and gave it a good shake. She took it away from him and set his bone between his front paws.

"I was planning on wearing that tonight," she told him. "If this is the night that changes my life, I can't go in wearing a chewed-up ballet flat."

Cash sat down and cocked his head. She almost wished she could take him with her tonight. She hated to leave him alone. She briefly indulged herself in a little fantasy where she called Sawyer: "Hey, Sawyer. I have a date tonight. Yes, a date. Would you mind watching my puppy?"

While Cash chewed madly on the bone, Montana returned her attention to the present moment and the dozens of outfits in her closet, none of which seemed quite right. Too casual for a restaurant with dancing, or too fancy for a Prescott Friday night. Finally, she settled on a pair of jeans and a light blue sweater she knew Sawyer loved.

Not that she should be thinking about Sawyer's reaction to the outfit she planned to wear to meet a new guy. But, hey, she was human, and this darn sweater made her think of Sawyer.

She'd bought it in downtown Prescott one winter while she was Christmas shopping. It was so, so soft. And it was her favorite color: the same light, crystalline blue of the ice that lined the little holes in a glacier. The night she bought it, she went straight home and put it on. Somehow, Sawyer showed up at her house, like he always did. Or, like he always used to. It was like yesterday. She was cooking. He came up behind her and put his hands on her upper arms, bending down to kiss her neck as she stirred her soup with a wooden spoon.

"Ooh, soft," he said, his lips still against her neck.

Standing behind her while she stirred, he ran his hands down the length of her arms, then back up. His palms then moved over her chest, and down to cup her breasts through the sweater. He continued rubbing, massaging, while she continued stirring. She was so aroused she could barely speak. That was how things always went with them.

She shut off the stove and turned around to face him. He pulled her close, and she could feel that he was already hard. They had sex, fast and desperate, right there in the kitchen. They ate dinner afterward.

Heart racing now, Montana reconsidered. Maybe she shouldn't wear the blue sweater for the double-blind date. She sighed, refolded it, and put it away. She chose instead a purple long-sleeved shirt. It was brand-new, no memories attached. Satisfied, she cut off the tags and put it on.

Abby said they would meet the two guys, Josh and Dave, at Tito's bar. The women decided to get there a little early, so they would be together and seated when the men arrived. They found two seats at the end of the bar and ordered glasses of wine. While they waited, Montana took in the bright colors and clean lines of the space. She'd always liked Tito's.

"Are you nervous?"

Only then did Montana notice she was bouncing her right foot.

"Yep. The foot-bouncing. Old nervous habit. Haven't done it in a long time."

"What, the foot bouncing? Or dating?"

Montana smiled. "Neither, I guess."

"Me, neither."

"But you're such a catch," Montana said. And she meant it. Abby was a successful businesswoman. A smart, savvy one. She was an interesting person. And, she was straight-up good-looking. The whole package.

"I don't know," Abby said, shrugging. "I think I'm too much for some men. Owning a construction company is traditionally something men do. So, when men hear that's what I do, it catches them off guard. I think they're afraid I'll be controlling or too independent or something. Or have bigger muscles than they do."

Montana gasped. "But you're just about the womanliest woman I know."

Abby lifted a hand. "I know. I like all the girly stuff: jeans with sparkly back pockets, mascara, fancy underwear. But most of the men I meet see me in construction boots and jeans. With dirty hands. And then they see me telling other men what to do."

"Well, when you put it that way." The two of them were silent for a few beats. Montana saw Abby notice something — or someone. She turned around and saw two men coming through the door.

"Quick," Abby said, her voice low. "What's your first impression?"

Montana gave the guys a quick once-over. They were both hand-some. Solidly built. Although they dressed differently (one of them wore dark jeans and a button-up shirt with rolled-up sleeves and the other wore slacks with a shirt and tie), they looked like — "Twins."

"Well, that is a twist I wasn't expecting," Abby said.

The discussion ended there, because the men were now standing in front of them. Montana and Abby stood up, and Abby put out her hand.

"You must be Josh and Dave."

"I'm Josh," said the one in jeans, and the other added, "I'm Dave."

After introductions and handshaking, the hostess signaled that their table was ready. The men stood back to let the women walk ahead of them, and as she passed them, Montana could feel Dave's eyes on her, appraising. And she liked it. It was nice to receive atten-tion from a man other than Sawyer.

Once they sat down, Montana found herself beyond relieved that this was a double date, and she wasn't there alone with a stranger. She'd forgotten how tough small talk was.

They went around the table sharing what they did for a living. Josh was a computer programmer whose bread and butter was software for restaurants, but he dreamed of being a video game designer. Dave designed computer programs for accountants. Montana stifled a yawn as he talked about his work, and then quickly reminded herself that she should be open-minded. Maybe this Dave had a secret wild side.

More than once during the meal, Montana caught herself comparing Dave to Sawyer. Which, she told herself, was perfectly normal. Wasn't it? Didn't a girl always compare dating prospects to the man she once thought she'd marry?

Where Sawyer's hands were calloused and often cut and bandaged, Dave's were clean and smooth. Where Sawyer always looked her right in the eye while they talked, like there was absolutely nothing more interesting in the world than what she was saying, Dave constantly glanced around the restaurant, his eyes landing on and following other people. When it came time to order, Dave requested several modifications to his meal. Silly ones, Montana thought: hold the cheese, no hot sauce, dressing on the side. She wondered if his mother had cooked him special meals growing up.

And before she knew it, her mind wandered off, concocting a

whole made-up childhood for this man she barely knew. She imagined if little Dave didn't like the tacos his mom was making, she'd whip up boring chicken. If he fell and scraped his knee, his mom probably sat him on the couch and made him cookies. By the time they finished eating, Montana knew: this guy was not for her.

Abby seemed to be having better luck with Josh. The two of them kept cracking up, like they were sharing one secret (and very funny) joke after another.

"Want to hit that piano bar over on Grove, grab a couple of drinks?" Dave asked after they'd paid.

Montana could tell Abby was on the verge of saying "yes," so she jumped in and said, "You know? I'm really tired all of a sudden. It's been a long week. Can we take a rain check?"

A few minutes later, Montana and Abby stood in the parking lot.

"Thanks for saying 'no,'" Abby said. "I didn't really want to go to the piano bar, but I felt like we should."

"I don't know," Montana said. "I just wasn't feeling it. Why don't the two of us go for a drink at the Watering Hole?"

Abby grinned. "Now you're talking."

Sawyer

THE WATERING HOLE was one of Sawyer's favorite Prescott hangouts. It was always hopping on a Friday night. So when Trace called him up and invited him to go out for a couple of beers, he didn't turn him down, even though he was tired and what he really wanted to do was sit on the couch with Dolly and watch some sports on TV.

The two of them sat at a high-top table in the corner. The barstools on either side were situated against the wall, so they each had a view of the entire room — the dance floor, the tables, the long bar, and the door.

Trace whistled when two women Sawyer didn't recognize came in. Sawyer just shook his head, and Trace said, "What, man? For once, there's a pair of ladies we haven't dated or wished we could date, and you're not even the slightest bit impressed?"

Sawyer just shook his head. It was going to take a lot to impress him that evening.

When the women headed for the bar, so did Trace, always anticipating his next move. He reached the bar at the same time they did. Sawyer watched with interest. Trace had always been good with women. He could strike up a conversation anywhere, anytime, about anything.

Both women looked at Trace, rapt. He was probably telling some story or joke. Whatever it was, he worked fast. Within a minute, the three of them were back at the table.

"Sawyer," Trace said, his voice confident as always. "This is Jessica, and this is Stacy."

Sawyer noted his first impression: Jessica was a tall, slender brunette and Stacy was medium in height with fiery red hair and intense green eyes. They both had killer smiles, and Sawyer felt his energy pick up, just the slightest bit.

"Nice to meet you, ladies," he said.

And so what if he didn't take them as out-of-towners and purposely enhance his Western drawl? "Can't say as I've seen the two of you around these parts before."

Out of the corner of his eye, Sawyer could see Trace shaking his head. But the ladies ate it right up.

"Oh, we're not from around here," Jessica said, and Stacy added, "We're from L.A."

"L.A., as in, Los Angeles?" Sawyer said.

"The one and only," Stacy said.

Immediately, some line about them surely being movie stars jumped to the forefront of Sawyer's mind. But fortunately, he managed not to let it come out his mouth.

Trace must have seen Sawyer's thought process because he jumped in. "What brings you ladies to Arizona?"

"We're here for work," Stacy said.

Trace and Sawyer exchanged a glance. That was the exact thing Tessa told Cody the night they met at the rodeo dance earlier that year.

"What do you do?" Sawyer and Trace asked simultaneously.

Sawyer noticed too late that his tone was far too intense for the conversation. But he shrugged it off. They would never see these women again.

"We're firefighters," Jessica said. "We're here for a conference. We're staying up at the resort."

"It's so nice," Stacy said. "There's an indoor pool."

Sawyer raised an eyebrow at Trace. Well. Her come-on sounded almost as desperate as his line about them being movie stars would have.

Sawyer relaxed back into his barstool. Firefighters were good. They weren't reporters there to get some scoop on the Mint Creek Ranch boys. Spending the evening with them was probably safe enough.

Trace snagged two barstools that weren't in use and brought them over to the table. The conversation flowed; strangers loved hearing about the Mint Creek Ranch and the men who ran it, and Trace loved talking about all that.

Although neither of the girls was really Sawyer's type (the thought, *Montana is your type, idiot,* rushed through his mind, but he pushed it away), he wouldn't mind showing them a good time. A good time did *not* mean ending up at the resort with its indoor pool and fancy mattresses (he'd seen them advertised in the local magazines).

But they could dance, couldn't they?

Neither Trace nor Sawyer had ever been the type to sleep with girls they met at bars. But they both loved a good night of dancing. The late-night crowd was coming in, and the energy was picking up. Sawyer loved nights like this. He loved that he could lose himself in the beat of the music. His body pulsing with the base, the sound drowning out any and all of the thoughts that were constantly rushing through his consciousness.

"Should we dance?" Stacy asked.

Jessica smiled at Stacy, and they each grabbed one of the men and pulled him out onto the dance floor. Stacy intertwined her fingers with Sawyer's. He felt nothing but skin against skin. No special electricity or energy or sexual tension — just two people heading out onto the dance floor. But boy, could she dance. Her body moved like liquid mercury. She twisted and turned, writhing and spinning. And *that* was fun. When they were face to face, she gave him a sexy, sultry smile, daring him to get closer. He put his hands on her hips, giving her what she wanted. Their bodies moved well together, and Sawyer was surprised to find he didn't get any more of a charge out of it. It was enjoyable, but he wasn't the least bit aroused.

That is, until Montana walked in.

No matter where he was, or when, or who he was with, as soon as Montana came into his periphery, he knew it. It was like their beings were somehow attached. He felt her come in before he saw her. He just knew. And sure enough, when he looked to the door, she and Abby were entering. They were talking, smiling. Montana laughed at something Abby said, and Abby's loud laugh carried over the music.

At that, Sawyer smiled. Stacy thought the smile was for her, and she grabbed his hips and pulled him closer. Naturally, Montana looked over right then. The eye contact was like a sucker punch. It was as if the air was vacuumed out of the room. And *now* he was aroused. Looking at the woman he'd loved for practically all his life, while dancing with a stranger he'd only just met, Sawyer was so turned on he could hardly stand it. Stacy seemed to sense the shift in him, and she ground her hips against his. She ran her fingertips up his arms to his shoulders and then slid her palms down his chest and grabbed onto his waist again. Sawyer closed his eyes, and imagined it was Montana touching him like that.

Guilt knocked on his consciousness. It wasn't right, him dancing with Stacy and imagining it was Montana. But dancing with Montana always felt so damn good.

He watched her as she and Abby made their way toward the bar. She acted like she didn't see him. But her spine stiffened, and her smile took on a frozen, mask-like quality. Abby must have noticed, because she glanced over at the dance floor. Her eyes widened in surprise when she saw Sawyer, still dancing quite suggestively with Stacy. Then, she put an arm around Montana's shoulders and steered her straight for the single open spot at the bar.

Although he tried to tear his eyes away from them, Sawyer noticed everything they did. They ordered shots, most likely of tequila, and Abby made some kind of toast. They tapped their shot glasses together and tossed them back. They repeated the process, this time with Montana making a toast. As she tipped her head back, Sawyer imagined running his lips along her throat. Then, even while he took Stacy by the waist and spun her around, he imagined doing body shots with Montana. A little salt here, a lick, a shot. A little salt there …

Abby and Montana wound through the crowd to the dance floor.

The two of them started dancing, holding hands, just like Montana used to do with her girlfriends at the high school dances. It seemed as though she had completely forgotten Sawyer existed. Which was the worst punishment she could ever dole out.

Suddenly, something like jealousy overcame all of Sawyer's other feelings. He wasn't jealous of anyone or anything specifically. He was just jealous that Montana seemed to be having a good time, and meanwhile, he should be having a good time, but couldn't, because he couldn't stop thinking about her. Suddenly, he wanted nothing more than to show her that he, too, could have a great time with someone else. He maneuvered the gorgeous, sexy Stacy over to where he was sure Montana could see the two of them. He turned up the heat on the dancing, pulling Stacy closer. Now it was him who trailed his hands over her body. And while the only thrill he got was seeing Montana watch him, it was thrill enough. She was jealous. Then, he turned the heat up even more. As one song ended and the next began, he took Stacy's face in his hands and kissed her.

She was surprised at first, and there was a split second when she paused and he wondered if he'd gone too far. But then she was kissing him back. His body didn't seem to mind. It was nice. Really nice. But, it wasn't Montana. He ended the kiss and gave Stacy what he hoped was a sexy-as-sin smile. She smiled back. They started dancing again. When Sawyer looked up, Montana had disappeared.

***

Montana

MONTANA WAS FURIOUS.

Not with Sawyer, for dancing with — and kissing! — another woman. In front of her, too. But with herself, for letting it upset her. He was entitled to dance with — and kiss! — anyone he wanted to.

So why was she so upset?

When she got home Friday night, all she wanted to do was wallow in self-pity. So she drew a hot bath, turned on some loud, feminist music, and submerged everything but her nose and mouth in the bathwater.

Even though she tried to focus on her breathing and eliminate any thoughts from her mind, she kept picturing the scene from the Watering Hole.

Why did she let Sawyer's dancing — and kissing! — that beautiful, sexy redhead get to her?

Was it, she wondered, pure and simple jealousy? Or something else? Was she upset because she couldn't bring herself to feel any sort of chemistry with Josh or Dave at dinner that night, yet Sawyer had obviously had quite a bit of chemistry with that other woman? Not that she could blame him. She was gorgeous.

Did it matter? Couldn't she just be infuriated without knowing why?

Breathe. Her entire body still submerged, she took a slow, deep breath through her nose, held it for a beat, and then exhaled through her mouth.

Cash, apparently intrigued by the noises coming from the bathtub, interrupted her serenity. She could hear the clicking of his toenails on the bathroom tile, coming toward her. She raised her face out of the water just enough to open her eyes, and she watched as the puppy put his paws on the edge of the tub and tried to lick her face. As clumsy as he was still, his paws slipped down into the water. Surprised, he tried to leap back, but couldn't unhook his elbows from the edge of the tub. There she was, trying to relax, and there *he* was, squirming and jumping from side to side, trying to get out of her bath. Suddenly, he was in the tub, a wriggling ball of fur that was anything but tranquil.

For a split second, Montana felt irritated with Cash. But then, she laughed. The tension from a moment before started to dissolve. She lifted up the puppy, who now looked a mere fraction of his usual size. She held him under the armpits, and he licked her face.

"Stop it," she giggled. He didn't. "Stop it, Cash. And congratulations on your first bath."

Feeling much better, Montana, still laughing, got them both out of the tub and dried off.

She had worried she wouldn't be able to fall asleep. But once her head hit the pillow, she was out.

CHAPTER TEN

MONTANA WAS REALLY LOOKING FORWARD to spending some time with Tessa — who really was her new best friend — on Tuesday. About a month had passed since they had worked together on a story for the *Daily Dispatch*. For the three months during Cody's championship bull riding tour, the two of them had spent almost every waking moment — and most of their sleeping moments — together. They shared an RV, spent all day side by side in the press box, and completed their nightly assignments across from one another in the RV's dinette. They ate breakfast, lunch, and dinner with each other, often splitting meals, sharing French fries, and talking each other into dessert.

But since they'd returned to Prescott, they didn't see each other nearly as much. All along, they both assumed Tessa would be heading back to Phoenix at the end of the bull riding tour. But then, Tessa and Cody fell in love, and the rest was history. Tessa ended up staying on as the education reporter at the *Daily Dispatch*. And although Montana often stopped by while Tessa was doing interviews, and they crossed paths in the newsroom, they didn't get a chance to talk very often. Tessa didn't have her own place yet, but she was staying with her parents in the cabin they were renting on the Mint Creek Ranch, just until the wedding. Montana knew Tessa spent most of her time at Cody's house anyway.

So, Montana was thrilled when Stanley Stephenson assigned her and Tessa to a front-page package about a new program through which one of the local farms taught kids all the aspects of running a farm. They would spend the entire morning there together.

Montana needed a dozen usable photos, which meant she would take about a hundred. It should be relatively easy: there was nothing cuter than kids and farm animals.

And, she would get the chance to catch up with Tessa without anyone else around. Apparently, Tessa was just as excited to spend time with Montana, because when they greeted each other at the farm's entrance, Tessa ran up and gave her a big hug.

"I've missed you," she said.

Montana felt her eyes smart from the sting of tears. "I've missed you, too."

"What's new?" Tessa wanted to know.

Montana shrugged. "Nothing, really. Same old, same old. Except for the puppy. But you already know about him."

Tessa inclined her head toward the farm's main office. They fell into step.

"I heard you and Abby went to the Watering Hole Friday night."

Montana sighed. "That's small-town living for you. Yes, Abby and I had a double-blind date and then we went to the Watering Hole for a couple of drinks."

"First of all, you didn't tell me you had a double-blind date. That's something new. And second of all, I take it the date didn't go that well?"

"I mean, it went okay. But — I don't know. No chemistry, I guess. The guys were both in I.T. There's nothing wrong with that. Just not my type, you know? I like tough guys. Guys with muscles and cuts on their knuckles."

Montana looked over to see Tessa smiling at her. "I never thought I'd say this, but so do I."

They checked in at the front at desk and got their press passes and schedules.

"Want to go watch goat-milking?" Tessa asked.

"There's nothing I'd love more," Montana said.

"I also heard Sawyer was dancing with a sexy redhead at the Watering Hole."

"Well, whoever you're getting your information from, it's a good source. That's also true."

"As you know," Tessa quipped, "I take information only from the best sources."

Montana loved being with Tessa. She loved their easy conversations. And she loved that they could be honest with each other.

"I take it Sawyer is your source," she said.

Tessa nodded, and then said in a confidential tone, "He's been spending quite a bit of time at our place since the two of you, you know, called it quits. Again."

"Has he?"

Montana kept her tone light, indifferent, but she *was* interested. If Sawyer was spending his time with Cody and Tessa, that meant he wasn't out on the town prowling. *Good to know.*

"Montana —"

a beat of silence.

"Yeah?"

"It's just — are you sure you and Sawyer are done? I mean, I know you called it quits. But are you sure that's what you want?"

"I've never been so sure of anything in my life," Montana lied.

Except for the fact that I want to buy one of Abby's properties, Montana thought. But she wasn't ready to tell Tessa that just yet. "Why do you ask?"

"Oh, I don't know."

Montana had come to know Tessa well enough over the summer to understand that Tessa *did* know. She had a reason for asking.

Fortunately, they had arrived at the goat pen. And they were coming up on a line of about fifteen of the cutest little future farmers.

Montana pulled her camera around to the front of her body. "Showtime."

There. That ought to put an end to the conversation. At least for the time being.

———

MONTANA SQUARED her shoulders and took a moment to compose herself before walking into the back room at The Steakout for the first meeting of the Sunset Valley First Owners Club.

The thought that she wasn't worthy enough — adult enough — to be part of this club kept worming its way into her consciousness. No matter how hard she tried to tell herself otherwise, she felt unqualified to be among those who would ultimately make decisions about an entire development.

She was unaccustomed to that level of power. As a photojournalist, she had a different sort of power: to share the truth as she saw it with the readers of her hometown newspaper. People could look at her photos and read the accompanying stories and decide what to do with the information she shared.

But she and the other members of the Sunset Valley First Owners Club would make decisions about how people lived.

Abby invited you to be part of this club, she reminded herself for what was probably the thousandth time. She placed her hands on the heavy wooden doors leading to the The Steakout's inner sanctum (*strike that,* she thought — *it's just the back room*) and pushed them open.

The space was swanky, all high-back leather chairs and framed paintings, and Montana figured Abby had chosen it on purpose. She wanted the Sunset Valley development to feel exclusive.

Abby was already there, seated at the head of a long, wide table. Sawyer and an older man — must be José Suarez, she thought, picturing the email Abby sent out — sat to Abby's left. Montana's heart beat a little faster. She took the seat next to Abby, across from Sawyer.

"We're just waiting on one more," Abby said. "Let's go ahead and order some drinks."

A few minutes later, their drinks on the table and their fifth member — Jacob Austin — seated next to Montana, Abby brought the meeting to order.

"As you know, we're the first five owners in the Sunset Valley development."

She put a hand on her chest. "I'm so excited. Beyond excited. For me, this is a dream coming to fruition. And you all are helping to make it happen."

Abby's words gave Montana chills. This was a dream coming to fruition for her, too. Finally, she would have her own place. Land, a house, a garden. She felt herself smiling, and when she looked up at Sawyer, she saw that he was smiling, too. She didn't need him to tell her that he felt the same way she did ... that his excitement was in complete alignment with hers. Truly, they had always wanted the same things. (Correction, she told herself. *Almost* always.)

How strange was it that they weren't embarking on this journey together? Not in the way she had always imagined. Suddenly, mixed in with her excitement, she felt a bit of sadness. Welcoming her own new dream was also saying goodbye to the one she'd had for two decades.

She could tell Sawyer recognized the sadness in her expression. His hand moved across the table toward hers. But before their fingertips touched, he drew it back.

So strange how he still wanted to comfort her. He'd told her before that comforting her was all he ever wanted to do.

She thought back to one morning in Albuquerque, a few months ago, when they were all on tour. It was the first night Tessa and Cody spent together. Montana got up early to go for a run, leaving Tessa and Cody sleeping in the RV she and Tessa shared.

As soon as she stepped outside, she saw Sawyer, also dressed in his running clothes. Running was something they used to do together. But on that morning, she wanted to be alone. She was feeling especially solitary because of the romance budding between Tessa and Cody. It renewed her awareness of everything she'd lost with Sawyer. So when she saw him that morning, all she wanted to do was take off.

Yes, they'd run hundreds of miles together. On tour, at home, everywhere. But that morning? Being in sync like that would just remind her of how good they were together.

She didn't want to run with him. She didn't think she could bear it. She didn't say so, but he should have been able to read her body language. When she started out, he fell into step beside her. They were in sync. Step for step. Breath for breath. He didn't even speak. He didn't do anything wrong. She tried to run faster, to put some distance between them. But he just increased his speed to match hers. She slowed down. He did, too.

"Why are you here?" she finally asked him.

"Figured I'd go for a run. Same as always. Same as you."

His tone was so casual. Like nothing bothered him. As if things were normal.

But things weren't. In fact, they were so far from normal, Montana's heart ached. Oh, how she wanted them to be. She wanted to run with Sawyer like she had a million times and then go back and squeeze into one of the RV showers together. But she couldn't. They couldn't. Montana stopped running. So did Sawyer. They stood there, facing each other. God, he was so handsome. The sheen of sweat, the slightly rosy cheeks, his arms muscular in that beat-up old tank top. She wanted to tuck his hair behind his ear, use her knuckles to wipe the sweat off his chin. She wanted to wrap her arms around his waist and just stand there with him. But she couldn't. So she turned around and hightailed it back to camp, crying all the way.

Looking back on it from the comfortable chairs in The Steakout's back room, she figured Sawyer could tell she was lonely that morning. Otherwise, he probably would've fallen back, run in a different direction when she tried to get away from him. But she'd been so hurt, so mad. And she wouldn't take his comfort. When in truth, that's all she really wanted.

Even months later, as they sat across the table from each other getting ready to help design the development where they would each become first-time property owners, she wanted to accept his comfort. But he'd already withdrawn it.

"Montana?" Abby said.

Based on Abby's expression, Montana realized she should be answering a question or responding to a statement, but as distracted as she was, she didn't know what to say.

"Sorry, can you repeat that?"

Abby narrowed her eyes at Montana. "I said, can you describe how you would like the development to feel to you? As a property owner?"

That, she could work with. Montana took a deep breath and made a decision. From this moment on, she would focus on what she wanted to experience … not what she was missing out on.

"Absolutely," she said. "I want it to feel spacious. Expansive. Like when you finally step outside a crowded room and get your first breath of fresh air. And yet, it should still feel like a neighborhood, like a community. Rural, but connected. Does that make sense?"

"Yes," Abby said, her eyes sparkling.

On a big sheet of paper, she wrote down Montana's words as Montana resisted looking around to see what the others thought of what she said. Within seconds, though, she was pleased to hear that their ideas echoed her own:

"I want to know I'm surrounded by friends, but not be able to hear their music when I sit outside on my patio," Jacob said, and Sawyer said, "Yes! I want to be able to see the stars and still walk to a neighbor's house to borrow a cup of sugar."

Montana was surprised to find that she was able to feel some of her sadness dissipate, and her excitement grow.

Even if she and Sawyer weren't living in the same house together, she didn't think he would mind if she came over to borrow a cup of sugar (although she doubted he would keep sugar on hand).

She kept catching him looking at her. She couldn't help but think back to the other night, when she saw him dancing with that sexy redhead at the Watering Hole. How could he dance with a woman that way and then look at Montana the way he was looking at her?

Abby asked the group what kind of amenities they'd enjoy in the development. As Abby wrote down ideas — a pool, a fitness center, a picnic area, a park, a community barn —Montana's heart felt so full, it could burst. Judging by the light in Sawyer's eyes, he felt the same way. This new dream meant as much to him as it did to her.

———

THE CLOSER MONTANA'S new home came to being a reality, the more she wanted to experience it.

So one evening, she dug a tent out of the very back of her coat closet and packed some pajamas, a change of clothes, and a cooler full of food. She loaded it all into her car, along with Cash's bed and his food and dishes. On the way through town, she stopped at the store to buy an air mattress. After all, she wasn't a teenager anymore.

At the last minute before heading to the register to check out, she grabbed a stake and tie-out from the pet section.

"Can't risk you running off while I'm setting up the tent," she told Cash when she got back in the car. "You're still little enough for an owl or coyote to snatch you up."

Driving past Mint Creek Ranch on the way out to her new property, she had the insane urge to cover her face with one hand, or turn away so no one would recognize her. Then she remembered that if they saw her car, they would know it was her, anyway.

Just past the Mint Creek Ranch, she slowed and turned off of Williamson Valley Road onto Saddle Horn, the two-track that led to Sunset Valley. And there it was: the little flag with her name on it — and Cash's.

"Here we are," she said to the puppy.

Whether it was because they were slowing down, or because he could feel her energy, the puppy uncurled and sat up straight, alert. He looked through the windshield like he knew they were arriving somewhere important.

"We're home," Montana said.

The puppy wagged his tail. Montana parked, then got out and walked around. The puppy trotted along next to her, nose to the ground. Every couple of minutes he looked up at her, as if to check whether she was still there. Or, maybe it was as if he were thinking, *Isn't this awesome?*

Wanting to feel the earth under her feet, Montana took off her shoes and socks. The grass was cool despite the warmth of the summer day. Briefly, she considered sleeping on the grass. She dismissed the idea; she wouldn't be able to sleep with Cash out in the open.

The sunset, brilliant spears of light shooting through low dark clouds against a peachy-pink background, reminded her that there was moisture in the air. A storm could blow in at that very moment. Moving with urgency, she returned to the car for the tent and Cash's stake and tie-out. There wasn't any place on her lot that was perfectly level, but she found a spot where the slope was gentle, and figured she could put her head on the highest side.

She put Cash on the stake and he plopped down to watch her.

As she pulled the tent out of its bag and unrolled it, she felt like she was unpacking so many memories. She'd always loved the smell of it. The material had its own distinct scent and it brought up camp- fires and listening to crickets before falling asleep and seeing the branches move against the moonlight through the screen windows. Mostly, it reminded her of Sawyer. Pretty much every memory in that tent included him. As teenagers, they took it out into the forest or onto the shores of the lake every chance they got. Depending where they were, they would spend the first night setting up and enjoying a good warm campfire. Then, they would spend the next day fishing or kayaking or laying in the hammocks. Or all of those things.

Pushing away those memories, Montana focused on the task at hand. When she'd first thought of sleeping under the stars on her new property, she worried she might not remember how to set up the tent. There were so many rods and little fabric loops. She wasn't sure she'd be able to keep them all straight, especially without Sawyer around to help her. But it was like muscle memory. She assembled all the rods and set them in stacks according to size. Then she laid out the tent itself and slid the rods into their proper places. She was done within fifteen minutes and had plenty of time to air up the mattress before the sunset. She laid out her sleeping bag and brought in her cooler and Cash's bed.

Back outside, she soaked in a final glimpse of the sun as it sank below the horizon, brightening the sky's colors to a fiery blend of orange and red.

"This is perfect," she said.

For a moment, she felt nothing but a deep gratitude, and the sense that she had made the right choice. It was a sense of peace — something she hadn't felt in a long time. In front of her, her dog perked up, his ears standing on end as he looked back toward town. That's when Montana heard it: the sound of an engine coming closer.

———

Sawyer

SAWYER PUT ALMOST no thought into the last-minute decision to spend the night out at his property. He didn't need a tent. He had a sleeping bag, a few beers, and a little food. He threw it all into the bed of his truck and headed out.

The drive between the Mint Creek Ranch and the future Sunset Valley development lasted only a few minutes. During that time, he felt an increasing sense of peace. He turned off of Williamson Valley Road and onto Saddle Horn, which led over a little knoll and down into the valley. He just had to go up one more rise, and then he would see his place. As soon as he crested that rise, he jerked in surprise. Someone was already here. There was a tent. Not just any tent. But *his* old tent. The one —

"Montana." The sight of her stole his breath. Her slender frame looked dark against the vivid colors of the sky. There was just enough light to illuminate her face. She was so, so beautiful. Just about the most beautiful thing he'd ever seen.

Not for the first time, he wanted to kick himself for letting her get away.

During the first meeting of the Sunset Valley First Owners Club, Sawyer had noticed how in alignment his ideas were with Montana's.

"And look, here we both are, having the same idea again," he said.

His puppy, who had been sniffing around on the floorboard of the passenger seat, hopped up onto the seat and looked out the window. She stilled as well, and Sawyer wondered if Dolly was noticing Montana, or her brother.

Although Sawyer was tempted to drive right past Montana and onto his own piece of property, simply so he didn't end up putting his foot in his mouth yet again, he decided to stop next to her setup instead. Just for a minute.

"Tread carefully, Nelson," he said to himself. "Not every darn thought that pops into your head has to come out of your mouth."

He parked next to her car and he and his dog got out. "Looks like we both had the same idea. Again."

She smiled, and he thought she was happy to see him. And damn it if that didn't make *him* happy. The dogs immediately became a single wiggling ball of fur.

"Thank goodness it's you," she said. "I heard a car coming, and I realized Cash here isn't going to be much in the way of protection at this point. I had no idea if it was some sort of hunter, or what. I'm relieved it's someone I know."

Oh. That's why she looked happy to see him. He'd mistaken her relief for happiness.

"Just me. I thought it would be nice to sleep out at the new place."

Montana gestured at the tent. "Same."

So far, so good.

"Want a beer?" he asked. "I brought a couple."

Again, she smiled at him. And again, his heart leapt.

"Sure. Thanks."

"I'll just stay a bit, and then I'll drive over to my own lot," Sawyer said.

"You're not bothering me, any," Montana said. "And now that I've thought about encountering a stranger, I'd rather you set up nearby."

The puppies, engaged in a rowdy tumble across the grass, growled and attacked each other and then separated and wagged their tails. Sawyer took a deep breath. He could do this. He could navigate a conversation with Montana without saying the wrong thing. He opened a beer and handed it to her. Then he opened his.

"Want to sit on the tailgate?"

They did, and sat without speaking as the sun finished its descent behind the horizon. The whole time, Sawyer was acutely aware of Montana's body next to his. He could feel the heat coming off of her. He didn't know how they ended up sitting so close together. Maybe it was just natural for their bodies to be in proximity.

"This is going to be so nice," Montana said.

Sawyer wished she was talking about this unexpected evening together. But he knew she meant living in the Sunset Valley development.

"It sure is," he said.

"You told Trace yet?"

Sawyer took a long drag of his beer. "Nope. You?"

Montana laughed. "I was hoping you would tell him first. Soften the blow. Then I'll mention that I, too, have gone over to the dark side."

"That's not fair. I was hoping *you* would soften the blow."

"You know he's going to be mad as a hornet, no matter which of us tells him first."

Sawyer grunted. "Maybe we should tell him together."

Montana swung her feet. "Maybe so. Let's not think about that tonight. Let's just enjoy our new place. Places."

Sawyer held up his beer and Montana tapped hers against it.

"Cheers," Sawyer said. "To a new beginning."

"Cheers," Montana said.

"Did you eat?" Montana asked.

"Not yet. I brought a couple hot dogs. You?"

She shrugged. "Same."

Hoping against hope that he wasn't saying the wrong thing yet again, Sawyer said, "Great minds, right?"

When she said, "That's right," he felt bolstered.

"Montana."

"Sawyer," she said, mocking his seriousness.

"Have you been noticing, lately, how it seems like we have all the same ideas? The puppy, the houses, the hot dogs ..."

Montana hopped off the tailgate. "Speaking of hot dogs, I'm going to start a fire."

Sawyer joined her on the ground, and they scavenged around for some leaves and sticks.

They moved in perfect time with each other, stacking the kindling and the bigger logs. He lit the match, and she blew gently on the baby fire. Once it was going good and strong, they stood back.

"You didn't answer my question."

"What? About how we've had a lot of the same ideas?"

"Yeah," Sawyer said. He shrugged, almost as if he wanted to seem indifferent, even though he wasn't. For weeks, he'd been building up to this conversation. What happened now meant everything.

"I noticed."

Again, she walked away. This time, it was to retrieve her cooler. She took out two hot dogs and put them on roasting sticks. Sawyer had to remind himself that she hadn't packed a roasting stick for him; they'd come in a two-pack and were tied together in the camping gear box. Montana offered him one. He took it, and watched her face in the flickering firelight.

Even though he had spent hours, maybe even days, of his life memorizing her profile and delicate features, he never got tired of looking at her. And he always discovered something new. This time, it was the way her eyelashes cast the most interesting shadow on her upper cheeks.

"And?" he pressed. She was really making this difficult on him.

"Sawyer, I can't tell you how many times I've wished that we wanted the same thing. And even though, right now, it seems like we do, I just don't think it's possible for this to continue, long-term. Every time we get going in the same direction, we either take two completely separate roads, or we crash. I just don't think I can do that anymore."

This time, she didn't sound mad or upset or even irritated. Just tired. Bone-tired. Like, if she could, she would toss her hot dog in the fire and go straight to sleep. Which, Sawyer thought, was better than her storming off and zipping herself inside the tent and refusing to speak to him for the rest of the night. After that, things were quiet between them. The puppies, who had continued to roughhouse while Sawyer and Montana made their hot dogs and had another beer, now lay at Montana's feet in a literal dog pile. It seemed as though the temperature dropped all of a sudden, and Montana shivered, but she declined Sawyer's offer when he held out his sweatshirt.

"Thank you, but I'd just as soon go to bed. It's been a nice evening. Do you have enough blankets? I could spare one."

Sawyer's heart broke all over again. He didn't want her to spare a blanket. He wanted to warm himself with heat from her body. But it was clear she didn't want that. Not anymore.

"I think I'm all right," he told her. "But thank you. Get a good night's sleep."

With that, they put out the fire, picked up their puppies, and went their separate ways.

CHAPTER ELEVEN

Montana

MONTANA KNEW what Sawyer was getting at. And she *had* noticed that they seemed to want all the same things. Even while she was telling him she wanted to walk her own path, her heart was trying to break out of her rib cage to be closer to him. And, even though she told him she was tired (which she was), she found that once she got inside her tent, she felt restless. She opened one of the single-serve wine bottles she'd packed. As she sipped, she thought. Sitting next to the fire with Sawyer, she realized that all she wanted was him.

There would never be anyone else.

The real reason she hadn't been interested in Josh or Dave on that double-blind date with Abby was because they weren't Sawyer. And that was the truth of the matter. She knew she couldn't have Sawyer, but she didn't want anyone else. She would probably go to the grave alone.

"Although," she whispered to her dog, "I have you."

She was sitting cross-legged on the floor next to his bed, and she rubbed his back. He stretched in his sleep, all four legs straightening out and his little toenails extending.

Plop. Plop. Montana felt moisture on her face.

"Is it raining?"

The puppy, too worn out to notice, didn't move at all. But the *plops* and drips and drops came faster. She hadn't really anticipated a monsoon storm, but she was glad she'd been prepared for the possibility. She quickly assembled the rain fly, running the rod across its peak, and then she took it outside and hooked it onto the tent. By the time she got back in, rain covered her arms and face. She shivered. During monsoons, the air could get cold, fast. It could be ninety-eight degrees one minute, and fifty-five (and wet) the next, with hail the size of marbles falling from the sky.

A mean, devilish part of her — the part born of jealousy after seeing Sawyer dance with that sexy redhead — relished the fact that Sawyer was in the bed of his pickup truck.

Then, a sensible, reasonable side stepped in and reminded her that he could get out of the rain. He could sit in the cab of his truck, recline a seat, and be just fine. In fact, she told herself, he was probably doing that even as she thought about it.

Still, she couldn't resist poking her head out to see if she was right. Even though it was almost pitch black, she could make out his silhouette in the bed of the truck, huddled against the cab. He was wrapped in a blanket, but she knew him well enough to know he only had one. And now it was soaked. She wondered why he wasn't getting in his truck. He was a smart guy. The rain pelted her head and roared in her ears.

"Sawyer!"

It was likely he couldn't hear her. The rain was so loud. A flash of lightning cracked across the sky. A loud boom of thunder followed. She called his name again, and when he didn't react, she put her fingers in her mouth and whistled, which, naturally, he'd taught her how to do. It worked. He sat up and turned his head. She motioned for him to come over and he wasted no time climbing out of the truck and running to the tent. He came right through the door even as she unzipped it the rest of the way.

"Where's Dolly?" she asked.

"Right here." He unwrapped the blanket and pulled the puppy out from under it.

"Aw," Montana said. "You're keeping her dry. You can put her in bed with Cash."

Cash woke up just enough to sniff Dolly, and the two of them snuggled in and went right to sleep.

"Good thing you didn't go all the way over to your lot," Montana said as Sawyer zipped up the tent.

"No kidding."

In semi-awkward silence, the two of them looked at the puppies.

"Well, I would say those two are tuckered out," Montana said.

"I'd say so."

"Why didn't you get in your truck?"

Sawyer offered her a sheepish smile.

"Locked my keys in it."

She raised her eyebrows. He wouldn't lie about that, would he? Was it possible he'd locked the keys in the truck on purpose? No, she told herself. It wasn't like he knew it was going to rain.

"Well, I guess you can bunk in here."

Again, Sawyer smiled, and she couldn't help but feel like maybe it wasn't an accident.

"Thanks. It's really coming down." He pulled the soaked blanket off his shoulders. He had taken off his flannel and was wearing only a white T-shirt with his jeans. Quite suddenly, Montana was awash in a range of very strong emotions. The first one — straight lust — hit fast and hard. Heat pooled between her legs, and she wanted nothing more than to strip down and throw herself at him.

And then there was love. Pure, unbridled love. Yes, they had their differences. But standing in that enclosed space with him, the rain hammering on the rain fly, their puppies asleep a few feet away, Sawyer looking adorably abashed at having locked his keys in the truck. It was right then, in that perfectly imperfect moment, that Montana knew: she was done with the on-again, off-again.

She wanted to be on. Maybe they'd never get married. Maybe they'd live in two separate houses. None of that mattered. All that mattered was that they were together.

"I can sleep on the floor," Sawyer said. He gestured at the space between the dog bed and the edge of the tent.

Montana shook her head. "Remember how you were asking me if I've noticed it seems like we're making all the same choices lately?"

Sawyer nodded.

"Well —" she started, and he cut her off. "You don't have to explain. I understand. It was silly of me to ask you."

She held up a hand. "Hear me out."

He nodded. Cleared his throat.

"Sawyer, all I have ever wanted is to be with you. I think you know that. And I don't know why it seems like, whenever we get together, things get all tangled up. I have so many feelings about our past, and our future. But the strongest feeling I have is love. I love you, Sawyer Nelson. I think part of the reason we are always on-again, off-again is because that's an option, you know? We always think, we're on-again, off-again. But what if it wasn't that way?"

"What are you saying?"

The rain pounded on the rain fly. Another flash of lightning, and another boom of thunder.

Montana gathered her courage. "I want to be with you, Sawyer. And that's it. None of this on-again, off-again stuff."

They were already standing so close together, all Sawyer had to do was lean forward and kiss Montana. She kissed him back, fiercely, hoping she could convey everything she felt. It all seemed so complicated, but wasn't it actually very simple?

———

Sawyer

THE NEXT MORNING, Sawyer and Montana experienced a rare first in their relationship: the two puppies, squirming, invaded their bed, licking their faces and walking all over them.

It wasn't the most romantic way to wake up, Sawyer thought. He slipped on his jeans and took them outside. Leashes in hand, he looked out over the view to which he would soon wake up every morning.

And he was awestruck.

While Mint Creek Ranch was built right around the creek, this property, nestled back into the foothills like it was, had a completely different feel. He loved Mint Creek Ranch and always would. But this — the rolling hills, the view of Granite Mountain — it felt like home in a different way. The puppies seemed to have finished their business because they were back to frolicking in the grass again, their limbs and leashes tangled. Sawyer brought them back into the tent. Montana was still in bed. She'd switched out the sleeping bag for a thin blanket, and through it, he could see every curve. Her hips, her thighs, her stomach, the rise of her breasts, even her nipples. He took off his jeans and, completely naked, lay beside her. She turned to face him, and looked into his eyes for a long moment before kissing him.

"Good morning," she said. "Thanks for taking the puppies out."

"Good morning, yourself," he said. "And you're welcome."

In response to that simple kiss, Sawyer felt himself standing at attention, hardening against Montana's thigh. Automatically, she reached down to stroke him.

"Not so fast," he told her. "I want to take my time."

He eased her hand away and gently rolled her onto her back.

"That's better."

The day was warming up fast, like it always did during the summer. He pulled the blanket off of Montana's body so he could look at her. Even though she was so familiar to him, he was newly captivated every time he saw her. She was so perfect — every inch of her. Now, she ran her fingers through his hair while he used his hands to explore her breasts, tease her nipples, trill over her rib cage. With one hand resting between her legs, cupping her warm center, he kissed her. She was eager, and her tongue moved against his with a hunger he hadn't felt from her in a long time. He began to move his fingers over her, using the lightest touch, stroking slowly, slowly. She moaned, and he increased the pressure just the slightest amount. She began to move against his hand, and he slipped a finger inside, letting his thumb take over on the outside. Again, she reached down to stroke him, and again, he told her, "Not so fast."

She chuckled, the sound deep and arousing.

"What are you doing to me, Sawyer?"

"You'll see." He worked his way down, moving his mouth to the spot just below her ear, trailing his tongue over her collarbone, down between her breasts. He paused there to flick his tongue over each nipple a few times. Then, leaving his hands on her breasts for as long as he could, he made his way down to her center.

Her hands rested in his hair, and she moved against him as his tongue caressed her. He could feel her rising.

"Sawyer." Hearing her say his name like that, when they were doing what they were doing, nearly drove him over the edge.

She wanted him to finish her, to take her all the way. But he wanted to be inside her for that. So again, he told her, "Not so fast."

He brought himself up, then, so they were face to face, and her eyes flickered open when he plunged into her. In that split second, he saw everything. He saw lust. Affection. Love. She was so, so close. Right at the edge. But he didn't want her to go over just yet. He slid an arm around her waist and flipped her over so she was on top.

"Ride me," he said.

And she did. She rode fast and hard and before he knew it, she was shuddering in an explosive orgasm. He came, too, gripping her hips and watching her beautiful face.

When it was over, she collapsed onto him. "Finally."

"That's what I was thinking," he said.

"Look at me."

It took a bit of effort for her to unbury his face from her neck. When they were eye to eye, she said, "I love you so damn much."

And Sawyer knew then that he would do anything and everything to keep himself from losing her again.

———

MONTANA

THE EVENING and morning Montana spent with Sawyer were wonderful. Beyond wonderful. Part of her thought, *Isn't it always like this, until it's not?* Another part of her believed things were really, genuinely different this time. There was something different about the way Sawyer looked at her. Something different, even, about the way he made love to her.

They were in Montana's car, driving to the Davises' house for more wedding preparation. At the thought of the delicious orgasm she had just an hour before, Montana shivered. Sawyer didn't ask if she was cold. He just gave her a devilish grin. She smiled back. They hadn't discussed what they would say to their friends when they showed up together.

"Do you think everyone will just assume you spent the night at my place?"

Sawyer nodded. "Yeah," he said. "I've been thinking about that."

"But how do we explain why we brought my car, instead of yours?" Montana said. "Everybody knows you love your truck."

Sawyer laughed. "I don't know. I mean, we could just say I locked my keys in it. At your place."

"But what if someone drives by and sees your truck's not there?"

They sat in relative silence, the putt-putt sound of Montana's car engine providing a soundtrack. Keeping their new houses a secret was going to be really hard, Montana thought.

For most of their lives, Montana, Sawyer, Cody, and Trace told each other pretty much everything. They had no secrets. Well, *almost* none.

There was the time in high school when Cody and Sawyer sneaked off to Chino Valley to meet some girls. Sawyer didn't want Montana to know, even though they weren't together at the time. So he swore Cody to secrecy. But then, Cody's truck broke down halfway home. If they didn't call for help, they'd never make it back for curfew, and then they'd have so many extra chores their hands would be blistered.

They tried Trace, but being the responsible one, he was already asleep, knowing they had to be up early the next day.

They had no choice but to call Montana.

She could remember their faces, plain as day, when she pulled up behind Cody's truck. Guilty, chagrined.

"Y'all are damn fools," she said to them. "You know if we don't make it back in time for curfew, we're all going to be doing extra chores for the next three weeks straight."

Sawyer had the common sense to say something about how she was right, and they wouldn't do it again. But Cody, always having to prove he had thought out a plan in advance, said something about how that's why they usually snuck out *after* curfew.

That's when Montana knew the two of them had been up to no good for a while.

"Tell me you guys aren't carrying on with a bunch of shenanigans," she said. "You can't be running off late at night without telling anyone where you're going. What if something happened?"

They didn't answer. Montana realized then that it was possible for best friends to keep secrets from each other.

Another time, *she* was the one hiding things.

It all started after that fateful night when she asked Sawyer — she couldn't bear to think about that, even ten years later. That horrible situation set off a chain of events she still regretted.

Montana had *needed* to get out of town. At least for a little while. She would come back, obviously. But she needed to be out, on her own, without leaning on the others. On Sawyer.

She needed to make sure she could do it.

College seemed like the only acceptable way. She knew none of the guys would like her leaving. There were perfectly good colleges right here in Prescott. So in secret, she started applying to out-of-town colleges. Not too many. Just the ones that had really great fine arts programs. She figured she would just apply. And if she didn't get in, then hey, she wasn't meant to go. But if she did … well, she would cross that bridge when she came to it.

And then she came to it.

She got an acceptance letter.

And then she enrolled, without telling anyone. She carried that secret around for weeks. It got heavier and heavier, until she felt like her entire consciousness would give way under its weight.

She did all the prep: she went shopping to outfit her dorm room, sent in a check for tuition and board, and even made the trip to New Mexico for the welcome weekend.

Finally, a couple of days before she planned to leave for her first semester, she knew she had to tell her friends. She decided on a casual delivery. She would act like it was no big deal. So, one night when they were all sitting around the bonfire, and there was a pause in the conversation, she said, almost offhand, "I'm leaving for college in two days."

If she thought there was silence before, there was true silence now, as if everyone had inhaled at once. Even the fire seemed to be holding its breath. Trace, Cody, and Sawyer looked at each other. And then, simultaneously, at Montana.

"Did I just hear you say you're going off to college? In a couple of days?" Cody said.

He was always the fastest to recover.

"Yeah." Montana looked at her hands. She noticed a piece of loose skin on the cuticle of her right thumb and used her left hand to pick at it. "I'm going to Taos Fine Arts College. In New Mexico."

Silence from Sawyer. Montana didn't look up.

"Has she mentioned this to either of you?" Trace said.

Montana looked up, then, to see Trace looking right at Sawyer. Obviously, if she'd mentioned it to anyone, it would be Sawyer. But Sawyer just shrugged.

In the two days between that moment and the moment she left, all three of the Mint Creek Ranch boys — her best friends in the world — went quiet.

At the time, Montana was so worried about them being mad at her for leaving town that she hadn't even considered how they would feel about her keeping a secret from them. A *big* secret.

———

*S*AWYER

MONTANA'S WORDS hit Sawyer harder than a punch in the gut. Much harder. They felt like the hard-packed dirt on the trail leading to the creek, when your horse bucked you off and you landed flat on your back, the wind knocked out of you, unable to breathe. That's what her words felt like. While Trace and Cody spluttered over Montana's decision to go to college (actually, her decision not to tell them she was going to college until two days before launch), Sawyer sat there with the wind knocked out of him.

He felt like he had to say *something*. But the words wouldn't come. Not that he knew what he would say. The words that came to him didn't seem right.

You can't leave me.

Please don't go.

Please stay here.

You belong with me.

He couldn't say any of that — not with Cody and Trace sitting around the fire with them. Probably he couldn't say any of it to Montana, either. Three months ago, he'd hurt her, deeply. It wasn't fair to ask her to alter her plans for him.

While the other guys talked to her, he watched her. He noticed her body language, the way she kept twisting her hands in her lap. The way her eyes darted around, coming to rest on the fire, the swing hanging from the big oak tree, the smoke rising into the air. They never rested on Cody, Trace, or Sawyer. She was nervous. Uncertain. But did those feelings relate to the simple act of telling her big secret? Or was she uncertain about going to college? The three of them were all talking, but Sawyer only half-listened. His brain was going a million miles an hour.

I could convince her to stay. But how? What would I say?

And then, the worst thought of all: *Maybe I shouldn't.*

No, convincing Montana to stay was the wrong thing to do. She deserved to experience her own adventure, separate from them. As much as it killed him to think it, he was going to have to let her go.

———

MONTANA

LATER THAT NIGHT, Montana went up to her bedroom under the guise of reading one of the texts required for her first college English class. She went through the motions, fluffing the pillows on her bed, finding a comfortable position, and opening the book to the first page. She *intended* to read. But she couldn't quite focus. Her mom's voice, coming from the living room, served as a welcome distraction.

"Montana! Sawyer's here!"

Well, *that* was an unwelcome distraction. Typically, Montana would rejoice at an unannounced visit from Sawyer. But that night, she knew he was coming to hold her accountable, to ask why she hadn't told him she was applying to colleges. Although she knew he deserved an answer, she didn't want to have the conversation.

"Montana?" Montana sighed. "Coming!" She set down her book, slid off the bed, and walked down the stairs.

When neither of them greeted the other, Montana's mom said, "I'll leave you guys to it."

Before she left the entryway, she asked, "Can I get you anything to drink?"

Montana offered her a grateful smile. Most of the time, she would chastise Montana if she didn't offer refreshments to a guest. And although Sawyer was practically a member of the family, he was still a guest. Manners should prevail. "Thanks, Mama."

Sawyer cleared his throat. "I'll take water. Thank you, Mrs. Hart."

"Same," Montana said.

They settled themselves on the couch in the living room, not so much as looking at each other until after Montana's mom came and went again.

"So..."

"Right," Sawyer said. "I'll go first."

Montana's stomach was abuzz with a flurry of emotions. Regret. Fear. Shame.

"Why didn't you tell me?"

Between Montana's palms, her water glass started to feel slippery. "Like I said earlier —"

Sawyer held up a hand, cutting her off. "I know what you said earlier. What I mean is, why didn't you tell *me*? Maybe I was wrong, but I thought I was, I don't know, separate from Cody and Trace. I thought I was, I don't know, special."

"You *are* special. It's just —"

There was that hand again. "No. I'm not. You made that perfectly clear by spending what? Months? A year? Researching colleges, applying, getting letters in the mail. And you never once thought to mention it to me?"

At that point, Montana started to feel sick. "I don't know what I was thinking. I wasn't sure I wanted to go. I wasn't sure if I would get in. I wasn't sure what it would mean for us. But I figured I could at least see if that door was even open to me. And if it was, then I could decide."

"I see. So when did you find out that it was, in fact, open?" His voice sounded borderline derisive, and Montana hated it. Finally, she ventured eye contact. "I started applying about three months ago. The acceptance letter came in about a month ago."

At that, Sawyer nodded. "So right before…"

His voice trailed off and she didn't bother finishing the sentence.

Montana shrugged, the movement feeble. "Yeah. Honestly, I thought you might not care if I planned on leaving. I mean, maybe our futures aren't as intertwined as we thought."

Again, Sawyer shook his head. Disgust radiated off him. "Of course you thought that. Because one thing — one thing! — didn't go the way you thought it should, you thought it meant we wouldn't be together."

"I'm sorry, Sawyer. I don't know what else to say. I'm going to college. It's only four years."

———

TEN YEARS HAD PASSED, and there they were, their lives still intertwined. She looked across the console at him, and when he smiled at her, he looked so happy. Which, naturally, brought tears to her eyes.

"I'm so sorry I didn't tell you I was going off to college."

His mouth opened in surprise. "Montana, that was a decade ago. What got you thinking about that?"

She returned her attention to the road. "I don't know. I just got to thinking about how you and I are keeping a pretty big secret from our friends. And how I used to think we never kept secrets from each other. But I kept one of the biggest ones of all. All I could think about was whether you guys would be mad at me for leaving town. I didn't even stop to think the secret-keeping would hurt your feelings."

Sawyer sighed. "That night when you told us, when we were sitting around the bonfire? I was shellshocked. I couldn't believe you would make that enormous decision without even telling me. Not that I expected you to ask permission. But I felt completely left out because I didn't even realize how much you wanted to get away."

Montana knew she had to choose her words carefully. "It's not that I wanted to get away. It's just that I wanted to experience something new, on my own. To prove to myself I could do it, you know? Growing up, I always wanted to do all the things you guys did. And I could — but I always had help. As gentlemanly as the three of you are, one of you always stepped up to help me, even when I thought I didn't need it. So I thought that if I went off to college, I could prove to myself I was capable. But I knew if I told you, you would try to talk me out of it."

"You're probably right," Sawyer said, letting out a breath. "Not only did I see absolutely no reason to leave this town, but also, I wouldn't have been able to bear the thought of you not being in it, even if it was just for a short time. No matter the timing of when you told me, knowing you wouldn't be on the Mint Creek Ranch would break my heart."

They'd come to the Mint Creek Ranch — their childhood home. Montana pulled her car into the driveway.

"I'm afraid Trace and Cody will feel the same way about you getting your own place," she said to Sawyer.

"Me, too. That's why haven't told them. But I take it you think we should?"

"Yes," Montana said. "Not only is it going to be so hard to keep our new houses a secret, but also I think they're going to be hurt that we didn't tell them."

She parked the car, and they looked at each other. Sawyer nodded. He leaned across the center console and kissed her. Immediately, heat shot to her core and only intensified when he caressed her breasts. She pushed him away, gently. "Save that for later. You're going to get me all hot and bothered, and there's nowhere to run off to, to release the tension."

His hands still on her breasts, still caressing, Sawyer smiled at her. "Oh, I think the teenaged versions of us would disagree. There's the barn loft, that granite alcove behind the big cottonwood by the creek, and surely a spot in the hay barn."

"Sawyer Nelson. Neither one of us is a teenager anymore. I'm a lady now."

With that, she grabbed Cash and got out of the car. He followed suit. As they walked up the drive, hand in hand, the puppies running along in front of them, Montana felt just about as content as she had in a long, long time.

CHAPTER TWELVE

*S*AWYER

HE KNEW IT WAS COMING. When Sawyer and Montana walked up to the group, there was that moment: everyone noticing they'd shown up together, holding hands, smiling and talking together. That moment was swiftly followed by that *other* moment: everyone trying to act like the first moment wasn't a big deal.

The women ran to greet the puppies, who were equally excited to see them. Tail-wagging and happy kisses ensued while the men shook hands and avoided talking about the elephant in the room.

Once everything settled down, Cody outlined the plan for the day.

"Ladies, you'll start building the arbor," he said, "and gentlemen, we'll work on the long table where we'll sit during the reception."

Sawyer, relieved the focus was on building things, said, "I don't want to imply we're not capable, but we're building a table? It has to be sturdy. Don't you think we might want to hire a professional for this?"

"I'm just doing what my future wife tells me to do," Cody said. "From what I understand, I'm getting in my practice for marriage. Tessa says it doesn't even have to look nice, because we're going to cover it with tablecloths. But she wants it built by the Mint Creek Ranch guys. So, that's what we're doing. We're building a table."

"All right," Trace said, sounding skeptical. "But she darn well better like it."

"Oh, I'll like it," Tessa said.

Still happy to be out of the spotlight, Sawyer laughed a little too loudly as the group walked around to the back of the Davises' house. Apparently, Tessa and Cody had spent the entire day before at the lumberyard. They had stacked what looked like a dozen trees' worth of wood behind the house. Cody pointed to the pile on the left. "That's the arbor. Or it will be. And that's the table. The sturdy table."

Sawyer looked at Trace, who returned his expression — humor, mostly, and a little fear. They both cracked up.

"I think your expectations might be a little high, Tessa," Sawyer said.

Tessa simply waved them off. Abby suggested building the arbor in exactly the place it would stand, so they wouldn't have to move it.

Sawyer suspected it was really so the women wouldn't be working side by side with the men. He was positive she didn't want Trace listening in on whatever she said. He knew from their limited conversations that Abby thought Trace thought she was bossy. Which was funny, because Trace was pretty bossy himself. In fact, even as the women carried lumber over to the arbor site, Trace took over the role of table-making boss.

"I say we make a frame for the top, first. And then put the actual surface on. Then put the legs on and finish it all. Or, should we finish the top and the legs separately, and then assemble it?"

Sawyer opened his mouth to speak, but Trace barreled on. "No, I think it would be better if we finish it first. What are we doing, staining it? Painting it? I think we should stain it. Yeah, that would look real nice."

While Trace went on, thinking out loud and conversing with himself, Sawyer walked over to stand next to Cody. "I say we just let Trace get this all figured out. And then do what he says."

Cody nodded. "That sounds like a plan. We're going to end up doing it his way, anyway."

Trace seemed to settle on a process because he wrapped up whatever he was saying and then said, "Sound good?"

Both Cody and Sawyer rubbed their hands together and said, "Sounds great."

"You two stopped listening five minutes ago," Trace said.

On a piece of paper on his clipboard, Trace started to draw a diagram, and as he did, he directed Sawyer and Cody to lay out the longest boards.

He tore off one end of the paper and handed it to Sawyer. "Here's a list of two-by-fours we need cut."

As they started setting up the sawhorses, the conversation Sawyer was dreading finally began.

"So," Cody said, and Sawyer knew. Trace said, "You and Montana, huh?"

At the memory of making love to her that morning, Sawyer felt himself getting hard again. He picked up a two-by-four and laid it across the sawhorses. "Yeah."

"Are you sure you know what you're doing, man?" Cody said. "Because — I'm just going to be the one to say it — I hate seeing the two of you get your hearts broken over and over again."

Sawyer knew Cody meant well, and he wasn't placing blame on either Sawyer or Montana. Still, his comment rankled Sawyer a little.

"And why do you think that's going to happen?"

Cody and Trace looked at each other and the two of them burst into laughter.

"Oh, I don't know," Trace said. "Maybe because history has a tendency to repeat itself?"

Sawyer felt like an idiot. Sawyer and Montana *did* have the tendency to hurt each other over and over again.

"It's different this time," Sawyer said.

He immediately regretted that announcement, though, because he wasn't ready to tell Cody and Trace about Sunset Valley and the fact that buying property meant he and Montana were finally growing up. He and Montana were going to make the announcement together.

"Golly gee," Trace said, his tone dripping with sarcasm. "Where have I heard that before?"

"You'll see," Sawyer said.

Even as the words left his mouth, he hoped they were true.

Throughout the day, Sawyer felt a little uneasy. How could he be sure this time was really different? And what about the fact that they were both buying houses, separately? What did that mean, long-term?

The group broke at lunchtime. Tessa ran out and picked up pizza, and they all enjoyed pizza and beer in the shade on the Davises' back patio. Conversation drifted among small groups. Tessa and Abby talked about the shape of the arbor and whether to paint it. Trace had Montana chatting about her new puppy. Sawyer suspected Trace's deep interest in Cash was a form of avoidance; it kept him from having to talk to Abby. Which left Sawyer and Abby to talk to each other. And darned if Sawyer couldn't think of anything to say that didn't relate to Sunset Valley. But that topic was off-limits.

"How's the table?" Abby asked.

"It's coming along."

"Same with the arbor."

"I'm not that great at small talk," Sawyer said.

"Me neither," Abby said, winking at him.

Thankfully, Tessa called Abby over and Sawyer was left alone.

After finishing off his pizza, he knelt down and gave Dolly a belly rub. Cash thought it was a game and pounced on Sawyer's hand, locked his jaw around his wrist, and shook. It hurt. The little guy had razor-sharp teeth.

While Sawyer was in the process of dislodging his wrist from Cash's mouth, Montana knelt down next to him. "Should we tell them after dinner?" She spoke in a hushed voice, and it reminded him of their teenage years, when they used to make secret plans to get together after a family gathering.

He grinned at her. Wiggled his eyebrows. "Are you talking about telling them, or is this code for something *else* we're going to do after dinner?"

She smiled back, but she looked nervous. "I'm talking about telling them."

Sawyer's stomach flipped over inside his torso. He was terrified of how Trace would react.

"I'm just wondering about the timing, that's all," he said. "This whole end of the summer, it's supposed to be about Cody and Tessa. Not about us. Maybe we should wait until after the wedding."

Montana chewed her lower lip, an old habit for which he had a long-standing response: he leaned in and gave her a gentle kiss. "True," she said. "But I'm remembering that secret I kept from you, and I'm afraid they're all going to be even more upset when they realize we've been holding out on them. I mean, this is huge."

"I guess I'm nervous," he admitted.

"Yeah. Me too."

They stood there for a few minutes without talking, watching a couple of ravens flying in big, lazy circles overhead. Thinking back to the way Montana acted that morning — as happy with him as he'd seen her in a long time — Sawyer realized it didn't matter: he would do anything to *keep* her happy.

So, he nodded. "Okay."

She read him like a book. "Okay? Okay, like you think that's a good idea? Or, okay, like you'll do it because it's what I want to do, but you disagree?"

He laughed. Montana's ability to intuit what Sawyer was thinking had always astounded, frustrated, and enthralled him. Two people knowing each other as well as they did was a once-in-a-lifetime deal.

"Okay, like I agree."

Satisfied, she kissed him again. The puppies circled their feet, growling, apparently thinking they, too, should be involved in the embrace.

"I'll let you tell them," Montana said. "When the timing's right."

"Sounds good," Sawyer said, even though it didn't.

Montana stood up and walked over to join Tessa and Abby. And even though Sawyer was happy to have given her the answer she wanted, he also realized that this was how things often went between them.

He often felt like he had to give in.

After giving each of the puppies one last belly rub, he rounded up Trace and Cody and they went back to where they'd been working on the table.

Sawyer thought some more about that conversation with Montana. The truth? He thought now probably *was* the best time to tell everyone about their plans to buy houses in Abby's development. The longer they waited, the bigger the secret would become. And the madder his friends would be. Spitting mad. Mad as hornets with a bear in their nest. Mad as a bull getting poked with a stick (he saw that particular kind of mad firsthand when he was nine years old and in his experimental phase—scared the tar out of him).

He just couldn't go through with it. He wasn't ready.

———

*M*ONTANA

"SO WHAT'S HAPPENING with you and Sawyer?" Abby wanted to know.

The heat rushed to Montana's face and she stammered, "We — spent the night together last night."

It was everything Montana could do to keep from glancing at Abby. She didn't want to reveal to Tessa that they'd been out on the property.

But she managed, and beside her, Abby kept working.

"Haven't you done that before? Many times?" Tessa offered her a wicked smile.

"We have," Montana said. "But this time, it's different."

After a few minutes during which they worked busily on measuring pieces of wood for the arbor, Tessa spoke again, proving why she'd quickly become a respected reporter. "What's different about this time? I mean, you've said that before ... so what's *really* different?"

If anyone else pressed her for details like that, Montana would feel put on the spot. But it was in Tessa's nature to ask questions. And her tone held nothing but pure curiosity.

Still working, still avoiding eye contact, Montana shrugged. "I don't know. It just feels like we're both ready this time. Ready for something different. Something more ... adult, I guess."

She could hear the smile in her friend's voice when Tessa spoke again. "That's good, Montana. I'm really happy for you."

Every time she and Sawyer got back together after a breakup, Montana told herself things were different. Including this time. But this time, they were.

She and Sawyer each had a new venture. They were buying houses; they'd gotten puppies; they were helping to plan a wedding. They were both ready to make a change. Weren't they?

Montana sighed.

"Everything okay?" Abby asked.

Montana offered her a smile. "Yep! Everything's great."

———

Sawyer

SANDING, measuring, cutting, drilling … it was all so rhythmic, so soothing. Sawyer loved the kind of manual work involved in making and finishing furniture. It gave his body something to do so his mind could relax and think clearly. For the rest of the day, working on the giant head table for Cody and Tessa's wedding, Sawyer thought. He considered how he could make sure things were different this time.

This time, he would put in true, renewed effort when it came to his relationship with Montana. Their relationship would no longer be based on impromptu sex — not that they'd never have it, because who wanted to go without that? — but this time, he was going to *plan* things. Dates. Day trips. Adventures. Things to show her how much he loved spending time with her. How much he loved her.

"Either of you check the weather for tomorrow?" he asked his friends.

"I looked earlier," Cody said. "Hot and partly cloudy. Windy."

Sawyer nodded, kept sanding the table leg.

"Why?" Trace asked. "What are you thinking?"

"I don't know," Sawyer said. "I was thinking of maybe taking Montana on a date. Maybe kayaking."

"You kayak?" Trace and Cody said.

Sawyer chuckled. "Don't you remember Montana and I kayaking when we were teenagers? We used to load those things up in one of the old farm trucks, and she'd follow me over to the Verde Valley in another. We'd leave her truck at the end point and float the river. At least twice a month from March to October."

"Now that you mention it, I do remember that," Cody said. "It's been a while, though, hasn't it?"

"It has," Sawyer agreed. "But it's like a bike, right? You never forget how to do it."

"Sounds like a nice idea," Trace said.

"I can't tell if you're being sarcastic," Sawyer said.

Cody chuckled. "He's not being sarcastic. He's just jealous because he can't find himself a woman."

If Sawyer wasn't mistaken, Trace was sanding his section of the tabletop with furious motions. "I can find myself plenty of women."

"Just none of them are interested in you," Sawyer and Cody said.

They high-fived each other and Trace shook his head. Sawyer could practically see the steam coming out of his ears.

"Hey man," Sawyer said, acting like he was about to propose a new idea. "What about Abby over there?"

Trace's response: a growl, from deep in his throat.

"Methinks he protests too much," Cody said.

Maybe he did, Sawyer thought. Was it possible Trace actually had the hots for Abby? If Trace finally started to like Abby — and heck, took it one step farther and started *dating* her — maybe Sawyer would be off the hook for buying a piece of property from her.

He felt like a scheming villain in a kids' cartoon. He imagined himself rubbing his hands together with an evil smile on his face. Still, making two people fall in love (okay, maybe love was too much — maybe making them fall in "like") was a good thing no matter what. When did having someone to like ever become a negative? And, maybe he could get Montana to help him with this plan.

Come to think of it, maybe not. Montana liked playing matchmaker, but her matches were rarely successful.

Throughout their teenage years, she tried to set up several different pairs of people. There were José Alcala and Melissa Yates, who shared a love of cranberry sauce but absolutely nothing else. He loved basketball, she hated it. She loved karate, he liked wrestling. Montana arranged for them to show up at the arcade at the same time, and they ended up having a screaming match over Pac-Man.

And then there were Nina Bombaderi and Eric Chen, the mathletics team captain and the star running back on the football team. Complete opposites.

"Opposites attract," Montana told Sawyer when he raised his eyebrows at her attempts to get the two of them together.

"I don't think that phrase holds true one hundred percent of the time," Sawyer told her.

It turned out he was right. They didn't even make it through the first date. Sawyer seemed to remember something about her storming out of the restaurant before dinner was even set before them because Eric couldn't tear his gaze from the TV broadcasting a college football game.

Maybe Montana wasn't the best partner in crime for matchmaking, Sawyer thought.

After the Kincaid-Davis Wedding Planning Team concluded the

day's work, it was time for dinner. Sawyer knew that no matter what he, he was going to let someone down.

The entire crew sat down at the outdoor picnic table. Steaks and racks of ribs sizzled on the grill, and the scent of the meat cooking made Sawyer's mouth water. Elaine and Cody came out the kitchen door, each carrying a giant bowl.

"Potato salad and watermelon," Cody announced.

Looking around the table, Sawyer thought, *everyone seems so happy.* Trace and Cody were entertaining Abby with a story about the first time Trace fell off a horse. They gestured and laughed as they acted out the scene wherein Cody found Trace, lying on his back on the trail, his horse standing lookout.

Tom removed the meat from the grill and placed it, one piece at a time, on the platter. He lifted the platter and turned around, a proud smile on his face. "This is going to be good, you guys."

Cody and Elaine brought out a stack of plates and silverware, too, and arranged them on the table. The only one who didn't seem caught up in the excitement was Montana, who took it upon herself to roll each place setting in a paper napkin. While everyone else talked and laughed, Montana kept her head down, nervous energy emanating from her.

Sawyer knew he couldn't do it. Announcing, right then, in the middle of all the festive energy, would ruin the moment. And this was Tessa and Cody's moment.

He looked at Montana, and she looked back at him, offering a weak smile and raised eyebrows as if to say, "Now?"

He shook his head, hoping the movement was imperceptible to everyone else.

Her shoulders slumped even more, and her silverware-rolling motions became jerky. Sawyer sighed. He knew he was letting her down. But he also knew the timing wasn't right. He wouldn't ruin this perfect afternoon for Tessa and Cody. However, he realized he had ruined it for himself. And Montana.

A heavy feeling of dread settled over him. Dinner continued in much the same fashion, with lots of talking, laughing, and compliments about the food. Despite how good everything smelled and the appetite Sawyer worked up throughout the day, he found he couldn't quite eat.

The fun and excitement swirled around the table, leaving Sawyer and Montana untouched. The two of them sat there, side by side, pushing food around on their plates. Sawyer was equally relieved and afraid, when, at the end of the meal, Montana said, "Sawyer and I will do the dishes."

———

Montana

MONTANA COULDN'T BELIEVE IT. The two of them had agreed that now was the best time to tell their friends about Sunset Valley.

So, why didn't he do it? Why wouldn't he tell them? She managed to get through dinner without elbowing him, kicking him under the table, or making some obvious opening into which he could insert their big news. It was all she could do to not somehow force him to say something. But, she had put the situation in his hands.

That's because you trusted him to tell them. Even to her own mind, the voice in her head sounded like a spoiled princess, complete with a tiara, arms crossed, nose turned upward.

By the end of dinner, she was fuming. She felt him tense beside her when she volunteered them to do the dishes.

The whole group carried plates, platters, bowls, and glasses inside, but after a few minutes, everyone else went back out to enjoy the summer evening, leaving Montana alone with Sawyer in the kitchen.

As the sink filled with warm water, Sawyer handed Montana dishes.

"I guess you're wondering why didn't say anything."

"Yeah," Montana said, hating the way her voice sounded, almost belligerent.

"I'm sorry," he said. "I just couldn't do it. Trace is going to be so mad. I was sitting there thinking how perfect the evening was, and I didn't want to ruin it."

Dishrag in hand, Montana started scrubbing. Sawyer moved to her other side to rinse and dry.

"How little do you think of Trace?" she asked. "I mean, how badly do you think he would react on an evening as perfect as this?"

Sawyer considered. "It's not only that. I mean, it is. He might temper his reaction here, when we're all together. But later? When us guys are alone? He's going to let me have it."

"Yeah." Montana said. Her heart beat faster, and she couldn't tell if it was from emotions or a result of her over-vigorous scrubbing. "But haven't you anticipated him letting you have it ever since you bought the property?"

"Yes. I have. But like I said, it's also about the timing. I think we should wait until after the wedding."

"I disagree. The longer we keep the secret, the more it's going to hurt their feelings that we didn't tell them."

"You said that." Sawyer added another plate to the dry stack, a little harder than he probably meant to. He picked up the plate and checked the bottom for chips.

The conversation was getting to him. Montana felt a little guilty. Through the open window, she could hear the group outside, chatting and laughing.

Maybe Sawyer was right. Maybe they should wait till after the wedding.

"Look," she said, drying her hands so she could take both of his. "I'm sorry. I understand. I disagree, but I understand."

"Thank you," he said, with a tone that implied that it wasn't the last they'd talk about it. "Let's get this done, so we can go out and enjoy our friends. Then, an early evening. I have something special planned for tomorrow."

CHAPTER THIRTEEN

MONTANA WOKE up feeling sick to her stomach over what happened the night before. Laying in bed with Cash nestled against her side, she did some soul searching. She was annoyed that Sawyer had gone back on their agreement. It was an adult version of the time in fourth grade when he promised her the last length of Bubble Tape and gave it to Trace and Cody, instead. The bigger emotion, though, was dread. Until she and Sawyer told the crew about their plans to build in Sunset Valley, she would dread their reaction.

How long she could go on like this, she didn't know.

Doing her best to shake off the negativity, she got up and fed the dog, made breakfast, and showered.

When Sawyer pulled into the driveway and Montana saw the kayaks in the back of his truck, her breath caught. He remembered: kayaking had been one of her favorite pastimes back in the day. By the time she opened the front door, he was there, holding a bouquet of sunflowers.

"For you."

"My favorite," she said, taking them, and he said, "I remember."

"Not the flowers."

She leaned in to kiss him, and when their lips met, her body responded. It was like coming home. Some of the weird tension dissipated.

"While it would be nice to do this all day," he said between kisses, "I do have something really fun planned."

"Fine," Montana said, feigning disappointment (the truth was, she was beyond excited to go kayaking).

She had so many memories of floating down the river, their kayaks side by side, the birds chirping overhead, lazy dragonflies in bright colors buzzing by. Every time they saw something interesting or beautiful — which was often — they looked at each other, sharing their appreciation without speaking.

People who didn't know Arizona thought it was a desert state. All cactus and rattlesnakes. But it was so much more than that. Just forty-five minutes from Prescott, the Verde Valley lay lush and green, thanks to a wide river that cut through, giving life to an ecosystem really unique from that of Prescott. And, up the mountains to the north, Flagstaff was home to a cool forest of pines and aspen trees with quaking leaves that revealed the prettiest colors in the fall.

As she trimmed the ends of the sunflowers, Montana chattered away to Sawyer. "I'm so excited to go kayaking again. I haven't been since the last time we went."

She paused and looked up at him then, and she knew they were both remembering how they had pulled their kayaks off to the side of the river and made love on a blanket on the soft sand. Afterwards, when they were lying there together, they heard another pair of kayakers coming down the river. It was the middle of the week, and they hadn't expected anyone else to be out.

In a panic, they got up and put on their clothes as fast as they could. Just in time, too, because the two older women floated into view just as they collapsed onto the blanket, laughing.

"That was a good time," Sawyer said, and Montana went from amused to aroused in an instant. She got a vase from the cabinet and filled it. As she arranged the sunflowers, Sawyer gathered up the cut ends and threw them away.

They drove back to Mint Creek Ranch to pick up another truck, and during the drive over to the Verde Valley, Montana followed Sawyer, her windows rolled down and her music turned up.

They put in at Green Bridge, where a little boat ramp jutted into the river. Weeds and trees grew lush along the banks and reflected in the river's calm surface. Even though the mercury would reach over one hundred in the town of Camp Verde that afternoon, everything was cool down by the river.

As soon as they'd loaded the kayaks and gotten in, Montana felt the familiar sensation of floating. Sunlight sparkled through the thick canopy of leaves, lending a magical feel to the scene. Her photographer's eye delighted in the brightness of it all: patches of bright-blue sky, dazzling green leaves, crisp greenish-blue water, the orange of the kayaks.

She'd brought her camera, and she raised it and absentmindedly took a few pictures of the scenery. Then she turned and snapped a few of Sawyer. He was so damn handsome.

For a while, they didn't talk; they just floated along, listening to the sound of the water lapping against the kayaks, their paddles slicing through the surface and coming back out. And although the current would have carried them to their endpoint on its own, they paddled their way with slow, lazy strokes.

"This is nice," Sawyer said.

Montana turned and smiled at him again. He wore a white tank top, and Montana found herself practically drooling while his muscles rippled. No wonder they stopped and had sex, riverside, the last time they did this.

"What are you thinking?" he asked, a devilish grin forming.

"Just noticing how good you look in that shirt," Montana said.

Saying the words out loud felt so good. When they weren't officially together, paying him a compliment seemed off-limits. Not that she didn't notice how good he looked pretty much all of the time. But a girl couldn't just tell her on-again, off-again boyfriend that he looked absolutely edible. They floated along for a while longer, until Montana's stomach started growling.

"Hungry?"

"How could you tell?"

They'd come to the spot where they always had lunch. A long stretch of river with no rapids allowed them to hook their kayaks together and place the cooler between them. They could float without steering or paddling for a good thirty minutes. Sawyer had brought the fixings for sandwiches, along with chips and fruit.

"You even thought to bring strawberries," Montana said. "That was really thoughtful."

Sawyer handed her the whole container. "Just for you."

Montana could tell he was making an effort. Strawberries always had been her favorite. In the past, she was the one to pack the lunch, and to remember what he liked. Not that he didn't remember, necessarily, but he didn't always put things into action.

He handed her a beer. She gasped. "You even got my favorite beer!"

"Honey wheat from the Red Rock Brewery," he said.

They popped the tabs on the cans, and each took a long drink.

"Can I ask you something?" Sawyer said.

Montana held up a finger and took a few more exaggerated gulps of her beer. "This sounds ominous. But I think I'm ready."

"That morning on tour a few weeks ago, when I came out and tried to run with you?"

Montana nodded. Licked her lips. Waited. Where was he going with this?

"Why did you get so mad?"

For a few seconds, Montana thought about how much she should tell him. She typically figured honesty was the best policy. But there *were* degrees of honesty. He didn't have to know quite how much she'd been hurting. He didn't have to know she'd been thinking about that night, all those years ago, before she started applying to colleges.

"That was the first night Cody and Tessa spent together," Montana said. "I guess I was a little jealous. Everything between them seemed so easy. It reminded me of how things used to be, between us. Before they got complicated. Anyway. I went for a run. And you were there. And my first thought was, *What a coincidence.* Right? Here I am, running. And here you are, running. We are so in sync. But then I thought, that's always what I think. I think we're in sync, and then something happens."

Sawyer nodded. He was silent for a few minutes. Montana had the urge several times to fill the space. But each time, she made the decision to let it be.

Finally, Sawyer responded. "What happened? When did things change?"

Montana knew exactly when things changed. Things changed the moment he rejected her. Was it really that he didn't know? If he didn't know, then maybe the moment was different for him. Or, did he just *pretend* that he didn't know?

One thing *she* knew was that she couldn't have that conversation, again.

So she lied. "I don't know," she said. "I'm not sure."

————

SAWYER

SAWYER COULD FEEL Montana's mood shift. He hadn't even meant to ask the question. Why should they go over the past when they were trying to make a new future? He wished he hadn't said anything. He also knew he'd better act quickly if he was going to salvage the day he planned. He had an idea.

"Tell me why you chose the lot you did in Sunset Valley."

He could see right away that the change in subject worked.

She smiled, and her eyes took on a dreamy expression. "First of all, the view. You can't beat that. And second, I like how there's that little valley there. Can you imagine how rich the soil's going to be? When I watched Abby give her presentation to the City Council, and I saw her rendering of the cottage, it had all these flowers. And I thought, I would love to have all those flowers. You know, in my apartment, I can only grow houseplants. But can you imagine the flower garden I can have in Sunset Valley?"

"I can," Sawyer said. "Maybe you could even sell them at the farmers market. I mean, we're going to have acreage, right?"

His own use of the word "we" tripped him up a bit. They had chosen adjacent lots. Adjacent, but separate. They wouldn't necessarily be doing all the same things. They hadn't even talked about living together. Should they? He didn't know. He felt a little panicked at the idea that she still planned on having her own place. But they'd only just gotten back together. And she likely felt like she couldn't assume a happily ever after with him.

"Sawyer?"

He blinked, realizing he'd missed her question. "What did you say?"

"Where'd you go?"

He smiled, lied through his teeth. "Just daydreaming. Sorry."

"I said, why did you pick your lot?"

Until then, Sawyer hadn't really had the chance to share his big dream with anyone. Well, he had mentioned it to Diego at the 5D Ranch, but that was all business, man-to-man. Not a fun, daydreamy conversation.

"I'm going to start my own cattle ranch."

She laughed out loud.

"What's so funny?" he demanded. "You laughing is the last reaction I expected."

"I knew it!"

"You knew it?" This was a surprise. He hadn't told anyone. "How'd you know?"

Montana wiped her eyes. "I'm not laughing at you, by the way. I'm just laughing because I had a sneaking suspicion ever since I found out you were buying this property. You think you're so sneaky. But you put the name of the ranch —"

"The name of ranch," Sawyer said, drawing out the words as the realization dawned. "Of course you saw it. On that first email about the First Buyers Club, right?"

"Right," she said, her voice weepy. "I've known from that moment. I was just waiting to see how long it would take you to tell me."

Sawyer just smiled. She knew him better than he thought she did. He went on to tell her about his visit to the 5D Ranch. He described his conversations with Diego, and told her how he got to see the calf nursery and all the different areas of the ranch. She listened intently. He'd forgotten how much he loved sharing his dreams with her. He always felt like she was truly listening. Interested. Invested.

"I think it's a great idea," she said. "I don't know what Trace is going to think of it. But we don't have to worry about that today. You're going to be great at it. You've always been so good at following the lines, knowing which cattle were going to have which characteristics and all that stuff. It's like you were born for it."

Montana's approval made Sawyer's heart soar. It meant so much to him that she thought he was capable.

"Hey," he said. "We can share a booth at the farmers market. You can sell your flowers, and I can sell steaks from my ranch."

She smiled, and he thought he detected a hint of sadness.

"That would be nice."

"There's the old Tree of Romance," Sawyer said, jumping on the distraction. "I guess we should pack up our stuff. It's time to paddle."

The Tree of Romance, a giant cottonwood, towered at the edge of the river. It was tradition for lovers to mark their initials in the tree's bark, to carve them in with a knife, a piece of broken glass, whatever was handy. Their initials — his and Montana's — were there, bumping up against dozens of others. As they packed away all the supplies from their lunch, he remembered the day they carved them.

They'd stopped on the bank because Sawyer saw some animal tracks and wanted to follow them. When the tracks petered out, they decided to walk along the river's edge for a while before getting back in their boats. They came across the tree by accident. Sawyer remembered being overcome by a sense of camaraderie with all the other couples whose initials were carved into that bark. He felt that somehow, this was a place that could make love stronger. It seemed like a good omen at the time.

"What can we use?" he said to Montana, and she was already pulling her pocketknife out of her pocket. She carved his initials, and he carved hers. They each carved one half of the plus symbol, and he carved a heart around their initials.

Montana brought him back to the present moment. "Think we'd still be able to see our initials?"

Sawyer nodded. "I'm sure they've stood the test of time."

———

MONTANA

ONE THING MONTANA loved about the river was that it was always different. Each visit, she and Sawyer discovered something new. Each time they put in, the landscape had shifted, even if just a little, from the last time they were there. The little section of rapids just past the Tree of Romance was no exception.

The first time she encountered rapids, Montana was terrified. Those kayakers in the Olympics wore helmets when they ran the rapids. Shouldn't she? But Sawyer coached her through it.

"It's really shallow," he told her as they approached. "If worse comes to worst, you can just hop out of the kayak and stand there."

"But won't the river push me over?"

At this, he laughed. "No. It's not moving that fast. Now, if we were here during or just after a monsoon, then maybe. Probably. But we're not. Just paddle as fast as you can to keep yourself pointed in the right direction. You'll be fine."

He went first, to demonstrate, and he swept his kayak right through the rapids like a pro. She did her best to replicate his motions, and found that making it through was much easier than she expected. And, it was absolutely thrilling. The water pushed her along, over the rocks, as if she were on some kind of amusement park ride. Even years later, having run the rapids dozens of times, she felt the same thrill, and let out the same loud laughter. She pulled her kayak up next to Sawyer's, and he said, "It never gets old."

She shook her head. "It doesn't."

"I don't mean the rapids, either," he said. "I mean your laugh."

They'd almost reached the end of their float. The second ranch truck was parked in a lot about a hundred yards downstream, which meant they had only a few minutes more together on the river.

"I don't want to get off the water," Montana said. "Do we have to?"

"If we stay in, we'll go all the way to the Salt River and have no way to get home."

A few minutes later, they pulled the kayaks out of the water, dragged them to the truck and strapped them down in the back before she drove Sawyer back to his truck.

"That was really nice," she told him before he got out. "Thank you for planning that."

"I have one more thing up my sleeve, if you have time."

"Yeah?"

She didn't know why her heart started to beat faster. Another surprise? She wondered what it could be. "I've got all day."

He leaned across the center console and kissed her. "I was hoping you would say that. Let's meet back at the ranch and I'll drive you home. We can both get cleaned up. You can put on something nice."

The tone of his voice sent goosebumps over Montana's skin.

"Oh, something nice? Or something … risqué? What kind of surprise is this?"

"Just wait and see." He kissed her again, then caressed her breast. Her body responded, arching toward him. She deepened the kiss. He groaned. "I wish we didn't have to drive separate trucks."

If they were back in their kayaks, on the river, Montana would insist on pulling over and making love on the bank again. Sawyer disentangled himself from her, climbed out of the truck, shut the door, and winked at her through the open window.

She took a deep breath to re-center herself while he walked around the hood. He came around to the driver's door of her car and gave her one more lingering kiss before they parted ways.

————

SAWYER

THE SIGHT of Montana dressed up for him took Sawyer's breath away when he pulled up in the small parking lot outside her apartment.

He got out of his truck and walked toward her, taking in every possible detail. The early evening sun cast a golden light on the whole scene. It played off her skin and white-blond hair, making them shimmer. The breeze pressed her long skirt against her legs, and her tank top caressed the curves of her breasts.

He was tempted to scrap dinner so he could put his mouth on her breasts, her collarbones, her shoulders.

"You look nice," he said.

Mentally, he kicked himself. What he *wanted* to say was that she looked way more than nice. There wasn't even an adequate adjective. Beautiful. Mouthwatering. Breathtaking. He should have said something better. Words always failed him around Montana. He should explain, tell her that the way she looked made him want to scoop her up and hold her and never let her go. That it made him want to spend the rest of his life — no, the rest of eternity — with her. But he always felt like he would sound stupid.

She took a few steps toward him and they met in the middle. When they kissed, he could smell her floral perfume, blending perfectly with the way her skin smelled when it was kissed by the sun.

"You don't look so bad yourself," she said. "Where are we off to?"

"It's a surprise," he said, hoping for at least the tenth time that she would like it.

"I thought about blindfolding you," he said as they got in the truck. "But I don't want you to get carsick."

"Ooh, now I'm even more curious," she said.

Once he pulled the truck onto the main road, he reached across the seat and took her hand. They'd held hands a million times, and every single time, he felt a thrill. He headed east on the highway. Montana turned up the radio, and the strumming of a guitar came through the speakers.

"I know I'm not supposed to be guessing," she said, "but I think I might know where we're going."

He didn't answer, just gave her hand a squeeze. Within half-an-hour, they'd come to their spot in Breezy Pines, a mountainous neighborhood to the south and east. Although the landscape around the highway was arid and grassy, the road to Breezy Pines wound up and into the shade of a thriving forest. About five miles off the highway, a little spring came out of a giant rock on the hillside, feeding a meandering creek. Sawyer and Montana had found it years ago while exploring, and had returned there many times over the years.

"I knew it!" she said as he pulled the truck off the road and put it in park.

"Your excitement's contagious," he told her, kissing her before hopping out and going to the back of the truck to grab the cooler and blanket.

"I haven't been here in forever," Montana said. While he spread the blanket on the bank of the creek, she walked around, exploring their little area, as if seeing it for the first time. This was one of the things he loved about her: her ability to see things with fresh eyes.

"Remember that time we found a hawk's nest over here?" She was standing at the base of the ponderosa pine tree, hands on her hips, head tilted back.

Sawyer did the only thing that felt right in the moment. He walked over to where Montana stood and wrapped his arms around her waist from behind.

"I do remember." He looked up into the treetops, too. "That was one of the coolest days up here, wasn't it?"

"It was."

They stood like that for a few minutes, and although Sawyer was replaying that day in his mind — the hawk screaming at them from the top of the tree, then swooping down to batter them each a couple of times before they ran away, arms covering their heads — he was also enjoying the feel of Montana's body against his. Before he knew it, his hands were traveling the familiar path of her torso, cupping her breasts. She moaned, and he turned her around to kiss her again.

"We should eat," he said, his mouth on hers. They sat down on the blanket, and he listened to the sounds of the water rushing out of the earth, bubbling by in the little creek. He took out a single-serve bottle of wine for Montana and a beer for himself. They sipped on their drinks for a little while before he pulled out the food.

"Did you make my favorite calzones?" Montana said when she saw the aluminum foil packages.

He loved the way her eyes lit up. That alone made all the work worth it.

"I did," he said.

After they ate, they took a walk through the forest, just like they had a million times before. Hand in hand, they walked between the trees, their feet stepping softly onto fallen pine needles. When it was almost dark, they returned to the truck. In the old days, he'd spread the blanket in the truck bed, and they would kiss and touch each other and make love under the stars.

But he was taking a new approach. He wanted to prove to her that their relationship was about more than sex for him … that they could enjoy an evening without getting naked.

So even though he hardened at the memory of lying next to her, the blanket scratchy beneath them, he led her to the passenger side. He didn't go completely chivalrous; before opening the door, he backed her up against it and kissed her until he could tell she was thinking about lying with him, too. Then he kissed her some more, letting his fingers get tangled up in her hair before trailing them over her neck and that collarbone and those breasts. He even ran his palm up the inside of her thigh, until he cupped her between the legs. She cried out, already ready to orgasm, and he gave her one more caress before moving his hand to her breast again. If there was one thing they weren't missing, it was this. They could do this so many times and never tire of it. He could, at least. His hand resting now on her waist, he looked into her eyes.

"We'll have to finish this up later, little lady."

It was an old joke; when they were kids, she wanted nothing more than to keep up with the boys. When they went to a neighboring farm to do chores and one of the farm owners made the mistake of giving her the "girly job" of oiling the saddles while the boys mucked stalls and herded horses, Sawyer, Cody, and Trace spent the rest of the day calling her "little lady." That lasted only as long as it took her to punch

Trace in the mouth, but it came up over and over throughout the years.

Montana's hand found Sawyer and stroked him a couple of times through the denim of his jeans. He was ready to let it spring loose, pull her panties aside, and take her, but she stopped just short of that.

"Rain check," she said, before giving him a smug smile, extricating herself from his embrace, and getting in the truck.

Sawyer wished the evening could last forever. He wished they didn't have to return to real life, where secrets hung in the shadows.

Still, as they drove home, Sawyer thought this was the best day he'd had in a long time.

CHAPTER FOURTEEN

AT TEN A.M. the following Saturday, mimosas in hand, Montana, Tessa, Abby, and Cody's sister Annie sat in the back of a limo headed to the bridal shop.

"I can't believe we're shopping for wedding dresses!" Annie said. "For my brother's wedding! This was so worth flying in for. I never thought I'd see the day!"

"Me neither," Montana said. "But I think we can all agree that we're glad it's Tessa who broke him."

"Absolutely," Annie said. "Here's to Tessa officially becoming a member of the Mint Creek Ranch family."

"And here's to the best friends — and future sister-in-law — anyone could ask for." Tessa sounded a little choked up, and Montana felt herself getting emotional, too.

"I'm so glad you guys could come down to Phoenix for the weekend," Tessa said.

"Are you kidding?" Abby said. "I would take dress shopping over manual labor any day."

They all laughed. "So not true," Tessa said. "You've made a career out of manual labor. But I appreciate the sentiment."

"You know," Abby said. "This is my first time shopping for wedding dresses. How does this work?"

Annie's eyes lit up. "First, we interview the bride. We ask her what she envisions. Then, we get to the wedding shop, disband, and do our best to snatch up any and every dress that meets her criteria. If any other brides-to-be or their shopping companions get in the way, we stop at nothing to snag the dresses we want."

Abby's eyes widened.

"Just kidding," Annie said. "Sort of. We carry all the dozens of dresses to Tessa's dressing room, and then we refill our mimosas and sit on the couch while she tries on every. Single. One. We give Tessa our opinions on all the dresses, eventually narrowing them down to *the one.*"

"Sounds exciting," Abby said, and Annie said, "Oh, it is. Exciting and exhausting. That's why I brought snacks."

"Should we start the interview, then?" Abby said.

Annie nodded. "Absolutely. Since it's your first time, you do the honors."

"I don't know where to start," Abby said, shaking her head. "Someone else had better handle this."

Not for the first time, Montana wondered about Abby's romantic past. She didn't have too much time to think about it, though, because Annie was nudging her. "You do it."

Montana nodded, sipped her mimosa. "So, Tessa," she said, "have you got any idea what you want for your dress? Any certain style? Traditional, modern, long train, short train?"

Tessa grinned. "I don't know," she said. "I mean, I've always liked the traditional look, with the tight bodice and big skirt and everything. But I'm going in with an open mind. You never know what might knock me off my feet."

Annie squealed, a sound so unlike her that Montana was laughing again.

"I am just so excited about this wedding," Annie said. Beaming, she lifted her glass again said, "Cheers to a great match."

Montana hadn't been paying attention to the changing landscape, but the limo had pulled into the trailer park where Tessa's parents lived. Droopy palm trees lined the cul de sac. The driver stopped in front of one particularly sad-looking home, and Tessa got out and quickly shut the door behind her. Montana remembered how ashamed

Tessa said she was of growing up in a trailer park. In fact, that shame had almost cost her her relationship with Cody.

"You're next, you know," Annie said, interrupting Montana's thoughts.

At first, Montana didn't realize she was speaking to her. But then she tore her eyes away from the little trailer where Tessa grew up and realized Annie was looking right at her.

"Me?" she asked, putting a hand on her chest. "What are you talking about?"

"I hear you and Sawyer are back together again. And I hear it's different this time."

"That's true. Don't rush into thinking I'm next. I don't think either one of us is quite ready to talk marriage."

Abby shrugged. "That's what Cody said, and look. He's about to get hitched."

Montana giggled. Tessa and her mom, Linda, were coming back down the walkway.

"Whatever you say, Annie," she said. "But let's not talk about me and Sawyer anymore, okay? This is Tessa's big day."

Annie gave her a knowing look, one that mixed together a bunch of messages:

Okay, the conversation's over … for now.

Okay, whatever you say. I'm pretty sure you're next.

You say things are different this time, but are they?

Montana wondered if she'd misread that last message. Or, was she sending that message to herself? Tessa opened the limo door and she and her mom climbed in.

"Hi Linda," Montana said. "Let me get you a mimosa."

"Next stop," Annie said, her eyes still on Montana, "Wedded Bliss."

WHEN THE LIMO driver pulled into a spot at the far edge of the Wedded Bliss parking lot, Tessa said, "Wait. Nobody get out yet. I have something fun I want to try before we follow Annie's protocol. I want each one of you to pick out one dress for me. I'll try on all of them, and then together, we can choose the one."

At this, Montana felt a little giddy. It would be so fun to pick out a dress for her beautiful friend. Where Montana was petite, Tessa was tall and slender, with long legs and a narrow waist. She would look so elegant.

Abby, apparently having similar thoughts (she was height-challenged, too), rubbed her hands together. "This is going to be so much fun."

"I'll meet you in the fitting area in twenty minutes," Tessa said. "On my count. Ready?"

She counted down from five, and they all jumped out of the limo and ran to the store. Inside, the group split apart. Montana headed toward a section labeled *Empire Waist*. She could never pull off an empire waist dress, but Tessa would look so beautiful in one, with heavy, silky fabric draping down to the floor. Letting in the excitement, Montana began to assess the dresses before her.

"Too sparkly," she said to one, and "not sparkly enough," to another.

"Who ever imagined there could be so many empire waist dresses?" a voice next to her asked, making her jump.

"Annie! You scared me."

Annie giggled. "Too sparkly," she said.

"I agree," Montana said.

"You know, I always thought we would be doing this for you, first. Not for Cody."

Montana shrugged. "I admit, so did I. But these things have a way of running on their own schedule, don't they?"

"I guess."

Montana slid another dress to the left and grabbed the next one. It had a beaded bodice and matching beaded pattern at the hem. Just enough sparkle, but not too much. "Perfect," she said, taking it off the rack and hanging it over her arm. "And what do you mean, 'I guess'?"

Annie sighed. "I don't know. I'm sorry. Forget it."

"No, it's fine," Montana said, a sense of dread growing. "I want to know what you're thinking."

Never one to pull punches, Annie looked Montana in the eyes and said, "I'm saying this only because I love you and Sawyer like siblings. I know you say things are different this time, but I don't understand how that's possible. Honestly, I'm tired of seeing you both get hurt. Every time you break up, you're as heartbroken as the first time."

Her words stung. Montana wanted to defend hers and Sawyer's

decision to be together. She wanted to explain that things really were different this time, that they were both being adults. They'd bought property. But she couldn't. She'd promised Sawyer she wouldn't tell anyone until they were both ready.

She blew out a breath. "Have you picked out a dress yet?"

Annie laughed out loud. "Okay, okay. Message received. You don't want to talk about you and Sawyer."

Montana shot her a grin. "Loud and clear, huh? Like I said, it's Tessa's special day. I shouldn't even be thinking about me and Sawyer. Because if there *is* a wedding for Sawyer and me, it's an eventuality, if anything at all."

"Fine, fine. I'm going to look for princess dresses or something."

"I'm not sure if they have those," Montana said. "Isn't that kind of old-fashioned?"

"They've got to have them," Annie said. "They might not be called 'princess dresses.' But doesn't every woman want to feel like a princess on her wedding day?"

She walked away, her body language conveying that she didn't have a care in the world.

Montana checked her watch. Half of the twenty minutes had gone by. Alone now, she continued perusing the dresses, and so what if she made a mental note of the ones she liked for herself? She might have even let her mind wander, and daydream just the tiniest bit about walking down the aisle to a waiting Sawyer.

When time was up, she made her way over to the fitting room. Tessa and her mom were sitting on a bright-pink leather couch that faced the pedestal in the middle of the fitting area. Her smile lit up when she saw Montana.

"Let's see! Let's see what you picked out."

"I couldn't choose just one," Montana said, shrugging. "I'm sorry. It's just that I pictured you in every single one of these, and every time, you looked amazing."

Linda came over to hold Montana's stack of dresses so she could display them, one at a time.

"I'm keeping a neutral expression," Tessa said, but Montana could see the excitement flaring up in her eyes.

Acting nonchalant, as if she didn't care too much about which dress Tessa chose, Montana glanced over at Linda, whose eyes already shone with the sheen of tears. Annie came over next, and although she, too, acted nonchalant, Montana could tell she was attached to the dress she found. It was beautiful. Simple and elegant. The fitted bodice sat above a skirt gathered so many times it looked like cotton candy. Abby's choice completely surprised Montana. It was hands-down the frilliest, most impractical, and the most glittery dress yet. White ribbon crisscrossed up the back, and the bodice had ribbon detail, too. The skirt was made of a fine, heavy tulle.

"Oh my gosh," Montana breathed. "That looks like something a magical ballerina would wear."

Abby laughed. "Well, I think we all know *I* would never wear this. But I'll bet we can also agree that our bride will look absolutely stunning in it."

Tessa, grinning, stepped out of her shoes and danced her way over to a dressing room. "Bring 'em over here, ladies. I suppose we won't know until I start trying things on."

After the women hung up the dresses, Tessa and Linda went into the dressing room, and everyone else settled on the couch and comfy chairs. For the first time that day, silence descended.

"The anticipation is killing me," Abby said after a few minutes, her voice practically a squeal.

"Me too," the rest of them agreed.

The curtain slid open, and all the women jumped to their feet as Tessa emerged.

Montana gasped. Abby put a hand over her heart.

A sob escaped from Annie, and she said, "That's it."

"Wait, wait, wait," Abby said. "She has to come stand on this pedestal thing so we can really get a good look at her."

Within seconds, it was unanimous.

The ballet-inspired marvel with the lace-up back and the frothy skirt was *it*.

Montana had always thought Tessa could be a ballerina, with her long, graceful-looking body. This dress proved it. Tessa *would* be a beautiful ballerina — and an even more beautiful bride.

"Cody's not going to believe his lucky stars!" Annie said.

And Montana had to agree. Unexpectedly, she felt her throat tightening, and the beginning of tears.

"That's the one," Abby said.

Linda, who'd bent down to straighten the skirt, stood up, wiping her eyes, and admired her daughter's reflection in the three-way mirror. "That's what I told her. It's perfect."

Afterwards, they went to lunch, and ordered champagne to celebrate.

Amidst all the happy chatter about flower choices and bridesmaid dress colors, Montana found herself wondering if she would ever have this.

In her role as bride-to-be, Tessa seemed so confident, so happy, so calm ... as if she knew she was on the right path. Montana wanted *that*. All her life, she'd felt like she was searching for some elusive thing that would provide her with it.

She glanced over at Abby and saw Abby watching her. Yes, they were relatively new friends, but Montana felt like Abby knew exactly what she was thinking and feeling. She smiled, and Abby winked at her. Suddenly, Montana remembered her excitement about her new house. Maybe that's where she'd find her sense of calm, of peace. Maybe that's when she would feel like she was right where she belonged.

———

AFTER LUNCH, the limo dropped off Linda, and then Annie, who was staying in Phoenix another day to, "take in a resort," which she described with a funny New York accent. Resorts with mazes of sparkling pools were uncommon in upstate New York, where Annie lived — as was desert heat — and apparently, Annie was missing both.

The limo was delivering Montana, Tessa, and Abby back to the hotel where they'd stayed the night before, and they'd ride back to Prescott in Abby's truck.

"I think, as the bride-to-be," Tessa said, "I'm entitled to one more glass of champagne before we get dropped off. I really should make the most of this experience, since I'll probably never have it again."

Expertly holding both glass and bottle aloft while the limo swayed, Tessa (at that point swaying, herself) poured herself more champagne.

"You never know," Abby said. "I never thought I'd ride in a limo, either, and yet, here I am, as natural as a pig in mud." She held up her workboot-clad foot, and all three of them giggled.

"You're next, you know," Tessa said, pointing at Montana with her full glass. A tiny bit of liquid sloshed over the edge, and Tessa rushed to take a sip.

Montana shook her head. "No. I've got other things on my mind. Getting married isn't one of them."

Abby, who'd made a point of staying sober because she had to drive home, shot Montana a warning glare. She must have been able to tell Montana was on the verge of spilling her secret. Not just *her* secret, but Sawyer's as well … and Abby's, too.

What a tangled web, Montana thought.

Montana pressed her lips together and gave Abby what she hoped was an imperceptible nod. The wedding was only a few weeks away. She could wait. She *would* wait.

"Oh, really?" Tessa said, her words running together and soft around the edges. "And what plans do you have, Montana?"

Montana's nerves prickled. Why did Tessa sound so disbelieving? And would she even remember this conversation tomorrow? Montana could probably mention home ownership with minimal damage. But, she couldn't ignore the message Abby was so clearly sending her. So, she went for a complete change of subject: "I'm going to fix Abby up with Trace."

That did the trick. Abby's eyes went round. She muttered something in Spanish.

"Are you crazy, woman? You will not be fixing me up with anyone, least of all Trace Walker. That guy despises me."

"Notice," Montana said to Tessa in a stage whisper, "she didn't say she despises him." She turned to Abby. "And what if he didn't?"

"If he didn't," Abby said, "we wouldn't be having this conversation. Because you mistake his hatred for chemistry or attraction. When really, he just can't stand to be in the same room as me. Which is fine." She held up her hands, a surrender. "I just wish he could learn to tolerate me for all of our sake."

When Montana looked over at Tessa, Tessa gave a tiny shake of the head, as if she was saying, *Drop it. Don't even think about it.*

Montana shrugged and looked out the window. She knew she was being sensitive. All the wedding excitement had her feeling jealous and stagnant. The limo had slowed to a stop and Montana realized they were back at Abby's truck. During the few minutes it took them to gather their belongings, tip the driver, and get into the truck, Montana's emotions whipped into a frenzy.

Suddenly, she blurted out, "I'll have you know, Tessa Kincaid, that I *do* have big plans. Just because I don't *usually* do interesting things doesn't mean I'll *never* do interesting things."

Abby's eyes met hers in the rearview mirror. Montana looked away.

"Okay," Tessa said, drawing the word out. "I'm sorry. I didn't mean to imply that you wouldn't have plans. I'm not sure I love the voice you're using right now. I'm scared of what you're about to say." Then, as if a realization struck her, she turned around in the passenger seat and said, "Wait. You're not planning to move away, are you? Like, all the way to a different state? Wait! Are you thinking about going back to New York with Annie? I mean, if you did, I would be happy for you. I would learn to be happy for you. But I would miss you *so much*. I mean, I have Abby," she said, reaching across the console to squeeze Abby's upper arm. "But I just love having you nearby, on Mint Creek Ranch."

Montana could literally feel Abby's glare on her, via the rearview mirror. She cringed. She knew they had to do everything in their power to keep Tessa (and, by association, Cody) from finding out Sawyer planned to buy a house. Still, she soldiered on. "I'm buying a house."

"A house? You did mention you wanted to buy a house, back when Cody's tour was finishing up. I just didn't realize you were that serious."

Abby, who could probably see steam coming out of Montana's ears, jumped in, making a noble attempt to put the conversation back on the rails.

"This has just been the best day," she said.

Montana could see the muscles in Abby's forearms flexing. *Poor girl, I'm probably giving her heart attack right now*, Montana thought. But, fueled by champagne and wistfulness, and the ever-present jealousy, Montana plowed on.

"Yes," she said. "A house in Abby's development."

The silence was almost comical. Montana would have laughed if she wasn't terrified. As soon as the words left her mouth, she regretted them. What was she thinking? In the passenger seat, Tessa turned her body so she was looking at Abby head-on. "I assume you knew about this?"

Abby grimaced, and Montana let a little giggle escape.

"I did, and I told Montana her purchase would remain private until she chose to disclose it."

Tessa rubbed her eyes with her knuckles. "I get that. If anyone understands that, I do. But." Now, she turned all the way around, so she was looking at Montana. "But what I don't get, is why you, as my friend, didn't tell me."

"Well…"

"Wait," Tessa said. "I already know. It's because Trace is so against the development. Right? You were — *are* — afraid Trace will be mad. And, maybe, that I would be mad on his behalf. Or, you thought I'd tell Cody. And Cody would tell Trace. And Trace would be mad."

A little relief crept in. Montana realized she'd gone from lounging comfortably in the back seat to sitting upright. Actually, she noticed, she was even leaning forward a little, shoulders tense. She took a deep breath and let herself relax against the back of her seat again.

"I should have trusted you," Montana said.

Tessa nodded, then crossed her arms and turned around to face forward. "I wish you had."

For a few minutes, the sound of the truck racing over the asphalt filled the space. Montana felt terrible. Abby leaned forward with robotic movements and turned on the radio. But since they were heading up the mountain, all she got was static.

"Wait," Montana said. "Did we just have our first fight?"

Tessa's posture relaxed, too. She didn't turn around, but there was a smile in her voice when she said, "I think we did. I can't believe you didn't tell me."

Another beat of silence. Then Tessa did turn around, her eyes bright and alert, and said, "So, now that you've spilled the beans, tell me everything. Which model did you pick? Which lot? What's your view like? Where are you putting your garden?" Before Montana could answer, Tessa said, "Wait a second. I do want all the answers to all the questions, but first — does Trace know?"

Montana shook her head. "Not yet. Which means —"

"Which means I can't tell Cody, right?"

With the same force and speed as she'd just shook her head, Montana nodded. "Right."

Tessa blew out a big breath. "This puts me in a real awkward position, Montana."

Montana could hear Abby thinking, *Way to go, Montana.*

"I know. I know it does. Which is why I didn't want to tell you. And I'm sorry. But I just had to tell you, because I am tired of everyone thinking I can't do anything on my own."

"Montana Hart, I never thought that, and you know it. But it's water under the bridge. Now that the cat's out of the bag, answer all my other questions. Go."

Montana spent the next half-hour or so talking about her new place. Abby filled in the answers to questions about the home design and the development.

Even though Montana had wanted so badly to share this news with Tessa, now she felt disappointed in herself. She was still keeping half the secret. She couldn't tell Tessa that Sawyer was buying a place, too. That was his secret to tell, and if Trace found out …

My head is spinning, she thought.

Eventually, the conversation wore itself out, and Tessa changed the subject.

Within a few minutes, Montana felt a rush of peace, of certainty. Finally, being able to talk to her friend about what was arguably the biggest decision she ever made felt so right. At least, until she had to face Sawyer and tell him what she'd done. They'd both agreed not to tell anyone, and she'd broken that promise. Even though it felt right in the moment, she knew that in hindsight, it would feel so, *so* wrong. It already did.

CHAPTER FIFTEEN

FOR SAWYER, the next few weeks were a time of great anticipation and excitement. He was invested in two thrilling projects: his own new house and the Kincaid-Davis wedding.

Growing up, it always seemed like it was the women who got worked up over weddings. But, helping Cody and Tessa execute the event that served as the symbolic beginning to their own little family, Sawyer felt like part of something big. And he loved it. They'd finished the massive head table and had begun working on a dance floor in the reception area. It was nothing fancy, just a raised platform made of two-by-fours and plywood. The women had finished the arbor and moved on to stringing fairy lights in the trees all around where the ceremony would take place. Sawyer thought the effect was going to be pretty magical, but he would never say that out loud to Cody and Trace.

Instead, he said, "This is shaping up real nice, man."

"I know, isn't it?" Cody said. They were working on the frame for the dance floor. Cody and Sawyer held some two-by-fours in place while Trace wielded the drill. They'd spent a good five minutes arguing over who would use the drill before agreeing to give it to

Trace. He couldn't give up control, and would be unbearably bossy if either Cody or Sawyer used it.

"You know, weddings — they're pretty cool," Sawyer said.

Cody looked up at him. "You going soft on me, man?"

Sawyer chuckled, letting his gaze follow the puppies, who ran back and forth between the men and the women, wrestling and tumbling all the way. "Not at all. I've just never been this involved before. I'm excited for you guys."

"You know what weddings do to ladies, right?" Cody asked.

Sawyer knew what was coming. "Makes them want to get married?"

"More than that," Cody said, and Trace laughed out loud before adding, "It makes them want to get married and have babies and buy puppies and kittens."

Fortunately for me, Sawyer thought, *Montana already has a puppy. And she'll probably never have the desire to get married again.*

He felt the surprising sting of sadness at that thought. *He* could ask *her*. In fact, all this wedding business was making him wonder about the likelihood of Montana saying "yes."

While Trace screwed two pieces of wood together, Sawyer looked over at Montana. Today, she was wearing a pair of thin leggings with a long shirt she called a "tunic." He thought that was a pretty fancy name for a long shirt, but there was something about the way the soft, thin fabric draped over her ass that got him all hot and bothered.

He knew he would never look at another woman the same way he looked at Montana. He knew he would never love a woman the same way, either.

In fact, the more he thought about it, the more he knew what he had to do. He had to ask her to marry him. But first, he had to convince her he was ready this time. Which, with any luck, would be fun.

Just then, the screw, powered by the drill in Trace's hand, came through the wood and ground against Sawyer's fingertip.

"Head in the game, Nelson," Trace said. "You should've seen that coming."

"He would have, if he wasn't so wrapped up in watching Montana hang those lights," Cody said.

Despite the fact that the screw had ripped open the skin on his finger — and the cut was now leaking blood at a pretty good rate — Sawyer's mind was still on convincing Montana he was ready … and, he thought, if he was going to show her, he was going to have to go big.

"Well, I must have been right," Cody said. "No response, even. He must be really wrapped up in it. It's that long shirt, isn't it?"

"It's a *tunic*, for your information." Sawyer stuck his finger in his mouth, and then swore. "I'm going to have to go in for a Band-Aid."

"Sissy," Trace said.

"Moron," Sawyer quipped back. "It was your bad aim that cut my finger."

"Correction," Cody said. "It was you being distracted by the *tunic*."

Smiling, Sawyer gave them a good-natured eye roll and headed toward the house. The puppies followed, and one of them nipped at his ankles. As he walked away, he heard Cody say to Trace, "You know, if you would just get over yourself and hit it off with Abby already, we would have even more fun."

"Yeah, at my expense," Trace said.

Sawyer didn't hear Cody's response, because Montana intercepted him on his way to the house. "I see blood," she said. "Everything okay?"

"Everything's fine," Sawyer said. "Trace just nicked me with the screw he was drilling in."

Montana was able to keep up with his pace, but just barely. "Let me see."

He slowed down and released his grip on the injured finger. Blood seeped out, immediately, and he clamped his hand around it again.

"Ooh. That's bad."

"Stitches?" he asked. "To tell you the truth, I didn't look at it that carefully. I was just trying to get the bleeding stopped."

"Maybe. Let's see if we can get you fixed up. If you won't stop bleeding, stitches."

In the Davises' kitchen, Montana steered him to the sink and turned on the water. She tested it and held up a finger. "Let it warm up just a little."

"I could get used to this," he said.

"What, nearly bleeding out through your fingertip?"

"No, you taking care of me. You have a real gentle touch."

Montana took his hand and held it under the running faucet. He winced.

"That's got to sting, right?"

"It does," he said. "But luckily, I'm distracted by the beautiful woman who's causing me this pain."

She was smiling, but she said, "Hey! Trace caused this pain, not me. I'm just fixing you up."

Once the wound was rinsed, Montana wrapped it in a paper towel and applied some pressure. After a couple of seconds, maybe half a minute, she lifted the paper towel to check for bleeding. "I think you're going to live."

She went to the cabinet where the Davises kept their first aid kit and brought back a Band-Aid. She put it on, nice and tight. Again, he winced. "That's going to smart for a couple of days."

"That'll teach you to put your hands anywhere near the end of Trace's drill."

"Hey, I rarely put my hands near the end of any man's drill," he quipped.

She swatted his arm. "You're good to go. Let's get back to work, or everybody will wonder what happened to us."

He winked at her as they walked out of the kitchen, and she swatted him again — this time on the butt. Dolly and Cash waited at the door, seated side by side, tails wagging. They leapt into action when Sawyer and Montana came out and chased them along.

Just a few minutes before, Sawyer had been brainstorming ways to convince Montana to agree to marry him. The fact that she was the one taking care of him at the moment didn't seem right. Maybe he should cook her dinner. Or buy her a gift. Too bad she'd already gotten her own puppy. He'd have to talk it over with the guys.

"Everything okay?" she asked as they walked back out to the work area.

"Yeah! Why?"

"You just seem distracted, that's all."

Sawyer offered her his best megawatt smile. "Just thinking how much I appreciate you taking care of me."

She returned his smile and brought his injured finger to her lips. She kissed it, gently, and then put a hand to his cheek. "You're welcome."

"See you in a bit. I can't leave Cody and Trace unsupervised for too long."

———

Montana

BACK AT HER post with Tessa and Abby, Montana decided to go to work on her *other* project: convincing Abby to give Trace a try.

"So. Abby."

Abby, atop a stepladder, a string of lights in her hands, looked first at Tessa and then at Montana. "Yes?"

Before Montana could answer, Tessa said, "Here it comes."

"As I mentioned on the ride up here the other day, I think you and Trace are a match made in Heaven."

Abby wrinkled her nose and reached up to hook the lights on a branch. "That's actually not what you said. And I'm inclined to disagree."

Now, Montana glanced at Tessa, who looked smug, like she had known how Abby would respond.

"Just hear me out," Montana said, before realizing the pleading tone in her voice. Abby didn't respond. She used a zip tie to attach the lights to the branch. She climbed off the ladder, moved it, picked up the string of lights again, and then climbed the ladder and began to attach the string to another branch.

"You're not even going to say anything?"

Abby made an exasperated sound, somewhere between a sigh and a laugh. "I don't know that I should dignify your idea with a response."

Her movements efficient, she relocated the ladder again.

"Montana, let's face the facts," Tessa said. "I've heard all the stories. You've never been that great at matchmaking."

"Haven't I?"

"I don't think so. At least, not according to the guys. Remember —"

"I remember," Montana said, huffing out a breath.

From her perch on top of the ladder, Abby turned around and put her hands on her hips. "Wait. You're telling me that you're trying to set me up, and you're not even good at matchmaking?"

"From what I understand," Tessa said, lips twitching, "it's not that she's *not good* at matchmaking. It's just that every match she makes ends in disaster. Ergo, she's *disastrous* at matchmaking."

Abby raised one eyebrow at Montana.

"I can't deny that's been the case in the past," Montana said. "But this time I really know the two people. You, Abby, are so smart and forward-thinking and clever. Not to mention beautiful. And Trace. Trace is —"

Abby cut her off. "Trace is a stubborn, backwards-thinking jerk. He might be smart, and he might be good-looking — *very* good-looking — but need I remind you that he despises me?"

No, Montana didn't really need a reminder about that. But Abby had just called Trace very good-looking. And hadn't Montana, herself, despised Sawyer a time or two? Or a dozen? And look how much she loved him now. She didn't bother sharing that rationale. Instead, she said, "I have a feeling that, as we continue to plan this wedding, the two of you are going to begin to find each other irresistible."

"I very much doubt that," Abby said. "But I wouldn't turn down your attempts to get him to tolerate me."

Montana took that as a green light. Of sorts.

The sound of the dinner bell rang across the yard. Just like Pavlov's dogs, the crew dropped their tools and trooped toward the kitchen, which they'd done since they were kids and Elaine bought the dinner bell so she wouldn't have to stand at the back door and holler.

"Everyone sit down, please!" Elaine called. "I've made way too much food, and I need your help eating it."

Montana noticed that despite everyone's protests, Abby and Trace ended up next to each other at the picnic table just outside the kitchen.

"So, Trace," Montana said. Everyone froze. "Did you know Abby likes riding horses?"

Trace gave her a look — it was one Montana couldn't quite read, but at least she'd planted the seed.

"No, I didn't know that," Trace said. And then, because everyone on the Mint Creek Ranch had learned impeccable manners in much the same way they'd learned to respond to the dinner bell — and were forced to use them — he turned to Abby and said, "Do you ride much?"

Oh, Montana wondered, a laugh threatening to burst out of her, *why did conversations about horseback riding always include so much innu-endo?* She should've chosen a different topic.

Trace, did you know Abby likes to build things?

Trace, did you know Abby grew up in Utah?

Trace, did you know Abby has never tasted a stuffed olive?

Abby cleared her throat and wiped her mouth. "Not as much as I'd like to. But once I move out here, I hope to get a couple of horses."

Montana braced herself, and she sensed that everyone else around the table did, too. Abby moving out here was definitely a sore spot for Trace. How would he react? Fortunately, those impeccable manners stepped in again. "That'll be really nice for you."

He took another bite of his lasagna.

Next to Montana, Sawyer perked up. "Oh yeah? What kind of horses are you thinking of getting?"

Abby's eyes lit up. "Ever since I was little kid, I've wanted a couple of Appaloosas. They're just so beautiful, so graceful. I first saw them at a rodeo in San Antonio. They were pulling this pretty little carriage. Don't laugh," she added quickly. "I was just a little girl. The carriage was wooden, and painted with all these bright colors. Those horses pulled the carriage out into the arena, and all these little clowns started jumping out. It was like that lady with the big skirt in the Nutcracker ballet. You can't believe any more people can fit in there, but they just kept coming out. Looking back on it, I suspect there were only about four or five guys in there, and a couple of them would distract the audience while the others went back inside the wagon and came back out. But at the time, to the little-girl version of me, it was really magical. Anyway. I *begged* my parents for two ponies exactly like those Appaloosas. Every Christmas, I asked for them."

Montana saw a little sadness cloud Abby's eyes and made a mental note to ask about that later.

"Those are beautiful horses," Cody said. Sawyer added, "I can keep my eye out for some, if you like."

Abby's cheeks flushed. "I should say 'no,'" she told him. "But please do. I'm not quite ready to bring them home yet. But, if it's meant to be, maybe you'll hear about it through the grapevine. Serendipity and all that."

Sawyer grinned at her and said, "Okay. Done. I'll keep an eye out, and I'll keep you posted."

Well, Trace hadn't completely rejected the conversation, Montana thought. Maybe she could build on this. She was building a little family with her new puppy, and she was building a new home. She was building love again with Sawyer. And maybe, just maybe, she could help Abby and Trace build something, too.

CHAPTER SIXTEEN

Montana

MONDAY MORNING, Montana received a text from Abby: *Special meeting of the Sunset Valley First Owners Club, tonight at 7. Same place as last time.*

Curious, Montana called to get the details, but Abby said she had a special announcement and wouldn't share it until the meeting.

"I hope she's not canceling the whole development," Montana said to Sawyer as they walked from the parking lot to the restaurant entrance that evening.

"She wouldn't," Sawyer said. "Would she?"

"I hope not."

In the back room, Abby waited, wringing her hands.

Finally, everyone was seated. "I wanted to make you all aware of a new opportunity. Technically, I could pursue this on my own, but I thought I would put it to a vote. I consider each of us a stakeholder now, so I didn't want to make any big decisions without hearing from you."

She looked nervous as she made eye contact with one person at a time, never letting it go on for very long before moving to the next person. No one spoke.

Finally, Montana said, "Well? What is it?"

Abby dropped her hands to her sides. "Oh! Right. We have the opportunity to put an RV Park at one end of the property. It would take the place of one permanent residence. I'm not asking you for advice about the zoning or anything like that. I've got that all taken care of. But I'd like to take a vote on whether we want to put an RV park on the property."

"What's it in it for us?" It was José Suarez, the Phoenix developer who was moving to Prescott for the country life.

"Good question, Abby said. "A businesswoman has come to me with a proposal. She wants to lease a section of land from me, and then build and maintain an RV park on it. Her people would handle the whole operation, and her company would keep the profits they earn from campers. But we — the Sunset Valley development — will get the lease money."

Montana tore her gaze from Abby and glanced around the table. Everyone looked interested, thoughtful. José had one leg crossed, his elbows on the arms of his chair, and his fingers steepled under his chin. Jacob Austin leaned forward, hands on his knees. Sawyer squinted, as if trying to envision the RV park and all its potential effects.

Abby went on, "I thought we could use it for something that benefits all of us. Maybe it could go into a community fund of some sort, for roads and tree-cutting and things like that. Or, maybe we could use it to build a community center or a park, or put in a pool. I think those things would attract more young families."

"Who said we want to attract young families?" It was José Suarez again.

Montana estimated he was about thirty-five — still in the potential-family-man category.

"I think it's a great idea," Montana said.

Abby's shoulders relaxed, just slightly.

"Sawyer?" Abby looked at him.

Sawyer froze like a deer in headlights. Then he looked at Abby, Montana, and José. If it weren't such a serious matter, Montana would've laughed out loud.

"I don't know yet," he said, finally. "Can you give us a little more detail?"

Now, Sawyer looked relieved as well; Montana suspected it was because he'd managed to avoid upsetting anyone with his opinion.

Abby licked her lips, took a deep breath. She was back to looking nervous.

"Well," she started. "I haven't thought of all the details yet. Ultimately, we want the park to be successful so the people managing it can continue to pay to lease the land. But, as nearby residents, we want it to look nice, right? We want it to *be* nice. With that in mind, I'd like to work up some different scenarios based on how many spots the park would have. That way, we can run the numbers and get a picture of how it would play out. Obviously we could talk about time limits on stays and that sort of thing. As you all know, Prescott is such a tourist hotspot that I don't think we would have any shortage of campers. People visiting family, taking vacation, whatever. And we could decide whether the RV park open year-round or just seasonally, throughout the warmer months."

"With all the activities the city puts on," Montana said, "we'd probably get a lot of visitors during the Christmas season."

Abby nodded, and Montana realized that the more she thought about it, the more she liked the idea of the RV park. It would be fun to have visitors. And it would be nice to have that income stream for the whole development. It was kind of like collecting money through a homeowners association, without all the rules.

"I don't think it's the best idea," Sawyer said then.

Montana felt her mouth drop open in surprise. Was he serious? Out of everyone here, she would have thought Sawyer would support an RV park on the property. He loved camping. And why wouldn't he want that income?

"Tell me what you're thinking," Abby said.

"I guess I just feel like, if this is our home, do we really want strangers in and out all the time?" Sawyer said.

"Right," said José. "I don't know if the money is worth the hassle of having people coming and going all the time. We'd have to consider the traffic, the noise, things like that."

"Okay," Abby said. "Those are great points. And, just so you know, the RV park would be at one end of the property."

"Well, that's not any consolation for me," Sawyer said. "If it's at the far end, the RVs and trailers will be driving past us day in and day out. And if it's at the close end, we'll be driving past that eyesore every time we come and go."

Montana couldn't believe what she was hearing.

"Some RV parks have restrictions on the age of the RVs that can camp at them," Abby said. "We could require that RVs be within a certain age range. And that would give us some peace of mind that they wouldn't be 'eyesores.'"

Sawyer seemed to consider it. But José didn't look impressed. "I'm a firm no," he said. "That's my official vote. And I won't change my mind. So, I guess I can leave this meeting."

He got up and walked out, leaving a cloud of expensive-smelling cologne behind him. Abby looked close to tears.

"Well, I think it's a great idea," Montana said.

"Do you?" Sawyer asked. "You won't mind all the RVs coming and going? The traffic? The noise? Strangers hanging out in our development?"

"Not really." Montana shrugged. She kept her tone nonchalant, but her heart raced. "The campground would be a great way to bring in some extra revenue. We could add some nice amenities. Don't you love the idea of a park? A pool? A community clubhouse?"

Montana felt her nerves melting away. She was a stakeholder now. She felt an obligation to speak up, to share her good ideas.

Abby smiled. "I think a pool would be a great addition."

"So do I," Jacob said, finally speaking up. "We could do so much. And think about how things like a pool or a park could increase resale value."

"I don't know," Sawyer said. "A pool would be nice, but I don't know if everyone would want to use it. If this community fund is truly a community fund, then shouldn't we all agree on how it's spent?"

"That's a fair point," Abby said. "I suppose we could put everything to a vote. Run it like a democracy."

"That's fine," Sawyer said. "You are, after all, our supreme leader."

Grinning, Sawyer bowed his head in deference. His humor worked. Abby laughed, and some of the tension dissolved.

But for Montana, the tension was just revving up. She thought she and Sawyer wanted the same things. So how could their views of the ideal development look so different? And how, so early in this supposedly different rendition of their relationship, could she be feeling so uncertain about whether they were headed in the same direction?

———

SAWYER

SAWYER LOOKED FORWARD to dinner all day, imagining that he and Montana would have so much to talk about after the First Owners Club meeting. When 6 p.m. rolled around, though, he found himself standing in his kitchen, waiting for Montana … and dreading it.

He'd already slammed one beer to calm his nerves, and he was sipping on a second. Yes, they would have a lot to talk about, he thought, but not in the fun, conversational way he'd imagined. No, the two of them were not cheerfully going to discuss their excitement for the future. Because, apparently, their visions for the future were not the same.

Ever since he'd realized they had completely different views of what the Sunset Valley development should be, Sawyer felt sick to his stomach.

Having two different visions of the future wasn't that big of a deal, but *these* two visions? They seemed to illuminate a complete difference in values. He could feel his rational side spinning out of control. Typically, he'd call Cody or Trace for perspective. But he couldn't, and that killed him. Maybe Montana was right about one thing: maybe they should tell their friends they were buying property from Abby.

But that wasn't the sticking point at the moment. How Montana could be okay with having an RV Park, typically a bustling center of activity, in their safe haven, the place where they should relax, was beyond him. What about all that traffic? All those people — strangers? Montana was okay with that?

She said she liked the idea of a park and a pool. Those two things made sense. She wanted kids. And kids loved parks and pools. But didn't she see the danger of all those strangers coming and going, sharing space with kids?

It was unlikely she'd even thought of that. Montana had a tendency to see the absolute best version of an idea through her permanent rose-colored glasses. So, maybe all he had to do was explain his rationale. She would understand. She would come around to his way of thinking. He went through this entire thought process while sipping on that second beer.

Finally, she knocked on the door. When he opened it, the puppies, who had been at Montana's place together all day, came rushing in, barking, wrestling, and tumbling, causing a commotion that distracted Sawyer and Montana from an awkward greeting.

When she did say, "Hey," the word came out covered in frost.

"No kiss?" he asked, trying for natural.

"I just saw you," she said.

It was true, but that didn't remove the sting. Maybe the lack of a kiss wasn't a sign she was upset … but he could tell. She couldn't hide her feelings from him. And it didn't take a genius to figure out why she was upset. Which made him mad. He was entitled to his own opinion.

His rational side piped up, reminding him that Montana was entitled to her own opinion, too. And that Sawyer had just spent the entire afternoon upset because the two of them disagreed, but he dismissed it. He was perfectly fine being irrational.

If Montana was mad because they had two different opinions, well, then, she was going to be in for a lifetime of anger. People — friends, family members, couples — had different opinions all the time. Some people liked wine, some liked beer. Some liked cake, some liked pie.

"I'm not mad because we had two different opinions," she said, icicles hanging off the words as she straightened up and put her hands on her hips. He wasn't surprised she'd practically read his mind. "I'm mad because we apparently have two different sets of values."

Sawyer, who had been midway to the fridge to get Montana a beer, froze. It was eerie, how closely her thoughts echoed his own. But he couldn't say that out loud. Not yet, anyway.

"Maybe we don't," he said. "I have a feeling that you like the idea of parks and pools and all that because you want to raise your family in a place where they can have fun, be kids, have experiences."

"That's true," she said.

"And I want that, too. But also, I want our new home to be a place where we can relax and feel safe. Having all that traffic going by, all those strangers hanging around, doesn't feel relaxing or safe to me."

"You act like all the people coming in will be crazy partiers or something, hanging out in our backyards," Montana said. "And I'm imagining them as families. Just bringing their kids to Prescott for a good time. And an RV park would bring in revenue without us having to pay a monthly HOA fee. Did you think about that?"

"I haven't heard anything about a monthly HOA fee yet," Sawyer said.

"You will, eventually," Montana said. "Almost every place like this has a fee. We don't think we need one now, but things come up. And before we know it, we'll have an HOA and the fees that come with it."

Montana's eyes were alight with intensity, and her cheeks were rosy. He handed her the beer he'd opened. She practically grabbed it with a muttered, "Thanks." Were they actually fighting about this? Sawyer couldn't believe it. They'd been getting along so well.

"Look," he said, and he could see Montana bristle at the single word, which usually signified he was about to start a debate. He decided to change his tactic. "Why don't you relax while I make dinner? This was supposed to be a nice evening."

"I'll chop the cucumbers," she said, gritting her teeth. He imagined her wielding the knife and almost asked her to choose a different job, but said, "Okay. I'll grill the meat."

He retrieved the cucumbers from the fridge, and then got out a cutting board and a knife. Moving stiffly, Montana came over to stand next to him. She picked up the knife. Sawyer moved quickly away, acting like he was afraid of her. That, at least, earned him a smile.

"Maybe we should just table this conversation for now," Sawyer said. "We're both feeling really strongly about it. Why don't we give ourselves some time to think it over, and then we can discuss it again later?"

"We don't really have to discuss it, do we?" Montana said. "It's not like we have to come to an agreement. We are two separate property owners. Two separate votes."

Those words hurt. Badly.

Sawyer clamped his mouth shut. He took the meat out of the fridge. Hyper-aware of the sounds of Montana's chopping, the raw meat hitting his cutting board, and his hands rubbing oil into it, he managed to say, "You're right."

And she was: they were separate property owners. They had no obligation to vote the same way on the RV park issue or any issue. Technically, they didn't have to agree. But their agreement felt very important to Sawyer.

If he couldn't convince her to come around to his way of thinking on the RV park, could he convince her to marry him? And even if he did, how many times in their marriage would they experience these fundamental differences?

———

AS THE TWO of them went through the motions for the rest of that evening, Sawyer couldn't stop thinking about that night, ten years ago. The Night That Changed Everything.

It came up in his mind often enough. Too often. But he always pushed it out of his consciousness. He couldn't bear to think about it. After that day's meeting, though, where his and Abby's major differences of opinion lashed out at each other across the table like a couple of warring dragons, he couldn't help but remember it. And replay it, over and over.

They were eighteen. *Just* eighteen. Just officially adults.

Throughout their childhood, Sawyer's and Montana's parents talked about them going to college as if it was the only path to becoming a responsible adult. Sawyer didn't want to go. It wasn't for him; he planned to work the Mint Creek Ranch, start his own line of cattle, and use the knowledge he'd gained throughout his life.

Stubborn, headstrong, and tired of his parents reminding him of looming application deadlines, he decided one fine spring day to tell them: he wasn't going. Period.

At first, their reaction was pretty much what he expected. His mom gave him *that* look: her expression a mix of pity and derision.

"You know why your father has been able to provide so well for us throughout your life, don't you?" she said to Sawyer. "It's because he went to college. He got a degree in business. And he has spent his entire adult life putting that degree to use. If Montana is going to college, I don't know why you can't go, too."

Before Sawyer could respond, his dad piped up. "You know, son. Montana's going to go off to college, and she's going to find her a man who is serious about the future. A man who is educated, willing to put in the time to ensure she and her children don't go hungry."

Things ramped up from there. By the time Sawyer's parents had finished lecturing him, he was convinced he would never be good enough for Montana, even if he went to college, and especially if he didn't.

"She deserves more than an uneducated hick."

"These days, you can't provide for a family without a college degree."

"You want to resign yourself to a life of poverty right now? Go ahead."

Still reeling from all the hurtful things his parents said, Sawyer sought solace in the one place he knew he could always find it: Montana.

Her parents were out of town, so she had the house to herself. She'd invited him over for dinner. When he walked in, his heart aching, he saw immediately that the entire place was candlelit. He had no idea where she managed to get all those candles, but they sat at the perimeters of the living room, dining room, and kitchen. Short, fat candles, tall, skinny candles, candles in glass jars and plain candles sitting on plates. Sawyer had never seen so many candles in his life. On the floor, rose petals made a trail from the front door to the kitchen. Two crystal goblets sat on the counter. Montana, who'd greeted him at the door, was wearing an apron — with nothing underneath. Sawyer gulped, and worried she could hear it, but fortunately, she had some nice jazz music or something playing on her parents' stereo system.

"Well, aren't you going to come in?"

Sawyer, his jeans feeling suddenly tight, walked across the room, picked up one of the goblets and sniffed its contents. "Wine?"

She smiled. "All I could find was brandy."

He set down the glass and automatically, he reached out, his fingers itching to touch her skin. But she moved away, as graceful as a cat. "Hold on, I need to talk to you before — well, before we, you know."

This made Sawyer nervous. What could they possibly have to talk about when she had set the scene like this? Thoughts of his parents were fading into the background, and all he could think about was sliding his hands under that apron. So why did she want to talk?

She couldn't be upset with him, could she? If she was, then she wouldn't have done all this. She would be fully clothed. Although, if she was feeling sinister, she could be luring him in just to give him a taste of what he was missing. But it wasn't that. She picked up a goblet and offered it to him. He took it. She lifted the other one and said, "Cheers."

Sawyer took a sip of the brandy, and it slid down his throat and warmed him right through. Montana took a sip of hers, too, and then ran the fingers of her free hand through his hair before resting her palm on the side of his neck, her fingertips curved behind his ear.

He gulped again. Why was he so nervous? He saw nothing but love and affection in her expression.

"Kiss me?" she said.

He did, and thanks to everything about that moment — the candles, the rose petals, the smell of something garlicky cooking on the stove, Montana naked under that apron — he was rock hard within a split second of their lips touching. Again, he reached for her, and again she playfully pulled away.

He groaned. "What did you want to talk to me about?"

She responded with a *tsk*. "Patience, my love."

A few minutes later, dinner was on the table. They sat side by side. Although he was starving, he could barely eat. His appetite was for one thing, and it wasn't baked manicotti. Finally, the plates were cleared, the dishes were washed, and Montana led him to the couch.

"Want to make out?" he teased.

"I do," she said. "But first I need to talk to you."

Sawyer felt like a rattlesnake had taken up residence inside his torso. His insides vibrated.

"So you said."

The sex-driven part of his teenage mind hollered, "Get to it, already," but suddenly, Montana seemed nervous. She took a deep breath. Sawyer did, too.

"Sawyer," she said. "I've been thinking. We're both going to graduate in a few months. And then we'll be free to do what we want."

He nodded. There was just one thing he wanted to do at the moment.

"Anyway. I had a question to ask you."

Maybe she was going to ask him to move in with her after graduation. Or go on a summer trip with her. Or travel the world before they started acting like real adults.

When she finally asked the question, it was none of those things.

"Will you marry me, Sawyer?"

Just like that. No reasoning, no explanation. It was so simple. Probably because for Montana, life really was that straightforward.

But for Sawyer, things were more complicated. He panicked as, in a rush, everything his parents said came back. He wouldn't be able to provide for Montana if he didn't go to college. It was only a matter of time before she realized the mistake she made. She deserved more.

Sawyer watched Montana go from expectant to uncertain to terrified. And then he thought, *What have I done?*

"Sorry," he said to her then. "I can't. I just can't."

And then, before he could watch her go from terrified to devastated, he fled.

Instead of just giving her a flat, "I can't," he should've said something like, "Yes — in five years." Or, "Yes, after I prove I'm worthy."

Because in every version of a future he envisioned, they were together.

He knew he'd never forgive himself, and he figured Montana would never forgive him, either.

CHAPTER SEVENTEEN

THINGS HAD BEEN tense between Montana and Sawyer since the RV park conversation. Over dinner one night about a week later, Montana said to Sawyer, "So. Are you going to help me with my little project?"

Mid-chew, Sawyer raised an eyebrow. He swallowed and said, "I can practically see you drumming your fingers together just before you cackle like a villain in a kids' movie. Does your little plan, by any chance, involve capturing two children and putting one of them in an oven?"

Montana laughed. Sawyer knew where she was going. The fact that he didn't bite instantly meant he didn't love the idea. But she did. "You're funny. Don't you think it would work?"

Mouth full once again, Sawyer said, "Do I think *what* would work? You playing the evil villain in a kids' cartoon?"

"No," Montana said. "Trace and Abby. Abby and Trace." She let that sink in for a few seconds, and when he didn't respond, she said, "I mean, come on. Can't you just feel the attraction between them?"

Sawyer cleared his throat. "Montana."

Uh oh. Whenever he replied to her like that, it usually meant he wasn't on board. Like the time she tried to rescue a bunny that had obviously been hit by a car. In hindsight, she could see that they should've left the poor creature to die in the bushes on the side of the road. At least it was familiar with those surroundings. But she'd suggested they put it in a cardboard box and take it to a veterinarian. After a serious, "Montana," he'd reluctantly lifted the barely alive rabbit into a box and driven it to the vet. By the time they got there, she was almost positive it was a lost cause. But she tried, and isn't that what really mattered?

And she was trying now. She couldn't quite put her finger on why getting Sawyer's buy-in felt so important. Still, she tried to keep things light. "Sawyer."

"Look, we've all seen the way they interact," he said. "And it's obvious —"

"That the two of them have so much chemistry, they don't even know what to do with it?"

Sawyer laughed, but it wasn't an amused laugh.

"Okay," he said. "I'll admit that when Trace first saw Abby, way back when she first came here and got lost and had the flat tire, he mentioned her. There was a spark. I've seen them look at each other like that a few times. But now? No. It's obvious that they can't stand each other. The only kind of chemistry they have is the kind that leads to a really great fight in a boxing ring. Or a UFC cage. But definitely not a good match between the sheets."

"Really?" Montana asked.

"Really. And I wish you would get this idea out of your mind. If they're going to be together, they'll get together. I don't think we need to play any role in it."

Montana moved her fork around on her plate, swirling some peas through the sauce from the chicken she made. "Don't you —"

"No."

The temptation to groan, or stomp off to the sink with her plate, was strong. It was also childish. It would be so much easier to set up Trace and Abby if she had Sawyer's help.

"Why is this so important to you?"

Once again, the urge to groan struck her. He knew her so well. It was infuriating. She had been about to ask herself that very same question. Why *was* it so important to her?

"I don't know," she said. "I guess it's just that Abby is such a great person. She has so much going for her. It would be so nice to, you know, bring her into the fold."

What Montana was really thinking was that Tessa and Cody were about to launch their own happily ever after. And now, more than ever, she wanted that with Sawyer. But also, now more than ever, she was uncertain about whether he wanted it with her. Sure, they were together, but meanwhile, they were pursuing their own separate futures.

Maybe this matchmaking was so important to her because if Sawyer helped her, that would signify that he believed in true, lifelong love. That he *did* want that happily ever after with her. But she could never say that to him. The last time she'd brought it up, he hightailed it out of her life.

He nodded. He must think her reasoning was sensible. He didn't need to know the whole truth.

"I agree that Abby's a great person," he said.

"I knew it," Montana said, excitement once again taking over.

"But," he said, and she groaned.

"But what?"

"But, if they're meant to be together, they'll get together. If we force it, then we may end up regretting it. Let things unfold naturally."

Deflated, Montana sighed. She took another bite of chicken. She would just have to do this on her own. Maybe after a few weeks, if Sawyer saw the progress, he would come on board. And if not, that didn't mean he wasn't interested in a forever relationship with her. Did it?

———

THE NEXT DAY, Montana launched her project.

She had done a lot of thinking and decided she was going to start making Trace and Abby cross paths whenever she could. To them, it would feel like serendipity.

But she would be the mastermind, the puppeteer behind the so-called chance encounters.

Soon enough, Trace and Abby would see they were meant to be together.

As she began to plan the first meeting, Montana had to admit to herself that she might be overstepping some kind of boundary. But she had a good feeling about it.

———

MONTANA PULLED her car up alongside the curb outside Abby's apartment building, and before she'd even put it in park, Abby's door swung open. Montana rolled down the passenger-side window and whistled. To her delight, Abby looked smokin' hot: she wore a short dress with a cinched waist and flowy skirt and strappy sandals with wedge heels.

"Oh, stop," Abby said with a grin as she got in. "You act like you've never seen a girl in a dress."

"I've never seen *this* girl in a dress," Montana said. "Lookin' good."

Montana imagined rubbing her hands together in anticipation of what she had planned.

"Thanks," Abby said. "I'm so ready for a night out, it's not even funny. Where are we going, anyway?"

"I thought we'd go to the Steakout," Montana said.

"Mmm," Abby said, leaning her head back against the headrest and closing her eyes. "Steak. My mouth is watering."

Perfect, Montana thought.

A few minutes later, they parked, and after a quick scan of the lot, Montana made a decision: "Want to grab a drink at the bar? Stretch out the evening a little?"

"As long as we can get some steak fries," Abby said. "I'm famished. I could eat a whole cow."

Montana chose a table in the corner so she could sit facing the door. Then, she crossed her fingers and hoped the seed she'd planted earlier was growing. They ordered drinks and fries, and chatted while they waited.

As the minutes ticked by, Montana became increasingly nervous. Maybe she didn't know Sawyer as well as she thought she did. Maybe she'd been wrong.

But then, finally, the door opened, and she recognized his profile, outlined in the setting sun. She let out a breath and took a long drink from her glass.

"Is that Sawyer?" Abby asked.

She was squinting, and Montana hoped that her hunger, the length of time they'd been in the bar, and the beer she'd downed hadn't combined to make her loopy.

"Oh! Yes, I think it is," Montana said, infusing her voice with as much surprise as she could.

As if she hadn't brought this chance encounter to life, starting earlier that day with a well-timed suggestion about Friday-night fish fry. With a friend.

And there, behind Sawyer, was Trace.

Montana and Abby saw him at the same time, and Abby inhaled sharply before saying, "Great," in a voice so melancholy, Montana had to laugh.

"What's wrong?" Montana asked, realizing the high pitch of her voice might give away the fact that she'd known he was coming.

When Abby's only response was to pop another fry into her mouth, Montana wondered whether her idea had been any good, after all.

The guys still hadn't seen them. Trace, elbows on the host stand, talked with the hostess, whose twinkling eyes and wide smile conveyed amusement and interest.

"Weird how he can be so charming when he wants to be," Abby said, her voice quiet.

When Montana looked over at her, she was surprised to see Abby's cheeks were pinker than usual. Was she *jealous*?

How interesting!

As Trace flirted his way into the hostess flirting right back with him, Sawyer's gaze made its way around the room. Montana couldn't decide whether to shrink back and become a wallflower, or sit up straight and tall and get the initial contact over with.

Fortunately (or unfortunately, Montana wasn't sure which), their eyes met then, and that initial contact was made. And Sawyer looked … unhappy.

Which she had (sort of) expected …

I will be unwavering, she thought, squaring her shoulders and grinning before giving Sawyer a hearty wave.

In return, he offered her a tight smile. He said something to Trace, who straightened up and looked toward the bar. And Montana saw it: his gaze landed on Abby and sharpened in interest. He offered her a genuine smile before making eye contact with Montana, his smile remaining in place.

Feeling triumphant, Montana gestured for Sawyer and Trace to join her and Abby. Sawyer looked more reluctant than Trace did.

He'll come around, Montana told herself.

"Hey," she said to the guys, feigning surprise.

"Hey," Sawyer said, conveying displeasure.

Montana wanted to laugh. Yes, she'd suggested he and Trace come to the Steakout for Sawyer's favorite: Friday night fish fry. And then, she'd invited Abby to join her there, as well. Couldn't he see this was an excellent plan? If he couldn't see it now, he would.

"Hey," Trace said. He looked at Abby and then Montana.

"Well, we're all here," Montana said. "Why don't we just eat together?"

Sawyer shook his head. Trace laughed. Abby scowled. Fortunately, the hostess led them to a regular four-top table and not a booth, so they didn't have to stand around awkwardly deciding who would sit next to whom.

SAWYER

AS SOON AS Sawyer saw Montana and Abby, *coincidentally* in the same place where Montana had suggested he and Trace have dinner that night, he knew what was going on.

Montana, acting like the sorceress she imagined herself to be, had mixed together a little of this and a little of that — a little Abby, a little Trace, and Sawyer's favorite Friday night fish fry — and was now using her long, magical finger to stir the pot.

He saw her expression the moment she knew he was on to her: happy, expectant, like she thought he would be impressed with what she'd arranged. But his reaction was totally the opposite. What was she thinking? Trace and Abby obviously just didn't click. Couldn't she just leave the two of them alone? And when Montana had asked his advice, Sawyer had said as much. She'd gone and created this *coincidence* anyway.

Plus, what if Abby, or even him or Montana, slipped and revealed that they were building houses in Abby's development?

"Fancy seeing them here," Trace said to Sawyer when they first spotted the women from the hostess stand. He had one eyebrow raised, and he might as well be saying it out loud: *I know what's going on here.*

Sawyer held up his hands up. "I didn't know, man."

Although Trace hadn't looked happy, per se, he recovered quickly enough and didn't seem too bothered by Montana's suggestion that the four of them eat together. Sawyer would be darned if he didn't notice a spark of interest in Trace's eyes as he talked with Abby over fried cod and French fries.

Darn it if Montana didn't sit there next to him looking smug and pleased with herself. Sawyer knew exactly what she was thinking: Abby and Trace have been sitting here talking, and they're not yelling yet. She was probably drawing an imaginary point in the win column under her name.

At one point, Trace said, "Actually, I'm kind of glad we ran into you guys. I've been wanting to install a new ceiling fan, but I wasn't sure about the wiring. I want to get one with one of those dimmable lights —"

"I'm sure all the ladies will truly appreciate that," Abby cut in.

Trace rolled his eyes, but he seemed otherwise unfazed.

"The only thing I know about wiring is that I shouldn't mess with it," Trace said.

"Well, at least you know that," Abby said.

Sawyer couldn't believe his eyes or his ears. A regular conversation, with what could be classified as flirting mixed in, never happened when Abby and Trace occupied the same space.

"I can help you with that," Abby said. "For a small price."

Trace opened his mouth to object, and Abby said, "I could use some advice about fencing. For the new development."

To Sawyer's complete and utter surprise, Trace just nodded. "Sure. I can help you with that."

While the conversation continued, Sawyer waited for the other shoe to drop. Sure, they might be getting along at the moment, but it was only a matter of time until they were at each other's throats.

"Well, let's hope Abby has the sense to listen to you," Sawyer blurted out, his tone a little harsher than he intended.

Abby's eyes darted over to meet Sawyer's. Montana rushed to intervene. "He didn't mean you, Abby. He meant me. Sawyer feels like I don't always listen to him, take his advice."

"Correction," Sawyer said. "I feel like she *rarely* takes my advice. Maybe even never."

He regretted the words instantly. Montana looked as if someone had slapped her.

———

MONTANA

MONTANA'S FACE burned with shock and embarrassment. She couldn't believe Sawyer was behaving that way. How could he be upset when things were going so well? She excused herself to go to the bathroom.

When she came out, Sawyer was waiting for her. Panic set in. Montana wondered what he was going to say. More importantly, he'd left Trace and Abby alone. Montana didn't see any smoke, so maybe that was okay.

"What are you doing?" he demanded, his eyebrows drawn.

"What do you mean?"

"I mean, why are we all here? How did this *coincidence* happen?"

"I expected you to be annoyed, but not angry," Montana said.

"I'm angry because you insist on playing matchmaker when it's obvious that neither half of the match is interested in the other. I don't know why you can't just let it go."

Because I want my friends to have the happily ever after we won't.

"I think they just haven't realized yet that they're great for each other."

"Are they?" Sawyer jerked a thumb toward their table and immediately froze when he looked over and saw Trace throw his head back in laughter while Abby watched him, grinning devilishly. Montana and Sawyer looked at each other, and Montana felt her face splitting into a smile, too.

Without another word, she walked back to the table, Sawyer close behind her.

"What's got you laughing so hard?" Montana asked Trace as she sat down.

Trace looked at Abby, who continued to grin. "Nothing appropriate to repeat."

Abby winked at Montana, and the server came over to take their orders.

Montana gave Sawyer another look, and he shrugged, implying that one scene didn't negate his feelings on the matter.

"As I was saying," Trace said, "That first night Cody and Tessa met, at the rodeo dance, I thought he was hooked. I thought there was no way he'd be able to resist getting her number, even though we'd agreed on a strict No-Lady Policy throughout the tour, which started the next day. And when we found out he wouldn't be able to resist spending time with her — because she was the reporter who'd be covering his entire three-month tour — I thought we were sunk. The situation had disaster written all over it."

"But it turned out better than you expected, didn't it?" Montana asked sweetly, earning her another glare from Sawyer.

"It did," Trace said. "As unromantic as I am, I can honestly say their meeting was the best thing that could have happened."

"I thought I was the only unromantic one around," Abby said. "It's so nice to be among my kind."

A look of surprise crossed Trace's face, but he recovered quickly and returned her smile. "And I thought we'd never have anything in common."

It was Abby who looked surprised, then, and she, too, grinned. "Same here. You just never know, right?"

"Right," Trace said, his tone thoughtful.

Montana shot another meaningful glance at Sawyer, who just rolled his eyes. She could practically hear his thoughts: *One thing in common doesn't erase all the ways they're at odds.*

From Montana's perspective, the rest of the evening went swimmingly. Sawyer loosened up, and the four of them chatted and laughed and shared stories for a solid two hours. It went so well, in fact, that Montana decided it would be the perfect time to break the big news to Trace.

CHAPTER EIGHTEEN

MONTANA DIDN'T SEEM to be reading the signs. Since the moment he and Trace arrived at the restaurant and saw Montana and Abby, his anger festered. Abby, Trace, and Montana acted like the meeting was a coincidence, but Sawyer knew better. She'd been behind the scenes, manipulating them all like unsuspecting puppets. He pictured her behind them, arms raised as she made the marionettes dance.

To be fair, Trace and Abby did seem to enjoy each other's company. Sawyer had thought about removing the steak knives from the table before they sat down, but fortunately, that hadn't been necessary.

Still, Sawyer's blood was pretty well boiling by the time they finished eating. He seemed to be the only one ready to hightail it out of there, because when Montana said, "Another round?" Abby and Trace said, "Sure!" before Sawyer could say, "I think we'd better get home."

They'd gotten through an entire meal without anyone wielding a steak knife as a weapon *and* without anyone slipping up and saying something about Sunset Valley, to Sawyer's great relief. But thanks to Montana, they'd now be spending even longer around the same table.

Sawyer groaned, inwardly. The server brought out their drinks.

"I think we can all agree we're surprised at how well tonight is going," Montana said, lifting her wine glass. "Actually, I'm not that surprised. I really love the two of you." She pointed at Trace and then Abby. "And I knew it was only a matter of time until you learned to like each other. At the very least."

Sawyer didn't miss the glance Abby and Trace exchanged. Was there something there? Or were they just sharing a moment, silently agreeing that Montana's matchmaking skills were less than stellar?

"I agree," Abby said. "This has been a very nice evening."

It looked like she might have more to say, but she pressed her lips together and took a drink. Trace nodded. Because it was obvious everyone was waiting for him to say something, he finally spoke. "I agree. This is the first time we've been in a social setting and Abby hasn't put up a forcefield between us."

"Me?!" Abby said, her cheeks immediately going rosy. "That was a forcefield of self-protection! From the fireballs you shoot at me every time we're in the same space!"

I knew it, Montana thought.

Sawyer held up his hands. "Okay, okay, kids. We were just talking about how well the evening was going. Can we keep things civil?"

Trace laughed. "I was just trying to get under her skin."

"And since the evening has gone so well," Montana said, shooting Trace a dark look, "I thought this would be the perfect time to share our big news."

Oh, no.

Was Montana about to say what Sawyer thought she was? How could she? She'd put the ball in his court, told him it was up to him to tell Trace. She wouldn't … would she?

He tried to get her attention, to capture it with his fierce energy. She studiously ignored him. Sawyer looked at Abby and saw that she, too, tried to get Montana's attention. But Montana only had eyes for Trace. On reflex, Sawyer kicked at the space where he imagined Montana's foot would be.

"Ouch!" Trace said, loudly enough for the people around them to turn and stare. "What did you do that for?"

"Sorry, man. Restless leg syndrome."

Trace leaned down and rubbed his shin. That, at least, got Montana's attention. She looked at Sawyer, eyebrows raised. He knew exactly what she was thinking: *What? You wouldn't tell him, so I have to.*

"What Montana's trying to say is —" he started. She cut him off.

"What I'm trying to say is that Sawyer and I are both buying property. We're both building houses."

Trace smiled. Abby tried to make herself invisible, looking down at her lap, shrinking back into her chair.

"That's great," Trace said. He turned to Sawyer. "So you're moving out?"

If Sawyer wasn't mistaken, there was panic in Trace's voice.

"Just next door."

Sawyer watched as the realization dawned. He looked at Montana, who nodded (with less resolve than she'd started the conversation with), and then at Abby, whose steady gaze met his.

"You're buying one of Abby's properties."

His voice sounded calm, but Sawyer knew what bubbled beneath the surface.

"Two, actually," Montana said. "One each."

"You knew about this?" he asked Abby, who simply said, "It wasn't my news to tell."

"How long?" Trace asked.

"Well, it's going to be a bit," Montana said. "Since we're still waiting on all the permits."

"No," Trace said. "I mean, how long have the three of you been keeping this secret?"

"Few weeks," Sawyer said, feeling like he should take some of the heat.

Trace shook his head. He gave Montana and Sawyer one more glare before folding his napkin and setting it on his plate. He got up and walked out of the restaurant without another word.

For a moment, the three of them sat at the table in stunned silence.

"Did you plan that?" Abby asked Montana.

"I mean—"

"She planned it," Sawyer said, his voice vicious. "She planned it, but didn't tell us."

Neither woman spoke, and that infuriated Sawyer even more. At the same time, he realized that if he had just told the group when he agreed to — at dinner the other night — Montana wouldn't have felt like she had to take matters into her own hands.

If he had been man enough to tell his friends the truth, and to stand up for himself and the new life he was so excited to build, Montana would not have felt like she had to step in.

Maybe, all those years ago, his parents were right. Sawyer wasn't man enough for Montana. It had nothing to do with college, a degree, or an income. It had everything to do with who he was. He wasn't strong enough to stand beside her and fight for their dream.

In the fraction of a second it took Sawyer to process all those thoughts, Abby had come to a decision, as well. "I'll talk to him," she said.

Montana set down her napkin, as if to follow Abby, but Abby waved her off. "Better me than you."

Montana settled back into her chair, looked strangely resigned, and looked at Sawyer expectantly.

"Montana," he started.

"I owe you an apology," she said. "I know you weren't ready to tell Trace, and I just blurted it out. Sawyer, I *had* to —"

"No," he said. "*I* owe *you* an apology. A decade ago, when you were ready to build your life, I wasn't. My parents had it right. Well, mostly. I'm just not enough for you, Montana. I thought I was, but I'm not. You go through life with so much confidence. You were afraid to tell Trace, but you were set on doing it, anyway. I was afraid, and I let fear stop me. You deserve more than that. All this time that we've been talking about our properties, I had a bigger dream for us. I dreamed that we would scrap the two-lot idea, and combine and do this together. But I was too afraid to bring it up. I thought you would turn me down, because you wanted your own place so badly."

"That's all I want, too," she said. "And I was just trying to help you, by telling Trace tonight. I understand that you're scared. Things are different between Trace and I than they are between the two of you. I figured it might hurt him less if it was coming from me."

Sawyer shook his head. "I appreciate your attempt. But the fact is, if we stay together, I'll always hold you back. I'll always feel like I'm not quite good enough for you. You deserve more than that. I just can't do this anymore."

Sick to his stomach, Sawyer stood up. His napkin fell to the ground, but he didn't pick it up. He walked out, keeping his chin up until he got to his truck. Abby and Trace were nowhere to be seen, so Sawyer got in his truck and drove away. He'd leave Montana to deal with that mess.

———

Montana

ALONE AT THE TABLE, Montana blinked back tears. That was stupid. She didn't have to tell Trace right then, did she? She hated herself for trying so hard to make a point. She'd hurt not just Trace, but Sawyer and Abby, too.

She'd hurt herself worst of all. Because Sawyer had just ended things, and there wasn't any coming back from it. Their relationship had been so fragile, and her stubbornness obliterated it.

She paid the bill, leaving a generous tip with the hope that their server, at least, would end the evening on a happy note. After picking up Sawyer's napkin, she folded it into hers, and left them on the table.

Sawyer's perspective was all wrong, she thought as she made her way through the restaurant. It wasn't that he wasn't good enough for her. It wasn't that he was inadequate. It was that Montana always had to have everything her way, on her timeline. Why? Because she was afraid that *she* wasn't enough.

Hadn't she proposed because she was afraid Sawyer wouldn't? Hadn't she avoided asking him if they could share a single property because she was afraid he wouldn't want to? Hadn't she tried to set up Abby and Trace because she was afraid that if she didn't, she'd miss out on the chance to say she had?

Because of her fear, she rarely left the space in their relationship for Sawyer to take action. So, she moved fast. That didn't mean everyone else had to move fast, as well. She was the one who needed to slow down.

Each time she acted out of fear, she drove Sawyer further away.

She pushed open the restaurant doors and saw right away that Sawyer's truck was no longer in the parking lot. A block down, she saw Trace and Abby getting into a taxi together. Under any other circumstances, she would congratulate herself on a matchmaking job well done. But that night, she couldn't do anything but chastise herself. Wallowing in misery, she got in her car and drove home.

She cried all the way home, vowing it was the last time she'd ever cry over Sawyer. A girl couldn't cry over a man she wasn't smart enough to hold onto.

CHAPTER NINETEEN

Montana

ALMOST AS SOON AS Montana started driving, her phone rang. Tessa's name showed up on the screen, and despite the promise she'd just made herself, Montana felt her throat tighten when she answered.

"What are you doing?" Tessa asked.

Montana took a deep breath. "Driving." Good. Her voice sounded strong and certain.

"Where are you going?"

"Home."

"From where?"

Oh. Montana could tell what was happening. Sawyer must have called Cody, who told Tessa. And here they were.

"I guess you already heard," Montana said. "Sawyer and I are over. For real this time."

"Want company?"

Montana glanced at her puppy and then at the scene before her, which, thanks to a sheen of tears, was now a kaleidoscope of lights. "Well, I do have Cash."

Tessa chuckled. "Do you want *human* company?"

This was one of the things Montana loved best about Tessa. No questions — well, after the initial ones — just an offer of friendship.

"I wouldn't turn down a girls' night."

"Okay. I'll be there in twenty minutes. But fair warning: I'm not changing out of my sweatpants."

True to her word, Tessa knocked on Montana's apartment door twenty minutes later, a bottle of wine in one hand and a plate of brownies in the other. She held them out in front of her, an offering.

"You're the best," Montana said. "Seriously."

"This is only half the brownies," Tessa said. "I'd just put them in the oven when Sawyer called. Had to leave some with Cody."

"You're still the best."

As they walked into the kitchen, Tessa said, "I don't know if I ever thanked you properly for coming to my rescue that morning in the RV, a few months ago. Remember that?"

"The morning after Cody broke things off because he thought you were in cahoots with that terrible reporter? On a mission to destroy him?"

"That's the morning, yes. You showed up with coffee and listened to my tale of woe. Now I'm here to do the same thing for you. Want to talk about it?"

Tessa was already pulling wine glasses out of the cupboard, and Montana uncorked the bottle. Even at the sounds of the cork leaving the bottle and the wine going into the glasses, Montana felt her shoulders relax.

"Not that much to talk about, really. Every time it happens, I feel like, 'Well, it's been a long time coming.' I thought things were different this time. But I guess we really need to call it quits. For real."

"What even *happened*?" Tessa wanted to know. "It seemed like you guys were getting along so well."

"You know," Montana said, her voice thoughtful, "it was the first time we really pursued something together. Only, we started out separate. Separate lots, separate houses, separate dreams. Each of us was pursuing a life separate from the other."

"Yes, but in the same place. Right?"

Montana picked up her wine glass. "In the same place, but two different places."

"I see." Tessa frowned.

"Anyway." Montana was eager to change the subject. "Cheers to another ending. I guess."

"And a new beginning?" Tessa said.

"*Your* new beginning. Let's drink to your wedding."

They clinked glasses.

The two of them settled on Montana's tiny deck, with Cash at their feet. Apparently, his roughhousing with Dolly had worn him out pretty good, because once he flopped onto his side, he didn't stir, except for the occasional dream-induced snuffle or half-bark.

"I'll bet you're looking forward to the big day." It was nice to talk about something other than Sawyer.

"Yes," Tessa said. "I'm a little nervous about how everything will turn out. I feel like I'm the new girl in town, you know? And we all know there's a lady or two who would love to be in my place."

"True," Montana said. "But there's only one lady who Cody wants in your place, and that's you. So who cares what the rest of them think?"

"Good point. What I'm really looking forward to is the honeymoon. I haven't been to very many places, and I've never been anywhere tropical. Hawaii is going to be amazing."

"Take me with you," Montana said. "I might just fit in your suitcase." Tessa smiled, and Montana said, "On second thought, never mind. I don't want to have to listen to all your newlywed lovemaking."

Tessa wiggled her eyebrows and Montana laughed. It felt so good to be there, like that, just the girls. They talked for another hour or so, reminiscing about their days living in the RV during the rodeo tour, talking about work, and discussing Abby and Trace.

"What I haven't had the chance to tell you is that the two of them acted like old friends this evening. Abby and I ran into Trace and Sawyer at the Steakout —"

"What a coincidence," Tessa said, her tone dry.

"Wait, what was that?" Montana said. "I figured Sawyer already ratted me out for arranging for all four of us to meet there. I suggested Sawyer and Trace go —"

"For the fish fry?"

"For the fish fry. And then I invited Abby to join me there, too. And we just happened to run into each other."

"I see."

"Wait, what do you mean, 'I see'?"

For the first time, Montana started to question her decision. Maybe she shouldn't have arranged that meet-up. If Tessa was saying, "I see," in that tone, maybe Tessa thought it was a bad idea, too. And if Tessa thought Montana had gone too far, well then, maybe she had.

She wrinkled her nose. "Think I went too far?"

"I mean, it sounds like they got along well. So, maybe you were right all along. But sometimes, it does seem like you can't quite pull your claws out of an idea after you've committed to it. You know? You're like that kitten who gets so excited, but then your toenail gets stuck in a piece of fabric. And you can't get it out."

Come to think of it, that's exactly what Montana was like. And, come to think of *that*, maybe that's what went wrong with her idea to propose to Sawyer, all those years ago. At the time, she thought it would be so cute to move away with her fiancé. Her betrothed. Imagine how fun it would be to go off to college and play house together. And when he didn't see her vision through the same lens, she couldn't let it go. Her claw was stuck in that idea, exactly as she'd dreamed it up.

Tessa's eyes narrowed as she looked at Montana. "What's going on in that head of yours? I can really see the wheels turning."

Suddenly, Montana was exhausted. She rubbed her eyes.

"I hope I didn't offend you," Tessa said, her words coming fast.

"No, no," Montana said. "You've just given me some food for thought. I never considered my relationship with Sawyer that way. But you really put it in perspective. I don't know if I'm quite ready to talk about it. Let's talk about something else."

SAWYER

ON THE FINAL work day before the wedding, the whole group gathered at the Davises' house. Although Sawyer set out with the intention of pretending Montana wasn't there — in fact, pretending she didn't even *exist* — he couldn't keep his eyes off her. She had taken a note from Abby's book and was wearing jeans and work boots with a snug white tank top. The jeans hugged her curves perfectly, and he couldn't stop picturing himself running a hand along her bottom every time his eyes happened to land there (which was often).

Her skin, tanned from all the summer sun exposure, gleamed. She wore her hair in two long braids, just like she used to when they were teenagers. He remembered wrapping them around his hands as he kissed her, winding them up until his knuckles rested just underneath her chin.

As always, Trace was in charge. Clipboard in hand, eyebrows closer together than usual, he barked out a bullet list of items they needed to complete that day. Sawyer knew he had to get Trace alone, so he could apologize, but the guy wouldn't even make eye contact.

"Set up the chairs for the ceremony and reception. Mow the grass around the ceremony and reception areas. Finish hanging the string lights. Set up all the tables for dinner."

While Trace kept reading, Sawyer let his attention drift back to Montana. She and Abby stood side by side, in the shade against the wall of the Davises' house. Their shoulders touched, and Sawyer knew Montana was leaning on Abby — figuratively and literally — for support. He could only imagine how bittersweet this experience was for her. She'd always wanted to get married, have a bunch of kids, a couple of dogs, a flock of chickens, and a big garden.

They'd almost had that, together. Until he'd gone and ruined it, again.

Now, Tessa was on her way to having it. And while no one had cheered on Tessa and Cody's relationship more than Montana, he could see the heartache in her eyes every time she thought no one was looking.

Trace finally stopped rattling off the items on his list, and Abby asked, "Is that all?"

Everyone laughed, and Abby looked at her watch and back at Trace. "You have high expectations, sir."

"I do," he said.

There was something in his tone … Sawyer couldn't quite place it. Surprisingly, whatever it was, it wasn't unfriendly.

"Tessa and I will start working on the chairs," Cody said, "if you want to mow the grass, Trace, since I know how much you love that ride-on mower. Abby, I think you said you had a few more steps to finish the arbor, right? And that leaves —"

Sawyer started to groan, but managed to catch himself before anyone else heard it. "That leaves me and Montana."

Montana didn't look at Sawyer. She stared hard at Cody. "What's our job?"

Sawyer could tell she was doing her best to infuse her voice with cheerfulness. He could also tell no one really bought it.

"Oh! Could you guys finish stringing the lights? I think we've got the trees pretty much done. Tessa just wanted some lights zigzagged over the dance floor. Isn't that right, Tess?"

"Yeah," she said. "But I can help Montana with that if you two want to set up chairs."

"No, no," Sawyer said. "No need. Montana and I can act like civilized adults. You guys are going to be married in a week. Now's the time to really start honing your teamwork."

Although Montana had hidden all her emotions up to that point, Sawyer didn't miss the giant sigh she heaved before she said, "That's right. Sawyer and I can handle the lights."

With that, everyone split up, scattering like billiards balls to leave the two of them alone.

"The lights are in the —"

"I know where they are." Montana was already headed for the shed. He had to jog a few steps to catch up with her. He knew better than to try to start a conversation. Small talk was absolutely the worst thing he could try to melt some of the ice. So, he simply took the box of lights Montana handed him and followed her back over to the dance floor. They set the boxes on the table the DJ would use.

"I think we should —" Montana said at the same time as Sawyer said, "What do you think about —"

Damn. Why did this have to be so awkward? Sawyer should've waited to break things off until after the wedding. That would've led to even more heartache, for both of them. Walking up the aisle arm in arm with Montana, dancing with her at the reception, making toasts together.

It would only remind him that what they had couldn't last. That they would never be the bride and groom.

No matter how hard he tried, Sawyer would never be quite enough for Montana. Better to endure these awkward days leading up to the wedding than to spend the festivities feeling gloomy.

"What were you going to say?" Montana asked, interrupting his visions of a depressing ceremony.

"Oh, I was just going to say, what if we unboxed a few strands, and then hook them together into one long strand, so we don't have to keep stopping to open boxes?"

"Sounds good. That's what I was thinking, too."

If nothing else, they worked so well together as a team. They often had similar ideas. Within a couple of minutes, they settled into an easy rhythm. Which meant they didn't have to speak much at all. They even skipped pleasantries like, "Here you go," and, "Thank you."

They just worked, steadily, seamlessly. It was the perfect example of what they could do together. Why couldn't they do it in their relationship? They were the first ones done with their job. Normally, he'd offer her congratulations and a high-five. But that day, he just headed to the gathering spot and got a drink of water. Montana did the same.

Instead of sitting there in awkward silence, Sawyer decided it was a good a time as any to make things right with Trace.

Finding him was easy. The ride-on mower hummed from the other side of the grass field. Gathering the courage to flag him down was a little more difficult, but Sawyer managed. Instead of walking over, Trace pointed the mower toward Sawyer and drove. Slowly ... stretching out the anticipation, letting Sawyer steep in fear.

After a long time, the mower came to rest next to Sawyer. "Yes?" Trace said.

Still icy.

"I owe you an apology, man," Sawyer said, getting right to the point. "I am sorry. Really sorry. I should have told you from the get-go. Not only about buying from Abby, but about buying at all. I was scared, and I wasn't man enough to face disappointing you."

Trace nodded. "Not to be all emotional, but it hurt. I wish you had trusted me."

"Me, too," Sawyer said. "It would have been even more exciting if I could have talked to you and Cody about it."

"Although, the way I was acting, you were probably thinking I'd handle the news like a real jerk."

"Truth," Sawyer said. "But still. You would have gotten over it."

"Eventually," they both said.

"Look, man," Trace said. "I'm sorry, too. Okay? For being such a jerk you didn't feel like you could tell me."

"Apology accepted," Sawyer said.

With that, Trace jumped off the mower and hugged Sawyer tight.

———

Montana

IF THE WHOLE WORKDAY — and a rushed apology to Trace halfway through — wasn't awkward enough, the rehearsal dinner was even more so. Montana dreaded playing her role as Sawyer's other half. But she vowed to put on a happy face. She wouldn't let her personal crisis interfere with the excitement of her best friend's big day.

There had been some discussion about whether Sawyer and Montana should be paired up. In the end, Tessa and Cody decided that's what they wanted. So, there they stood, at the end of the aisle, about to rehearse for the ceremony.

Annie, back from New York, was officiating. She stood at the other end of the aisle, her black binder in her hands. Abby and Trace would walk up first. Even in her less-than-stellar mood, the way Abby and Trace smiled at each other before proceeding warmed Montana's heart. That was something.

As Tessa had instructed her to do, Montana slipped her arm through Sawyer's just as Trace and Abby passed the front row of chairs. Why did she still feel a surge of sexual energy as her fingers wrapped around his bicep? Why did she still wish the two of them were rehearsing for their own wedding?

She *had* to give up on that vision. Quite suddenly, she was blinking back tears. Fortunately, Sawyer stared straight ahead, obviously making a point of not looking at her. Montana forced herself to smile. She'd once heard that smiling released endorphins, feel-good chemicals. Then, she madly started doing her multiplication tables. She'd also heard that doing some sort of rational task would make the emotions subside. These two strategies seemed to work: by the time she and Sawyer reached the arbor and went their separate ways, her eyes were dry.

At least if she cried during the ceremony, everyone would think she was crying tears of happiness. Which she would be. Of course she would. But there might be a tear or two of sadness mixed in there. Tessa, already glowing, came up the aisle next. Her dad walked next to her, smiling with so much pride, Montana thought her heart might burst.

"Once you get to the end of the aisle, I'll say a few things," Annie said. "And that's when Cody will take Tessa's hand. And then,

George, you can sit down in the front row, and then the ceremony will begin."

"So when do I get to kiss her?" Cody said.

Everyone laughed.

"You can kiss her right now, if you like," Annie said. "But please, keep it PG."

Cody wrapped his arms around Tessa's waist and slowly tipped her back in a dip, kissing her all the while. Trace and Sawyer whooped and hollered, and then everyone, even Montana, was clapping and laughing.

At long last, Cody ended the kiss, righting himself and Tessa, and then giving her one more peck on the lips.

"Ew," Annie said, wrinkling her nose. "Now that *that's* over, I'll present you as Mr. and Mrs. Cody and Tessa Davis, and the two of you will walk back down the aisle."

The procession happened again, in reverse. This time, when Montana put her arm through Sawyer's, she managed not to feel anything. By the time they were seated at the table at the restaurant thirty minutes later, she had her emotions in check.

She didn't notice the way his eyes sparkled when he laughed at something Trace said, or the way his voice sounded, deep and gravelly, when he serenaded Cody and Tessa with his favorite country love song. No, she didn't notice, and she definitely didn't feel the cracks in her heart becoming even bigger.

CHAPTER TWENTY

Montana

FOR THE MINT Creek Ranch women, the Kincaid-Davis wedding would be the highlight of the year. They'd planned to spend the night together at the hotel Saint Michael, where Tessa was staying when she first met Cody. Montana, Abby, and Annie put together a special basket of goodies for their slumber party: nail polish, sparkling water, and snacks, along with a couple of movies, celebrity gossip magazines, and a bottle of wine they could all share between them.

The hotel was old-fashioned, but the modern amenities in the top-floor suite were nothing to sneeze at. When they all walked in together, Tessa gasped. "This is magical! So far beyond anything I ever imagined for myself on my wedding day."

Montana had to agree that the place was really special. A wide window overlooked the Courthouse Plaza, where the trees leafed out in all their summer glory, providing a shady canopy for the people enjoying the lawn. A fluffy white comforter covered the king size bed. Through double doors, a second room held two queen size beds. A small living area sat off to one side, complete with a dining table and kitchenette.

"If I wasn't building a house, I would live here," Montana said.

It was an innocent comment. She really *could* live there, in luxury.

She could slip between the one-million-thread-count sheets every night, lay her head on the down pillows.

But she realized too late that she had just spilled her own secret.

The room went silent. Montana had told Tessa about the new house on the way home from wedding dress shopping ... but Annie didn't know. At least, not until that very moment.

This would be a disaster. Annie would feel so torn. On one hand, she'd feel obligated to tell Cody and Trace, knowing Trace's beef with Abby. On the other hand, she'd feel obligated to keep Montana's secret.

Montana's nerves went on high alert as she waited for Annie's reaction. Was it possible her comment would slip under the radar? Annie could be distracted, thinking about her role in the ceremony the next day.

While Montana's mind searched frantically for a subject change, Abby seemed occupied with the minibar.

Thankfully, Tessa recovered quickly and changed the subject: "This is going to be so much fun! Thank you guys so much for sleeping over with me. I'm pretty nervous about tomorrow, so it'll be nice to get some girl time."

Annie closed the minibar and turned around. "Why are you nervous?" she asked, a wicked gleam in her eye. "Isn't marrying my brother going to be the best day of your life? Or are you now terrified to join the Davis family?"

"No, no! It's not that. It's just, all those eyes on Cody and me. I'm used to being the one asking questions, not the one center stage."

Abby sighed and flung herself backward onto the bed. "Exactly why I'm never getting married. At least, one of the reasons. It's going to be such a special day, Tessa. Just remember, it's an open bar. By the end of the night, no one will remember anything you say or do."

"Probably true," Tessa said. "I'm getting hungry, are you guys?"

They ordered room service and lounged on the giant bed, talking, while they waited for it. While they did, Montana's mind wandered. She wondered what her own wedding would be like. Would they all get together the night before? She thought she would like that. That is, if she ever had a wedding.

"So which song are you and Cody using for your first dance?"

"It's that 'Last First Dance' song," Tessa said.

"Oh, I love that one!" Abby said. "One of my favorites."

At it again, Montana thought about which song she'd choose for her first dance with her husband.

When a knock at the door interrupted her, she hopped up to answer it, relief propelling her forward. She really had to stop thinking about her wedding. It wasn't going to happen, no matter how much she wanted it.

———

WHEN TESSA'S alarm went off the next morning, a collective swell of energy rose. *Wedding day.*

Montana could feel it, zipping around the room, thrumming through her body, straight to the tips of her fingers and toes. Any residual sadness she felt over the end of her relationship with Sawyer was gone (or, at least, in hiding for the moment).

A wedding day was for joy, and only joy.

She got out of her bed and went over to sit next to Tessa on hers. Within a couple of minutes, Abby joined them, while Annie went to work brewing coffee.

"It's the big day," Montana said.

Tessa stretched, arms in the air. "I can't believe it. Not that we had a particularly long engagement or anything, but still. This thing we've been thinking about, talking about, planning for … it's finally here. I don't know what we're going to do when it's all over."

Abby winked at her. "Oh, I think you'll find some ways to keep yourself busy."

The four of them ate breakfast in their pajamas, cross-legged on the bed.

While they devoured the quiche and muffins and fruit, Annie went through the list of everything they had to do that day: put up the flowers and decorations at the Davises', get their hair and makeup done, and finish working on the wedding favors.

A few minutes later when Montana walked out to her car to get the supplies for the favors, she could feel the storm building. The forecast called for a hot day — with only a thirty percent chance for a monsoon storm — but Montana had always considered her body kind of a human barometer, and she could feel the air pressure. The forecast said rain was unlikely, but everyone knew a monsoon storm could blow up out of a clear blue sky within mere minutes.

It was early September, and Tessa and Cody had known when choosing their wedding date that monsoon season would be in full swing for a couple more weeks. The air was already sticky despite the early hour, and when Montana opened her car door, heat waves rushed out.

She pulled out the pallet of cacti in their mini terra cotta pots and shut the door. Maybe she was just imagining an impending storm, she told herself. She shook off the feeling of doom and went back into the hotel.

A half-hour later, the women, dressed and caffeinated, headed over to the Davis home to begin setting up.

Dana, the florist, was already there, unloading buckets and buckets of flowers. Cody's mom, Elaine, and Tessa's mom, Linda, carried armfuls of table linens from the back of the house. While the two of them spread tablecloths, Abby tightened all the screws on the arbor, and Tessa and Montana unfolded chairs.

"It's not going to rain today, right?" Tessa said as they worked. "I mean, a little rain would be okay. But in the summer, you never get a *little* rain."

Although Montana wanted to reassure Tessa that the weather would be perfect, her inner barometer still said the pressure was rising. The best she could offer was, "No promises. If there *is* a storm, maybe it will just zip right around us."

"You think it's going to rain, don't you?" Tessa said.

Montana kept her eyes and hands busy arranging the flowers. "I don't know," she said. "But even if it does, you can still get married. No one ever said a couple can't get married in the rain."

Tessa sighed. "I know. But isn't rain on your wedding day a bad omen or something?"

At that, Montana did look at Tessa. "You listen to me, Tessa Kincaid. Rain brings life. In the desert, rain is *never* a bad omen. I mean, it might come with bad timing. But it's never a bad omen."

Tessa nodded, sighed again. "Okay. You're right. Thank you."

For the next few minutes, they didn't speak. Chairs unfolded, the two of them moved on to centerpieces. The florist had set them all on one table, so each carrying one vase at a time, Tessa and Montana completed the table décor. Montana loved the flowers Tessa had chosen: pastels and creams and whites.

Elaine and Linda finished with the tablecloths and headed back to the house. "Those look beautiful, girls," Elaine said as they passed.

"They do," Linda said. "This is all turning out just beautifully."

By then, Abby and Annie were inside, cooking the big Italian dinner Tessa and Cody had decided on. The scent of spaghetti sauce — spicy meat, plenty of garlic, and ripe tomatoes — drifted down from the kitchen.

Montana inhaled deeply. "I'm getting hungry already."

Tessa laughed. "Aren't you always?"

Vases placed, Montana and Tessa began the next step: affixing a bouquet to the chair that would sit at the end of each row during the ceremony. They cut lengths of white and pink ribbon and tied the bouquets on with tidy box knots.

"This is just perfect," Montana said.

"I know, I love it," Tessa said. "It's exactly what I pictured."

Montana checked her watch. "Two hours till go time. Aren't we supposed to meet the photographer and do hair and makeup?"

"Yep, it is. Shall we?"

Tessa and Montana stood, arms crossed, surveying the scene before them.

"It's perfect," Montana said.

Tessa raised her hand for a high-five. "We did good."

———

MONTANA SENSED it the instant she walked back out to the ceremony site an hour later, her hair up and makeup on: the storm had arrived. A quick glance upward revealed her intuition was right. The leading edge of the storm — a heavy, dark gray cloud and a wall of rain beneath it — moved closer, and at that very moment, a strong gust of wind came through with so much force, Montana actually took a few steps back. Visions of storm-caused damage she'd witness over the years flashed through her mind: a flooded creek rushing along, carrying a car with it. A twelve-foot trampoline bounding through a yard. Patio furniture flipped upside down.

This kind of storm, the kind that moved in with almost no warning, hit hard and fast, and did lots of damage.

As Montana surveyed. the scene before her, she imagined what was coming. The storm would toss aside all those vases on the tables, sending them to the ground to shatter. A few fat drops plopped onto the crushed granite where she stood. *Plop. Plop. Plop.* One landed on her head, going straight through her hair to her scalp. She shivered, realizing that she'd better cover up the fancy 'do she'd just paid big bucks for. There was only so much hairspray could do against a desert monsoon storm.

The wind would tip over the tables and chairs, destroying all the work they'd done this morning. Another gust of air, this one colder, whipped through. The tulle strung across the backs of the chairs lifted up, threatening to detach in the wind. The tablecloths ruffled.

And just like that, the storm was in full force. The wind seemed to be coming from every direction. The raindrops no longer plopped slowly. No, they roared down, so loud Montana fought the urge to cover her ears. But she had to do *something* to stop the impending disaster. Although, just like the hairspray, she could only do so much against nature.

A movement at the other side of the ceremony area caught her eye. It was Sawyer, emerging from the office building attached to the barn, where the men were getting ready. His gaze locked onto hers. For a fraction of an instant, he grinned. His expression turned serious so quickly, Montana thought maybe she'd imagined the smile. But no, it was there. He'd smiled at her.

And she knew they were both thinking of the same thing. They were remembering a once-in-a-lifetime moment they'd always agreed signified the depth of their love.

One beautiful summer morning between their sophomore and junior years, they planned to ride their horses to the granite dells, an area where suede-colored boulders rose up in clumps, as if some ancient god had spent hours or days or eons rolling and stacking them. Sometimes, Montana swore she could see a fingerprint on a boulder's surface.

Montana had looked forward to that day since earlier in the week when the professor for her community college photography class assigned students to photograph their favorite places in different light. She couldn't wait. But even more than the photography, Montana looked forward to being out in nature with Sawyer.

Tucked away amongst the boulders, innumerable crevices and nooks provided perfect locations for making love. And where they were going, it was unlikely they'd be disturbed. She spent the days leading up to that weekend imagining all the ways she could please Sawyer. Over and over, she pictured him, his shirt unbuttoned, his jeans pulled down to reveal the lower half she loved so much.

That morning, the two of them woke before sunrise, so she could capture the early-morning light. It only made sense that she was more than a little distracted. The dark didn't bother her; they rode with headlamps and flashlights fairly often. Besides, even though the sun hadn't peeked over the horizon just yet, the sky was already lightening, and within a few minutes, their eyes would adjust, and they'd be able to see just fine.

Sawyer insisted Montana lead the way, so he wouldn't be in front of her if she saw a scene she wanted to photograph.

"Also, I like the view from back here," he said, giving her a sexy smirk that reminded her of her secondary mission on the trip.

As they rode, the sky changed color, from inky black to dusky gray to dusty blue. Finally, the top edge of the sun peeked out above the horizon, and the sky turned lavender and then pink. A few times, Montana stopped her horse so she could take a picture. But when the light exploded, gilding the undersides of a few wispy clouds and turning the sky into a brilliant watercolor with so many shades of orange and red, Montana knew she had to dismount.

Her horse, Bright, used to this sort of thing, stood patiently. She didn't mind if Montana bumped up against her while looking through the lens. Behind her, Sawyer was silent. He knew better than to start a conversation. She must have pressed the shutter button about five hundred times in a five-minute span. She felt certain she had a sunrise image that would work for her assignment. When she finally lowered her camera, Sawyer spoke.

"Quite a view."

"I know," Montana said, her voice dreamy and her eyes still on the sky.

"I love watching you work," he said.

And that was all it took. Two teenagers, hormones running rampant through their veins, out in their favorite part of nature. Sawyer dismounted, too, and in the next instant, they were kissing, bodies pressed together. Sawyer wrapped Montana's braids around his hands and tugged, pulling her chin back and exposing her throat. Then, his mouth was there, in that spot just underneath her ear. She shivered, even though the day was as warm as could be. Her hands found his belt buckle, loosened it, pulled down his zipper. His hands found her breasts, first through her shirt, and then underneath.

She gasped when she wrapped her hand around him. He was hard, ready. He moaned as she started to stroke him. They made their way across the trail, where Sawyer put Montana's back up against a slab of granite. Still kissing her, he unfastened her pants and tugged them down, all the way to her ankles. He lifted one of her knees up, so she straddled him, and he drove into her. She came instantly, and he followed.

And, at the same moment, a bolt of lightning and crack of thunder shook the very ground they stood on, just as the rain started to pour.

"Must be some lovemaking," Sawyer said, his mouth still on Montana's.

Laughing as they reassembled their clothes, they led their horses to shelter under an overhang in a nearby boulder and waited out the storm. Giddy and breathless, Montana and Sawyer kept looking at each other and laughing.

There was a photo shoot at high noon, and another at sunset. And there were plenty of places to make love in between.

CHAPTER TWENTY-ONE

BACK IN THE PRESENT, as a massive summer storm unleashed just before Tessa and Cody's wedding, Montana knew Sawyer was remembering that day, too.

She could feel him reminiscing right along with her. In fact, he reached down and adjusted his jeans. A little flame of satisfaction ignited in her belly, and she gave him a smug, knowing smile.

That's when the first few fat, plopping raindrops turned into a torrential downpour. On instinct, Montana touched her hair. Her focus shifted when a gust of wind lifted one of the round tables onto its side, throwing the centerpiece to the ground. Miraculously, the glass remained intact. The flowers scattered, and the table went spinning across the reception area.

She and Sawyer jumped into action at the same time, running after the wayward table. Sawyer, in the jeans, collared shirt, and vest he would wear for the wedding, made better time than Montana did in her long, flowing dress. He got there first and managed to stop the table from rolling. The tablecloth lay crumpled on the grass, stray flowers strewn across it, blotches of rainwater making dark stains in several places.

Montana collected the flowers and vase, and then picked up the tablecloth, thinking she'd put it back on the table.

While she was shaking it out, Sawyer yelled, "Don't bother! It's never going to get dry out here!"

He was right — and they had bigger problems. The wind blew another table onto its side. The chairs underneath caught it, but only for a moment. The next gust was powerful enough that the table toppled right over the chairs and then whirled away as if to join the first one. The rows of chairs on either side of the aisle, connected by the tulle Montana and Tessa fastened earlier, began to tip backwards. Sawyer ran after the second table, so Montana headed for the chairs. On her own, it was nearly impossible to right them one at a time, and literally impossible to stand up the entire row.

"I think this might be a two-person job!" Montana yelled just as lightning cracked overhead. Running full speed after the third table, Sawyer looked back over his shoulder and yelled, "What?"

A massive boom of thunder tore through the air.

If it were her own wedding, Montana might start laughing right about now. She'd throw up her hands and get married inside. But it was the wedding of two of her best friends. She had to fix this. It didn't have to be perfect, but darn it, it was going to be close. Another flash of lightning, and the accompanying thunder, almost simultaneously — which meant that lightning was *close*. Montana nearly jumped out of her skin.

Suddenly, Sawyer was beside her, his voice in her ear. "That was close."

Montana nodded. She was soaked. Rainwater ran down her scalp and neck and dripped off her fingers.

"We've got to fix this," she said, hearing the desperation in her own voice.

"We will," Sawyer said. "But we're never going to fix it if we get struck by lightning. I think we've got to go inside, wait this out. Then we'll come back."

"Tessa and Cody can't know." Even though he was behind her, and she couldn't see his face, Montana could sense that Sawyer thought this was another one of her big ideas. She could practically feel him inhaling, preparing to argue. But then, nothing. Except the pounding of the rain, against the ground, her head, her shoulders. She turned to look at him and saw that his mouth was set in a grim, determined line.

He gave a short nod before grabbing her hand and pulling her in through the Davises' kitchen door.

Once they were inside, and Sawyer got a good look at Montana, he inhaled sharply — and then stopped. It was too late. She could read him like a book.

My hair.

———

SAWYER

"OH NO!" she said, carefully running her fingertips over her hair. "Is it bad?"

"It is. It's trashed."

She grimaced, and he thought her hair looked as soggy as an old wet hen who didn't make it to the coop on time to beat the rain. Even then, she looked the most beautiful he'd ever seen her. He always liked it down anyway.

"I can tell it's bad," she said.

Another flash of lightning, and a roll of thunder that shook the kitchen window. That's when Sawyer noticed goosebumps all over Montana's skin.

"You're freezing."

He couldn't say what came over him, but he felt a fierce need to take care of her. He grabbed a kitchen towel and began to dry her off — arms, shoulders, upper back. Although he told himself his own goosebumps were the result of wearing wet clothes, he knew the truth: being in close proximity to Montana, so aware of her bare skin, he was unbelievably turned on. While the rain continued to hammer the roof, Sawyer continued to move the towel over Montana's arms. After a few more minutes, she said, "I think I'm good and dry now, thank you."

She took the towel from him, gently, and set it on the counter. "I'd better go see what I can do about this hair."

"And your makeup," Sawyer said. He used a thumb to wipe some mascara from under her left eye.

She nodded. "Thanks again. Hopefully by the time this rain stops, I'll be presentable."

"It's going to take a minute, I'm afraid," he said.

She smiled at him before heading through the kitchen to the room the women were using to get ready. And as he watched her walk away, his heart broke just a little bit more.

———

Montana

STILL BREATHLESS, Montana and Sawyer stood arm in arm at the end of the aisle. They'd accomplished a tremendous feat: as soon as the storm cleared out (as quickly as it had come in), they'd run outside and done the best they could to put the ceremony and reception site back together. It wasn't perfect. The storm had crushed a few flowers beyond repair and the tablecloths were still wet. But Montana doubted whether any of the guests could tell that just a few minutes ago, the site had been in shambles.

She gave Sawyer's arm a little squeeze, and he flexed his biceps, giving her hand a little squeeze in return. She giggled. Trace, who stood in front of Sawyer, his arm linked with Abby's, turned around to glare at Montana — a silent *shh*. She offered him a sweet smile. The music started. Trace and Abby began to walk.

Montana inhaled deeply and felt Sawyer do the same.

"Shall we?" he said.

She looked up at him, and what she saw in his eyes took her breath away. There was so much tenderness. And maybe even love. It wasn't the right kind of love, she reminded herself, but it was something, and it would have to do. Not for the first time that week, tears pressed against the backs of her eyelids.

She gave Sawyer a nod, and they began to walk up the aisle. It took everything she had not to look up at him as they did, but the last thing Montana wanted was to make a spectacle of herself at Tessa and Cody's wedding.

So she smiled, and made a point of smiling at the guests she recognized as they walked. There was Mama Martin from the llama farm, who'd done nothing to stop a llama from spitting on Tessa during her first visit. Montana wondered if Tessa knew she was here. There was the family from Bright Moon Ranch, and the other reporters from the *Daily Dispatch*. These were all the people Montana had always imagined would be at her own wedding one day.

It came time for Montana and Sawyer to part ways, and she took her spot next to Abby. The music fell silent. The air filled with suspense.

The Bridal March began to play. Tessa emerged from the back of the Davises' house, her father walking with her. Instantly, Montana's eyes started to sting. Again. Yes, she had been with Tessa all day. She'd seen every part of the transformation, from just-got-out-of-bed sleepy to dazzling bride, rotating in front of the mirror, wearing the lace-up spectacle of a dress they'd chosen. And yet, in that moment, she thought Tessa was probably the most beautiful sight she'd ever seen. She wished desperately for a tissue or handkerchief.

The guests shared a collective gasp, and Montana wasn't surprised. Tessa was always pretty. But, aside from the horrible pencil skirt outfits she wore when she first showed up in Prescott, none of them had ever seen her in anything other than slacks or jeans.

Montana glanced at Cody. She was jealous, not only because he'd thought ahead and had a tissue in his pocket, but also because of the way he looked at his bride as she approached. His expression radiated pure joy.

That's the right kind of love, Montana thought.

CHAPTER TWENTY-TWO

Sawyer

OF *COURSE* SAWYER looked at the bride. He knew as well as anyone that the bride's big entrance was The Number One Wedding Moment.

Tessa looked beautiful. Radiant. Stunning.

Sawyer thought back to the first time he saw her. The private investigator Trace hired to research Tessa — since she'd be covering Cody for the duration of his final rodeo tour — put together a packet that included Tessa's headshot. In the picture, she looked plain, bordering on homely. She wore some godawful noncolor and her hair looked droopy. A half-smile played on her lips, but her eyes didn't convey a trace of happiness.

It was no wonder that when the three of them — Sawyer, Trace, and Cody — saw Tessa at the rodeo dance they didn't recognize her as the reporter from the headshot. She'd come with Montana and was nothing short of drop-dead gorgeous. And the moment Cody laid eyes on her, he was a goner. Who would have imagined their story would take this path? If it were even possible, Tessa looked about one hundred times as beautiful on her wedding day as she did that night at the rodeo dance.

Still, Sawyer found his gaze drifting over to Montana. Every time he'd seen her that day, her beauty had stolen his breath: that morning when she'd arrived at the Davises' in her sweatpants; early that afternoon, when she snuck into the kitchen in her bathrobe for a snack; later, wet and bedraggled, her hair and makeup a mess. And standing next to the altar, put back together masterfully. If he didn't know she was a soggy mess an hour ago, he would never guess as much during the wedding. She was glowing.

The ceremony started. Annie, as the officiant, welcomed the guests.

"As you know, we've had beautiful weather today," she said. "I'm supposed to have you take your chairs over to the tables after the ceremony, but as soggy as the grass is, I'm not sure you'll be able to remove the chairs from the grass after sitting in them. We'll make this short."

Cody looked at his sister with pure adoration, and again, Sawyer found himself thinking about how life always worked out. Just a few months before, Cody and Annie hadn't been on speaking terms. Sawyer couldn't think of anyone better to pronounce Cody and Tessa a married couple.

For her part, Montana watched intently. This wedding was serious business. She had just risked life and limb to make it possible in the wake of that once-in-a-lifetime storm.

"Well, I'm off the hook," Annie was saying. "Since the two of you decided to write your own vows, you've made things easy on me. Tessa, would you like to go first?"

Tessa cleared her throat, took a few nervous steps in place.

Cody said, "Go on. Although I should have insisted on going first. You're the writer, and you're going to set the bar high."

Everyone chuckled, and Tessa cleared her throat again before speaking.

"Cody," she said. Her voice wobbled, and Sawyer felt his own throat getting a little tight. Again, he looked at Montana. This time, she was looking right back at him. They continued to look at each other while Tessa spoke, her voice gaining strength.

"The first time I saw you..." she paused, and Sawyer thought she'd forgotten what she was going to say. But then she laughed. "I can't really share the thoughts that went through my mind the first time I saw you. Let's just say I knew you were special. I've never met anyone who made me feel that way before. You were a stranger, but somehow, I felt like I'd known you forever. That is, until you discovered my true identity."

A few people laughed, sounding nervous. Then Cody flashed the grin that helped make him famous, and the laughter spread.

———

SAWYER COULDN'T EVEN LOOK Montana in the eye as the two of them linked arms to walk back up the aisle. He wished desperately that they didn't have to stand around for pictures.

Watching Cody and Tessa declare their love for each other was almost more than Sawyer could bear.

He was beyond happy for his best friend. At the same time, hearing Annie pronounce the couple husband and wife, hearing that declaration of impending happily ever after, broke Sawyer. He wanted that. And he wanted it with Montana.

When the two of them were out of the guests' sight, they released each other's arms. Sawyer thought Montana separated herself from him, as if the contact burned her skin.

She had made her way over to the bride and was hugging Tessa tightly. A tear made its way down her cheek. As she and Tessa broke apart, she wiped it off, laughing.

Sawyer went up to Cody, offering him yet another handshake. Then, he said, "Oh, what the hell," and pulled him in for a hug.

The photographer was there, capturing all of these moments, and all Sawyer could hope was that she wasn't capturing his heartbreak. He managed to plaster on his best Sawyer-Nelson smile for all the pictures: the whole wedding party together, the groomsmen lifting Tessa and her giant lacy wedding dress, the bridesmaids surrounding Tessa, gazing at her with adoration. And even though he forced himself to grin and bear it, Sawyer was relieved when the photographer cut the wedding party loose to take pictures of the newlyweds.

Montana grabbed Abby's arm and spirited her away, Sawyer assumed to the bar … which he thought was a good idea. He made eye contact with Trace and nodded in that direction, and they walked over.

"That was a really nice ceremony," Trace said, "but I'm so glad it's over. If I have to be paired up with Abby Flores for another moment, I'll —"

They'd reached the end of the line for the bar, and, as Sawyer suspected, Abby and Montana were already there. The bartender handed each of them a cocktail. Sawyer avoided eye contact as they turned around and walked past him, making their way to the table. Next to him, Trace hissed out a breath. "I don't know what it is about that woman, but she really gets to me."

"If I didn't know you better, man, I would say you've got the hots for her."

"Before today, I would've said you are full of it. Crazy as a soup sandwich. But now I've seen her in a dress. I've felt her skin on mine. And I don't know if those are things a man could soon forget."

Sawyer chuckled. "Who would've thought? A romance unfolding between Mint Creek Ranch's own Trace Walker and his arch nemesis, Abby Flores."

Trace shrugged, took a swig of his beer. Grinned at Sawyer.

Sawyer said, "Think you can get her to go home with you tonight?"

"Go home with me? Heck, I'd settle for a dance."

Sawyer let his mouth drop open and his eyes go round in exaggerated shock. "A dance? Well, our man Trace must think highly of Miss Flores. I'm willing to wager you can get her to dance with you. I mean, she's practically obligated, being your bridesmaid and everything."

Trace scoffed. "Don't let her hear you calling her *my* anything. She'll punch you right in the nose."

"Well, that might be true."

About fifteen minutes later, everyone was seated at the head table and dinner was served. Sawyer was grateful that Tessa had decided to have all the men on one side and all the women on the other. It meant Sawyer didn't have to sit next to Montana, breathe her scent, and wish he wasn't such an idiot. As they dug into the spaghetti he'd been smelling all day, Trace said, "So, you going to do your typical thing tonight, man?"

"What you mean?" Sawyer knew exactly what Trace meant, but it was safer to play dumb.

"You know what I mean."

Sawyer rolled his eyes, then grunted and took another big bite of spaghetti. Trace did the same. Instead of coming up with something clever to say, Sawyer surprised himself by speaking the pure, unfiltered truth. "I wish things were different."

He took a giant bite of garlic bread.

"If you mean you wish Montana had always been head-over-heels in love with you, then I don't know what you wish would be different, man, because she always has been, and still is."

Sawyer shook his head. He wished that were true. He wished Montana were truly head-over-heels in love with him. But how could she be?

Sawyer was relieved when Tessa stood up, microphone in hand. As she thanked everyone for coming, he got nervous. Soon, it would be his turn to speak. Sure enough, within what felt like a few seconds, people were clapping for Tessa. She was saying Montana's name, and Montana was standing up and taking the microphone from Tessa. Her hand was shaking. She took a deep breath, and the sound of her exhale was loud coming out of the speakers.

"For those of you who don't know, I saw her first."

The guests laughed, and Montana's shoulders relaxed just the tiniest bit.

"When I met Tessa at the *Daily Dispatch*, I knew she was special. She was a city girl, sure. But as soon as I took her to that rodeo dance, I realized it immediately: she was a country girl in a city girl's clothing. Which, thank goodness, we got rid of." As an aside, she mock-whispered to Tessa, "I burned those suits."

Tessa gasped, and everyone laughed again. Sawyer smiled. Montana was nailing this. And she was adorable.

"I'd be lying if I said I thought Tessa and Cody were headed to this moment. Actually, I thought they were headed for disaster. But this, this moment right here, it proves that when two people are meant to be together, love finds a way."

Sawyer could hear the emotion in her voice. He wondered if there was any small part of her that wanted love to find a way with the two of them. He did, with all of his being.

"I wanted to keep this speech simple, because more than anything, Cody and Tessa's love story proves that even when life seems complicated, the answer is simple. The answer is always love."

There was a collective, "Aw," from the guests. And then, more laughter. Sawyer found himself wiping a tear from under his eye, and then Montana was handing him the microphone. Once again, she avoided looking at him. He stood.

"Wow. Tough act to follow." A few people chuckled, probably just to humor him. Then, silence while everyone waited for him to speak.

"The first time I saw Cody and Tessa together, I thought to myself,

'Wow. I've never seen him look at a woman like that before.' He took one look at her, and it was like there was no one else there, to the general dismay of every woman who showed up there that night."

Good, more laughing. Maybe his little speech wouldn't be too much of a bust.

"He found out she was the reporter he'd been spending three months with." Another heavy silence.

"You should've seen his face." This time, laughter erupted. Sawyer laughed too, gave himself a moment. "I mean, he was thrilled. Trace and I both saw the excitement, right before he shut it down."

Trace whistled, to more laughter and some cheering.

"Then," Sawyer went on, "he was mad. But you know what? That proved that he saw the potential. He was mad, because he never felt that way about anyone before, and he thought she was off limits. But then, here she comes, being all professional and charming. And as they say, the rest is history. Although their relationship started in the most interesting of ways, and it's been the most interesting journey, it's been clear from the start that these two are a match made in heaven. So, without further ado, please join me in congratulating Mr. and Mrs. Cody and Tessa Davis."

Sawyer sank into his seat to a round of generous applause. He watched as Tessa and Cody kissed yet again. Then the music started, and he was out of the spotlight.

———

MONTANA

NOW THAT HER speech was over, all Montana had to do was have fun. She finished off the champagne from her toast and invited Abby to the dance floor. A few minutes later, when Tessa tapped her knife against her own champagne glass and waited for everyone to get quiet again, Montana felt butterflies flapping around in her stomach. She couldn't even say why.

The DJ's voice came over the speakers, then: "The newlyweds will now share their first dance."

Beaming, Tessa set down her glass and took Cody's hand. As they walked onto the dance floor, a few people whistled. Montana took a spot with the other guests to watch. The scene shimmered.

"For the next song," the DJ said, "the happy couple would like to invite their wedding party to join them on the dance floor."

The first notes of the song began to play. At the edge of the dance floor, Abby took Montana's hand, pulled her close and swayed in time to the music.

"Why don't you dance with Sawyer, and I'll dance with Trace?" Montana said.

"Psh," Abby said. "I would never get between you and Sawyer. Plus, it's been kind of fun hanging around with Trace today, me in my fancy dress and all."

"Ooh," Montana said. "Are you telling me you and Trace were actually experiencing some chemistry?"

Abby shivered. "You have to admit, he does look darn good in that outfit."

"Oh, you're right about that. And you look darn good in yours."

It was just one dance. Montana had danced with Sawyer countless times. It wouldn't do any harm to do so once more at Tessa's request. As Tessa and Cody's song ended and the next one began, Sawyer was there, swooping Montana into his arms in a big, romantic gesture that had her giggling. The silliness of it all, the over-acted romance, wasn't enough to dampen the flames of desire that sparked up when he touched her.

"Nice speech you gave tonight," he said to her. His voice, deep and scratchy, gave her a fresh round of chills.

"Same to you."

"Do you really believe it?" he asked.

"Which part?"

He paused, and in that space, Montana was keenly aware of his body against hers, the firmness of his muscles in his chest, the warmth of his hand on her bare back. Why did Tessa choose these low-cut dresses? His calloused thumb made circles at the lower edge of the fabric, the lowest part of her back. She'd be lying to herself if she said she wasn't imagining removing his clothes right there on the dance floor.

"The part where you said, 'love finds a way.'"

Oh. That. "Of course I meant it," she said.

Sawyer put his forehead on hers and looked into her eyes. "Then why doesn't it work for us?"

Montana's heart thundered in response to his question.

"What do you mean?" She knew exactly what he meant. But she wanted to hear him say it.

He closed his eyes now, and his voice was quiet when he spoke. "I just love you so damn much. But I feel like no matter what I do, I'm always screwing things up."

His voice sounded tight with emotion. Montana felt like crying, too. She ran her fingers through Sawyer's hair, interlaced them behind his neck.

"You're not," she said. "I am. I never leave space for you to do things. I always take over. I make you feel like you're screwing up, but it's really me."

"Because I never take action."

They could talk in circles all day, Montana thought. "We always find our way back to each other, though," she said, her voice practically a whisper.

"We do," Sawyer said. The song went on. Montana laid her head on Sawyer's chest. After a few seconds, he said, to "Do you remember that day you asked me to marry you?"

Montana froze, tilted her head back to look at Sawyer. "Obviously I do, you silly man. Sawyer Nelson, you know me well enough to know that was one of the defining moments of my life."

Even as she spoke the words, her entire body vibrated with emotion. It was probably some combination of anxiety (why was he bringing this up, now?), fresh anger, and lingering hurt. And maybe, if she were being honest with herself, the tiniest flicker of hope. When Sawyer put a little pressure on her waist to start her swaying again, she obliged, but only because she didn't want anyone to notice them frozen on the dance floor.

"I know," he said. I didn't mean to imply that you would forget. It's just — that probably wasn't the best way to start the conversation."

"What conversation?"

"Let me start over."

What is he getting at?

He took a deep breath. "Montana. I've never wanted anyone but you. Since I met you, you've been the only one for me. I know, you're thinking, 'What about that girl you went to prom with?' Or, 'What about that girl you dated while I was in college?' Well, you should know that every time I dated anyone else, all I could think about was you. Every woman I was even remotely interested in, I compared her to you. Did her hair smell as good as yours? Did she look at me the same way? Was her laugh as contagious? The answer in every case was no. Not a single woman has ever measured up to you."

Montana's heart once again hammered at her rib cage.

"I never told you this, but that day you asked me to marry you? My parents had just given me a big lecture on how I wasn't going to amount to anything. They wanted me to go to college. And, you know, really make something of myself. They wanted me to be an accountant, or a doctor. But all I've ever wanted to do was build my own ranch, from the ground up. With you."

Shock hit Montana like a blast of cold air. "Your parents said that to you? Why didn't you tell me?"

"At first, I was ashamed. As time went on, I realized that was their idea of a pep talk. They were trying to inspire me. Meanwhile, all I've wanted to do, my whole life, is to prove to my parents, to myself, to *you*, that I'm good enough for you. Except, instead of doing it, I spend all this time questioning whether I should."

"And I make things worse by taking over. My so-called 'vision' doesn't give you a chance to make your own. There's no reality where you're not good enough for me."

Sawyer nodded. "You know how it is. Certain ideas, certain thoughts, they just stick. Lately, I've come to realize that we both want the same things. We both want our own place. We both want rambunctious puppies. We both want to live in Sunset Valley."

"And we both want each other," Montana finished for him, her throat tight.

"And we both want each other," he echoed.

With that, he brought his mouth to hers. Everything else fell away, and Montana felt like it was just the two of them on the dance floor, just the two of them in that moment.

"Will you come with me?" Before Montana had time to answer, Sawyer had her by the hand and was leading her away from the dance floor, between the tables they'd set up only a couple of hours before, and back around to the front of the Davises' house.

"Where are we going?"

"You'll see."

He led her over to the golf cart and helped her tuck her dress around her legs so it wouldn't get caught under the tires. Then he got in and drove toward the pasture. Montana's mind flashed on the barn where they'd made love so many times. But that's not where they were going. Around the side of the barn, a giant old oak tree stretched its branches into the sky. A wooden swing hung there, as it had for years. It wasn't always the same swing. Tom Davis replaced the ropes and the board whenever they got old and damaged by the sun. All the kids had spent countless hours on that swing. While the others had gradually lost interest as they got older, this had always been a favorite spot for Montana and Sawyer. He parked the golf cart and came around to take Montana's hand. Fingers interlaced, they walked over to the swing.

"Sit," he told her, gesturing, palm up. She did as she was told.

"We'd better not spend long," she said. "Someone is sure to miss us."

"Yeah?" Sawyer said. "And so what if they do?"

Montana smiled. A wave of desire rushed through her body. She realized that she'd unconsciously begun swinging herself, pushing against the ground with the balls of her feet. Then, Sawyer knelt in front of her and the swing gently bumped against him. She thought he was going to kiss her, but he didn't. He looked at her for a long moment and then caressed her face. When he reached into his pocket, Montana could've sworn her heart stopped beating.

"I've dreamed of doing this for years," he said. "But, like I said, I never felt like I was worthy. I couldn't bring myself to believe that you would say 'yes.'"

"But I'd already asked you!" Montana was surprised to hear her voice was tight with emotion. Then she was laughing. "I can't believe you're saying this."

"I thought you were the one who got away. I pictured myself, a hundred years old, sitting on my porch swing, alone. Looking back and thinking, Montana's the one who got away."

He opened his hand and revealed a black velvet bag, closed with a satin drawstring. His hands shook as he opened it. He turned it upside down over his other hand, and a ring tumbled out.

Montana gasped.

"I bought it forever ago. I have planned so many times to give it to you. But always, I put it off. We'd fight over something stupid, or I'd see you dancing with some cowboy at the Watering Hole, or I'd get the sense that you're mad at me, even though we haven't spoken."

Tears flowed freely down Montana's cheeks. "We fight about the stupidest things, don't we?"

"We do," Sawyer said. "But I'm hoping this can be a new chapter. Where, instead of getting our feelings hurt because we're so afraid of getting our feelings hurt, we put all that energy into loving each other."

"I like that."

"So? What do you say? Will you marry me?"

"Absolutely I will."

Sawyer took the ring and slid it over Montana's finger. The stone sparkled in the moonlight.

"It fits perfectly."

"It ought to. I stole one of your other rings to make sure I got the right size."

Montana laughed, and kissed Sawyer long and deep.

CHAPTER TWENTY-THREE

SAWYER

FINALLY, after all the years that had passed, Sawyer and Montana would get to make their happily ever after.

They had a real, concrete plan, and were beginning to make it reality.

The two of them would consolidate. They would keep both pieces of land and build two houses: the model he'd chosen, for them and their dozen children to live in. Just a stone's throw from the main house, the cottage she'd chosen, which Montana would use as an office as she built her graphic design business.

Although she wanted to continue working at the *Daily Dispatch* for now, she knew she would work from home once they started having kids. But that was a few years down the road.

Two weeks had passed since Cody and Tessa's wedding — since Sawyer proposed to Montana. The newlyweds were just back from their honeymoon, and Sawyer had invited the guys over for dinner and after that, a tour of the new property.

Trace was there first, naturally. Early. He walked right into Sawyer's house and helped himself to a beer from the fridge. That told Sawyer things were back to normal. Trace leaned against the counter, one hand wrapped around his beer, the other in his pocket. He gave Sawyer an appraising look.

"I think home ownership will suit you," he said. "But don't make yourself too scarce, okay?"

"Oh, don't worry. I'll be coming to your house, getting beers out of your fridge," Sawyer said. "Plus, I have a feeling you're not going to be lonely. How are things with Abby?"

Trace looked away, taking a sudden interest in the refrigerator door.

Sawyer almost expected him to start whistling, like some cartoon character. Silence.

"Well?"

Trace did whistle, then, through his teeth, like the prodding stung. "Why does everyone keep asking me that question? There *are* no things with Abby."

"No?"

Trace, set his beer on the counter and rubbed the back of his neck. "No."

"Not even after the way I saw the two of you dancing two weeks ago at the wedding?" Sawyer asked.

Trace picked up his beer. Again, took a long drink, long enough to nearly drain it. "We weren't dancing."

Sawyer laughed. "You kidding me? You might not have been on the dance floor, but I saw you."

"How'd you see us?!"

"Ah. You don't deny it. And you'd have to be a fool not to notice that chemistry."

"I don't know, man. She's only just recently stopped shooting daggers at me with her eyes. I don't think we're making the leap to romance just yet. Dance partners? Maybe. But romance? I don't know."

Well, that's interesting, Sawyer thought. Trace wasn't a flat "no" on the romance. Now that Sawyer finally felt secure in his own romance, he wanted it for everyone else.

A knock on the door distracted Sawyer before he could answer.

"That'll be Cody," he said.

"Thanks, Captain Obvious," Trace said.

Cody strode in then, looking as tanned and as happy as Sawyer had ever seen him. Trace whistled again. "Man, I haven't seen you that tan since that summer we turned fifteen," he said to Cody.

"Those sun rays coming off the beach sand in Hawaii do a body good. Oh, and so does a week-and-a-half of almost constant sex."

Trace covered his ears and Sawyer faked a gagging motion.

"Too much, too much," Sawyer said, and Trace said, "Yeah, man. She's Mrs. Davis now. You're supposed to keep that stuff private."

Cody laughed. "Bunch of sissies. You're just jealous. So, what's up? And where's my beer?"

"This guy is getting a little big for his Wranglers," Trace said, even while he pulled another beer from the fridge. "I suppose you expect me to open it, too."

Chuckling, Cody pulled his keys out of his jeans pocket and used the bottle opener on his keyring to open the beer. Trace pulled open the drawer with the garbage can in it, and Cody flipped the lid right into it.

"Well, I'm glad to see marriage hasn't made you lose your touch," Sawyer said.

"Nah," Cody said. "If anything, it's made me better than average. Anyway, dish, man, on the property. I can't believe you didn't tell me before the wedding. Made Tessa tell me on the honeymoon."

"Yeah," Trace said. "We never really got to talk. When did this all come about?" Cody leaned back in his barstool and crossed his legs at the ankles.

It felt so good to finally share this news, this dream, with Cody and Trace. "Well, you guys know I've always wanted my own ranch. And I know I could have started my own brand on the Mint Creek Ranch, but I wanted something of my own ... not something someone gave me."

"But you know any success you have on Mint Creek Ranch is a result of work you've put in," Trace said. "Yes, maybe our parents handed it down to us, but it's our hard work that's made it successful. There's no shame in that."

"I know," Sawyer said. "And I've thought of that. I guess it's a pride thing. A long time ago, my parents told me I wouldn't amount to anything. They said I didn't have it in me. I'd never be good enough for an ambitious girl like Montana."

Even now, the memory hurt. Reliving that conversation was like poking a sleeping bear with a stick.

"They said that?" Disbelief twisted Cody's features.

His surprise made it obvious his parents had never said anything like that to him. Sawyer sighed. "They did. I mean, they probably thought it'd inspire me. But it was rough."

"That's bull," Trace said. "Why didn't you ever tell us?"

"I mean, that's embarrassing, right? Your own parents say something like that, and you believe it's true. What if I brought it up to you guys and you said, 'Yeah, your parents are right. You're a loser'?"

"Sawyer," Cody said. "Come on, man. We'd never say that."

"I know," he said, and he believed it. "But what if you were thinking it?"

"Never," Cody and Trace said.

"Thanks, you guys. Really. This is just something I felt like I had to do. For me."

"But what about Montana?" Cody wanted to know. "I mean, she just bought a property, too, right? Talk about timing."

Sawyer explained the plan, and he couldn't have said why he was so relieved and pleased when Cody and Trace seemed to think it was a good one. He hoped that one day, he would outgrow the need for other people's approval. For now, though, at least he sought it from those who supported him.

"Thank you, guys," he said again. "I can't tell you how much I've been dreading this conversation. How hard it was to keep the secret."

His friends made matching dismissive gestures, and Trace said, "Don't get me wrong, I can see why you were hesitant. You probably thought I'd blow a gasket. But I'm happy for you, man. And you know I've been real worried about the kind of people who would buy one of Abby's properties. I thought they'd be wannabe ranchers who try to turn Prescott into a big city. But now that I know you're one of them, I feel good about it. At least I know if we have any neighborly disputes, I can kick your ass."

Sawyer grinned. "I wouldn't be so sure."

Montana

THE RAYS of the early-evening sun bathed Williamson Valley in soft, golden light. Montana and Sawyer got out of Sawyer's truck.

"This is ours," Montana said as they met in front of the truck and took each other's hand. "Can you believe it?"

"I can't," Sawyer said.

They walked hand in hand across the piece of property Montana chose. She pictured her little cottage tucked up against the foothills.

"I'm so glad you were open to my crazy idea, keeping both properties."

"I wouldn't take that from you," Sawyer said. "I know how much you always wanted a place of your own."

"Just one of the many reasons I love you," she said. And it was true: there were so many reasons. "Another is that you are incredibly sexy."

He stopped walking and turned to face her. She wrapped her arms around his waist. He brought his lips to hers and she felt the thrill of the contact through her whole body.

"How did I get so lucky?" she asked.

"I've been wondering the same thing," he said.

They heard the sound of a truck engine approaching, and then another.

"The whole gang's here," Sawyer said. "You ready?"

Montana was more than ready. She'd been keeping one last secret from Sawyer, and she couldn't wait to reveal it while they were surrounded by their closest friends. She was nervous. She'd taken a big step, made a big decision without talking to Sawyer about it. But she had a feeling he would be thrilled.

The trucks — belonging to Cody and Trace — pulled up next to Sawyer's. Cody, Tessa, and Abby got out of one, and Trace got out of the other. All of them smiling, they came to stand with Montana and Sawyer.

"Pretty awesome place," Cody said.

"Would you like a little tour?" Montana tried to sound nonchalant even though her heart was in her throat.

"I hate to admit it, but I've already seen the place," Trace said.

When everyone looked at him, heads snapping to attention, he laughed and held up his hands. "What? I had to see what Abby was up to, didn't I?"

Abby, laughed, her face flushed.

"Enough about me," Trace said. "Yes, we'd love a tour, from the new property owners."

Taking her time, Montana led the group around her piece of property, showing them the footprint of the cottage and where she planned to put her garden.

"I can see why you fell in love with this spot," Tessa said. "It's perfect. And, when the sun sets … Exquisite."

Montana looked at Sawyer and smiled. "I like that. *Exquisite.*"

He put an arm around her shoulders and squeezed. "It is. All of it. Especially you."

There was a collective, "Aw," and Montana felt herself smiling ear to ear.

"And now, for Sawyer's half of the property," she said, leading the way, trying to stay a little ahead of Sawyer.

He noticed. "You in a hurry? I feel like you're about to pull my arm off."

Everything was perfect. She and Sawyer were in the lead, their friends behind them. The sun was shining, and she could hear some birds chirping. They'd made their way down into the little valley between two gentle, grassy swells. As they walked up the second one, any minute now, Sawyer would be able to see the surprise.

In fact, as they ascended, she could see the tops of the temporary corral. Sawyer hadn't noticed yet. He was still looking toward the sunset. Montana couldn't breathe. She was so excited. Her knees felt weak as she trudged along.

"What's that?"

He saw it. She wondered what he was thinking. Maybe he would imagine someone had come out to the property. It wasn't unheard of for people to camp in undeveloped areas. A few more steps and she could see the calf's ears, twitching. As they approached the peak of the little hill, she could see its head. The fur stood thick and curly between its ears, and its eyes were enormous and rimmed with the longest lashes. Montana hoped he was friendly. He wasn't a bull for riding, but for breeding.

"Is that —"

"That's a bull," Montana said. "You should know that."

She leaned against his body and smiled up at him.

"But where — how —"

"He's yours."

"Mine?"

"Well, I wanted him to be a wedding present. I called up Diego at the Five D Ranch, because I knew you had your eye on a couple of lines up there. I told him what I wanted, and he insisted on making the first Leaning S Ranch bull a gift from him, as well. He's pretty cute, isn't he?"

"Well, I wouldn't say *Diego's* cute," Sawyer said.

"I meant the bull."

"Oh, right. But we don't want them to be that cute. He's going to be the sire of a championship line of rodeo bulls. *Mean* rodeo bulls who make cowboys weak in the knees."

"True."

They'd made their way down to the temporary corral. The bull walked up to them and stuck his head between two of the railings. Sawyer put a hand on his head. "Hey, buddy."

The bull blinked.

"Montana, I don't know what to say. I don't know how to thank you. I never would've dreamed of a steer as a wedding gift. But he's perfect."

"Just build us the second most beautiful ranch in Prescott."

Stepping back to admire the bull, Sawyer took Montana's hand. Behind them, Trace whistled long and low. "Well, he's a real beaut. Montana, you told me he was a good-looking guy, but you didn't do him justice."

When Sawyer turned around and said, "You knew about this?" Montana couldn't help but smile. Trace said, "We've all got our secrets. Montana told me she was keeping him on Abby's property, but now I know there was more to it."

Cody stepped up and slapped Sawyer on the back. "This is the start of something wonderful, Sawyer. Not just the bull, but all of it."

"It is," Sawyer said. He looked at Montana and asked, "And what do you think about this view?"

He gestured to the land, their land, the steer in his pen, and the friends gathered there with them.

She looked up at him and smiled. "It's my favorite."

———

The End

PREVIEW: MY FAVORITE PLACE
BOOK THREE IN THE MINT CREEK RANCH
SERIES

MY FAVORITE PLACE: CHAPTER ONE

ABBY

ABBY FLORES REMEMBERED the exact moment she realized construction was a man's world. It was the same moment she made the decision to prove she could thrive in it.

She'd just turned fifteen, and even though her parents planned to throw her a massive quinceañera, she was even more excited about what was happening the day after the party. She was finally old enough to have a real job. To be on the payroll at her father's construction company, to pay taxes, and to open a bank account.

Even though she stayed up long past midnight dancing with her family and friends, she was awake well before her alarm went off at six.

Her dad walked into the kitchen as she was pouring him a mug of coffee. He accepted it, and his eyes twinkled at her through the steam. "Big day?"

"The biggest." She held up her own coffee mug for a toast. "To finally being a legal employee."

"Cheers," her dad said, lifting his mug to touch hers. "Although I have to admit, I'm sad to lose my free child labor."

They both laughed at the standing joke. Abby hadn't been on the payroll, but since she turned twelve and was able to work right along-side the crew, Ernesto had paid her in cash.

He reached out and curled a strand of her hair around his forefin-ger. "Your fancy hairdo held up."

"I know," Abby said. "I can't believe it. I'm going to have to braid it before we go."

Her dad made a dismissive sound. "Leave it. For the day."

It was still so dark outside that the kitchen window acted like a mirror. The hairdresser had worked magic on her long, thick hair, twisting the upper half into intricate swirls and letting the lower half hang long and curling down her back. Abby patted the top half. "It's not my normal work 'do," she told her dad. "But you're right. I should keep it as long as I can."

"You should do something about your face, though. All that makeup. All those young men."

He stood behind her, looking over her shoulder at her reflection. It was true: the mascara and eyeliner weren't normal for her. They made her look older.

She chuckled. "Daddy, you taught me early on how to handle the guys. I'll be fine."

Still, when they showed up at the jobsite — Ernesto's company was building a new hotel in their Utah hometown — he handed her his framing hammer. "Keep this in your toolbelt today. I have a feeling you're going to be fighting off the summer crew."

Abby had worked as something of a junior member of Ernesto's main crew since she was able to walk. Her role had evolved from a tagalong to gofer (the guys would often send her to retrieve certain tools or supplies), to apprentice, to, in more recent years, a full-fledged crew member.

Although construction was a nomadic business and workers came and went, Ernesto had a few loyal crew members who were like family to Abby. There was Joseph Scott, the foreman, who'd been with Ernesto since the early days of the company. And Christopher Hernandez, crew leader. The two of them oversaw everyone else. None of them had ever so much as looked at Abby sideways. They regarded her as another one of the guys.

But she had noticed that as she got older — and turned into a young woman — her father kept a closer watch.

Plus, school had gotten out the week before, which meant local teens and college students were looking for work. But Abby could handle herself.

When Ernesto handed her the hammer, she kissed him on the cheek before tucking it into her toolbelt. "I'll be fine, Dad."

And she was. More than fine. Her excitement over finally being on the payroll, officially, stoked the fire that fueled her productivity. All morning, she swung that hammer, helping frame in the walls for several rooms on the second floor. By noon, her arm was burning and her palm was blistered.

On a big project like that one, the construction manager usually set up an office — a portable building with enough space for a couple of desks, a filing cabinet, and a fridge. There was no official break room, so the crew members usually picnicked somewhere onsite. After retrieving her lunch from the fridge, Abby headed back up to the second floor. She sat down, her feet hanging over the edge, above what would eventually be the hotel's main entrance. And that's when it happened.

A kid about her own age, who she'd never seen before, came sauntering across the plywood that made up the unfinished floor. Abby figured he belonged to one of the subcontracted crews her father hired to help with such a large-scale project.

Come to think of it, judging by the stubble on his jaw, maybe he was a year or two older than she was. He wore construction boots and jeans, but he'd taken off his shirt and tucked it into his back pocket, the white cotton hanging down the back of one leg. And he had muscles. A deep tan, and really nice muscles. He was definitely older than her.

The onceover she gave him was unintentional, but the one he gave her seemed *very* intentional. He looked at her face for a full second — eyes and then lips — before his gaze traveled down to her breasts. She, too, sported a white T-shirt as part of her standard building uniform — and she was still wearing hers! But the way he looked at her, it was as if she were already naked.

He licked his lips, and she felt a shiver travel over her scalp. It was not an aroused shiver. She felt threatened, violated. So, she did what her dad had taught her. She stood up, gave him her biggest grin and offered him a hand to shake (he'd once told her she should spit a giant loogie or summon up a fart, but she couldn't bring herself to do it). "I'm Abby Flores. And you are?"

He blinked, stunned, which meant her confidence took him back a little. Abby was relieved. Maybe he was just a run-of-the-mill teenage boy gawking at a teenage girl who, if she did say so herself, looked drop-dead gorgeous with her fancy hairstyle and professional makeup job.

"Miles Taylor. Nice to meet you."

There was a beat of silence. Miles cleared his throat. Thankfully, he looked a little uneasy. "Mind if I join you?" He gestured at the spot where her lunch sat.

She didn't want him to join her, but her parents had taught her to be polite.

"I guess not."

There. That wasn't top-of-the-line politeness, but it would do. Only then did Abby notice that Miles was holding a paper bag, his palm curled around the top of it.

"Cool. Thanks."

She let him sit first, so she could leave some space between them.

Abby's acquiescence gave Miles some of his confidence back. He unrolled the top of his bag and peered inside, then looked at her and said, "You know, I think you might be too pretty to work here."

Abby's mouth would have dropped open, but, manners. She finished chewing her food, took her time swallowing, and then offered Miles the most withering look she could muster.

"Oh, do you, now? I'll bet you a hundred bucks I could frame more walls in an afternoon than you can, hands down."

"All I'm saying is, shouldn't you be, I don't know, in the office or something?"

That, right there, was the moment. It was the moment Abby made up her mind that she would become a successful builder. She was good, even at fifteen. She'd been taught by the best. Quality was everything. Mistakes happened, and they were fixed. All the elements of a project worked together like cogs in a motor: timing, precision, rhythm. The finished product was exquisite.

How many hours had she spent with her dad at construction sites, looking over blueprints and finding creative ways to give clients what they wanted, while staying within budget? This business was part of her blood. It was part of her family. And it would be her livelihood and her legacy. She would do it for herself … and despite Miles Taylor and all the people like him, who thought women belonged in the office ... who thought women couldn't swing a hammer.

Abby never ate lunch with Miles again. In fact, she never spoke another word to him. If he said, "Hello," she responded with a curt nod. She would ignore him, but if her father ever saw that, she would hear about it.

Instead, she gave him a wide berth, and gratitude: he uttered the words that ignited her desire to prove that she, a young woman, belonged.

———

TRACE

AS AN ADULT, Trace Walker liked things just so. Every morning when he got up, he went straight to the kitchen, where his coffee sat, already brewed. He poured himself a cup before walking down the driveway to grab his copy of the *Daily Dispatch*. Then, he sat at his kitchen table, next to the window that overlooked Mint Creek itself, and read the paper front to back. After that, he ate and showered, then dressed and left the house. He fed and watered the horses, often along with his co-owners in the ranch, Cody Davis and Sawyer Nelson. They'd generally spend the morning tending the livestock, shooting the breeze, riding the fences, and making repairs around the property.

One hot, windy spring day, he went about his chores with his trademark work ethic and the enjoyment of checking off the boxes on his to-do list: *Repair the irrigation line. Check. Wash out the horse troughs. Check. Muck the stalls. Check.*

As he walked back toward his house, though, he saw a brand-new sports car coming up the driveway — *his* driveway.

For Trace, an unexpected visitor was almost always unwelcome. He felt his mouth settle into a grim line, and knew that his own mother would chastise him for greeting a stranger with such an unfriendly expression. Squaring his shoulders, he approached the driver's side as the car stopped. After a long couple of seconds, the window rolled down.

And Trace, despite the disruption to his normal routine, found himself grinning like a lunatic at the driver. She was stunning, to say the least. Eyelashes for days, an adorable dimple on each cheek, and a smile so bright, it almost blinded him.

As his eyes drank her in, his heart danced. It knocked against the inside of his ribs as if to say, *Are you seeing this?*

"Good morning," the woman said.

"Hi there," Trace said.

The eye contact made him freeze. It seemed to do the same to her. They remained there, staring at each other, grinning.

She recovered first. "I'm Abby. And I'm lost."

"Trace. And maybe I can help, Abby-and-I'm-lost. Where are you headed?"

He hoped she would say Mint Creek Ranch was her destination. Which was absurd, because nobody driving a car like that could possibly think they belonged in Prescott, Arizona.

She said, "I'm looking for an intersection, I guess. Williamson Valley Road and Saddle Horn?"

Why on Earth anyone would be looking for that intersection, Trace couldn't say. The two roads formed one half of the property line on an old piece of land that was overrun by weeds. But his mother would tell him it was rude to say so.

He couldn't stop himself from asking, "What are you doing out in these parts?"

Her smile disappeared. "Exploring."

Okay, Trace thought. *She's a closed book.*

He could understand that. A woman traveling alone probably didn't want to share too many details.

He relied again on the manners his mama taught him and said, "You're nearly there. It's been unmarked since three summers ago, when a microburst came through here and tore down the sign. Back out to the main road, hang a right, and go slightly less than three quarters of a mile. Saddle Horn Lane is a dirt road. Looks almost like a two-track these days. I would say you can't miss it, but really, you can."

She nodded. "I know exactly what you're talking about. I think I sped by it on my first pass. I was so caught up looking for a street sign, I figured that was someone's driveway. Anyway, thanks a lot. I really appreciate it."

As she rolled up her window, Trace tried to think of a way to ask for her number. His mind was so scrambled from the chemistry that he came up blank. She finished rolling up her window, then backed expertly out of the driveway. As she got back onto the main road, he waved, hoping she could see him in her mirror.

———

THE MINT CREEK Ranch changed Trace's life. He owed the place — and the city of Prescott — a debt of gratitude. Before Trace was one of the Mint Creek Ranch boys, he was a gangly, awkward eight-year-old. He wasn't one of those cliché loners, at least, not from the outside. Kids tolerated him. He never ate lunch alone or spent recess looking for someone to play with. But, he never really felt like he belonged, either. He felt *different*. Until he was eight, he could never put his finger on it.

Western-style decorations hung on the walls of the tiny two-bedroom house where he lived with his parents. Ceramic horse figurines and cowboy statues sat on the shelves. His dad, a car mechanic, and his mom, a teacher, dressed in leather boots, jeans, and button-up shirts. He did the same.

He had a bigger interest in Legos and library books than he did in fashion, and never even thought about how his wardrobe compared to those of his classmates. That is, until one hot spring day in the third grade. The air was stifling, and the school playground felt like an oven. When the teacher sent the kids outside, every part of Trace's body felt hot immediately: between his shoulder blades, the backs of his knees, especially his ankles in his leather cowboy boots. Sweat dripped from his hairline, and as he walked out to the playground, he wiped his forehead on his sleeve.

"Hot, huh?" Mindy Ray, his classmate, swung from the metal rings of the play structure, her long, dark hair swishing down to her waist. Trace took a moment to look over her outfit. The bright-yellow skirt and white striped t-shirt she wore looked about a hundred times cooler than his jeans and tucked-in plaid shirt. But, he didn't really have an answer for her — sure, it was hot, but wasn't that pretty obvious? He gave her a nod and climbed onto the platform to take his turn on the rings.

"Yeah, but Trace don't care if it's hot." The voice came from behind him. Trace turned around to see Jaden Billings giving him a once-over, like someone might examine an alien species. "He's some kind of cowboy, or something. Ain't that right, Trace?"

Trace recognized an unusual tone in the kid's voice. Him calling Trace a cowboy was definitely not a compliment.

Mindy, still swinging, giggled. "I know. It's like he thinks we live in Texas, or something. Giddyup." She landed neatly on the platform opposite Trace, and a couple of other kids laughed.

"Hey, y'all," one of them drawled.

Shocked, Trace felt his mouth drop open. If it were possible, his face felt even hotter, and he could feel his pulse in the tips of his ears, reminding him of the way he'd like to pummel Jaden's face, since he'd started the whole thing. Instead, he did what his mama taught him to do when someone was rude or disrespectful. He walked away. He jumped down off the platform before ever reaching for one of the metal rings. As he walked, his feet plowing through the wood chips, he heard the squeal of metal on metal. More laughter. More words spoken in fake Western accents. He made it to the edge of the grass before he felt the hot sting of tears in his eyes. And he kept moving.

A kid noticing the way he dressed was one thing. But *all* of those kids noticing the way he dressed, and acting like he was the only one who *didn't* notice? He felt blindsided.

When the bell rang and everyone went back to class, his classmates acted like everything was perfectly normal. But for Trace, everything had changed. That afternoon, as soon as he walked into his house after getting off the bus, he pried off his boots and threw them across the living room.

"What's the matter?" His mom came out of the kitchen just in time to see the second boot spinning through the air as it careened across the room.

"I need new shoes," Trace said. He could hear the pout in his own voice, and he was ashamed. He knew how hard it was to keep him in shoes. His feet always grew so fast.

"You didn't outgrow those already, did you?" his mom asked. "Darn it, Trace, those are brand new."

For the second time that day, Trace felt his face burning hot. "No, Mama. I didn't outgrow them."

He knew he shouldn't ask, but the words tumbled out of his mouth. "Do you think I could get some different shoes? Like tennis shoes or something?"

As he expected, the answer was a firm "no." Okay, not exactly, but a, "Well, I suppose we could go on down to the secondhand store and see if they've got a pair."

If anything was worse than cowboy boots, it was secondhand shoes you bought because kids teased you about your cowboy boots.

For the next week, Trace wore his cowboy boots to school every day. And every day, he avoided talking with the other kids. After all, who knew what else they were thinking when they saw him?

Exactly one week after he came home and flung those boots across the living room, Trace came home to his parents waiting for him in the kitchen, a plate of freshly baked chocolate chip cookies on the table alongside a full glass of cold milk.

Something strange was happening.

"Trace, honey," his mom said. "We have something to tell you."

His dad cleared his throat and drummed his fingers on the table. He must have come straight from work. Trace could see grease under his fingernails.

Trace couldn't imagine what they were going to tell him. Was something wrong? Had one of his grandparents died? Did his dad get laid off?

"Son," his dad said, "we're moving."

MY FAVORITE PLACE: CHAPTER TWO

TRACE

TWO WEEKS LATER, the Walker family packed their belongings into a single moving truck and headed north.

"You're going to love your Aunt Elaine and Uncle Tom, and your Aunt Lola and Uncle Wyatt," Trace's mom said, her voice different than he'd ever heard it, almost as if she might explode from excitement.

"If I'm going to love them so much, how come I've never met them before?"

His mom laughed, a high-pitched, birdlike sound. "It's so wonderful, honey. I grew up with Elaine and Lola. We were the best of friends. And as a life so often does, it took the three of us in different directions. We got busy and drifted apart, is all. But neither time apart nor distance have lessened my affection for them. They've asked your dad and me to be partners in the ranch up in Prescott."

"The ranch?" Trace wrinkled his nose.

"Yes! A real, working ranch. Trace, you're going to love it. And they each have a boy your age. I can sense this is going to be a great new beginning for you. For our whole family."

Eyes shining, she reached across the front of Trace to grab his dad's hand. They looked at each other over the top of Trace's head, and when Trace glanced from one to the other, he saw they were both smiling.

As they drove further and further north, the buildings seemed further and further apart. Dry, dusty cement and heat waves gave way to trees and shade and space. Lots of space. After about two hours, they came into a tiny, old-fashioned looking town, with a giant white building in its center.

"What's that?" Trace wanted to know.

"That's the county courthouse," his mom said. "And that, right there, is Two Scoops, the best ice cream place in town. And that —" she pointed at a bench sitting in the lush grass surrounding the big white building — "that's the best place to eat said ice cream."

"Can we get ice cream now?"

Trace's dad laughed. "Well, I don't think I can park this thing downtown. But we'll go this weekend and get a scoop."

"A double scoop?"

"Sure, a double scoop," his dad said.

Well, Trace thought, if his dad was agreeing to a double scoop, he must be really happy.

If Trace thought the little downtown looked nice, Mint Creek Ranch itself looked like heaven on earth. After turning off a long road flanked by wide green fields with plenty of trees, the moving truck made its way under a thick canopy of leaves and emerged onto the ranch property.

"This is it," Trace's mom breathed.

It wasn't as neat and tidy as Trace had imagined it. The grass and weeds were overgrown, and the buildings looked a little worse for wear. But he knew instantly: this was home. Everything seemed to sparkle in the early evening light.

"That's the main house, over there," Trace's dad said, pulling alongside a different building and putting the moving truck in park. Before they'd even finished climbing out of the cab, a stampede of people came through the front door. In the lead: two boys Trace's age. There was a jumble of adults, a bunch of laughing, and loud talking.

Suddenly, the two boys were right in front of Trace.

"Hey," said the taller one. He flashed a grin so wide, Trace immediately felt like they were friends. He stuck out his hand. "Cody."

"Trace."

Cody gave Trace's a good, hearty shake.

"Sawyer," said the other kid, whose shaggy blonde hair was a little too long. He, too, smiled and shook Trace's hand.

"Want us to show you around?" Sawyer asked. "Our parents said we had to."

Cody elbowed Sawyer, who laughed out loud. Trace found himself laughing, too.

"What? They did!"

"I know," Cody said. "But I don't think we're supposed to repeat that."

He looked at Trace and shrugged. "Well, you want to see the place?"

The two of them started to run — the precursor to the days and years that would follow — and as Trace jogged to keep up with them, he noticed something interesting: they were both wearing cowboy boots. And when he thought back to the moment before, when everyone had emerged from the house, he realized they were, too.

The three of them ran all over the ranch, from the first house to the second, third, and fourth, and then to the barn. They walked carefully through the yard of discarded farm stuff, tractor tires, fence panels, and giant wooden spools.

"Want to play hide-and-seek?" Trace asked, and within a few minutes, they were hiding and seeking and finding and laughing, and doing it all again. After a few rounds of that, Sawyer announced, "I'm hot. You guys want to go in the creek?"

Trace looked down at his clothes, and then said, "I've got no idea where my swim trunks are."

Cody made a dismissive gesture. "Go in your jeans."

The idea seemed impractical (what would the kids at his old school think about swimming in jeans?), but Trace was hot, and besides, he didn't want to disappoint his new friends. So he ran with them to the creek. Without even slowing down, the other two boys pulled off their boots and socks and shirts and splashed into the water. Trace followed suit, and gasped at the temperature of the water on his skin.

"Refreshing, right?" Sawyer hollered, pushing his arms over the creek's surface to splash Trace.

The sun sank lower in the sky and cast a golden light over the whole scene like magic. A while later, the sound of a bell ringing broke through the noise of splashing and shouting.

"Dinner bell!" Sawyer hollered.

"Good thing, too, because I'm starving!" Cody said.

"Me too!" Trace said.

They threw on their boots, grabbed their shirts, and ran back to the main house, where they ate a meal better than any Trace had ever tasted: smoked brisket, green beans, and biscuits with honey. After dinner, someone started a fire in the giant fire pit out front, and the boys roasted marshmallow after marshmallow. Their parents were so caught up in conversation, they lost count, and the boys polished off the whole package. Then, bellies full, almost sick on sugar, they flopped down on their backs on the grass.

"Boy, you can really see the stars up here," Trace said.

"Sure can," Sawyer said.

"Pretty incredible," Trace said.

"Sure is," Cody said.

After packing, loading the moving truck, driving, and the excitement of arriving, Trace was so tired he felt his eyelids getting heavy. Right before he drifted off to sleep, he thought, *This is perfect. This is exactly where we are supposed to be. This is home.*

———

THE NEXT DAY, Trace received his first up close and personal introduction to horses. The many long hours he'd spent admiring his parents' paintings did almost nothing to prepare him for that moment. Looking at two dimensional images was one thing. Sure, the oil-on-canvas horses hanging in his home looked athletic. Even in that format, a kid could tell horses were beautiful, powerful. But it wasn't until Cody led a massive chestnut horse out of the barn that Trace realized how big and imposing the creatures could be.

"This here is Shirley," Cody said, and Trace could swear his new friend was exaggerating his drawl. "Like Shirley Temple, the actress."

Even though the horse plodded toward him at a walk, and it seemed good-natured enough — she let a boy a fraction of her size lead her without ever once putting tension on the rope — Trace took a step back. His head came up to what he thought was the animal's shoulder. He had to tilt back to see her eyes. When he took the time to really look at her, he felt a bit calmer. Her eyes were a clear, warm brown, like the brandy his dad sometimes had before bed.

"She has really long eyelashes," Trace managed, and Cody and Sawyer chuckled.

"Well, that's not the first attribute a guy looks at on a horse," Cody said, "but maybe on a lady."

They were in stitches, clutching their sides as they cracked up. Trace couldn't be certain whether they were making fun of him, but he found the corners of his mouth tugging upward in a smile. As if Shirley understood that he'd relaxed, the tiniest bit, she lowered her head so her nose was directly in front of his face. Trace couldn't help himself. He reached out to touch her nose. He had to know if it felt as velvety soft as it looked. And it did.

"Careful," Cody said, his voice sharp. "You don't want her to mistake your fingers for carrots. Make sure to keep your palm flat like this." He held up his hand to illustrate. Trace flattened his hand.

"Want to ride her?" Cody asked.

A rattlesnake shook its rattler inside Trace's stomach. "I don't know."

"You ever ridden before?" Sawyer wanted to know.

Trace ran his palm over the massive cheek, which was sleek and smooth. The horse pressed her face against his hand. "Naw," he said, trying on the drawl. "My parents always told me we could get a horse one day, but that day hasn't come."

"The way I hear it, you'll be getting a horse of your own lickety-split." Cody spoke with such certainty, Trace didn't bother to question him.

"Which means," Sawyer said. "You might as well learn how to ride."

They didn't wait for him to answer. Sawyer took the lead rope from Cody, and Cody moved to Shirley's left side. "First thing is, you've got to learn how to mount."

He put his hands on the saddle horn.

In a move so effortless, Trace thought it resembled teleportation, Cody swung his right leg up and over Shirley's back. "That's it," he said. "Up and over."

As easily as he had mounted, he dismounted, and then he motioned for Trace to try. Trace copied Cody's motions: he put his left foot in the left stirrup, grasped the saddle horn, and hoisted himself up. It didn't feel nearly as easy as Cody made it look, but he did it, first try. Shirley seemed way taller, once he was on her back. He looked down at his friends. They both grinned up at him.

"You're a natural," Sawyer said.

Trace felt himself beaming with pride. "I am?"

"You are," Cody said. "But we're not going to let you loose quite yet. Let's do a few laps."

Cody picked up the lead rope again, and Trace was surprised to see no one had been holding it. The horse stood there, patiently, as if she were waiting for someone to tell her what to do next. This gave Trace a little comfort. He felt his shoulders relax.

"That's it," Sawyer said. "Keep your body relaxed."

"Ready?" Cody asked.

Trace nodded. Cody clicked his tongue and started to walk. Shirley started to move, and again, Trace marveled at how huge she was. After a few steps, he settled into the rhythm. It reminded him of a boat rolling over the choppy surface of a lake: up and down, up and down. Cody led Shirley into the corral and started a wide circle around the perimeter.

"So far, so good," Sawyer said. "If I didn't know better, I'd guess you grew up right here on this ranch."

"True," Cody said, his voice conveying surprise.

In that moment, basking in the glow of compliments from his new friends, Trace felt like he was on top of the world.

That feeling stuck with Trace throughout his childhood. Mint Creek Ranch was the first place where he really felt like he belonged. Not only with his parents, but with other kids, in his new hometown.

Eventually, Trace learned how to really ride. Not just sit astride a horse while someone else lead it around the property, but to trot, then gallop, then rope steers and horses. He was as comfortable in the saddle as he was on foot.

He, Cody, and Sawyer became like brothers, and when the Hart family moved onto the property, Montana Hart became like a little sister to him. The four of them played together, worked together, and squabbled now and then. But through it all, Trace knew his life was perfect. He wouldn't change it for anything.

———

TRACE'S first encounter with horses kicked off a lifelong love affair. He'd admired the horses in his parents' paintings, but no artist, no matter how skilled, could replicate what it felt like to stand right next to a horse, one hand on its warm neck, looking into its eyes.

Every chance he got, Trace ran to the barn. He became so efficient at his household chores that his parents joked they should've introduced him to horses long before moving to Mint Creek Ranch.

Soon enough, caring for the horses became one of his daily duties. His dad taught him how to feed and water them, how to clean their stalls, how to brush them, and eventually, how to rope and herd. Once he'd mastered those essential skills, he was allowed to take the horses out on the trails.

On his first solo ride, he did everything himself. He put the saddle blanket over the horse's back, and the saddle on top of that. He cinched it down and fastened it before adjusting the stirrups. He put on the bit and the bridle, laying the reins over the saddle. Then, with a growing sense of excitement, he mounted. And for the first time on his own, he led the horse out of the barn. As soon as he felt the afternoon sun on his shoulders and face, he smiled. He smiled so big that he was glad no one else was there.

At first, he let the horse walk. But he was a ten-year-old boy. And pretty much every boy he knew liked to go fast — even his dad. Sometimes when he and his dad went for a ride in the car and his mom wasn't there, his dad would look across the cab at Trace and say, "Pedal to the metal, right buddy?" And then he'd press the gas pedal practically down to the floor, making the car go so fast, Trace's stomach floated inside his body. Trace would give his dad a thumbs up and a grin — probably similar to the goofy expression he wore as he rode that horse out of the barn.

He didn't know how his parents would feel about him going too fast, so he kept the horse at a walk until they were around the corner. Then, he gave her a gentle nudge with his heels. She picked up speed, but barely. He couldn't blame her. The nudge had been somewhat ... *tentative.* "Tentative" was one of his vocabulary words: *Done without confidence; hesitant.*

It seemed almost as if the horse could read Trace's mind or sense his feelings. Although he wanted to go faster, he wasn't quite sure if it was the best idea. But then something grabbed ahold of him. Something like courage. Or maybe stupidity. He leaned down over the horse's neck and gave her a nudge quite a bit more certain than the previous one.

They were off.

The acceleration was faster than Trace expected. He almost slid right off the horse's butt. He grabbed the saddle horn to keep himself in the seat. They were flying. He could hear the beat of the horse's hooves on the ground beneath them, but still, he felt like they were flying.

"Faster," he yelled, even though he knew that wasn't one of the commands the horse understood. Or maybe she did. She went even faster. She ran and ran. And she ran some more. She ran so fast, for so long, that Trace got tired of holding on. He'd heard from Cody, Sawyer, and all of their parents that he didn't really have to hold on tightly. But as new as the sensation was, he had a death grip on the reins. He brought the horse to a halt, marveling again at how she seemed to understand what he wanted.

When he turned her around, though, a realization knocked the wind out of him, as if he had fallen off the swings at school and landed flat on his back: when a horse runs really fast, for a really long time, she goes really far. Although it felt like they were running in a straight line, Trace had no idea where they were. The sun was a lot lower than he expected, too.

That excited feeling in his stomach did a one-eighty and turned to dread. What if he couldn't find his way back home? Boy, he would be in a world of trouble. More than once — more than one hundred times, maybe — one of the parents had mentioned that if a boy got lost on the property, he could die of starvation, dehydration, or hypothermia. In fact, Cody, Sawyer, and Trace had heard it so often that they usually rolled their eyes, figuring their parents were being dramatic.

But here he was, lost, with no idea how to get home. Just about sunset, too. How long had that darn horse run? Why hadn't she turned them around? Oh, but it had been so much fun! He couldn't decide whether to laugh or cry. At least no one was around to see the tears if he did. But still. Like his mom always said: crying didn't solve the problem.

"Put on your thinking cap, Trace," he said to himself.

Ah. Nature offered him one important clue: the sun was setting in the west. The creek ran north to south. And it ran along the western edge of the property. If he headed toward the sunset, he should come across the creek. And then, all he had to do was follow it south to the Mint Creek Ranch. Feeling better already, he turned the horse around. And because the sun seemed to be making a faster descent than ever, he nudged the horse, so she would go a little faster. She moved with confidence, and that's when yet another realization struck him: the horse would know how to get home. No one had taught him a command, like, "Go home." He said it anyway. Ears pricked, the horse picked up her pace even more. Not the full-out canter they'd done heading north, but fast enough. After what seemed like an eternity, the buildings of Mint Creek Ranch came into view. Trace couldn't believe the relief he felt. For a few minutes there, he really thought he might die out in the elements. He felt that grin spreading across his face again.

Something about the horse's run seemed a little jerkier, and he felt the saddle sliding around her midsection. As it slid, so did he. Within a few more steps, Trace felt himself unable to hold on to anything. His hands slipped off the horse's sweaty neck, and although his fingers could probably grasp her mane, he didn't want to hurt her. Grabbing the saddle horn didn't help. As he finished that final thought, he found himself flat on the ground, the wind knocked out of him again. For a split second, he had the thought that the horse might step on him, and he was terrified. Not for himself, but for her. His parents had told him that if a horse stepped on a human, it could break a leg. Most of the time, the damage was permanent, and the vet would have to put the horse down. Trace already felt guilty over it, and it hadn't even happened.

Fortunately, she was nimble. She stepped right over him. Her back legs didn't even touch him. He lay there, flat on his back, breathing heavily.

Less than a second later, the horse was back, the saddle hanging upside down below her belly. Suddenly, her giant, soft nose was inches from his face. She sniffed him, and he figured she was checking to see if he was all right.

"I'm all right, girl," he told her, and after a quick mental scan of his body, he realized he was. He might have a few bruises, and he definitely felt a little breathless. But he was all right. A few seconds later, he heard another horse approaching. He couldn't make out the rider right away, but then he heard the voice. "Well, what do we have here?"

"Cody. Thank goodness it's you."

"You're lucky it's me. Any one of the parents would whoop you."

They both laughed then, because none of their parents had ever whooped any of them.

"Looks like you didn't cinch the saddle tight enough."

"Yeah, I figured that one out."

Cody sighed. "Rookie move."

Trace sighed as he sat up. "I know."

"What are you doing out here?"

"Thought I'd go for a ride. Solo."

"Didn't you tell anyone you were going?" Cody asked. He took off his hat and examined it, much the way Trace had seen Cody's dad do.

"No," Trace said. "But I should have. Right?"

"Right. What if you didn't come back?"

"Right. Then no one would know where I'd gone." Trace sighed again. "Maybe I should give up riding."

"Nah," Cody said. "Gotta get back in the saddle. I'd tighten it up first, though."

Trace did, and they rode home, side by side.

The more Trace rode, the more he wanted to ride. Over the next couple of years, he spent all his spare time in the barn or on the trails. He watched the more experienced riders take care of the horses and memorized as much as he could of what they told him. *Check the hooves daily. Feed grain, morning and evening. Always look for lumps and bumps or sores during grooming. Exercise a horse every day.*

One evening after a big winter storm blew through, Trace went to the barn to put blankets on all the horses. Sure, they had their own fur coats, but he'd overheard his parents talking about how temperatures would dip into the single digits that night. Even if the horses huddled together, he thought, they would be freezing, and he couldn't stand the thought of that. So, wearing his clunky snow boots, his puffy jacket, and his knit hat, he trudged to the barn. His gloves made his hands clumsy, but he managed. For their part, the horses seemed grateful. Some of them bobbed their heads in thanks, and some nuzzled his ear with their velvety noses. As he was tying a blanket around Cody's mare, Cinnamon, he heard someone come through the barn door, stamping their feet.

He turned around to see who had joined him. "Dad! What are you doing down here?"

His dad didn't answer right away. He unwound his scarf and brushed ice off it before pulling off his own hat. Trace could see kindness in his smile. "Your mom and I saw you heading out, and she asked me to come keep you company."

"That was nice of you," Trace said. "But the horses are keeping me company just fine. I didn't mean for you to come out into the cold."

His dad shrugged. "Can I give you a hand?"

Trace nodded and they walked together to the closet that held the blankets. "I've got almost all of them done. Just a couple more."

"It's nice," his dad said, "how you've been caring for the horses."

Trace shrugged. "I'm finding that I like them better than most people."

His dad laughed then, a great big belly laugh. "Me too, son. Me too."

Trace walked over to Sawyer's horse and laid a blanket across her back. As was her habit, she leaned into him. Sawyer said that's how she gave hugs, and it was the first hug Trace had received. He gave her neck a good rub.

He bent down to tie on the blanket, and as he stood up, he spoke without thinking. "It would be so nice to have a horse of my own."

His dad didn't respond right away, and Trace regretted his words instantly. Horses were expensive. He knew that as well as anyone. He had a good set of ears and a good memory. He could recall countless adult conversations at the dinner table.

He started to apologize, but his dad said, "I know you really love them, son. And you're great with them."

And that was it. Trace didn't say anything else, and neither did his dad. He figured he'd better stop while he was ahead, before he said something to upset his dad.

"I didn't tell you this before, because I didn't want you to worry," his dad said as they tied the last two blankets on the last two horses. "But your mom said they're expecting another storm. The real reason she sent me down here was so that you didn't get stuck in a blizzard between the barn and the house when you came back up. Now that you've got these guys all tucked in for the night, we'd better hustle."

Together, they closed up the barn. As they began the trek back up to the house, Trace's dad put an arm around his shoulder. Trace matched his dad's strides, his arm wrapped around his waist, and even though the first flakes of the new storm brushed his skin, he felt warm.

———

A WEEK LATER, the smell of bacon frying woke Trace up. Then he remembered — it was his thirteenth birthday. His mom was cooking his birthday breakfast, like she did every year: bacon, eggs, and chocolate chip pancakes.

His mouth watered as he sat up. Although he could hardly stand the thought of waiting, he shoved his feet into his winter boots and pulled on his winter coat. He had to feed the horses before breakfast. They always came first.

When he walked into the kitchen, his mom smiled at him and gave him a big hug. "Happy birthday to my favorite son."

"Smells good," he said. "Thank you for making breakfast."

"You know I'd never skip a birthday breakfast, even on a school day."

"I know. That's why you're my favorite mom."

She laughed at that, and then seemed to notice his jacket and boots. "Oh, your dad already went down to take care of the horses. Being as it's your birthday and all."

"I'll go help him finish up," Trace said. "We'll get it done faster that way. Then we can all enjoy breakfast together."

"No, no," his mom said. "The birthday boy can't eat a cold breakfast. I've already dished you up. Sit down and eat. Your dad shouldn't be much longer."

Trace pulled off his jacket and boots and set them by the door. By the time he sat down and picked up his fork, his dad came in, grinning. "Happy birthday, my boy!" He ruffled Trace's hair. "Eat up. It takes a lot of energy to be a teenager."

"Thanks for feeding the horses, Dad. I guess I'll go say goodbye to them before I leave for school."

His mom set his dad's plate in front of him and added another slice of bacon and another pancake to Trace's as she joined them at the table.

"So. What's your biggest wish this year?"

Of their own accord, Trace's eyes looked over at his dad for a beat, and then back at his mom. His dad could probably guess what his greatest wish was. But he wouldn't say it out loud. It was too big. He'd been expecting the question. Answering it was a birthday ritual. He'd prepared in advance.

"My biggest wish is to have the best year ever."

His parents looked at each other. Almost as if they knew. Almost.

"Can you be a bit more specific?" his dad asked. His eyes twinkled.

"I mean, I guess — I want to explore more, have more adventures, that kind of thing."

His parents nodded.

"What kind of adventures?" his mom asked.

Trace shook his head, stabbed a piece of scrambled egg with his fork. "You know. Camping. Rock jumping. Skydiving."

By the time Trace was finally dressed and ready for school, he didn't have time to stop by the barn.

"They'll be fine until you get home from school, sweetheart," his mom said, pushing a tray of cookies into his hands. "Be careful on the bus. I'd hate for you to spill the cookies."

With that, Trace was off. A minute later, Cody, Sawyer, and Montana joined him, and they walked down the long driveway to the bus stop together. None of his friends said so much as, "Good morning," and Trace was feeling a little miffed by the time the bus got there. They took their usual seats, the three boys squishing into the row directly behind the driver, and Montana across the aisle. They rode in silence, Trace getting madder by the minute. By the time they got to school, his face felt hot. Was it possible they'd forgotten his birthday? If it was, it was also pretty darn depressing. They'd remembered each other's birthdays. And Trace had been talking about it nonstop.

They got off the bus and walked to their respective classes. Trace, teeth clenched together in anger, didn't say, "Goodbye."

Idiots, he thought as he stomped off to his homeroom class. *You'd think the fact that I was carrying a plate of cookies would clue them in. But no. They can't be bothered to remember my birthday.* He fumed about it all morning, and then at lunchtime, he decided he didn't want to be mad anymore. He would give them a hard time, and then let bygones be bygones. Water under the bridge and all that. But when he got to their normal table, they weren't there. He scanned the hot lunch line, but they weren't there either. He couldn't remember whether he'd seen them carrying lunches that morning. They always sat together, and they always sat at the same table. So where were they? Maybe they'd made plans without him. He sat down and ate his lunch as quickly as he could, hoping no one would notice he was alone. Then, instead of heading out to the basketball court like he usually did, he went to the library.

"The library," he muttered to himself as he walked. "On your birthday. You're a loser, man."

Cody, Sawyer, and Montana weren't on the bus home, which puzzled Trace. Had they left school? And if so, why did they get to leave school on his birthday, and he had to stay? Again, he was fuming by the time the bus rolled up in the driveway. He half expected his friends to be there, waiting for him. Maybe even laughing at him for being the lone sucker who had to finish out the school day on his own birthday.

But they weren't. Sure he was being watched because his friends must be playing some practical joke on him, he hiked his backpack up on his shoulders, put his head down, and marched straight to his house. He put his backpack away, washed his hands, and went to the kitchen to get a snack. The house felt eerily quiet. Often, his mom was home to greet him. Even if she came home from her work on the property to chat with him for a few minutes before heading back out, there weren't many days when she wasn't in the kitchen to ask him how his day went.

And that day — his birthday — was one of those very infrequent days.

Trace wanted to cry. Instead, he grabbed an apple and a couple of cheese sticks and headed out to find the friends who never let him down: the horses. He stuffed the cheese in his pocket and took large, angry bites of the apple as he walked. He reached the core of the apple and the barn door at the same time. It was all part of his ritual. One lucky horse would get the core, and munch on it while Trace ate the cheese. He pushed open the door and then jumped. Cody, Sawyer, and Montana were sitting on the fence railing directly in front of him. Trace looked hard at Cody, then at Sawyer, then at Montana, and made a point of not saying anything.

"You think we forgot your birthday," Sawyer said, and Trace detected something in his voice. He couldn't quite put his finger on what it was, but it was something. And then Cody said, "Just so you know, we didn't."

"Yep," Montana said. "We didn't."

Nice of you to wish me happy birthday, Trace thought. He felt his eyebrows pressing down and inward. They were probably almost touching, he was so mad. He muttered, "Great," as he took a left to head toward the row of stalls.

"Hey, bud."

He jumped — again. "Mom."

She was smiling so big, Trace felt some of his own anger slipping away. "What are you doing out here?"

His dad was there, too, standing behind his mom. "There's something we wanted you to take a look at," he said.

Trace's heart raced. What could they possibly want him to look at? Had something happened to one of the horses? But no, they wouldn't all be standing around so calmly if one of the horses was sick. Maybe one of them had had a baby. Although surprise foals weren't common, they weren't unheard of, either. He took a few cautious steps toward the stall where his parents were standing. "What is it?"

"Come on over here and see," his mom said.

If anticipation could ever be an emotion, it was at that moment. Trace could feel his heart pumping the blood through his body. He could hear it whooshing in his ears. His feet moved in time to each pulse. He saw his parents glance at something behind him, but he was too focused on whatever was in front of him to look back. After what felt like about a hundred years, Trace was standing in front of his parents. His dad leaned casually on the half-door of one of the stalls, his elbow propped on top of it, his chin in his hand. His mom played casual, too, hands on her hips. But the energy in the air was anything but casual. Trace could feel it, zapping around between his parents, off of him, off the walls. That's when his dad tilted his head toward the open half-door. Trace crept forward, and looked in. He was eye to eye with a horse. One he had never seen before. When it saw him, its ears shot straight up and its nostrils flared. Its eye appraised him. Darn it if that horse didn't take a step forward and kiss him on the cheek. Trace's hand, with a mind of its own, reached up to touch the horse's cheek. They stood there for a moment, looking at each other. Then, Trace's mom said, "Well, what do you think?"

"What do you mean?" Trace said, afraid to believe it.

"Meet your new horse," his dad said.

Something exploded inside of Trace right then. He would call it pure joy, or straight-up happiness. It was like nothing he'd ever experienced. He wanted to shout, to scream. To run around the barn like a wild animal. But he didn't want his horse's first memory of him to be of a crazy kid. Still, it was as if she could sense his excitement. She pawed the floor with her right hoof. Even gave a little whinny.

"*My* horse?"

He almost couldn't believe it. He looked at his parents, whose eyes were shining.

"You've been so responsible," his mom said, and his dad said, "You've done such a great job with the horses. You're really turning out to be a great young man. We're so proud of you. Happy birthday."

Trace wrapped his arms around his mom's waist, and his dad encircled both of them in a big hug. After a couple of seconds, the events of the day made sense. Trace released his parents and turned around to face his friends. He pointed at them, accusing. "You *knew!*"

They were all grinning ear to ear. They said, "We knew."

Cody pointed at him. "You thought we forgot! We've been working on this surprise for weeks!"

"We agreed not to talk at all this morning. We didn't want to ruin the surprise," Sawyer said.

"You were so *mad,*" Montana said.

"At lunch —"

"We begged our parents to let us come home," Montana said. "We knew they were bringing the horse this morning, and we wanted to help get everything set up."

"You *all* have been working on this for weeks?" Trace said. His voice was thick with emotion, but he was too happy to care.

"We got to help pick her out," Cody said, and Montana asked, "You really didn't know?"

Trace shook his head. "No clue."

Sawyer said, "We think you're going to love her. She's so smart. And she handles great."

"She's *fast,*" Cody stage-whispered, and they all laughed.

"You want to take her for a spin?" his dad asked.

"Can I? She's brand new."

"Of course you can," said his mom. "We wouldn't get you a horse that we didn't think you could ride."

Trace turned to his friends. "You want to go?"

"We're ready," Cody said. "Our horses are saddled. We've been waiting for you."

Trace walked over to the saddles, but his dad put a hand on his shoulder. "We got you a new saddle, and gear, too. It's only fitting for a new horse."

Trace couldn't believe his ears.

"Everything's in her stall," Montana said.

Trace felt a little uncertain about going into a stall with a new horse. But when he opened the door, she stood calmly. Watchful, but serene.

"Why don't you talk to her for a few minutes?" his dad said. "Let her get to know the sound of your voice."

So he did. He put his forehead against hers and told her how excited he was to have her. Trace could've sworn she was listening, and that she actually understood his words.

After a few minutes, Trace rubbed her neck and ran a hand over her back. She remained still. He went ahead and put on the saddle blanket and the saddle, which didn't seem to faze her. Next, he gave her the bit and put on the bridle. Then he looked at his parents. His mom nodded. "Go ahead."

Trace took the reins and lead his horse (*his* horse!) out of the stall and through the barn.

Cody, Sawyer, and Montana were mounted up and waiting.

"Oh yeah," Cody said. "Happy birthday, man."

"Yeah," Sawyer said. "Sorry we didn't say so, earlier. We were afraid we'd ruin the surprise."

"But just know that we were *so* excited," Montana said. "We couldn't *wait*."

"It's okay," Trace said, and his friends burst out laughing.

"*Now* it is," Sawyer said, and Cody said, "But you should have seen your face on the bus this morning. Maddest I've ever seen you."

Smiling, Trace said, "Want to head down to the swimming hole?"

"You take the lead," Cody said.

Trace was grateful. If he was in front, they couldn't see him cry. As he brought his horse up to a trot, he felt the first tears running down his face.

He heard his dad call, "You're going to have to name her!"

And, as he brought her to a gallop, the tears really started to come down. He couldn't believe it. His very own horse.

MY FAVORITE PLACE: CHAPTER THREE

ABBY

ABBY NEVER THOUGHT of construction sites as dangerous places. No, a job was more like a giant jungle gym. As a little kid, fear wasn't even part of her vocabulary. She hopped from one floor joist to another, climbed unfinished walls, and swung from the ceiling.

Her dad's calls to, "Get down from there!" evolved to, "Be careful," and he shouted those two words more times than she could count. His crew members saw her coming and hollered, "Watch out! Here comes the tornado!"

The way everyone watched out for Abby, she never thought to watch out for anyone else. It never even occurred to her that a jobsite could be dangerous for the others.

Abby was twenty-two when it happened. She'd been a full-time crew member for seven years. They were building a commercial building — three stories. Her dad had come from another site to do an end-of-the-day walk-through. Abby was on the first floor, circular saw in hand, cutting two-by-fours for the guys framing in the interior walls. The sounds — the saw whining before it touched the wood, grinding while sawdust flew, and the end of the board clattering to the concrete foundation — were so loud, Abby didn't even hear her dad walk up. She jumped at the hand on her shoulder, but her sawing hand remained steady.

"You startled me!"

Her dad chuckled. "I'm glad to see you're such a focused worker. How's it going here?" Hands on hips, he surveyed the space. Abby felt at once proud and nervous. It had been a productive day. Also, he was a stickler. Every member of the crew knew that if something wasn't done right the first time, he would ask them to redo it. Although Abby was tempted to follow him as he began to walk around the first story, she instead picked up another two-by-four and set it across the sawhorses. Out of the corner of her eye, she could see her dad walking, examining. He ran a thumb over the head of a screw on one wall, then gave that board a gentle tap with his knuckles. He went all the way around the room this way. Abby was holding her breath by the time he made it back to her workstation.

"Looking good," he said. "If you aren't careful, you're going to become the foreman when Joseph retires." Abby stopped sawing and grinned at her dad. "That's fore*woman* to you."

"I suppose that's true." He gave her shoulder a squeeze. "I'm going to head upstairs, take a look."

Modern-day Abby didn't know why she hadn't said, "Be careful," like he'd said to her so many times. She winked at him and carried on with her work. He climbed the stairs, a hand against the unfinished wall for balance.

Once he was gone, Abby lost herself in the rhythm of the job. Choosing a board, measuring, sawing, setting it down. Lift, measure, cut, set down. And although the noise continued all around her as her crewmates hammered and drilled and sawed and shouted, the sound of the accident was unmistakable. A clatter, and then a shout. The sounds of a body thumping against wood, irregular. Grunting, more shouting. And then, the worst sight Abby had ever seen: the body of her father, limp, falling between the joists above her. He landed inches from where she stood. His hips hit first, and his back arched over the ends of the cut lumber. His head hit the concrete foundation with a sickening *crack*.

And then, complete silence.

Abby, the saw still in her hand, froze. She had the bizarre thought that she should scream, to somehow alert the rest of the crew that something was terribly wrong. But she couldn't find her voice. Or her feet. Fortunately, everyone else seemed to have found theirs. They came thundering down the stairs, emerging from the various corners, rushing to her father's side.

"Boss!" someone was yelling. "Boss!"

And then, "Someone call an ambulance."

"Don't move him," someone said. Someone else said, "Did someone call an ambulance?"

"I-I will," Abby said, her voice cracking. "I've got it."

She had a mobile phone in her car, and on numb legs she ran out to get it. She fumbled with the door handle, and with the phone. Her fingers shook so badly. It was everything she could do to press the right buttons. But once a dispatcher picked up, her voice sounded strong and clear as she gave the woman the address and asked for an ambulance.

She ran back inside, where most of the crew members had taken a step back from her dad. Only Joseph, the foreman, knelt next to him, a hand on his shoulder. Abby ran up and knelt on the other side.

It was bad, she knew that. She knew from watching her dad fall and seeing him land. But the expression on Joseph's face — and the fact that he avoided eye contact — made her think it was even worse than bad.

ABBY GLANCED in her rearview mirror and saw the rancher, Trace, give her a wave. She wished she had given him her business card, or something. Then he'd have her number. But her brain was fried from everything that had gone wrong that day, from the mix-up at the rental car company (she'd never drive a hot rod, if it were up to her) to the flat tire on the interstate, and she hadn't thought of it. She supposed she could go back there after checking out the property she hoped to buy.

If she did, though, she would have to come up with some kind of plausible excuse. The Mint Creek Ranch (there was a sign), a breathtaking property with rolling hills, old-growth trees, about a zillion head of cattle, and one very fine cowboy, wasn't a place where someone simply stopped by. If she hadn't been able to guess that from the geography alone (the place was practically in the middle of nowhere), the beyond-unfriendly expression on the rancher's face when she pulled up to his house would have been a dead giveaway.

But, that smile. When she rolled down her window and their eyes met, that smile had sent a buzzing energy straight to her lady parts. Which was very out of the ordinary. Most of the time, guys, even good-looking ones, didn't get Abby's libido going like that. Not at first sight, anyway.

She remembered Trace telling her to go less than three-quarters of a mile. In reminiscing over that one-minute encounter, she'd gone at least a full mile. She preferred her pick-up truck, but one benefit of a sports car was that she could do a quick one-eighty. This time, on her third pass, she saw the road. She took the left turn, enjoying how well the car handled compared to her truck. It didn't do quite as well on Saddle Horn Lane's washboard surface, but it wouldn't hurt to slow down and enjoy the scenery.

From what the real estate agent told her, this piece of property, a 100-acre parcel in Williamson Valley, had been a wedding present to a pair of city dwellers from the groom's parents.

The family came from a long line of northern Arizona ranchers, but the young couple chose to stay in Phoenix, where they both worked in electrical engineering. No matter how much the groom's parents pushed and prodded, the engineers couldn't be persuaded to move north, or even to put a weekend home on the property.

Real estate prices in Arizona had skyrocketed during the twenty years since, and the electrical engineers, no longer a young couple, wanted to sell the land to fund their retirement. So, Abby thought, it had served its purpose. They could use the land to live happily ever after.

And so could she.

She crested a little hill and got a view of the acreage below. She gasped — the landscape literally took her breath away as she stopped the car. She couldn't think of a more perfect place to build her dream development. All green grass and rolling fields, the land lay before her like an offering. Rock formations in tans and brown, evergreen trees in a deeper green, and smaller, flowery shrubs dotted the landscape.

Abby's hands came to her chest, and tears came to her eyes. Which was silly. It was a piece of land, that was all. But it was a beautiful piece of land. And her dad — her dad would be so proud. She parked the car, right there on the road, and got out. She would walk the place, step by step, yard by yard, acre by acre. She already knew in her heart that the land was *it*.

As reluctant to leave the pristine piece of property as she was an hour later, Abby had a flight to catch. And even if she wanted to (which she admitted to herself, she did), she didn't have time to revisit the Mint Creek Ranch.

As soon as she turned on the car, it made a loud beeping sound.

Abby groaned. "What now?"

The display on the dashboard read, "Low tire pressure."

Abby tightened her grip on the steering wheel and hit her forehead against it a few times, wailing, "Whyyyyy?"

She supposed she could take it as a sign. But she didn't know which way the sign was pointing. Was it saying, *You should stay here, in Prescott?* Or was it saying, *Everything about this trip has been doomed from the start. You absolutely should not build a life in this town?*

Leaving the car running, she got out and walked toward the rear. The driver's side tires looked fine, but the back one on the passenger side was completely flat. The only thing between the rim and the ground was about a centimeter of rubber. Abby groaned again. If the whole trip hadn't been going so terribly, she would probably cry. But the flat tire was the icing on the cake. So, she did what her father had taught her to do when everything was going wrong: she laughed. Perhaps the laugh sounded a little weepy, a little insane. But she didn't care. There was no one around to hear her.

Only, there was. "Hello," said a sexy, smooth voice behind her. "Flat tire, huh?"

Startled, Abby jumped as she whirled around. "You wouldn't believe it —" she started. Then she saw who the voice belonged to, and found herself speechless.

It was him. The guy from the ranch next door. He was still gorgeous, and his horse was even more so.

She chuckled, to herself. *The guy from the ranch next door.* That had a nice ring to it. Realizing that she might sound insane, Abby sucked in a breath and said, with as straight a face as she could muster, "Yep. About par for the course today."

She congratulated herself on the use of a golf metaphor. Golf was something all men could understand. Maybe that would impress this manly rancher. The guy from the ranch next door.

As she stifled another laugh, he said, "I fail to see the humor in this, being as you're a young lady out in the middle of nowhere." He pulled off his sunglasses, and his eyes smiled at her. "Ma'am, I've got to tell you, I've never seen someone laugh about a flat tire."

"You wouldn't believe it," Abby started again. "This is about the tenth thing today that's gone wrong. I'm only laughing because otherwise, I'd cry. If I don't hurry up and get this fixed, I'm going to miss my flight. Which ordinarily wouldn't be too big of a deal, but someone's waiting for me."

She was being purposefully cryptic, something she normally didn't do. But she normally didn't have a reaction like the one she was having to the guy from the ranch next door.

"That thing got a spare?"

Abby sighed. "I'm sure it does, but I haven't had a chance to look. I'd rather take your real horse back down to the airport than drive this thing."

As she spoke, she walked around to the driver's door. She hadn't even used the trunk yet, but the lever was easy enough to find. Sure enough, a panel in the bottom pulled up to reveal a spare tire.

"Yep, there's a spare," she said.

The rancher was already dismounting. In any other situation, Abby would feel a bit prickly about that. Did he assume she couldn't handle changing a tire? But in this case — only because she was in a hurry and *not at all* because he was five-star sexy, and cowboys were known for being chivalrous — she found the gesture sweet.

Still, she went ahead with assembling the tools and unscrewing the spare tire.

"You know your way around a tire change, I see," he said.

"I do," Abby said. She left it at that. She did know her way around a tire change, but still felt relieved when he said, "If you don't mind my help, the two of us can probably get you on the road a little faster. Give you some chance of catching that flight."

"Actually," she said. "I would appreciate it."

They worked together seamlessly, and within ten minutes, he was loading the flat tire into the trunk while she folded up the jack. He grabbed a rag out of the saddle bag and offered it to her just as she was wondering how she'd get her greasy hands clean.

"Thank you so much," she said, and he tipped his hat at her. To this, too, she had an unusual reaction: she wanted to kiss him.

"Any time. I hope you make your flight."

"Me too," she said. She glanced at her watch. "In fact, I think I will — thanks to you. As long as nothing else goes wrong."

"It'll be smooth sailing from here," he said. "I can feel it."

With that, he mounted that gorgeous horse and rode away.

Abby took a quick look at Mint Creek Ranch over her shoulder as she sped by a minute later. The drive back to the Phoenix airport was right about two hours, which meant Abby had plenty of time to take action. And to think. In that order.

As soon as she got on the highway, she called her real estate agent, who picked up right away. "What did you think?"

Lucy Marino was all business, straightforward, no-nonsense. Abby loved it about her.

"I want to put in an offer. Full asking price. Thirty-day escrow."

"That's it?"

"That's it," Abby said. Her voice held confidence. Sure, she felt a little nervous. But anytime a person made a big leap, nerves were part of the equation.

"Okay," said Lucy. "I'll write it up and send it in. I'll let you know the instant I hear back."

"I know you will."

Abby and Lucy had worked together on a few projects already: a commercial lot in Utah where Abby was building a retail building, a run-down ex-supermarket she'd remodeled into a strip mall, and a lot zoned for multi-family housing. While each project hit a snag or two, they were always able to get a deal through. So Abby was fairly certain Lucy could help her bring her vision for the property to reality, too.

"If you get this place, you going to move to Prescott? Wait — that's not how the locals pronounce it, right? 'Rhymes with biscuit.'"

"Right," Abby said. "I don't know if I'll ever pronounce it like the locals do." She sighed and looked briefly around at the mountains silhouetted against the pristine blue sky. "I *want* to move here. I really do. When I get this place, it's likely. Although, I'll have a hard time parting with my dad's house in Utah."

"You could always keep it," Lucy said. "The way you run your business, I think you'll have the cash flow."

"True. It's something to think about, anyway."

"Agreed. All right. I'll get this offer in and talk to you soon, okay?"

"Okay, thank you so much."

"Anytime, Abby. Drive careful."

The call ended, and music blared over the premium stereo system. Abby would love nothing more than to live in Prescott. Although that particular trip had been a bit of a whirlwind, especially with the travel delays, it had also been a nice break.

Instantly, Abby felt guilty for thinking that way. She'd spent the past several years being a caregiver for her dad, and while she *was* exhausted, she wouldn't have it any other way. She'd learned absolutely everything from him. It was only because of him that she was in the position to buy the property for her new development. And, if she could push it through, she'd have enough money to bring him out, too, and hire people to care for him.

———

THE SIGHT of her father in a wheelchair always gave Abby a little start. When she was a tiny girl, he seemed bigger than life, and she'd scramble up his back like she was climbing a mountain. She would stand on his shoulders, feeling like she was at the top of the world.

The way she thought of him — still — didn't jive with the reality: his body folded into the wheelchair. His shoulders were still broad, his long legs still sturdy looking, but he seemed smaller, somehow.

"My girl!" His voice reverberated throughout the room, strong despite the fact that he could no longer walk on his own. "I've been waiting for you."

Abby walked up to him and leaned down for a hug. His arms encircled her, and she was grateful that whatever else had changed, the comfort she experienced from his hugs remained the same.

"Well, how was it?" he asked at the same time she said, "Dad, it was perfect!"

"Tell me everything," he said. "I wish I'd been able to go with you in person."

It wasn't that Ernesto *couldn't* travel. But even though several years had passed since the accident, he didn't feel confident enough to navigate his way through a busy airport in his wheelchair, and he always said he didn't want to slow Abby down while she was working.

She insisted he wouldn't, but he insisted she go without him.

"Let me get us some drinks, and we'll go out onto the porch," she said.

"I'll get the drinks," he said. "You must be tired."

It was true. She rode the wave of exhilaration all the way down the mountain to the Phoenix airport. She was still flying high as she went through airport security and power walked to the gate. She felt alert with excitement as she sat in the chair, her thumbs flying over her phone screen, checking her emails and text messages for any news about whether the seller had accepted her offer on the property. There were no new messages by the time she boarded, and she shut off her phone as soon as she sat down. The next thing she knew, the plane was touching down in Utah. She jolted awake, but the adrenaline rush lasted only a couple of minutes before the bone-deep exhaustion set in as she drove to her dad's house. While some of the excitement was returning, thanks to sharing the news with him, she could definitely use a cold beer and a minute to sit.

"Meet you on the deck," she said.

Her dad nodded and powered his wheelchair toward the kitchen.

Immediately after his injury, she'd doted on him, trying to anticipate his every need before he mentioned it out loud. She felt like a butterfly. She would light on his shoulder, flutter away to get him something, and then return for only the briefest moment before going on another errand. At first, he needed it. Fighting through his own grief, he felt like his body failed him. Although his physical therapists marveled at how strong he was, how much he could do so quickly after his fall, Ernesto was beyond frustrated.

Over time, acceptance set in, and although he could do more for himself, Abby didn't let him. She wanted to take care of him in the same way he had always provided for her. She felt that somehow, if she cared for him, she could lessen his frustration, take away some of the sting.

She later realized that only Ernesto could do that for himself. Her realization came about the same time his did, and he sat her down and told her that she had to get on with it.

Remembering the conversation brought a smile to Abby's face as she pushed open the French doors that led to the deck.

Outdoor spaces had always been one of the best in Ernesto's designs. This one jutted out from the house in a way that made Abby feel like she was floating when she stepped onto it. A table and chairs sat at one end, and another row of chairs backed up to the house, positioned with a stunning view of the red rocks beyond.

A minute later, Ernesto joined Abby on the deck. He handed her a glass of seltzer water, with plenty of ice.

"Thanks," she said. "I needed this."

"I've got something stronger, if you want."

Abby smiled at him. "I could probably use that, too," she said. "The way my trip went. But I'm afraid I'd be snoring on the porch before you could get me home."

"I thought your trip went well. You said the place was perfect."

Abby took a long drink of the water, let the bubbles burst in her mouth before swallowing. "It is."

Evening sunlight poured over the landscape in front of them. The scene looked so soft. For a moment, Abby wondered how the sunset looked in Williamson Valley right then.

"The land *is* perfect. The trip — kind of a nightmare."

She told him all of it: the long security line at the airport, the flight delay, the rental car mix-up, the flat tire. When she got to the part about missing her turn and asking for directions at the Mint Creek Ranch, her dad's eyes started to sparkle.

"What?" she asked.

"What are you leaving out?"

Abby's body betrayed her. She felt herself blushing. "Nothing."

"Lies!" Ernesto pointed at her, as if to say, "Gotcha."

Abby laughed. "Well, if you must know, the rancher who gave me directions — let's just say he was easy on the eyes."

"Easy on the eyes, huh?"

"That's about the best description I can give, to my *father*!"

"Did you get his number?"

"Dad! No! I was there on business."

"I mean, did you get his number for business purposes? He could be a good ally, you know, in a neighborly way."

"Somehow, I didn't get the impression that he wants anything to do with an out-of-towner. He was pretty prickly when I drove up unannounced in my rented Mustang."

Ernesto shrugged. "Probably because he thought *you* were easy on the eyes, too."

"Da-ad," Abby said, breaking the word into two syllables, like she had as a teenager.

"What? You ought to be good-looking. You have my genes and

your mother's. God rest her soul. You know what they say about the acorn."

"It's the apple. Not the acorn."

"Whatever. I see some potential here."

"Let's talk about the property."

Eyes still twinkling, Ernesto chuckled. He took a drink of his water. "Okay. Let's talk about the property."

Abby pulled out her sketchpad and got to work, giving Ernesto the lay of the land, the hills and valleys, Granite Mountain. She held up her sketch for her dad to examine, and watched as his vision took shape. Instead of reaching for her pencil, though, he asked, "What are you thinking?"

She grinned. "I was hoping you'd ask."

ABOUT THE AUTHOR

Hilary Dartt loves great adventures, whether she's writing, reading, or living them. The author of twelve novels, Hilary lives in Arizona's high desert with her husband, their three children, her Weimaraner and running partner, Leia, and a failed barn cat, Striker. She loves camping, exploring in the Jeep, and dance parties with her kids. Learn more and sign up for her newsletter at www.hilarydartt.com.